Big Bad
Beast

Big Bad Beast

Shelly Laurenston

BRAVA

KENSINGTON PUBLISHING CORP.
www.kensingtonbooks.com

BRAVA BOOKS are published by

Kensington Publishing Corp.
119 West 40th Street
New York, NY 10018

All Kensington titles, imprints, and distributed lines are available at special quantity discounts for bulk purchases for sales promotions, premiums, fund-raising, educational, or institutional use. Special book excerpts or customized printings can also be created to fit specific needs. For details, write or phone the office of the Kensington special sales manager: Kensington Publishing Corp., 119 West 40th Street, New York, NY 10018, attn: Special Sales Department; phone 1-800-221-2647.

ISBN-13: 978-0-7582-3170-3
ISBN-10: 0-7582-3170-9

First Kensington Trade Paperback Printing: May 2011
10 9 8 7 6 5 4 3

Printed in the United States of America

PROLOGUE

It wasn't his idea of an ideal place to discuss such matters, but he was willing to be flexible considering whom he was meeting with. And, to be honest, Niles Van Holtz—Van to his friends and family—preferred that this meeting take place in a large, open area, in neutral territory with lots of people around.

He stepped out of his car and allowed his young cousin to follow. Six-year-old Ulrich was staying with Van and his mate for the summer because, to quote his relatively new bride, Irene, "That young man needs to realize that his father's an idiot now rather than later when the damage is done." The kid wasn't exactly a challenge, though. All he did was read and work on his knife skills in the kitchen. He didn't even need TV, and seemed to find it a distraction from his books. He didn't talk much at first, but Irene had a surprising way with kids, drawing Ric out of his self-imposed shell until he'd turned into quite the chatty pup when the mood struck him.

So Van knew he could have left the kid back in Seattle, but in just a few weeks, Ric had become, as Irene called him, Van's "shadow." And that meant that leaving him behind just didn't sit right.

Besides, it was just a business meeting. Nothing dangerous or anything. Even if it was with one of his Pack's sworn enemies.

Business was business to Van, and he assumed everyone else felt that way as well.

"Stay right here, Ric." Van placed the kid on the hood of his rental car: a speedy little Porsche he'd picked up near the Memphis airport before traveling out for the meeting in this neutral territory. "I'll be right over there, okay?"

"Okay." The kid pulled out a book from his backpack and began to read. *The Count of Monte Cristo.* A six-year-old was reading the *Count of Monte Cristo.* A book Van had been forced to read in high school and only after the teacher warned him that the CliffsNotes edition wouldn't help him during the midyear exam. But the kid had picked out that book himself at the store. Along with twelve others and a pocket dictionary for any words he might not understand.

And the newest handheld video game Van had gotten for Ric straight from Japan? That was still sitting on the kid's bed, in the box, untouched.

Van patted Ric's head, adoring him despite his lack of priorities, and turned to head off to the meeting, but he quickly jerked back. The wolf he'd been coming to see stood right in front of him in a worn Led Zeppelin T-shirt, torn jeans, and old combat boots. A long chain hooked to one of the front loops of his jeans snaked around his leg to his back pocket and probably his wallet. His dark brown hair reached his shoulders, the front nearly obscuring yellow eyes. His beard was full and covered the entire lower half of his face. He looked like a crazed homeless vet who hadn't yet gotten over what he'd been forced to do during the Vietnam War.

"Mr. Smith?" Van asked, almost hoping he was wrong.

He wasn't. The grunt told him this was, in fact, Egbert Ray Smith of the Tennessee Smith Pack.

"Niles Van Holtz." Van held his hand out. "Nice to meet you."

The wolf didn't take his hand or look away from glaring into his face. Van had to remind himself he was the Alpha Male of his Pack now. He wasn't going to be intimidated by this possible serial killer.

"Watcha want, boy?"

This wasn't exactly starting off well, now was it? "I'm here to offer you a job, Mr. Smith. With my organization. The Group."

"The Group's a bunch of pussies."

"Perhaps, but I've taken over and I'm moving them forward. Making them more like the Unit." Smith's eyes narrowed a bit. He'd been in the Unit for years—and it showed. From every line on his not-that-old face to every scar on his neck and probably all over his body. But things inside the Unit had changed recently, the shifter-only military team within the U.S. Marine Corp was planning to move its members out of the Unit—whether they wanted to go or not—after ten years. Smith had been in the Unit for nearly the entire time he was in the Corps and he'd been the first casualty of the new procedures. From what Van had heard, Smith had been non too happy with his choices of taking an honorable discharge or assimilating with his full-human Marine brethren. He'd taken the discharge, but that was probably because he would never assimilate with anything full-human. Smith had gone straight from boot camp to the Unit, and in the process made quite a name for himself. As a killer.

Because that's what Egbert Smith was. He was a killer and a very good one. And Van was sure that Smith would be a perfect addition to his team, because he was moving the Group in a new direction. Molding it into a protection unit that would neutralize any dangers to shifters within the United States. *All* shifters.

An important step now that things were getting more and more dangerous for their kind every day.

"I need people like you on my team, Mr. Smith. The pay will be excellent with full benefits, safeguards for your immediate family, and the kind of flexibility a man like you needs." Van's nice way of saying, "We both know you could never hold down a real day job, sport."

The wolf grunted again, his yellow-eyed gaze unwavering.

Van dug into the back pocket of his jeans and pulled out a slip of paper. He handed it to Smith. "That would be your starting salary. *Yearly.*"

The wolf glanced down at the piece of paper, looked at Van, then glanced at the paper again. Van was sure that Smith had never expected to get that kind of money from any job, but the Group had ample resources and had no problems using them for the right recruits.

"That sum will, of course, go up the more time you put in with us and depending on how well you do your job."

The wolf glanced off across the big parking lot where the flea market had been set up on this Saturday afternoon. He cleared his throat and finally admitted, "Promised my mate I'd settle down." His voice was low and gravelly and, if Van looked close enough, he could see an old scar right over where the wolf's vocal chords should be. "Don't think she'd like me leaving her again for so long."

"You won't need to relocate for this job, Mr. Smith. There's no base for you to live on, no country you'll need to go to. Although, trips to Alaska and Hawaii may be necessary. Short trips. To be honest, I'll need you to merely be available when you're called. But whether you're working a day a week, every day for three months, or sitting around with nothing to do for six months, you will get paid. Every other week, like clockwork."

"And if something happens to me?"

"Your family will be taken care of and your Pack reimbursed for the loss of its Packmate. The Group takes care of its own, Mr. Smith."

While Van waited for the wolf to say or do *something* in response to his offer, a young girl walked up. She couldn't be more than nine or ten, unable to even shift yet. But she had her father's eyes. Bright yellow and cold. So very cold.

She glanced at Van, seemed to deem him non-threatening, and tugged on her father's shirt. "This one," she said.

Her father looked down at the enormous bowie knife she held in her hand. He took it from her, examined it closely. "Why?" he asked.

"It's a good weight. The blade is well-made steel and a length that'll penetrate chest bone. The handle is strong, and when my fingers get longer, I'll still be able to use it. I thought I'd want one of those folding knives, but I'll be able to pull this out faster and use it quicker. If I have to use a weapon, I won't have time to be fumbling around with a folding knife to get it open."

Her father nodded in agreement while Van could do nothing but gawk at the girl. Sure, he'd spent the last few weeks with Ric teaching the kid how to use his knife set to quickly and efficiently butcher deer and wild boar, but that was for cooking purposes only, so he could one day take his place in their Pack's restaurant business. This little girl, however, was talking about knives going through chest bone—Van didn't think she meant the chest bone of a zebra.

"How much?" Smith asked her.

"He wanted two hundred for it. I got him down to eighty."

"How'd ya do that?"

"Stared at him 'til he made it eighty."

The wolf dug into his pocket and gave her four twenty-dollar bills, then handed over the blade. "Take good care of it, it'll take good care of you, Sugar Bug."

"I will, Daddy." She ambled off to the vendor and Smith faced Van again.

They locked gazes and stayed that way for how long, Van really didn't know. But it must have been long enough, because Smith finally said, "Don't much like feelin' hemmed in."

"You won't be. You have my word."

The wolf snorted. "The word of a Van Holtz. That don't mean much."

"To *me* it does." Fed up, Van finally asked, "In or out, Mr. Smith?"

Smith looked him over one more time and said, "In."

The little girl returned, her new knife clutched in her hand. "He even gave me a sheath, Daddy. It's real leather."

"Good girl." He motioned to Van. "This is one of them Van

Holtz wolves I'm always warning you about. They all look like him. Kinda skinny and snobby. Smell like him, too. Avoid 'em, if you can. Gut 'em if you can't."

"Yes, sir."

Not exactly the introduction Van expected but . . . whatever. It didn't matter.

At least it didn't matter until he realized that his young cousin was no longer on the hood of the car but standing right next to Van, leaning against his side, wide eyes fastened on Smith's little girl.

She scowled down at Ric, but as he continued to gaze up at her in awe, her scowl faded and she smiled. "What'cha lookin' at, shorty?" she asked, her young voice teasing.

Ric didn't answer—Van had the feeling the poor kid couldn't answer—but he did hold out one of the plain Hershey bars he kept stashed in his bag.

She looked at the candy bar, then up at her father. He nodded and she took the candy from Ric. After a moment, she said, "Thank ya kindly," and her smile grew.

Ric let out a sigh and blurted, "Marry—"

Van slapped his hand over Ric's mouth before he could finish. He might only be a defenseless six-year-old with more brains than sense and caught up in his first childhood infatuation, which he probably wouldn't remember in another day or two, but something told Van none of that would matter to Egbert Smith when it came to protecting his daughter.

"All right then," Van said, dragging his struggling cousin over to the car. "Time to go. I'll be in touch, Mr. Smith."

Van got the car door open and shoved his cousin inside. He followed, throwing the kid's pack into the back seat. Once he had the door closed and saw Smith and his daughter walking off, Van let out a breath.

"Kid," he said, "you have *got* to learn about timing."

"But she's perfect, Uncle Van. I think I love her."

Van glanced over at the still-growing She-wolf. A too-skinny little girl with long legs and arms in a T-shirt and denim cutoffs and no shoes.

"Ric, you're way too young to love anybody but your parents and, of course, me."

"She needs to eat more," Ric observed, ignoring Van's comment. "And I'll be the one to feed her!"

Rolling his eyes, Van started the car.

"Come on, Ric," he tried desperately to reason with the kid. "You're too young for all this crazy mate stuff. You need to focus on other things first."

"Like what?"

"Food, your hunting skills . . . even other girls," he answered honestly.

"I hate girls." He was six. *Of course,* he hated girls. "She's not a girl, though. She's *amazing.*"

The first time the kid had spoken so many words in a solid five-minute stretch and he was doing nothing but absolutely freaking Van out.

"She's perfect for me, Uncle Van."

"No, Ulrich. She's not. From what I can tell she's just like her father and that means she needs to be avoided at all possible costs. Understand?"

Ric nodded, carefully buckling his seatbelt and pulling out his book again.

"I understand, Uncle Van."

"Good," Van said, reversing out of the parking spot.

"I'll wait until we're both older," the kid went on, "and then I'll *nail her.*"

Van hit the brakes. "What?"

"Like you and Aunt Irene."

Panic beginning to set in, Van asked again, "*What?*"

"That's what you told her last night when I was scrubbing the pots from dinner. You were going to nail her. Then you laughed."

Oh, shit. "Uh, Ric . . ."

"And so I'll just wait until my future mate and I are older and then I'll nail her. Or we'll nail each other. That sounds like more fun. Nailing each other."

"Listen, Ulrich—"

"What is that, anyway? Nailing? The way Aunt Irene smiled when you said it, I'm guessing it's fun, right?"

Van rested his head against the steering wheel and wondered how bad a meltdown Ric's father would have over this. Uptight, rich snob that Alder Van Holtz was, Van was guessing . . . bad.

Eggie Ray Smith closed his truck door and let out a breath. His baby girl went up on her knees in the passenger seat and faced him. "You're leaving again, ain'tcha, Daddy?"

"Off and on."

"Momma won't be happy."

"I know." His mate liked having him around. Not underfoot, mind you. She couldn't stand that. But she liked to know he was just a "holler away" when she sent the call out that dinner was ready.

"But you have to go," his little girl said, her hand pressed against his shoulder. "You've got important things to do, Daddy. And like Big Poppa always says, you can't do 'em if you're sittin' in the backyard having tea and cakes, now can ya?"

Unable to stop his grin, Eggie looked at Dee-Ann Smith. Of all the things he'd done over the years, being the father of this little girl was definitely the most important and fulfilling. "You're right, Sugar Bug. I can't."

"Besides, I can watch out for Momma. Nobody's gettin' past me to get to her."

Eggie knew that. He'd made sure that if there was one thing his baby girl could do, it was protect herself and those she loved. Not just fight, mind, but protect herself. He'd learned in the Corps that there was a difference between scrappin' and protection. An important difference. Because any idiot could fight.

"That's right. They won't." He stroked her cheek with his fingers. "You like your gift, Sugar Bug?"

Her grin was wide. "Yep."

"Good. Happy birthday." He started the truck. "And don't tell your momma. We'll pick you up something else on the way home. But the knife is between us for a few more . . . well . . . *years*. Understand?"

She tucked the knife in the back of her denim cutoffs and sat down in the seat. "Yep."

"Good girl. Now eat your chocolate."

She studied the still-wrapped bar of chocolate. "That was a cute kid," she said.

"Still a Van Holtz," Eggie reminded her. "You've gotta avoid the Van Holtzes."

"But he's so cute and little," she argued. "And he looked smart, too. Bet he could help me build a real nice fort so I can fight off those savages, the Reed boys."

"Don't care how cute and smart a Van Holtz is, Sugar Bug. They can't be trusted. You keep to your own. Understand?"

"Yes, sir."

Dee-Ann broke off a piece of the chocolate she'd unwrapped, handing it over to her father without even taking some for herself first. As Eggie took the candy, he realized that he had the best little girl in the world, and if taking this job with an enemy wolf would ensure she'd always be safe and happy and financially stable, he'd do it.

Because he wanted better for his baby girl. He didn't want her running 'shine or, like some of his idiot cousins in other parts of the country, guns. He also didn't want her risking her life every day fighting the world's worst scum.

But what he definitely didn't want for his little girl was for her to spend a second of her precious life working for some sneaky, know-it-all, rich wolf who thought because he could cook a steak he was better than everyone else. Nope. That wouldn't be for his Dee-Ann. Not ever.

Eggie would make sure of it.

Chapter I

Twenty-five years later . . .

Ulrich Van Holtz turned over and snuggled closer to the denim-clad thigh resting by his head. Then he remembered that he'd gone to bed alone last night.

Forcing one eye open, he gazed at the face grinning down at him.

"Mornin', supermodel."

He hated when she called him that. The dismissive tone of it grated on his nerves. Especially his sensitive *morning* nerves. She might as well say, "Mornin', you who serve no purpose."

"Dee-Ann." He glanced around, trying to figure out what was going on. "What time is it?"

"Dawn-ish."

"Dawn-*ish*?"

"Not quite dawn, no longer night."

"And is there a reason you're in my bed at dawn-ish . . . fully clothed? Because I'm pretty sure you'd be much more comfortable naked."

Her lips curved slightly. "Look at you, Van Holtz. Trying to sweet talk me."

"If it'll get you naked . . ."

"You're my boss."

"I'm your supervisor."

"If you can fire me, you're my boss. Didn't they teach you that in your fancy college?"

"My fancy college was a culinary school and I spent most of my classes trying to understand my French instructors. So if they mentioned that boss-supervisor distinction, I probably missed it."

"You're still holding my thigh, boss."

"You're still in my bed. And you're still not naked."

"Me naked is like me dressed. Still covered in scars and willing to kill."

"Now you're just trying to turn me on." Ric yawned, reluctantly unwrapping his arms from Dee's scrumptious thigh and using the move to get a good look at her.

She'd let her dark brown hair grow out a bit in recent months so that the heavy, wavy strands rested below her ears, framing a square jaw that sported a five-inch scar from her military days and a more recent bruise he was guessing had happened last night. She had a typical Smith nose—a bit long and rather wide at the tip—and the proud, high forehead. But it was those eyes that disturbed most of the populace because they were the one part of her that never shifted. They stayed the same color and shape no matter what form she was in. Many people called the color "dog yellow," but Ric thought of it as a canine gold. And Ric didn't find those eyes off-putting. No, he found them entrancing. Just like the woman.

Ric had only known the She-wolf about seven months, but since the first time he'd laid eyes on her, he'd been madly, deeply in lust. Then, over time, he'd gotten to know her, and he'd come to fall madly, deeply in love. There was just one problem with their becoming mates and living happily ever after—and that problem's name was Dee-Ann Smith.

"So is there a reason you're here, in my bed, not naked, around dawn-*ish* that doesn't involve us forgetting the idiotic limits of business protocol so that you can ravish my more-than-willing body?"

"Yep."

When she said nothing else, Ric sat up and offered, "Let me guess. The tellin' will be easier if it's around some waffles and bacon."

"Those words are true, but faking that accent ain't endearing you to my Confederate heart."

"I bet adding blueberries to those waffles will."

"Canned or fresh?"

Mouth open, Ric glared at her over his shoulder.

"It's a fair question."

"Out." He pointed at his bedroom door. "If you're going to question whether I'd use *canned* anything in my food while sitting on my bed *not* naked, then you can just get the hell out of my bedroom . . . and sit in my kitchen, quietly, until I arrive."

"Will you be in a better mood?"

"Will you be naked?"

"Like a wolf with a bone," she muttered, and then told him, "Not likely."

"Then I guess you have your answer."

"Oh, come on. Can I at least sit here and watch you strut into the bathroom bare-ass naked?"

"No, you may not." He threw his legs over the side of the bed. "However, you may look over your shoulder longingly while I, in a very manly way, walk purposely into the bathroom bare-ass naked. Because I'm not here for your entertainment, Ms. Smith."

"It's Miss. Nice Southern girls use Miss."

"Then I guess that still makes you a Ms."

Dee-Ann Smith sat at Van Holtz's kitchen table, her fingers tracing the lines in the marble. His kitchen table was real marble, too, the legs made of the finest wood. Not like her parents' Formica table that still had the crack in it from when Rory Reed's big head drunkenly slammed into it after they'd had too many beers the night of their junior-year homecoming game.

Then again, everything about Van Holtz's apartment spoke of money and the finest of everything. Yet his place somehow managed to be comfortable, not like some spots in this city where everything was so fancy Dee didn't know who'd want to visit or sit on a damn thing. Of course, Van Holtz didn't come off like some spoiled rich kid that she'd want to slap around when he got mouthy. She'd thought he'd be that way, but since meeting him a few months back, he'd proven that he wasn't like that at all.

Shame she couldn't say that for several of his family members. She'd met his daddy only a few times, and each time was a little worse than the last. And his older brother wasn't much better. To be honest, she didn't know why Van Holtz didn't challenge them both and take the Alpha position from the mean old bastard. That's how they did it among the Smiths, and it was a way of life that had worked for them for at least three centuries.

Hair dripping wet from the shower, Van Holtz walked into his kitchen. He wore black sweatpants and was pulling a black T-shirt over his head, giving Dee an oh-too-brief glimpse at an absolutely superb set of abs and narrow hips. No, he wasn't as big a wolf as Dee was used to—in fact, they were the same six-two height and nearly the same width—but good Lord, the man had an amazing body. It must be all the things he did during the day. Executive chef at the Fifth Avenue Van Holtz restaurant; a goalie for the shifter-only pro team he owned, The Carnivores; and one of the supervisors for the Group. A position that, although he didn't spend as much time in the field as Dee-Ann and her team, did force him to keep in excellent shape.

Giving another yawn, Van Holtz pushed his wet, dark blond hair off his face, brown eyes trying to focus while he scanned his kitchen.

"Coffee's in the pot," she said.

Some men, they simply couldn't function without their morning coffee, and that was Van Holtz.

"Thank you," he sighed, grabbing the mug she'd taken out for him and filling it up. If he minded that she'd become quite familiar with his kitchen and his apartment in general, after months of coming and going as she pleased, he never showed it.

Dee waited until he'd had a few sips and finally turned to her with a smile.

"Good morning."

She returned that smile, something she normally didn't bother with with most, and replied, "Morning."

"I promised you waffles with *fresh* blueberries." He sniffed in disgust. "Canned. As if I'd ever."

"I know. I know. Sacrilege."

"Exactly!"

Dee-Ann sat patiently at the kitchen table while Van Holtz whipped up a full breakfast for her the way most people whipped up a couple of pieces of toast.

"So, Dee"—Van Holtz placed perfectly made waffles and bacon in front of her with warmed syrup in a bowl and a small dish of butter right behind it—"what brings you here?"

He sat down on the chair across from her with his own plate of food.

"Cats irritate me."

Van Holtz nodded, chewing on a bite of food. "And yet you work so well with them on a day-to-day basis."

"Not when they get in my way."

"Is there a possibility you can be more specific on what your complaint is?"

"But it's fun to watch you look so confused."

"Only one cup of coffee, Dee-Ann. Only one cup."

She laughed a little, always amused when Van Holtz got a bit cranky.

"We went to raid a hybrid fight last night—not only was there no fight, but there were felines already there."

"Which felines?"

"KZS."

"Oh." He took another bite of bacon. "*Those* felines. Well, maybe they're trying to—"

"Those felines ain't gonna help mutts, Van Holtz, you know that."

"Can't you just call me Ric? You know, like everyone else."

And since the man had more cousins than should legally be allowed, all with the last name Van Holtz, perhaps that would be a bit easier for all concerned.

"Fine. They're not going to help, *Ric*."

"And yet it seems as if they are—or at least trying."

"They're doing something—and I don't like it. I don't like when anyone gets in my way." Especially particular felines who had wicked right crosses that Dee's jaw was still feeling several hours later.

"All right," he said. "I'll deal with it."

"Just like that?"

"Yep. Just like that. Orange juice?" She nodded and he poured freshly squeezed orange juice into her glass.

"You don't want to talk to the team first?"

"I talked to you. What's the team going to tell me that you haven't? Except they'll probably use more syllables and keep the anti-feline sentiment out of it."

She nodded and watched him eat. Pretty. The man was just . . . pretty. Not girly—although she was sure her daddy and uncles would think so—but pretty. Handsome and gorgeous might be the more acceptable terms when talking about men, but those words did not fit him.

"Is something wrong with your food?" he asked, noticing that she hadn't started eating.

She glanced down at the expertly prepared waffle, big fresh blueberries throughout, powdered sugar sprinkled over it. In bowls he'd also put out more fresh blueberries, along with strawberries and peaches. He'd given her a linen napkin to use and heavy, expensive-looking flatware to eat with. And he'd set all this up in about thirty minutes.

The whole meal was, in a word, perfection, which was why Dee replied, "It's all right . . . I guess."

A dark eyebrow peaked. "You guess?"

"Haven't tried it yet, now have I? Can't tell you if I like it if I haven't tried it."

"Only one cup of coffee, Dee. Only one."

"Maybe it's time you had another."

"Eat and tell me my food is amazing or I'm going to get cranky again."

"If you're going to be pushy . . ." She took a bite, letting the flavors burst against her taste buds. Damn, but the man could cook. Didn't seem right, did it? Pretty and a good cook.

"Well?"

"Do I really need to tell you how good it is?"

"Yes. Although I'm enjoying your orgasm face."

She smirked. "Darlin', you don't know my orgasm face."

"Yet. I'm ever hopeful."

"Keepin' that dream alive."

"Someone has to." He winked at her and went back to his food. "I'll see what I can find out about what's going on with KZS and get back to you." He looked up at her and smiled. "Don't worry, Dee-Ann. I've got your back."

She knew that. She knew he would come through as promised. As hard as it was to believe, she was learning to trust the one breed of wolf her daddy told her never to trust.

Then again . . . her daddy had never tasted the man's blueberry waffles.

"But do me a favor, Dee," he said. "Until I get this straightened out, don't get into it with the cats."

Dee stared at him and asked with all honesty, "What makes you think I would?"

CHAPTER 2

The first punch to her face sent Dee-Ann stumbling. But that wasn't surprising. They didn't call the tigress Marcella Malone "Bare Knuckles" for nothing. And Dee's big mistake had been turning her back on her. She knew better than to turn her back on the treacherous feline and former Marine originally from Mineola, Long Island, New York. Or, as Dee used to put it when they trained together—"that Long Island whore."

It had been a lot of years since they'd seen each other, since they'd started together in the Marines Corps' shifter-only Unit until their commanding officer had placed them on separate teams because, as the polar bear had explained, "Some dogs and cats will just never get along."

"I'm sorry, Dee-Ann," the feline told her without any remorse whatsoever. "My fist slipped."

"It happens," Dee replied seconds before she swung her own fist, connecting with Malone's face.

The She-tiger snarled, her head coming up, blood streaming from the cut on her cheek, eyes turning bright gold and angry. Seemed fair, though, since Dee had the same amount of blood coming from her nose.

The pair sized each other up. Dee quickly remembered all the strengths and weaknesses the She-tiger had. About Dee's age, thirty-five or so, Malone had come into her full adult power with strong arms and thighs. She'd be fast, but her stamina would be nothing like Dee's. At six feet, Malone weighed a bit more and had more curves in her human form. She still kept her black hair with white and red streaks long, and Dee had no qualms about using all that hair to her advantage if she had to.

Their teams spread out around them in a circle and Dee knew on some deeper, more humane level that this was wrong. They were here on a hot, late-June night in this Brooklyn warehouse for bigger issues than a bitch-fight between former Marines. But Malone had always brought out the worst in Dee. The absolute worst.

So ignoring the bigger issues—like what had happened to the fight ring that was supposed to be having an event tonight at this location—the two She-predators removed their jackets and brought up their fists.

Malone was and always would be a brawler. It ran in her tiger bloodline. She was the daughter of one of the greatest early shifter hockey players, "Nice Guy" Malone. And, like her father, she'd gone from the Marines to playing right defenseman for the Nevada Slammers. She was pretty good, too, but spent a lot of her time in the penalty box because she simply couldn't stop from beating the hell out of people when they irritated her.

But hockey wasn't all that Malone was part of. She also worked for Katzenhaft Security or KZS for short. The feline nation's security team. Dating back several hundred years, KZS had bases all over the world, their job simply to protect all felines. It was rare for Dee or the Group in general to come face to face with a KZS team. Especially when dealing with hybrids. The cats were notorious for having no interest or patience with mixed breeds of any kind. As it was, they barely tolerated the feline crossbreeds—tigons, ligers, cheetah-leopard crosses, etc.—but when fellow felines bred outside their species or KZS teammates were dealing with canine mixes in general, they often showed more disdain than usual. Which meant they normally didn't involve themselves with hybrid issues.

Until recently. Something that made Dee-Ann all sorts of distrustful.

That two-ton truck Malone called a fist rammed into Dee's cheek, followed by a right cross to her already battered nose. Dee ignored the little yellow birds twirling around her head and blocked the next punch with her right forearm, smashing Malone's nose with the palm of her hand. Malone's head snapped back and Dee followed up with a punch to the stomach. Malone caught Dee around the neck with both arms and came in close, bringing her knee up into Dee's gut, twice. Dee slammed her head forward into Malone's.

"That's it!" a female voice yelled.

Strong hands yanked Dee and Malone apart and the fact that their feet weren't touching the ground told Dee they were being held by something really big.

"Dee-Ann?" That female voice again. It didn't belong to whatever was holding them.

Dee wiped blood out of her eyes and looked down into a familiar face. "Evening, Desiree."

Wearing a bulletproof vest over a light T-shirt, her gun drawn—she always had more than one on her at any given time—her bright grey-green gaze quickly taking in the room, Desiree MacDermot-Llewellyn seemed much more at home with shifters than with her own. It wasn't just her choice of mate either, the lion male Mace Llewellyn whom Dee had known for years through her cousin Bobby Ray. No, it was too easy to dismiss Desiree as a full-human who didn't find her own way until she'd met her mate. Because the truth was, Desiree MacDermot-Llewellyn was as much a predator as anyone Dee had known.

Desiree shook her head, blew out a breath, and put her weapon back in the holster at her side. "What the hell are you doing, Dee?"

"Don't know what you mean."

Rolling her eyes, Desiree looked over at Malone. "And you?"

Malone snarled, baring her fangs. A move that didn't bother Desiree one bit based on that snort she gave in return.

"Check the place," Desiree ordered. She was NYPD and had not come alone tonight. Besides the bear holding Dee and Malone like two rag dolls, there was a S.W.A.T. unit from the Brooklyn precinct that was made up mostly of shifter cops who'd worked for other precincts throughout the five boroughs until they got this gig. Unlike the Group or KZS, their job was to keep the peace between the species throughout the city, not protect or wipe out. And although Desiree was full-human, she had three things going for her that made her perfect for this particular job: She was mated to a powerful lion male, she'd bred a lion male of her own, meaning she'd do what she could to protect him, and the woman was a damn good cop.

"Dez," one of her team called out. "You better see this."

Desiree walked off and Malone said to the one holding them, "Think you could put us down now, sport?"

The roughly seven-ten polar's gaze went back and forth between them before answering, "No."

After several minutes, Desiree returned, her expression direct and not too happy.

With a swirl of her finger, Desiree ordered her team to, "Bring 'em all in."

"What the hell for?" Malone snapped.

"There are about twenty bodies back there," she informed them. "Some in their human form, some not so much. Maybe you two would have noticed if you weren't busy having a caged death match." Disgusted, she shook her head. "Until we straighten this out, everybody goes."

Desiree turned to her team, barking out orders.

Feeling downright shamed, Dee glanced over at Malone, who raised her head at the same time. And, for a moment, Dee guessed they both felt the same bone-deep disappointment in themselves for not keeping their eyes on the bigger issue. But then it seemed they both got tired of that and began snarling and snapping, trying to claw at each other from a distance, ignoring the bear ordering them to settle down.

Dee had to admit, it felt better doing that than feeling sorry for herself.

Ric pulled three plates from the overhead grill. He slammed the door shut with his elbow and slid the plates of sizzling sea lion blubber onto the saucier's station for the final touch.

"Let's go, people!" he yelled out, seeing the number of tickets piling up. "Let's pick up the speed. We've got a full house out there!"

"Yes, chef!" was the answer he got back, followed by several muttered "Asshole." But Ric didn't mind. He kind of deserved it.

"Ric!" he heard his younger cousin Arden yell out as she stormed into the kitchen. If a Van Holtz didn't want to work in the kitchen, then they worked front of house. At least until they got through college.

Arden held a large platter in her hand. A full salmon, head and all, that Ric had sent out ten minutes earlier.

"What is it?"

"The grizzly on six says there's not enough honey in your honey sauce salmon."

Knowing that his honey sauce glaze was, is, and always *would be* perfection, Ric understood what the disgruntled bear really wanted. Reaching down to one of the cabinets, he grabbed one of the fifty bear-shaped bottles of average, everyday honey he kept there. He wouldn't waste the good—and expensive—European stuff on Philistines.

Pushing past his sous-chef, Ric unscrewed the top and dumped half the bottle of honey right onto the salmon, stole a knife from one of the nearby stations and smeared the honey over the fish. Taking the platter from his cousin, he tossed it into one of the industrial microwaves and re-heated the fish for a few seconds. Again, someone with an actual palate might deserve better treatment, but this idiot bear was lucky Ric didn't drag the damn fish across the bathroom floor.

When he knew enough time had passed, he opened the microwave and pulled out the fish. "Here. With compliments from the chef," he practically snarled.

Grinning, his cousin walked out.

"They're all Philistines!" he announced to his kitchen.

"Yes, chef!"

Ric went back to work, his unwavering focus on getting the food done and getting it done well. He was happily in a zone when his phone vibrated from the pocket of his black sweatpants.

"This is Ric."

"Hi, Cousin."

Ric smiled. "Uncle Van! How's it going?"

"Great. Great. I know you're busy so I'll make this quick. I'm having something messengered over to your apartment in the next day or two."

"Okay."

"You're not going to ask me what it is?"

"Should I?"

"Probably."

Ric grimaced. "This involves my father, doesn't it?"

"Possibly. I'm sending you copies of the books for the Van Holtz restaurants in the tri-state area. I want you to look them over, closely, and tell me what you think."

Ric's grimace turned to slack-jawed panic. He could feel his mouth dropping open in shock. "Pardon?"

"You know what I'm asking, Ric."

"Yes, but—"

"And you're the one I trust to be honest with me."

"But it sounds like you already know the truth."

"I'm guessing. *You* are the one with the head for numbers. Or so my beautiful wife keeps telling me. Her exact words were, 'Please don't try to think. It's painful to watch. Send the damn things to Ulrich.' And, as always, she's absolutely right. Will that be a problem?"

Investigating to see if Ric's father, Alder Van Holtz, was robbing his own family and Pack of funds for whatever reason he might have? Gee . . . why would that be a problem?

"No, sir."

"Excellent. Let me know when you have something."

"Okay."

The call disconnected, Ric went back to his work, glad that he would be turning over his kitchen to his sous-chef soon because he had guests coming over in a bit. But before he could get lost in the food, his phone went off again.

Dreading that his father had already heard all about it through his spies, Ric went out to the back alley to answer the call.

"This is Ric."

"Mr. Van Holtz?"

Ric almost sighed in relief when he heard a woman's voice on the other end. "Yes."

"This is Detective MacDermot. NYPD."

He knew her. Mace Llewellyn's wife. Not exactly the type of woman Ric would expect a lion like Llewellyn to choose for his mate. Not that there was anything wrong with Desiree MacDermot. Far from it. But a Puerto Rican–Irish street cop from the Bronx wasn't exactly a blue blood, was she? Something that the Llewellyns usually insisted upon.

"Yes, Detective. What can I do for you?"

"My boss was wondering if you could come in tonight for a meeting."

Ric frowned. "I'm working tonight and have plans, so I'm not sure that's going to—"

"We have your team, Mr. Van Holtz."

Ric blew out a breath. *Dee-Ann.* "I understand. I'm heading right over."

"Thank you." She ended the call and Ric slipped the phone back into his sweats. Already irritated, now Ric was extremely annoyed. He glanced at his watch, making sure he had enough time to deal with whatever drama Dee-Ann and her team had gotten into and then get back to meet his friends without being forced to cancel the entire evening. He could do it, even though he might be a little late, but they'd wait for him.

Already thinking of what he'd have to do in his kitchen before he could cut out, Ric gazed down to the end of the alley that led out to the street. That's when he saw him. Their eyes met and the kid took off.

Ric ran to the end of the alley, looking up and down the busy street, trying to catch sight of him again. Nope. Nothing.

Damn it. This night was simply not getting any better, was it?

Dee sat in the cage, her elbows resting on her knees, her chin resting on her fists. She sat in the cage and waited while the She-tiger in the cage next to her paced back and forth like she was about to be dragged off to the Bronx Zoo tiger display.

"How can you just sit there like that?" Malone finally demanded.

"What do you expect me to do? Pace around like an idiot?"

"I expect you to do *something*."

"Don't see the purpose of gettin' all upset."

"When do you ever?"

"That was always your problem, Malone. All emotion, no sense."

Malone faced her, gripping the bars with her still-bloody knuckles. "At least I give a shit. At least I care about those people they found."

"That's real Yankee of ya, Malone. But your big emotions don't really help nothin', do they?"

"Cold as your precious daddy, I see."

That had Dee up off the bench she'd been sitting on, across the cage, her arm through the bars, and her hand wrapping around the back of Malone's head. She jerked her forward, slamming her forehead into the titanium metal they used for these cages since they were built specifically for shifters.

Malone's fist came through the bars, punching Dee in the eye.

Fangs bared, the two females held on, trying to drag each other through the bars.

"*Dee-Ann!*"

Dee stumbled back, the pair releasing each other at the bellow.

Trying to see through her already swelling eye, she blinked in surprise.

Van Holtz . . . er . . . Ric, stood outside the bars, absolutely seething. He was in his black sweats, black Van sneakers, and black T-shirt, but the scent of his busy kitchen still lingered all around him. The predator cops sitting at their desks lifted their heads and tested the air, probably trying to figure out why they were suddenly so hungry.

"Get out here," Ric ordered and Dee walked forward. She reached through the bars and fussed with the lock that held her for a bit. It opened easy enough, and she heard Malone gasp in surprise behind her. Poor felines. They just didn't have the same way with locks as wolves and foxes.

"Why didn't you do that before?" Malone wanted to know.

"Because knowing I can do it is just as good as doing it. Just like *knowing* that I can cut your throat while you sleep—"

Ric placed a hand over Dee's mouth and pulled her down the hall. "Bathroom?" he asked Desiree, who was unlocking Malone's cage.

"At the end of the hallway."

They found the room and Ric pushed her in.

"What is wrong with you?" he demanded.

And all Dee could do was shrug and admit, "She irritates me."

Ric opened the first aid kit tacked to the wall and took out some gauze and antibiotic cream. He wet the gauze and began wiping the blood off Dee's face and her knuckles. Once the blood was gone, however, he still had bruises and cuts to deal with.

"She irritates you? She irritates everyone."

Dee gazed at him through the one eye that wasn't swollen shut. "You know Malone?"

"I hired Malone. She plays on the Carnivores."

"What the hell did you do that for?"

"Have you seen the way that woman plays?"

"I don't care how she plays, supermodel. She's with KZS. Did you know that, too?"

He gazed into her eyes and answered with utter honesty, "Of course, I knew."

Dee shoved him aside. "You're working with *them* now?"

"They're not our enemy, Dee-Ann."

"Like hell they're not. Maybe you don't remember when they tried to move on wolf territory, but I sure do."

Ric scratched his forehead. "You mean in 1832?"

"Yeah."

"Wow. Smiths really don't let a grudge go, do they?"

"Not unless we're contractually obligated to like we were with y'all."

"I'll keep that in mind. But we don't have time for this, Dee."

"What does that mean?"

"Come on."

Dee waited while Ric threw out the bloody gauze, slathered some ointment on the worst of her cuts, washed his hands, and took Dee to the main office on the floor: a glass room with a door and a view of the Brooklyn Bridge from the window behind the desk. Sitting at the desk was a black bear sow. Desiree stood next to the desk and Malone sat in a chair beside another feline. A lynx, who seemed way overdressed for this meeting.

"There you are," the lynx complained, pointing at her watch. "Have date. Not missing. Let's move this along, people."

Ric closed the door and, always the gentleman, began introducing everyone to Dee. "You know Detective MacDermott, and this is her boss Lynsey Gentry. She runs this division of the NYPD. And you know Marcella Malone, and this is her boss, Nina Bugliosi. She's Cella's supervisor, but speaks for KZS as I speak for the Group."

Dee gazed at him. *Cella? He's calling her Cella now?*

"Sit, you two. Sit." The sow motioned them down and began. "I'll keep this short because I don't see a point in making it long-winded. Here's the deal. These fight rings have popped up all over the city and they're multiplying. Now, I won't get into the concern over protecting who we are from the full-humans who know nothing about us. That's a given, I think. The more important issue is that we can no longer ignore what's happening to the hybrids in this city and the other boroughs, nor can we continue to try and strike at these small dogfights that we've been stumbling across. It's not effective. So after talking to Niles Van Holtz, who runs the entire Group from East Coast to the West, and Victoria Löwe who represents Katzenhaft Security in the States, we've all decided to join forces."

"Which means what, exactly?" Malone asked.

"That means we're putting a small team of our best people on this to get to the heart of where it's all stemming from. I want to know who's the money behind this. Once we find the money, we can take it from there. But we've got to find the money."

"And who's gonna be on this team?" Although Dee already had a bad feeling she knew the answer.

"Desiree will take lead. She represents NYPD and can keep the full-human precincts off you, something she did earlier tonight after the residents of that neighborhood complained, so you should thank her. I don't know what we could have done if anyone else had found you in that warehouse with all those bodies."

Together, Malone and Dee looked over at Desiree and sneered, "Thank you."

Desiree laughed and Gentry continued. "To represent KZS, we'll have Miss Malone and for the Group, Miss Smith."

Canine and feline scowled at each other across the room. Then Malone roared and Dee barked multiple times, lips pulled back over fangs.

The lynx snapped her fingers in Malone's face. "Date!" she bellowed. "Was I not clear I have a date? I don't have time for this bullshit." She pointed at Dee-Ann. "From you either. So let's cut to the chase rather than wait for the bear to make her slow, *plodding* way to it. We've already looked at your records, ladies.

All three of you are former Marines, and both Smith and Malone have Unit training. So you're going to get over whatever bullshit issues you have and fix this problem before I get really fucking cranky." She stood, smoothing down her mini-dress. "Is that it?"

"Well—" the sow began.

"Good. See ya!" Then she was out the door and gone.

Dee turned to Ric, waiting for him to say something. He did.

"So . . . are you hungry?"

CHAPTER 3

R ic paid the cabbie and stood, Dee-Ann glaring at him from
the front stoop of his family's restaurant.

"What did you want me to do?" he asked.

"Tell them no."

He shrugged. "I like the idea. Besides, we should all be working together to stop this—don't walk away from me, Dee-Ann."

His stern warning ignored, Dee kept walking, but Ric caught
up with her and pulled her into the alley between the restaurant
and the deli next door.

"Don't you find it curious," he asked, standing in front of her,
"that felines who are so into pure bloodlines they could be
British royalty are suddenly concerning themselves with hybrids?"

Folding her arms over her chest, Dee did that thing he hated
where she looked right past him. Then again she only did that
when he was right about something and it pissed her off.

"If you're really adamant about not working on this, I can put
someone else on it." He tried to think of the one person who'd
really set Dee off and he realized that one person was waiting for
him right inside one of the private dining rooms. "I'll give it to
Blayne."

Ric took a step away, but Dee's hand shot out and caught hold
of his arm. "Pardon?"

"I said I'll put Blayne on it since you don't want to—"

"Teacup? You're going to put Teacup on *this*?"

"She's a great ambassador for the Group, gets along well with felines *and* bears, and she already knows Dez MacDermot."

"She *babysits* for Desiree."

"She's also taken on bigger responsibilities with the Group and that's worked out just fine."

"With the hybrid pups and cubs. It's not like she's ever been in the field."

"But she handled herself just fine in Ursus County." Ric still had a hard time believing that his goofy, loveable wolfdog buddy was the same She-predator he'd seen decimate a gang of full-human males trying to kill them. And she'd done it with nothing more than a couple of blades in her hands and sheer willpower. Then again, Blayne's knife skills only made a real appearance when she was backed into a corner with no way out. Of course . . . he didn't have to mention he knew that to Dee.

"Ursus—" The She-wolf gritted pearly white fangs and snarled at him like he was trying to take her favorite chew toy. "The only reason she lived through Ursus County was 'cause of me. The only reason she has a job with the Group is 'cause of me. The only reason she breathes my precious, precious air is 'cause of me!"

It was true. The one person who could really set Dee-Ann Smith off was and perhaps always would be Blayne Thorpe.

"I understand that, but—"

Dee's head dipped low, bright gold eyes looking up at him through dark brown lashes. "Fine. I'll do it."

"Not if you're just going to use this as an opportunity to beat up on Cella."

If it was possible, Dee-Ann's expression turned even angrier. "That's true. I wouldn't want to hurt your girlfriend."

Ric blinked. "My what?"

"Forget it." She stepped around him, ready to leave, but Ric caught hold of her wrist, keeping her in place.

"I promised you food."

"I don't need you feeding me, Van Holtz. I'm not some charity case."

"I never said you were. And what happened to Ric? It sounded so nice when you called me Ric. And you have to eat, Dee-Ann." He gripped one of the loops of her jeans, tugging at it.

"Hands!"

"One good tug and these will come off. You're too skinny."

"When did you become my mother?"

"See? Even your mother is concerned."

"No, she's not."

He led her to the back door. "Come on. You have to eat, otherwise I'll be up all night worrying you've passed out somewhere. Unable to take another step due to lack of nutrition."

Ric had his hand on the doorknob, giving Dee a wink over his shoulder. But the door swung open from the inside, shoving him back and right into the She-wolf. He slammed into her, his body pushing hers into the wall behind them.

"Sorry, boss," one of his crew said, tossing a bag of trash into the Dumpster. "Didn't see you there."

Ric didn't reply. He was too busy being seriously aware of the woman he had pressed against the wall.

"You planning to get off me anytime soon, supermodel?" she asked.

"Or we can stay this way forever. That's an option." One he was more than willing to explore.

"Good Lord!" Dee pushed him back and walked toward the alley door. "If Cella's not your girlfriend, we need to get you one."

"Cella's not my girlfriend. She works for me. It would be inappropriate."

Dee-Ann stopped in the open doorway and faced him. "So do I, but that hasn't stopped you from demanding I get naked every other day."

"True, but I don't sign your checks."

"Which means what exactly?"

"I don't know, but if you give me some time I'm sure I can come up with something completely logical that could be argued in front of the Supreme Court."

"Ya know . . . I bet you could."

Dee didn't know why she should suddenly care if Ric was going out with Malone or not, but she'd admit to herself that she kind of did care. Maybe she was just feeling moody. Maybe a little homesick. Whatever. She'd get over it.

She stood outside the kitchen while Ric went back in and got their food. It seemed to take longer than she thought it would, which meant that he was cooking it himself. But when he finally came out, he smiled at her—back to his happy-go-lucky, goofball self because he'd cooked something up in a pan—and motioned down the hall toward the private dining rooms. Figuring he probably wanted to discuss next steps before she had to deal with Malone on a daily basis, Dee started walking. One of the waiters slipped past her carrying a big tray piled with more food.

"Here," Ric said, when the waiter stopped at one of the rooms.

That seemed like a lot of food for the pair of them, but maybe he was hungrier than she realized.

Once at the door, Ric reached around her with his free hand and pushed it open. The waiter went in and Dee followed, but she froze at the doorway and snarled, glaring back at Van Holtz.

"What?" he asked, trying to look innocent.

"I really should have killed you when I had the chance, supermodel."

"And where would the fun be in that?" He pushed her into the room before she could make a break for it, and that's when she was noticed.

"Deeeeeeee-Annnnnnnnnnnnnnnnn!" she heard seconds before a crazed wolfdog female wrapped herself around Dee and held on, hugging her tight.

"You've been missed," Van Holtz whispered in her ear before

he walked into the room, grinning at the table filled with a small group of people she tolerated but didn't necessarily want to spend much time with.

"I'm so glad you're here!" the wolfdog said, arms tightening so that Dee's air was almost cut off.

"Get off me, Blayne."

"You're staying, aren't you?"

"Get off me, Blayne."

"You have to stay so we can eat and talk. It's been ages!" She rested her head against Dee's shoulder. "I've missed you so much."

That's when Dee reached for her bowie knife, but Ric caught her hand before she could clear the sheath and held it behind her back.

"Why don't we all sit down and eat before the food gets cold?" he offered.

"Okay!" The wolfdog released her death grip on Dee's neck and skated back to the table—why she was wearing roller skates in the middle of a restaurant, Dee didn't want to even hazard a guess—unaware as always how close to death she came every time she insisted on the touching.

"Put it away," Van Holtz whispered in Dee's ear, "or I'm taking the whole hand."

With a grunt, Dee shoved the knife back. "There, supermodel. Happy?"

"Thrilled." He released her, but not before she felt his fingers slide across her forearm. "You have the smoothest skin," he murmured, looking down at her arm.

"Yeah. It's the scar tissue from all those knife fights. After a few years, it heals up real soft."

Ric got Dee-Ann seated at one end of the table and Blayne Thorpe at the other—not easy when Blayne kept insisting on wanting to hug Dee again. It was like she had a death wish. Then he and one of his runners went about taking care of the rest of his guests.

Lachlan "Lock" MacRyrie, Ric's best friend since they were both ten years old, was still laughing when Dee sat down kitty-corner from him. Whether he was laughing at Blayne's attempt to show Dee affection, Dee's reaction to that affection, or Ric's constant attempts to keep Dee from wiping Blayne from the face of the earth, Ric didn't know. It was hard sometimes to believe that this nearly seven-foot-tall grizzly taking up a lot of space in the good-sized private dining room had once been the same medium-sized kid who'd run face first into Ric's locker on a dare. A dare that had been issued by Ric. He'd felt bad about it, too, when Lock had knocked himself out cold.

Ric placed a full-sized platter in front of the grizzly. "Salmon and my perfect honey glaze for you."

Lock stared at the fresh, ten-pound wild salmon in front of him. "Did you put in enough honey this time?"

Snarling, Ric pulled the plastic honey bear out of his pocket and chucked it at his friend's big grizzly bear head. "Philistine," he snarled.

Turning away before he could watch the brute desecrate his perfectly prepared food with all that honey, Ric leaned in and kissed Lock's mate and Blayne's best friend, Gwen, on the cheek before placing a plate of food in front of her. "Wild boar stew for you."

"Yum. Smells fantastic."

Next came the simple New York steak with sautéed green beans for Blayne since she could be a little finicky about her food.

"To drink?" he asked the table.

"Wine?" Gwen asked.

"Excellent choice." He'd introduced the Philly feline to the higher-end wines in the last few months and it had turned out she had a wonderful palate.

Her grizzly bear mate, however . . .

"Mil—" the bear began but Ric held his hand up, cutting his friend off.

"Can't you at least *try* some wine?" Ric nearly begged. "I have a splendid nineteen thirty-two—"

"I want milk. Cold. A vat please."

Shaking his head, disgusted, Ric turned his attention to Blayne. "And you, Miss Thorpe?"

"Nothing with caffeine or sugar!" she crowed. "Or I'll never get to sleep tonight! Woo-hoo!" When they only stared at her, Blayne's shoulders slumped and she calmly stated, "Diet Coke please."

Ric turned to Dee-Ann, who seemed to still be seething. "Dee?"

"Water."

"Sparkling or flat?"

The confused expression on her face was priceless when she snapped, "Tap."

"Flat it is." As if he'd ever give her regular, everyday tap water. He nearly shuddered at the thought.

Ric gave the runner their drink orders and suggested he bring more bread now rather than later because Lock was gnawing his hand off in hunger. He caught hold of the door and opened it, the runner shooting out and leaving Bo "The Marauder" Novikov standing there. Novikov was a godsend to Ric's hockey team and Blayne's mate, but he was such an irritating asshole that Ric couldn't help slamming the door in the polar bear–lion's face.

A roar shook the door and walls, and Blayne jumped out of her seat and across the room to snatch the door open. "Do not"—she ordered—"rip those hinges off!" She took Novikov's hand. "Just come in and be *nice*." She glared at Ric. "You too, Ulrich."

"Me?" Ric placed his hand against his chest. "What did *I* do?"

Fresh from his daily—and brutal—training, Novikov tossed the bag with his hockey equipment to the floor. He glanced around and asked, "Is there food for me?"

"Are you paying this time?" Ric asked, which got him a slap on the arm from Blayne. "Ow!"

The runner returned with their drinks and Ric had Novikov

give him his order since Ric didn't deem him worthy of his brilliant expertise in guessing—always correctly—what his friends were in need of at the moment.

The seven-foot-one hybrid dropped his nearly four-hundred-pound weight into one of the restaurant's best chairs with no regard for the furniture and looked around the table, his blue eyes stopping on Dee-Ann. "What's she doing here?" he asked Blayne.

"I invited her," Ric told him, sitting in the seat across from Lock and kitty-corner from Dee. "Although I don't remember seeing your name on the e-mail I sent out."

"Both of you stop it," Blayne snapped. "And Dee's here because I want her to be here," she told Novikov.

"She tagged you like a wildebeest."

"Would you let that go already?"

"Here." Lock reached over to the sideboard, grabbed one of the big baskets of bread, and slammed it in front of Novikov. "Shove this in your hole and keep quiet."

Snarling a little, the rude bastard continued to glare at Dee-Ann, and Ric was ready to climb across the table and tear the hybrid's face off with his teeth. But Blayne had a good handle on her mate, pulling a notepad out of his back pocket and proceeding to write on it.

"What are you doing to my list?" he demanded as if she'd stolen his wallet.

"Just making a few . . . changes." She held up the list. "I drew hearts and flowers on it!"

"Give me that!" Novikov yanked it back from her and so began another lecture on the proper use of lists.

How Blayne tolerated it, Ric had no idea. To each their own, he guessed.

Ric picked up his fork, ready to dig into his medallions of gazelle and deer in wine sauce. But finding only an empty plate where his food used to be, he decided that he'd been right. Dee-Ann had been hungry.

"What?" Dee asked around his gazelle when he raised a brow in her direction. "You were busy talkin'."

*   *   *

Dee ate the most amazing angel's food cake with white icing and listened to the chatter going on around her.

It seemed wedding plans were not going well for Lock and his mate because their mothers had different views on pretty much everything. Blayne was worried her wedding would top five hundred guests "easy," and Ric was arguing with Novikov about . . . well, about pretty much everything, but mostly about who to add to their team and who to drop. Since she had no interest in weddings, Dee listened mostly to the hockey discussion. Especially since Reece Lee Reed was on the team now.

Dee had grown up with the Reed boys. Although she'd always been closest to Rory, the eldest, she was tight with all of them. Ricky Lee Reed was currently in Tokyo, working in the Japanese division of her cousin Bobby Ray's security business. Yet all the Reed boys were as close to her as her cousins Sissy Mae and Bobby Ray. Then again, her cousins had never faced the wrath of Eggie Smith when caught trying to sneak her drunk ass back into her parents' house. So, like Lock MacRyrie, the Reeds had earned her loyalty.

After a few minutes, the conversation turned to Cella Malone, and MacRyrie said to Dee, "By the way . . . Malone moved back to the city. She's on the team now."

Dee gazed at the bear while Ric chuckled beside her. "I know," she said.

"Oh." The grizzly's head tipped to the side and he asked, "Did you know you have a bunch of bruises on your face?"

"I'm aware."

He thought a moment and added, "It's not because of Malone, is it?"

"Do I really need to answer that?"

He shook his head, dug into his platter-sized slice of berry-nut cake. "I'm thinking, no, you don't."

"Do you know Marcella Malone?" Teacup asked.

"My face does," Dee muttered.

"Isn't she great? She's so nice and sweet. I met her at team practice the other day. Her dad is 'Nice Guy' Malone."

"Fascinating," Dee lied, then slammed her fork into Ric's before he could get some of her cake. "Don't you need that hand to work so you can keep cooking?"

"You won't share?"

"Not without a fight."

Ric leaned in a bit, the rest of the table having a discussion about something else she couldn't care less about. "And don't let this thing with Marcella Malone bother you, Dee. You have more important work to do. I expect you to impress me."

"Because that's my life goal," she replied dryly. "To impress a Van Holtz."

"All the Packs would be better off if that *was* their life's goal."

"Y'all born with that level of arrogance?"

Ric grinned, showing perfect, gleaming white teeth. "It seems that way. Although my Aunt Irene says she hasn't quite figured out if it's an inborn personality trait or a genetic defect. But she's working on it."

Ric walked his guests out of his restaurant. It was a hot, muggy night and he couldn't wait to get home. But he still had to ensure the kitchen was shut down properly, that he knew what was being delivered tomorrow so he could start working on the menu for himself and his Aunt Adelle, who shared executive chef duties with him, and that he dealt with any complaints that may have come up in the evening if they had to do with his crew.

"Everything all right?" Lock asked him, the pair standing off to the side while the others watched a hyped-up Blayne do backflips in her skates. He could only guess that there was some processed sugar in the honey cake the pastry chef had made. He'd have to check since it was listed on the menu as a sugar-free dessert.

"I thought I saw Stein earlier."

Lock turned toward him, eyes blinking wide. "Are you sure it was him?"

"Not really. But it *looked* like him."

"Your father's going to have a fit if the kid's back."

"I know."

"Are you going to help him?"

"No."

"Ric—"

"I'm not." The kid had broken his heart. Ric wasn't about to help him now. Those days were over. "The kid's on his own, which—according to him—is the way he likes it."

"Stubborn."

"It's a flaw I've learned to live with."

By now Novikov had a wriggling "I need to run and be free!" Blayne over his shoulder. "Anyone need a ride?" he asked, heading to what Lock called the man's "military transport." A vehicle so big, it could get an entire Roman legion in it.

"No, thanks. We have our truck."

"Okay. See you at the game tomorrow." He started to open the door of his truck, but stopped and faced them. He thought a moment and said, "And thank you for dinner."

Ric, confused by the sudden bout of politeness, answered, "You're welcome."

With a nod, he suddenly slapped Blayne's rear and said, "Happy now? I said thank you to your loser friends and Gwen."

"It's progress! Now let me go to run free!"

"You'll be in Connecticut before I can catch you and I have a game tomorrow."

He got her into his vehicle and put a seatbelt on her. It appeared to be a standard seatbelt but, for whatever reason, Blayne seemed unable to get it off, giving Novikov time to get around and inside the vehicle before his mate could make a run for it.

Watching her try to wiggle and fight her way out of that seatbelt, Ric stated, "I feel like we should be rescuing her."

"Really?" Gwen asked, slipping her arm around Lock's waist. "I always feel like I should be rescuing *him*. He's gotta go home and deal with a hyped-up Blayne for the next few hours."

Ric shook his head. "I need to talk to Jean-Louis about his honey cake. It's supposed to be sugar free."

"You gonna tell him, hoss?" Dee suddenly asked from behind Ric. To be honest, he'd thought she'd left a while ago.

Lock, appearing caught, shrugged. "Don't know what you mean." He grabbed Gwen's hand. "Let's go."

"Wait. What's the redneck talking about?" Gwen demanded, forced to follow her mate to their truck.

Ric sighed. "Okay. What's going on?"

"I'm only telling you 'cause I don't want Jean-whatever—"

"Jean-Louis."

"Yeah. Him. He makes the best angel's food cake I've ever had and I don't want him fired over something not his fault. But when Novikov wasn't looking, MacRyrie put sugar in Blayne's *soothing* chamomile tea."

Ric, working hard not to laugh, said, "Oh. That's *horrible*. I'll talk to Lock about it tomorrow."

"What about you re-organizing Novikov's hockey bag while he was in the bathroom? You gonna tell MacRyrie about that, too?"

"Probably not . . . right away."

She grinned. "Y'all are so mean to that boy."

"You act as if he doesn't deserve it."

"I didn't say that, but where I come from, we tolerate our rude ones when they play a sport that well. We put up with Mitch Shaw for the town's football season."

"Mitch isn't rude, though. He's just"—he thought a minute and finally finished—"Mitch."

"That don't make it right." She winked and began to amble off. He'd never met anyone who ambled in Manhattan, but Dee managed to.

"Uh . . . need a lift home?"

"Not going home. Got that meeting with that idiot feline and Desiree early in the morning and it's too far to travel."

"You can stay at my place," he offered, hoping to look innocent and helpful rather than lustful and desperate.

"No, but thank you kindly. I'll crash at Rory Reed's tonight. He's staying at Brendon Shaw's hotel with the rest of the Pack, so he's got room service and a real comfortable couch."

"But my place has me and my waffles with blueberries."

"I can't keep living off you, Van Holtz."

"It's not living off me if you're going to be my wife anyway."

Turning around and walking backward, she said, "Huh?"

Ric decided this wasn't the time. "Nothing. Have a good night, Dee-Ann."

"You, too." She turned back around and quickly faded into the shadows. "And thanks for dinner."

He sighed, thinking about another lonely night in his bed. "Anytime."

CHAPTER 4

Rory Lee Reed was lying in his bed, wondering how much longer he'd have to sit here and hold this full-human female, when—finally!—his bedroom door slowly creaked open.

The full-human raised her head from his chest and, in a panicked whisper, "Rory . . ." She tapped his shoulder. "Rory. Wake up!"

He pretended to come awake, and looked across the room at Dee-Ann. She stood in his doorway, one denim-clad leg crossed over the other, Big Betty—the name he and his brothers had given her bowie knife—in one hand while she cleaned under the fingernails of the other.

"Dee . . . Dee-Ann? What are you doing here?"

"Came for my man," she growled low and turned her head a bit so the early morning light made the yellow of her eyes stand out that much more. And, if he didn't know her, he'd be terrified.

Heh.

"You told me you were single," the full-human accused.

"Uh . . . well . . ."

"It doesn't matter," she said quickly and Rory stopped just short of rolling his eyes. She was one of *those*.

"You need to roll up out of here, darlin'," Dee explained in a slow drawl. "Before I start gettin' cranky."

"Rory's with me now," the full-human told Dee. "I'm sorry if that hurts, but that's the way it is."

Dee's eyes flicked over to his and without saying a word, he begged, *Please don't leave me. Please don't leave me.*

They'd only been on three dates! Three dates that led to one night of solid, entertaining sex. But, as was the way with some of these full-humans, that was sometimes enough.

His daddy had warned him. Warned him but good. "Stay away from the full-humans, boy. They're clingy and don't know when to walk away. They'll put up a fight."

Of course, that warning came when Rory was sixteen. He was now thirty-five and, he just decided at this moment, way too old for this shit. By the time his daddy was his age, he had a mate, four healthy pups, and a decent business to keep them all going. And what his father hadn't needed at the age of thirty-five was his best friend trying to help him get rid of his latest conquest . . . who wasn't much of a conquest anyway. She'd practically dived into his bed.

"You gonna take care of our six kids, too?" Dee asked.

Six? Good Lord.

The full-human blinked. "Six?"

Tapping her knife against the tip of each finger, Dee named each imaginary offspring. "There's Benny Ray, Johnny James, Jackie Duke, Juney Peach"—*Juney Peach?*—"Sadie Mae, and Sassy. She's gonna be our pageant queen, ain't she, Rory Lee?"

"You have six children?" the full-human demanded.

"And each one gets child support," Dee added. "A real good amount, too. And with the oldest only seven . . . that's a whole bunch of years of financial care he owes us. Ain't that right, Rory Lee?"

Rory stared at the full-human and answered, "I take care of my kids."

The poor room service waiter looked absolutely terrified when an hysterically laughing Rory answered the door. And with

Dee on the couch laughing so hard she had tears, he placed the tray, got the signature from Rory, and took off.

"Juney Peach?"

Arms around her stomach, Dee replied, "Couldn't use names of my kin. Didn't know if she'd met them or not."

Dropping on the couch across from her, Rory shook his head. "That's it, Dee-Ann. I'm not doing it anymore."

Wiping tears from her eyes, Dee-Ann sat up. "Not that again," she sighed. "You always say that and I always end up rescuing your ass the morning after from clingy full-humans."

"I'm thinking it's time for me to settle down. I got a good job. The Pack's in a secure place." He looked her up and down. "You busy?"

"Oh, that's nice."

"You're not still waiting for *love* are you?"

"When was I ever—"

"Third grade. 'Rory. One day I'm gonna find true luuuuu-uvvv.' "

"I never said that."

"Mind like a steel trap. Trust me, darlin'. You said it. Meant it, too."

"I meant lots of things when I was in third grade. So did you. If I recall, you were gonna be 'president of this here United States.' "

"I still could be."

"That's all we need. A Reed in the White House."

"I'd make you my Secretary of Defense."

"You'd better." Dee glanced at her watch. "Shit. I gotta eat and get out of here."

"Work?"

"I'm working with KZS now."

Rory laughed. "Kitty, Inc.? Have fun with that."

"More like watch my back."

"If you're worried, why are you—"

"Too much to explain. Not in the mood." She dug into her bacon and waffles and no, it wasn't nearly as good as Ric's.

"Call me if you need something. Things are kind of quiet right now at the office, so I have time."

"Everything all right?"

"Things have definitely slowed down, but we are still getting more work than most agencies. I think things will pick up when Bobby Ray's back at the office full time."

"He's not?"

"Spending time with his pup."

Dee wasn't surprised by that. Wolf males often invested as much time in their pups as the females.

"What about Mace?"

"He's got the name that gets the wealthy in, but his personality . . . we're better with Bobby Ray handling that end."

"You do it. Until Bobby Ray gets back."

"Me? Why me?"

"You're as smooth as Bobby Ray, and don't pretend you're not. At least don't pretend to me."

Dee glanced at her watch again, shoveled the rest of the food into her mouth, followed by a few gulps of scalding hot coffee.

"All right. Gotta go."

"See ya."

Dee left her friend's hotel room and headed out. She wasn't looking forward to this day, but the faster she could get it over with, the quicker she could be done with Marcella Malone.

Ric was on his computer, playing with his money in his home office, when Mrs. M. walked in. She'd been Ric's housekeeper for years and she always took good care of him. She was older now, though, and only worked three days a week, but that was okay with Ric. When one found good staff, especially staff that made the best soda bread and brisket this side of Ireland, one remained flexible.

"Your mother's here."

Ric looked up from his financial reports and he knew he was frowning.

"Are you too busy?" she asked.

"No. No, of course not. Just give me a minute."

"Of course."

Ric piled together all the paperwork and put it away in his big safe. It wasn't that he didn't trust his mother, but if she was coming to see him, unannounced, it most likely involved his father. And Ric would rather that she didn't see anything his father would feel the need to drag out of her. His mother was not a very good liar and his father always knew when she was hiding something.

He was back at his desk when Jennifer Van Holtz walked in.

"Ulrich."

"Mom." He came around his desk and kissed both her cheeks. "You look wonderful."

"Thank you."

He held a seat for her and she sat down. Rather than return to his own chair, he rested his backside against his desk and smiled at her. "So what brings you here?"

When she twisted her hands in her lap and looked away, Ric answered for her. "Dad?"

"Well," she began, "you two have never gotten along and he thought it might be better coming from me."

"What might be better?"

"You know your father has always wanted to try his hand at something a little different."

"Like being a coroner?"

First she looked stern, then she gave a little laugh. "I meant with his restaurants."

"That's down to Uncle Van." But why Alder Van Holtz would want to change the theme of their restaurants when they were doing so well, Ric didn't know. To quote Dee-Ann, "If it ain't broke, leave it the hell alone."

"He knows that. But nothing can stop him from doing something on his own."

"Absolutely."

Ric did all sorts of things on his own and Uncle Van never once complained, which he appreciated.

"And he has some backers already who are more than willing to invest in a new restaurant."

"A new restaurant? Now?" In this economy? Ric was just grateful the Van Holtz Steak House and Fine Dining chain was doing so well *despite* everything else that was going on. But shifters did like their "natural" foods, as they called it. Polars wanted their seal blubber, lions wanted their gazelle legs, wolves wanted their deer marrow. . . .

"I know it sounds very challenging. He understands that, but he's really got some great ideas and plans—"

"But?"

"He could use another backer."

"Preferably his son, who he probably won't bother paying back because he wants to believe that my money is his money?"

"Ulrich—"

"Mom." He crouched in front of her and took her small hands into his own. "I know you want to help him, and maybe he's got the best idea for a new restaurant chain that will make him a ton of money. And maybe it would be something I'd love to invest in . . . if I trusted him. I don't trust him."

"He's your father."

"He hates me."

"That's not true."

"Mom." Ric laughed. "Come on. You sent me to Uncle Van's every summer rather than risk me spending days home alone with just him and Wendell while you were out. Probably because you were afraid of what he'd do while you were gone."

She snatched her hands back from his and stood, stepping away from her son. "Ulrich Van Holtz! That is a horrible thing to say about your own father."

Ric stood, shrugged. "But not exactly inaccurate."

Dee walked into the Group offices cafeteria and immediately noticed how quickly all conversation stopped.

"What now?" she asked the room.

One of the coyote weapons technicians, with his legs up on

one of the tables, grinned at her and asked, "You're working with KZS?"

"Yeah. And?"

"You? *You?*"

"What's that supposed to mean? I work with the worthless, lazy evil felines around here all the time. It don't make me no nevermind."

"Perhaps," one of the cheetahs sweetly suggested, "referring to felines as lazy and evil—"

"Don't forget worthless," Dee reminded her with a smile.

"Right. Perhaps . . . that might suggest that you, of all beings on this planet, shouldn't be working with the pro-feline, non-canine-fan Katzenhaft members."

"But why? When I'm willing to overlook y'all's flaws and annoying feline habits?"

"This isn't just some feline," a sloth bear pointed out over canine laughter. "This is Bare Knuckles Malone. She used to play with the Nevada Slammers before she came out here. She ranks third in all-time penalty minutes behind The Marauder and that polar bear who tore off a hyena's jaw with his teeth."

Dee sweetly crossed her hands over her upper chest. "Are y'all worried about me?"

"No," the entire room kicked back, making Dee laugh until that hand slammed down on her shoulder, nearly ripping it out of her socket.

"Smith," Malone said, smiling.

"Malone." Dee glanced at the hand gripping her shoulder. "You wanna keep those fingers, feline?"

"You wanna take your best shot, backwoods?"

"Wait, wait," a male wolf injected. "Don't do this . . ." He stood. "Until we pull the tables back."

Blayne Thorpe wiggled her cute little butt out from under the restaurant's kitchen sink. "All done!"

Ric finished up the eggs, bacon, and toast, and placed it on the counter where Blayne would have her late breakfast.

"Thanks for getting here so quick," he said, before wiping down his pans. "We're completely booked for lunch and dinner, so a backed-up sink would have killed us."

"No problem." Blayne scrubbed her hands clean before hopping up on a stool and enjoying her food while watching Ric's crew get ready for their lunch service. She managed to light up the room without being intrusive. It was definitely a gift, especially in a busy restaurant kitchen.

"So," she asked, "are you going to give your dad the money?"

Ric rested his elbows on the counter and his chin on his raised fists. "No, which is going to irritate him."

"But don't you have to give him what he wants when he asks for it? Isn't that Pack rules or something?"

"Not unless you no longer want to have a Pack." Although Blayne was half wolf, her father hadn't been part of the Pack since she'd been born. The Magnus Pack Alphas—like most wolf Packs at the time and some still today—refused to let him stay if he insisted on keeping Blayne. So she had little experience with Pack law. She did, however, have a great father. Moody, a tad terse, but he loved his daughter. Ric briefly wondered what that was like—to know your father loved you. "Due to the opposable-thumb flaw all shifters have, you take a huge risk that they might leave the Pack if you attempt to abscond with their money."

"Aaaah. I forgot about the opposable-thumb flaw." She held up her hands, wiggled her thumbs. "Damn these thumbs. Damn them!"

Ric laughed, so glad now that he'd had sink problems. Blayne always had a way of getting his mind off . . . well, pretty much everything.

"So here's my plan," she said, pouring herself more orange juice. "July Fourth is coming up and I'm thinking about getting Bo to throw a party for all my friends. Doesn't that sound great?"

"Why would you do that to us, Blayne?" Ric asked honestly. "You know we love you and you abuse that by trying to force us to spend time with that cretin."

"He is *not* a cretin. He's misunderstood!"

"I'm surprised his knuckles aren't dragging on the ground and that he can create whole sentences with subject-verb agreement."

She shook her finger in his face. "I *will* make you and Lock and Bo get along. Nothing will stop me from making you three the best of friends!"

"You mean besides my and Lock's moral outrage on Novikov's existence on this very planet? Allowed to breathe our precious air?"

Blayne's lips twisted briefly before she asked, "Can't you just say you find him annoying?"

"I find Lock's insistence I don't put enough honey in my honey glaze annoying. I find Novikov offensive and barbaric."

Blayne let out a big sigh. "Yeah . . . so does everyone."

"But everyone loves you," he reminded her.

"Of course, they do. I'm Blayne." She grinned. "They can't fight my charm."

At that point, they both started laughing and it took them forever to stop.

They had each other in a headlock when the front desk admin, Charlene, walked into the cafeteria. "Dee-Ann!"

"What?"

"Detective MacDermot's here. And you know there's no interspecies fighting allowed on Group territory."

Dee and Malone immediately separated and Dee said, "We weren't fightin'. Right, Malone?"

"Right. We were . . . training."

Charlene folded her arms over her chest. "Training? Really?"

"I'm hearin' tone," Dee warned. She motioned to the door with a tilt of her head and headed out of the cafeteria. "Where's MacDermot?"

"Waiting out front for you—and you did hear tone," Charlene called after her.

Dee was passing one of the training rooms when Malone caught the sleeve of her denim jacket. "You're gettin' them kinda young, Smith." Malone motioned to the young hybrids getting trained in hand-to-hand combat.

"Those are kids we've been finding around town."

"Shouldn't you take them to social services or something?"

"They're hybrids."

"All of them?"

"Yep."

"Were they all used for fighting?"

"Just a couple. Like that girl sitting in the corner, glaring at us through the glass?"

"Yeah."

"That's Hannah."

Malone glanced at Dee. "You brought her back? 'Cause she looks a little . . ."

"Dead inside?"

"Yeah."

"Didn't have much choice. Couldn't handle the whining."

"She whines?"

"Not her, but a teacup poodle."

"Canines have teacup poodle shifters now?"

Dee was about to answer, then realized it was a stupid conversation, and instead just walked away. She went out the front doors and immediately smiled. "Who is that handsome cat?" she asked, reaching down to pick up the young cub who'd charged into her legs.

She tossed Marcus Llewellyn high in the air, loving the laughter she got from him.

"Not too high," Desiree squeaked. "As we've found out a few times, too high and he'll hook himself to overhangs."

"Are you still bringing that up?" Mace Llewellyn demanded, coming around the couple's car to give Dee-Ann a hug and kiss.

She still remembered the day the cat rolled into Smithtown, with Dee's cousin Bobby Ray, acting like he owned the joint. Although he had the protection of Bobby Ray, Mace didn't really need it. He'd grown on them all and was like family. Hell, Sissy

Mae, Bobby Ray's baby sister—and the single living reason Dee-Ann got into so much trouble when she was growing up in Smithtown—was godmother to Marcus.

"Mace, this is Marcella Malone."

He shook Malone's hand. "Bare Knuckles. I heard you're with the Carnivores now with Novikov." Mace gave a little laugh. "Didn't you get into a fistfight with him after a game?"

Malone scowled. "That fucker pitched me into and *through* the glass in front of the penalty box during the game. So afterward I hit him in the nuts with my stick and spit in his face. And he threw his fox goalie at me! Skates first. Hit me right in the head. I was out for like twenty minutes and you can still see the scar from where the goalie's skate split my head open." She shrugged and added casually, "But we get along now."

"Let's go," Dee said, exhausted just from hearing that stupid story.

She handed Marcus back to Mace. He took his son, but leaned down and whispered into her ear, "I don't actually have to tell you that you'd better watch out for my wife, do I? Or how much I'll hurt you if anything happens to her?"

"Mace Llewellyn, are you tryin' to sweet-talk me? Right here with your wife staring at us?"

"Stop threatening people, Mace," Desiree told him, well aware of the Smith female "code" when it came to their friends' mates. Besides, Desiree knew her husband well.

"He's just watching out for you, Desiree." Dee patted Mace's arm. "Bless his heart."

Mace growled. "I know that's not a compliment, Dee-Ann."

Although he'd managed for an entire hour not to let one puck get by him, it was the one that did finally get past him that had Novikov screaming about what an idiot he was and how he would never amount to anything if he didn't play like he had some "purpose."

Ric, used to it by now, let the oversized hybrid rant like they were playing for the world playoffs rather than merely getting in some early ice time before the rest of the team came in. But when he saw Lock speeding across the ice, Ric scrambled to get between the two. He barely managed, Lock reaching over Ric's head to shove Novikov and Novikov reaching over Ric's head to shove the grizzly back.

"Can we not do this?" Ric demanded. "There are kids watching!"

"They have to learn sometime," Novikov spat out. "Either they're winners or they're losers! There is no second place except for loser grizzlies!"

Lock roared, his grizzly hump growing under his practice uniform.

"Cut it out!" Ric ordered, expecting them to actually obey. Not only because as team owner he could fire them both—something he'd most likely never do—but because he was also team captain. That meant something!

"Novikov, run drills." As it was something that the man did obsessively anyway, Ric knew it would be done without question. And, with a little snarl, the Marauder skated off to run his precious drills.

"Why do you put up with him?" Lock demanded once Novikov was at the other end of the ice.

"Because he's one of the best players of all time, because we win, because—"

"Blayne would hysterically sob if you traded his ass?"

Ric couldn't lie to his best friend of twenty years. "Yes."

"Your weakness sickens me."

"I know. But if Blayne Thorpe was miserable, she'd cry about it to Gwenie, who'd complain about it to you, and then *you'd* make me hire Novikov back anyway."

Lock's grizzly hump quickly deflated. "You're right."

"I know. But we can be weak together. Besides, even that Neanderthal can't ignore the pitiful tears of a wolfdog."

"True."

Ric patted Lock's shoulder. "Do me a favor. Go run some drills with him until the team gets here. Keep him busy and out of my hair."

"Yeah. Sure."

Lock put on his helmet and gazed down the length of the ice as if Ric had just asked him to face an entire army of samurais completely alone.

While his friend skated into battle, Ric left the rink and went into the team's locker room.

"Hey, Bert," he said to the black bear tying up his skates, and the only other player there.

"Hey."

Ric walked past him and to Novikov's locker. He played with the new lock the hybrid had just purchased, opening this one as easily as he'd opened the others. Once inside his locker, Ric proceeded to move around all his meticulously laid out items, including shampoo, soap, razor, bandages. He took his time, enjoying what he was doing as much as he enjoyed making a really good crème brûlée. Once he felt he'd done enough, he closed up and engaged the lock.

Bert watched him until he was finished, then remarked, "You've got kind of a mean streak, Van Holtz."

"Only a little one."

"True." Bert got to his feet. "You could have pissed in his locker instead and we both know he would have spent hours cleaning it up."

"Don't tempt, Bert. Don't tempt."

Van buried his face in his hands and sighed—loudly.

He'd come to loathe these meetings with the Board, the representatives of every major Pack, Pride, and Clan, as well as some reps for the non-social breeds. The meetings were long and tedious but he wasn't ready to step down from his position for no other reason than he didn't trust any of these people to do what had to be done. The grizzly and black bears with their philosophical debates. The polars with their inability to take anything seriously. The lions with their blatant boredom. The tigers and leopards with their constant plotting. The foxes with their sticky fingers and the wild dogs with their patience-rendering goofiness. And then there were the wolves. His own kind. Even the damn boardroom table was merely another area for them to fight over territory. He'd become so fed up with the constant snarling and snapping that he'd actually outlawed it during meetings. It was the only way to get through these things in a somewhat timely manner.

"Is there anything else?" he asked over the current argument. And what were they all arguing about? Where to hold the next Board meeting. The Magnus Pack was down for Arizona so they could attend a thousand-mile ride with a bunch of other lowlife bikers. The Löwes wanted to meet in Germany, probably for the multi-band rock concert that happened every year. The Llewellyns wanted to go to the French Riviera, and several of the grizzlies, polars, and a couple of tigers wanted to go to Siberia—because that would be fun.

"Yeah," Anne Hutton, a middle-aged tigress from Boston who made most of her money by laundering gangster cash, said. "What's going on with all that half-breed shit in New York? And why are we giving so much money to the Group? *Your* Group?"

"It's hybrid, you fucking idiot," said the always delicate Alpha Female of the Magnus Pack, Sara Morrighan. She reminded Van of a dog that had been kept in a cage twenty-four-seven for the first half of its life until someone had let it out in the backyard to go completely wild. "Half-breed is rude."

"Shut up, Fido, no one's talking to you," Hutton shot back.

"Don't you have a hairball to cough up?"

"All right," Van cut in. "That's enough." He held his hand out and his assistant placed the file he'd brought with him. "And why we're putting so much money toward this situation is simple." He pulled out the stack of photos and tossed them across the glossy table. Some glanced, but quickly looked away. Others leaned forward to take a longer look. Some didn't look at all.

"There are so many," Morrighan whispered.

"Too many." Van gestured to the photos. "And we can't let this go on."

Slinging her arm over the back of her chair, Hutton said what Ric was sure many of the others were thinking. "They're mutts. Are we really going to go through all this effort for mutts?"

Van saw Morrighan's left eye twitch the tiniest bit. The only sign she'd show just before she went completely postal and attempted to kill everyone in the room. Holding his hand up to stop her, he said, "They start with them, but they'll end with us. We protect all of us. You. Them. All of us." He grabbed one of the pictures: a lovely shot of a young female dog-tiger hybrid torn in half with her insides spread out across the dirt floor she'd died on. "This is Trisha Barnes. She worked full-time as a waitress in a diner and went to nursing school in the evening. One night she was snatched off the street and used as a bait dog for the screaming entertainment of a myriad of scumbags." He picked up another photo. He knew the victim in each one. Had studied the information about each, knew how they'd died, how they'd suffered. And he'd done all that just for this reason. For what was happening right here—at this moment. "This is Michael Franks. A mechanic. Had a wife and four pups. His injuries were so bad, we were forced to put him down on-site." And another picture. "And this is—"

"All right. All right." Hutton cut in, waving her hand dismissively. "I get your point. God, you're such a drama wolf."

"But now that Katzenhaft is involved," Matilda Llewellyn suddenly volunteered, "perhaps they can take the lead—and the financial hit." Matilda was one of those ancient shifters who just wouldn't die. She-lions had a tendency to live a long time anyway and Matilda seemed to be ready to outlast everyone if she could manage it. Van was afraid that she could manage it quite nicely at the rate she was going.

"Katzenhaft is involved now?" Melinda Löwe sat up straight. "Katzenhaft doesn't get involved in anything to do with hybrids."

"Apparently their philosophy has changed—as has ours. And perhaps you should talk to your niece Victoria, since she runs KZS."

Melinda, who'd known him for what felt like centuries, rolled her eyes. "Oh, come on, Van. This is KZS we're talking about. Even the Prides don't have control over them."

"That's probably why they get things done," Clarice Dupris of the Dupris hyena Clan muttered loud enough for everyone to hear.

Seeing where this would quickly be heading, Van stood. "Meeting adjourned. Because I'm rather sick of all of you right now."

With shrugs and eye rolls, the predators he was forced to work with for the good of his kind, got up and headed out for the lunch he had set up in one of his Pack's restaurants on the top floor of this Chicago hotel. Really, Van would rather get to his jet and head home to his wife, kids, and kitchen, but he'd make it through lunch. That was the great thing about predators—little talking while they ate, and they all ate quickly. In another hour, he would be heading home.

Thinking about that, he motioned to his assistant and began to pull the papers together when Matilda made her slow way to his side with the help of a cane and one of her young great nieces.

"So young Niles," she greeted, flashing those fangs that could no longer retract. That's how old she was. It was like she was turning into a very large and lean cat full time. It was weird. Even for fellow shifters . . . it was weird. "How's it going with that She-wolf? Egbert Smith's daughter."

"She's working out well." Matilda always had problems with the hiring of Eggie Smith and then Eggie Smith's daughter. Van didn't know why, nor did he care. What Matilda always failed to understand was that sometimes one needed killers when they were protecting more than a few dollars in the bank or some jewels in a safe. And Eggie and Dee-Ann Smith were both born killers.

"Best watch her, though," Matilda warned, slowly moving around him, and heading toward the door. "Just like her father, she kills for fun."

Van's assistant stood next to him and noted, "You didn't really argue that point with her, did you?"

"There's no point in arguing the truth."

Chapter 5

R ic walked into his apartment, placing his hockey bag right by the closet. Yawning, he headed down the hallway toward his kitchen, but stopped when he saw light coming from his office. Without thought, he pulled out the .45 he kept holstered to the back of his jeans more and more these days. Checking corners as he went, Ric made his way to his office, but stopped right inside the doorway.

"Dee-Ann."

"You gonna shoot me, supermodel?"

"If you keep calling me supermodel." He put the safety back on his weapon and pushed it back into the holster. "What are you doing here?"

"Needed some information and knew your computer was linked in to the Group's database."

"True. Of course, you can also access the Group's database by using one of the PCs at the Group office. As opposed to illegally breaking into my apartment, I mean."

"Where's the fun in that?" She pointed at his TV. "Plus you have a plasma flat screen and a real comfy office chair. Ergonomic and all that."

Ric walked over to the desk and yelled, "What I'm trying to say, Dee-Ann, is that you can't just keep coming in and out of my apartment whenever you like!"

Startled, Dee gawked up at him, which was when he added with a smile, "Unless you're naked."

She rolled her eyes and shook her head. "Like a wolf with a bone."

"Don't I deserve to get a little something out of it if you're going to come and go as you like?"

"You get the blessing of my company."

Ric resumed his trip to the kitchen. "I'll make your blessing something to eat."

"You don't always have to feed me, Van Holtz."

"If I don't, who will?"

Tonight all Dee got were ham-and-cheese sandwiches with some tomato soup. That is, the sandwich was freshly carved Black Forest ham with some fancy French cheese with a name she couldn't pronounce, seasoned with cracked black pepper on fresh baguettes, and toasted in the oven. The soup was made from scratch with tomatoes he grew in the hot house he'd had built into part of his big penthouse apartment so he could have fresh vegetables and herbs for his home cooking. She was surprised he didn't have a cow in there somewhere for the milk he gave her. She wouldn't put it past him.

"What were you looking for on my computer?" Ric asked her.

"We're trying to track down the owners of the properties that have been used for fights in the past. They've all been empty locations, but each one has been owned. The list is long, so I took half and Desiree took the other."

"What about Cella?"

"She's not too good with the thinkin'. Must be all those hits to the head."

"Dee-Ann . . ."

"What?"

"Make this work. Don't push her out because you don't like her."

"That's not what I'm doing. She admitted she's not good with the computer stuff, so I took part of it and Desiree took the rest."

"That works."

"I know."

"Not sure how the headlock in the cafeteria fits, though."

"It was a mutual headlock and that Charlene's a tattletale."

"The lovely Charlene is my eyes and ears, so be nice to her."

"Lovely, huh?" The wording bothered her—she told herself she didn't know why—so she suggested, "Maybe you should take Charlene out sometime. It's been ages since you've been on a date."

"Dee-Ann, I work with Charlene. That would be grossly inappropriate."

And he wasn't joking. "How is *that* inappropriate but telling me to get naked isn't?"

"First off, I don't *tell* you to get naked. I suggest it in a completely nonthreatening and non-sexually harassing manner. And second, you and I are far beyond the boundaries of workplace etiquette that I normally abide by."

"And why is that?"

"Because you constantly break into my apartment, wear loose-fitting clothing that simply begs for me to feed you so that they won't be so loose all the time and, to be quite blunt, you're damn cute."

"Cute? I'm cute?"

"Damn cute." He tapped the table with his forefinger. "*Damn* cute."

"Charlene is lovely and I'm . . . cute?"

"Damn cute. You keep forgetting the damn part of it."

Disgusted, Dee went back to her delicious sandwich. No wonder the man made such good food. It was the only reason she hadn't chucked it at him.

"Almost every one of these properties is shifter owned."

Dee leaned over his shoulder to get a better look at his computer screen and Ric worked not to bury his face in her neck and sniff. Something she'd already caught him doing more than once.

Honestly, how could the woman be so oblivious to the attraction between them? Or, at the very least, his attraction to her.

It had been ages since he'd been on a date? He knew that! Because he was waiting for her! What was the point of going on a date with a woman he knew would never be who he wanted? It wasn't that he was a saint or anything, but Ric had never been one of those one-night stand guys. He never knew how to extricate himself from those situations the day after. It was a skill he simply lacked. Like his inability to golf well.

"Do you know any of these people?" Dee asked.

"Some of them. I've heard or know of others."

"Can you get me some home addresses?"

"Why?"

She briefly chewed the inside of her lip. "No reason?"

"Is that a question or a statement?"

"Both?"

Ric turned his chair, facing her. "You can't harass these people, Dee-Ann."

"Harass? Who says I want to harass anyone? I'll just ask a few questions."

"Uh-huh."

"What's that look mean? What do you mean by that look?"

"That—and I'm only suggesting—that you let Cella and Dez handle interviews."

Slowly, Dee stood up straight, her hands resting on her hips. "And why would you suggest that?"

"Let's just say your strengths aren't in that particular area."

"I am damn good at interviews."

"No. You're good at interrogations. Interviews are not your strong suit."

"Since when?"

"Since you made that six-year-old cry."

Dee stamped her foot. "She was hiding something!"

"And she was *six*!"

He made her use the front door like some common guest, walking her to it, and handing her a paper bag with several slices of that angel food cake she loved from his restaurant.

"You still mad at me?" he asked.

"Probably."

"The cake didn't help?"

"Maybe a little."

He leaned up against the doorway. "Don't be mad at me, Dee."

"You accused me of terrorizing children."

"No. I accused you of being really good at your job, where little things like age or infirmity or the inability to count past ten without your mommy's help don't really stop you from getting the truth."

"Man," she griped. "You kick one walker out of an old sow's hands and suddenly you're all levels of evil."

"Are you kidding? You're the best thing that's ever happened to the Group and to shifters. You're a protector, and I can't think of anything that means more to me or to the people you protect."

Damn him! Damn him to hell and back! Being all nice and well-spoken. Thank the Lord he was actually a good guy, because if he decided to become a serial killer, he could be worse than Ted Bundy! Luring girls in with his supermodel looks, sexy body, polite ways, and damn waffles!

"Are we okay?" he asked, and she hated him a little for making her want to ease his worry.

"Yeah. We're okay."

"Good. I'll talk to you later." Then he leaned in and kissed her cheek, taking Dee completely by surprise because he'd never done that before. He kissed his female friends all the time, like Teacup and Gwen, but Dee usually just got a little pat on the shoulder or back.

Before she did something weird like analyze what a kiss on the cheek from Ulrich Van Holtz meant, she simply walked away.

Once she was outside, she realized that she didn't want to take the long trip home. Especially since the cabbies would never take her all the way to her apartment. God, when was the last time she'd been at her apartment anyway? It didn't matter. She'd go stay with Rory. Maybe she'd get to toss another full-human female out on her ass. Much to her private shame, she enjoyed doing that sort of thing way too much.

CHAPTER 6

"*Coffee! Coffee! Coffee!*" Dez MacDermott barked until Cella Malone handed her the Starbucks cup.

Once she had several sips, she smiled at the taller female and said, "Thanks."

"Are you like this every morning?"

"Not a morning person until I get the coffee."

"Then maybe you should have coffee *before* you come to meet us."

"I would have, but my fuck session with Mace this morning lasted longer than I thought it would, and then I had to shower, walk the dogs because Mace was all, 'They're not my dogs' and I was all, 'Fuck you, we're married, they *are* your dogs' and then I had to feed the baby and he was all fussy and clawing and then I had to feed Marcus, who was busy imitating his father by being all fussy and clawing."

"Wow," the She-tiger said. "You *really* needed that coffee. And kind of deserved it."

"That's my feeling."

Dee-Ann walked up to them and now that Dez had her coffee, she greeted her with a cheery, "Hey, Dee-Ann!"

"Am I intimidating?"

Since Dez had bent back to nearly a U-shape because Dee was all up in her grill, Dez decided to lie. "Of course not."

"It's your freak eyes," Cella told Dee-Ann while she buffed her dark-red painted nails and popped gum. Dee always wondered if that was a skill taught in all Long Island high schools. Like in Home Ec or something.

"My freak eyes?"

"Yeah. They're freaky."

"My eyes are not freaky. I got my daddy's eyes."

"Heard his eyes are freaky, too."

Dez quickly stepped between the two females. Something Mace had made her promise not to do from the moment he'd heard about this new assignment.

"My eyes," Dee-Ann said over Dez's head, "are the same color as yours."

"They are so *not* the same color as mine. My eyes are a beautiful, feline gold with a touch of green for mystery. Your eyes are a direct, blunt canine yellow." She pointed to a pitbull tied up to a fire hydrant outside the café. "Like his."

"You're comparing me to a pitbull?"

"No. I find pitbulls sweet and cuddly and misused by man. You . . . not so much. Except maybe the misused part."

"*Ladies*," Dez cut in, desperate. "Can we please get to work?"

Dee-Ann held up several sheets of paper. "A list of fight locations that are owned by our own kind with addresses."

"Great. I have a list, too," Dez said, patting her backpack. "I had Mace take a look at them, see if he recognized anyone or had any juicy gossip."

"Oooh," Cella cheered, eyes gleaming. "Anything really good?"

"As a matter of fact, you will not believe what he told me about Lattie Harlow of the Harlow Pride out of Queens—"

"Work," Dee-Ann pushed. "More work, less bullshit."

Cella snapped her gum. "Fine, Working Dog." She snatched the pages out of Dee-Ann's hand. "Let's get to work. Especially since I have an exhibition game tonight with the Carnivores."

With one more snap and pop of her gum, Cella walked out.

"Don't let her get to you, Dee-Ann." Dez told Dee.

"I'm not. And maybe I can handle a couple of the interviews."

"Or," Dez hastily countered, "you can start off with basic questions."

"What do you mean?"

"I'd like to hit public records before we see these people directly. See if there's anything else there."

"Okay, but what does that have to do with me—"

"If you can handle public servants, Dee-Ann, you can handle interviewing *anybody*. As a cop . . . I know this."

Dee-Ann grunted in reply and walked out, and Dez went back to the counter and ordered herself two more cups of coffee. Because she knew this was going to be a really long day.

It was a busy, midweek lunch rush and Ric's kitchen was one dropped pan away from being "in the weeds." Thankfully, they'd managed to avoid that and keep the food going out as quickly as possible without any major errors that would have his head exploding and him ripping into one of his crew.

He slammed two plates down on the board. "Table ten up!" he called out and spun toward his oven, but stopped short when he scented one of his own through all those meats, herbs, blood, and other breeds.

Ric looked up, his eyes narrowing, fangs sliding from his gums. With one leap, he was over the kitchen island, ignoring his scrambling-away crew, and latching on to the arm of the wolf trying to slink in. He yanked him into the hallway and out the back door into the alley. With one shove, he sent the kid slamming into the opposite wall.

"What the hell are you doing here, Stein?"

Stein Van Holtz, one of Ric's younger first cousins, winced and moved his shoulder around. "No need to be so pushy."

"Out," Ric ordered. "Or I'm sending my chief sommelier after you. She's a sloth. She'll beat you to death with one of the wine bottles." Ric turned to walk back into his restaurant.

"Wait!"

Ric stopped, his hand on the alley door.

"Please."

Ric glanced back at the kid. He didn't look good. He was too lean, looked too old. He wasn't getting enough food and his body was beginning to feed on itself.

"I know how you feel about me," Stein said. "I know how all of you feel about me. And . . . and you're right, too. I fucked up. I know." He scratched his forehead, struggling to find the right words. "I just need you to give me one more chance, Ricky. I hate that I have to ask. I hate that I have to beg, but I need—"

"What?" Ric demanded, facing him. "Money? How much do you owe this time?"

Stein winced. "I don't want money." He stopped, shook his head. "That's a lie. I do want money."

"Of course."

"But I want to work for it. I'm not asking for a handout."

"You expect me to trust you in my kitchen again? After last time?"

"I have no excuse for what I did last time. I know that." Stein looked down at his feet. He wore Keds. Worn ones that seemed to be holding on by a few threads. His T-shirt and jeans didn't look much better, and the denim jacket would be too small for him if he were his proper weight. This definitely wasn't the cocky con artist who had sold spare equipment and expensive cuts of meat and seafood out of the back of Ric's kitchen for three months. Right under Ric's nose, too. And, because of that, Ric had felt certain he'd lose his kitchen to one of his other relatives. Losing one's kitchen was the worst thing that could happen to a Van Holtz wolf, but Uncle Van had stepped in and overruled Ric's father.

A decision that, three years later, Alder had still not forgiven Van or Ric for. But dealing with Stein had been left up to Alder and he'd gone even farther with the twenty-year-old-kid—he'd forced him out of the Pack. And the kid had walked off without once looking back, his middle finger raised high in the air, heading right for Atlantic City, and based on the look of him, even more trouble.

Back then, Ric had wanted to stop Stein. He'd wanted to explain that a wolf needed his Pack, but Alder wasn't having that either. Because once Alder made up his mind, that was, tragically, the end of it.

As for Ric, there were few things he would not forgive, but making him look bad in front of his father was incredibly high on the list. So he had no intention of forgiving Stein now or ever.

But still . . . the kid looked like hell. Ratty clothes, dirty hair, and he kept pressing his left forearm into his side.

Ric stepped forward and Stein immediately backed away, eyes down, head dipping low. If he were wolf, his tail would be tucked between his legs, and he'd be pissing himself. Definitely not the kid Ric had known.

Once Ric backed Stein up against the alley wall, he took hold of the kid's T-shirt and lifted. Stein immediately pulled away from him, eyes still down, but Ric had seen enough.

Catching him by the neck, Ric dragged Stein back into his restaurant.

Dee-Ann circled around to the back of the Queens house. She kept low, and stayed down wind. She peeked around the corner, but saw no one in the backyard. She hated dealing with hyenas but it seemed the most logical place to start. At least one of the properties that had hosted a hybrid fight belonged to the Allan Clan, although they'd buried the fact that they owned that property under many layers. Why they would bury that information was what Dee wanted to know.

True, she could ask that question directly of the matriarch of the Allan Clan, but after what had happened earlier in the day it was decided that wouldn't be a good idea.

"If we want them beaten up and terrorized, Smith, we'll call you," Malone had snapped at one point, after they'd left a cheetah sobbing in the middle of Public Records.

All right, so maybe Ric was right. Her strengths lay in other areas. At least she had a supervisor who understood that and appreciated the skills she did have.

The Allan Clan territory was a simple place. Nothing re-

motely fancy, although large enough for a Clan of its modest
size. The backyard was spacious enough and had its own swing
set. There was also a detached garage, locked. Dee got the lock
open and eased inside. It seemed the Clan had a healthy taste for
really nice cars, but still . . . nothing that suggested they were
rolling in money covered in the blood of hybrids.

Not finding anything that she could yell out "a-ha!" over, she
slipped outside, barely ducking in time to avoid the baseball bat
aimed for her head.

Snarling, she looked up into the faces of two male hyenas. The
one with the bat was pulling back for another swing, while the
other one had a small blade, lashing out with it and slicing
across Dee's arm.

She felt the first trickle of blood slide down her forearm and,
Dee would admit later, that's when she got a little ornery.

Cella Malone sat across from the three hyena females in the
Clan living room and tried to figure out how she'd gotten here.
Not the physical place she was in at this moment, but more a
philosophical question.

She had the full-human sitting next to her, reeking of lion—
one of her least favorite scents—and a She-wolf, who'd always
annoyed the fuck out of her, outside. And she had to work with
them. Maybe her father had been right. Maybe she should have
just focused on playing hockey. Or she could have joined the
family business.

But Cella always believed in protecting her kind. It was a flaw
that her parents blamed on Cella's grandmother. She was another "helper," and the one who'd suggested Cella should join
KZS after her time in the Marines. Katzenhaft Security might
sound like any old security company where you get big guys to
cover the front door of your daughter's sweet sixteen party, but it
was much more than that. For hundreds of years, KZS had protected felines from all over the world. It was necessary, since
most cats were solitary. They might live with their families, if
they settled down like Cella's parents did, but unless they had the

power of a Pride behind them, the lone tiger or leopard or any other feline could find him or herself in serious trouble with nowhere to turn.

She'd been proud of her work over the years and loved that the job still allowed her to play pro hockey, something that meant a lot to the Long Island girl who started skating with her father when she was barely three years old. And with four, not-too-much younger brothers hoping to beat their father's record, she'd had to learn hard and fast how to survive on the ice. It was worth it in the end, though. She still wasn't as great as her father, but she held her own and had a great time doing it. Plus, she had a bit of a reputation that she enjoyed. But what could she say about that? Cella loved a good brawl.

"Why were you trying to hide that you owned the property?" MacDermot asked the three hyenas. Sisters, the one in the middle was the matriarch of the Clan. They were an odd-looking bunch, though. Maybe because if she shut her eyes or it was slightly darker in the room, Cella wouldn't know if she was talking to men or women.

"We weren't trying to hide anything. It was a simple business transaction set up by our accountant."

"So you're trying to evade paying your taxes."

"Did we say that?" the matriarch asked. "I don't remember us saying that."

Cella had a feeling this wasn't going anywhere. Like the bear territory in Ursus County a few months back and the other territories they'd checked during the day, it seemed that someone knew about these properties and used them for the fights—unbeknownst to the owners. But MacDermot had been determined to check the Allan Clan out. The former Bronx girl had a real hard-on for the hyenas and Cella could only figure she must have picked that up from her lion mate.

As a tiger, Cella found the hyenas annoying and, if she was bored, she had no problems slapping them around, but other than that . . . they just didn't get to her the way they got to the gold cats. Then again, the wind blew wrong and the lions got bitchy.

About to shut this meeting down at the first opportunity—especially since she needed to get back to the city and ready for the game—Cella glanced out the big picture window behind the hyena females' heads. That's when she saw a male hyena run by, followed by another . . . and then Smith. Carrying a bat. A few seconds later, the males ran by the other way, but this time Smith caught one of them, yanking him back by his sweatshirt and dropping him to the ground. She hit him a few times with the bat and went after the other one.

Cella glanced over at MacDermot, but the full-human's focus was still on the females in front of her.

"So you had no idea what was going on inside your own building?"

"We never use it," one of the younger females argued. "It's there, we own it, but we never use it."

Smith stumbled into sight, the bat she held raised as a lead pipe came down at her. She blocked it, but the power of the hit drove her back a few feet. She swung the bat, smacking the lead pipe out of her way and slammed her body into the male's, knocking them both out of sight.

Must be like fighting one of the New York Jets. Sure, Cella was always willing to take Smith on, but that's because she'd been trained to fight opponents four times her size. Like most female felines, Cella was long and lean, just hitting six feet. Only the wolves and bears seemed to grow their females so ridiculously . . . large.

Cella saw a rope flip up in the air, tossed over something. Smith jogged into view again and grabbed the end of it, hoisting the male up and into the air. She tied the end of the rope off, and proceeded to beat the poor bastard like a birthday piñata.

Once she was done hitting him, Smith started to walk off, stopped, came back, hit the one on the ground a few times for good measure, then was gone.

"Okay then!" Cella said, standing. "Time to go."

Confused, MacDermot stared up at her. "What?"

"I've got that exhibition game with the Carnivores tonight, re-member?"

"No."

"We have to go."

"But I'm not done."

Perhaps not, but when Cella saw Smith spring by that win-dow again, a gang of vicious, baby-fanged hyena cubs chasing after her, she knew they *had* to leave. She grabbed the full-human under the arm and yanked her off the couch, heading to-ward the door. "Thank you for your assistance in this matter. We'll let you know if we have more questions."

They were outside on the stoop when Smith hurtled around the side of the house toward their SUV. MacDermot stopped short. "What in—"

"Let's go." Cella yanked the full-human off the property and to the car. Smith was already inside with the engine revving. Cella and MacDermot scrambled inside, but before they got their seatbelts on, Smith hit the gas.

As they headed back to the City, Cella asked herself again, *How did I get here?*

CHAPTER 7

"Tell me you didn't take him back," Lock said while they sat on the bench, waiting for the second string to get through the next few seconds of the game.

"I had to. He's my cousin."

"He's your thieving cousin with a gambling problem. And have you forgotten your father's edict?"

"Hardly."

Lock blew out a breath. "He's going to blow an artery."

"Are you two focusing on the game?" Novikov demanded.

The pair gazed at the hybrid for a moment until Ric turned back to Lock and said, "You didn't see him, though, Lock. They'd already beaten the hell out of him. He hasn't been eating. I couldn't just leave him like that."

"But he's out of the Pack, Ric, which means he's out of the restaurant."

"I can hire who I like, and someone has to wash those dishes."

"What did Adelle say?"

"We haven't discussed it yet, but I'm sure she won't be pleased."

"Don't you have enough problems with your old man, now you're going to piss off Adelle too?"

"Stein needs help."

"Why? Who does he owe money to this time?"

Ric grimaced; he'd hoped Lock wouldn't ask that question. "Polars. Dave Smolinski and his brothers out of Atlantic City."

"Jesus Christ, Ric."

"I know. I know."

"Do you think you two *girls* could table this discussion until after our game?" Novikov snarled. "Maybe when you have a sleepover and you're braiding each other's hair."

Ric stared at his least favorite human being and replied, "I think you'd look pretty with ponytails."

"A single ponytail," Lock insisted. "With front bangs."

"Awwww. Now that would be lovely."

Novikov stood. "I hate both of you."

They followed him out onto the ice, Ric taking his position in front of the goal. Cella skated behind the net and around it, passing Ric with a smile.

"Everything go okay today?" he asked.

When she only laughed, he didn't know how to take it.

Dee was sitting in the stands, watching the game. She didn't want to, but she was too tired to get up and leave.

"Dee-Ann?"

She sighed, recognizing the wolfdog's voice and praying the woman wouldn't hug her. She couldn't fight her off at the moment. "Yeah?"

Blayne leaned in closer. "Hon, you're leaking."

"Pardon?"

Teacup pointed at Dee's arm. "You're leaking."

"Shit." She'd thought she'd stopped the bleeding.

"Come on."

Blayne grabbed her arm and helped her out of her seat.

"You'll miss the game," Dee told her.

"These days I *live* hockey. I can miss a game or two."

Unable to fight, Dee let the wolfdog lead her to the hockey team's locker room and into the medical unit that was always on standby during their games.

"Blayne!" the four technicians and three sports doctors called out.

"Hi, guys. You don't mind if we use your facilities for a bit, do you?"

"Be our guest."

Blayne helped Dee up onto one of the tables and went off to get supplies. She returned a few minutes later and helped Dee take her jacket off. She pulled off the towels Dee had wrapped around her wounded arm and, after some *tsking*, went about cleaning off all the blood.

"How did this happen?"

"Hyena cut me."

"Oh, Dee . . ." Blayne said sadly. "You didn't kill him, did you?"

She almost smiled. "Not this time."

"Good. All this killing can't be healthy for you."

Blayne leaned in and studied the wound. "This is going to need stitches."

Dee pointed at one of the doctors. "He can do it."

"You're not on the team. He won't touch you."

"Fine. I'll go to the hospital then."

"I can do it." Blayne reached for a small plastic package.

"You must be joking."

"Nope. But you have nothing to worry about. I've been sewing up O'Neills since I was fourteen. You know, when they couldn't go to the hospital because it would have to be reported to the cops or something."

"Watch me not even respond to that, but my answer is still no."

"Dee-Ann, I'm *trying* to be nice here. But you're testing my patience."

"Sorry if I don't trust you to start sticking needles into me considering our past."

"Are you still harping on that?" Blayne demanded. "So I broke your nose and shot you that day in Ursus County . . . I can't believe you're still holding that against me."

"I know. So irrational." Especially when Dee had to let her hair grow out just to cover the damage to her dang ear from that gunshot.

"It is. Especially when I'm trying so hard to be nice. The least you can do is appreciate the gesture for what it is and let me stick this curved needle into your flesh over and over again. Understand?"

"Well—"

"Good! Now, hold on!" Gripping the pre-packaged needle with surgical thread in one hand and Dee's wounded arm in the other, Blayne cheerfully chirped, "This is gonna hurt!"

"I know this was an exhibition game," Novikov told them while the team tried to shower, change, and get out for the evening. "And I know that we won . . . but there are some things that you guys suck at. I have a list."

He pulled a list out of his hockey pants and Ric jumped in front of Lock before he could get his hands around Novikov's throat. "Why don't we discuss this at the next team practice?" Ric suggested to Novikov, barely able to hold the grizzly back.

Novikov held up his sheet of paper. "But I have a list."

Lock snarled, trying to push Ric out of the way, but somehow Ric managed to hold him back. "I know. But I think that list will be much more effective when we're all rested and relaxed before a practice."

Novikov took a moment to think about it, and finally agreed. "All right. But next practice—you'll all get to hear how you suck *and* how to fix that suckiness."

Ric waited until Novikov walked off to the shower before he told his best friend, "Let it go."

"I should twist him into a pretzel."

"What's the point of that? Especially when there's a risk he might twist you back. Let's just take a shower and get out of here."

Grabbing his towel, Lock stormed into the shower, Ric about

to follow. But he took a moment to unlock Novikov's locker, move his deodorant, hairbrush, and mouthwash around, and lock it all back up again.

He was heading to the shower when Blayne walked into the locker room.

"Blayne!" the entire team called out.

"Hey, guys!" She leaned in and whispered into Ric's ear, "Dee got hurt."

"What?"

"Don't panic. She'll be fine. I think the bleeding's stopped."

"Wait . . . *what?*"

"You're still panicking. Anyway, I can take her home, but then I realized that *you* should take her home. Or, if you're worried about how she'll heal . . . take her to *your* home."

Confused by all of this, Ric asked, "I don't understand what you're—"

"You. Take poor, wounded Dee home." She winked. "It's all part of my 'Project: Wolf-Wolf' plan."

"I thought you were coming up with a less appalling name."

She shrugged. "Nothing worked. So Project: Wolf-Wolf it is! It's cute!" When he continued to scowl, "Suck it up, Van Holtz, and take her home."

"Shouldn't I take her to the hospital—"

"So cute," she snapped, cutting him off. "But sometimes so freakin' dumb."

"Yes, but if she's badly wounded—"

"Ulrich. Did my Project: Code Name Bear-Cat not work for Lock and Gwenie?" Blayne's ridiculous but fun-loving plan to get their two best friends together forever, although to anyone with eyes that pair had seemed destined to be together—with or without Blayne's help.

"Yes, but—"

"Then my Project: Wolf-Wolf will work for you. But you must listen to me and trust me implicitly."

"I understand that, but—"

"Just take her home already! *Geez!*"

"Okay, okay!" He grabbed a towel, preparing to shower first. "I'll be right out."

"No problem. She's hanging with the Babes." Blayne's derby team.

Now Ric did panic. "*What?*"

"She'll be fine. They love the Dee-ster."

"Good God, woman. You don't call her that, do you?"

"Well . . ."

Deciding the shower would have to wait, Ric threw his clothes on.

"What are you doing, baby?" Blayne asked Novikov once he'd returned from his shower.

"Someone keeps moving the stuff in my locker around. It's driving me nuts!"

Blayne rolled her eyes and circled her forefinger around her temple while mouthing, *He's so crazy,* at Ric.

Shrugging, Ric grabbed his bag, and rushed out of the locker room.

When Ric got down the hall, he found Dee-Ann surrounded by the derby girls of Blayne's team. Like Blayne they were a loud, fun-loving, *chatty* bunch . . . and Dee looked seconds from killing them all. Seeing the desperate rage in her eyes, Ric quickly walked over and caught her arm. "Hello, gorgeous ladies."

"Ulrich!" they all cheered and a few hugged him.

"Did we tell you how much we love the jackets?" They all turned and showed off the light jackets he'd purchased for them that not only had the team name, their derby name and number, but also the Van Holtz name as he was one of their biggest sponsors. What could he say? The sponsorship drove his father crazy, but there was nothing the older wolf could do about it—not legally anyway.

"I'm so glad you guys like them."

"You two should come out with us!" one of the girls begged. "We'll get coffee or something."

"We'd love to," he began, but before he could finish, Dee dug particularly sharp claws into his hand, "but we can't."

"Oh." The entire team eyed them then, together. "Ohhhhh."

"Got it," another said. "You guys go. Have a great night."

Ric laughed, tugging a snarling Dee-Ann through the group.

He led her down the hall until they reached the elevator. Once inside, he asked, "What's going on?"

With a sigh, Dee pulled back the sleeve of her denim jacket. He saw the stitches. "Malone?" he asked and Dee chuckled.

"Nah. She's not a fan of knives. It was a Hyena. It's not that bad. And Teacup didn't do a bad job."

"You let Blayne sew you up?"

"It was either that or hear the sobbing."

"Excellent point. And you handled the derby girls very well, too."

"That took a lot out of me. They were watching the game, but when Blayne didn't come back, they all went looking for her. Like she was some lost kitten. But when they all started talking at once . . . that's when I thought, 'Time to start the killin'.' "

"Good thing I rescued you when I did then," Ric teased.

"Yep."

The doors opened and they walked out into the underground parking lot. "I'll take you home," he said, not bothering to frame it in the form of a question or an offer.

"Don't need you to take me home," was Dee's immediate response.

He pressed his hand against her forehead, ignoring the way she slapped at him. "Until I'm sure you don't have a fever, get used to having me around."

"Great. First Teacup, now you gettin' all pushy."

"I'd like to think I rank a little higher than Teacup." He stopped and glared at her. "And now you've got me calling her that!"

Chapter 8

Dee was busy trying to think of ways she could ditch Ric. Not that she didn't appreciate his trying to help, but she didn't need a babysitter and she wasn't in the mood to share a cab to Rory's hotel so that Ric could complain about her needing a place of her own. She had one, she just never went there. She always meant to but then something came up and by the time she got around to heading home, it was just easier to head to the hotel or Bobby Ray's place.

Thinking she had a good excuse, Dee began to lie but stopped when she saw it. It sat in its own little spot, all by itself, freshly washed and detailed by the staff kept down here, Dee was betting. But worth it, she had to admit. So worth it. Because if there was one thing Dee didn't believe in scrimping on, it was an automobile. And good Lord, but Ulrich Van Holtz had the best automobiles.

Now, it was true, she leaned toward American muscle. Cars from the sixties and seventies that, with the right engine, could hit speeds that would have troopers on her ass for days. But unlike her cousins, Dee had no problem with small foreign cars that just reeked of speed and sex. And that was the one thing she really liked about Van Holtz. The man knew how to pick his cars. Most of the time, they weren't even on the market yet in the

States. Instead, he had them shipped over from Italy, Germany, and Asia.

Today he'd gone for a Mercedes-Benz so new that it wasn't even on the market in Europe yet. She knew because she'd read the article about its upcoming European release in one of Sissy Mae's magazines.

While Ric tried to force his hockey bag into that tiny trunk, Dee dragged her fingers over the rear fender and moved around the vehicle to the passenger door.

How Ric managed to get the American version of a German car not yet available in Germany, Dee didn't know. She didn't ask. To be honest, she didn't care. Because the mystery made it even sexier.

"You like?" he asked. "Just picked it up."

"Nice."

He grinned and unlocked the doors by remote. Dee slid into the leather seat and her entire body tingled from the contact. Now this was luxury. These Manhattan females with their obsession for shoes and bags and designer clothes that were out of style a nanosecond after they were sold could keep all their fancy crap. Instead, Dee would take *this*, thank you very much.

Dee buckled her seatbelt and, without thinking, gave Ric the address of the apartment she never went to. In fact, she was so busy touching and admiring the man's car that she didn't even know they were moving until they stopped in front of her building.

"This is where you live?"

Busy opening and closing the glove box, Dee snapped her head up, quickly taking in her surroundings and the scum that were eyeing Ric's car—and probably Ric—from the various alleys and dark corners of the neighborhood.

What had she been thinking? Why didn't she tell him to take her to the hotel? Especially since her apartment had no damn furniture in it! And to be honest, the whole street was nothing but a gangland horror show, filled with junkies, pimps, and murderers. A place where Dee-Ann could get information when she needed it without worrying about asking nicely or that the cops would show up should things get ugly. Although one could hear sirens going off all night long, cops and emergency personnel rarely came to *this* part of town until the sun came up and any bodies lying on the ground could be clearly seen.

Scrambling to get Ric out of here, Dee said, "Well, thanks and—"

"I'll walk up with you."

"No!" Dee cleared her throat. "What I mean to say is . . . not necessary. Besides, you can't leave your car here anyway."

"I can't leave my car here, but I'm supposed to leave *you* here? And that makes sense because . . ."

Stubborn. As stubborn as a mule. Even worse, Ric's technique was to keep questioning her until he either wore her down or the entire street descended on them in a mass attack.

No, what Dee needed to do was get this over with quickly.

"Come on then," she snapped and got out of the car.

She stood on the street and glared down one end of the block to the other. She saw bodies step back into the darkness, not wanting to be seen by her. No one wanted to be seen by Dee. She didn't know why specifically, but she didn't mind. Not around here.

Together they quickly walked up the stairs of the building, Dee finding herself more and more embarrassed as they stepped over trash and filth and a couple of piles that were breathing and smelled like ninety-proof liquor. Trying to be rich or look like she was rich was not something Dee-Ann ever thought about. Normally, what people thought of her or how they saw her, didn't matter much. But, for the first time that she could remember, Dee was embarrassed. Terribly embarrassed that Ulrich Van Holtz of the mighty Van Holtz Pack was seeing a Smith—any Smith—living like *this*.

Lord, she hoped her momma never found out about this. That She-wolf would have a fit! Where Dee-Ann and her daddy usually couldn't care less what people thought, they did care an awful lot what Darla Lewis thought.

Finally at her door, Dee quickly unlocked it. "Thanks," she said and stepped inside. She turned to close the door behind her but Van Holtz had already walked in. Normally as polite as any Southerner Dee had grown up with, Van Holtz would never do such a thing. But when it came to Dee-Ann, he seemed to be less about polite and more about getting his own damn way.

"Oh, Dee-Ann."

She could hear the horror in his voice and she forced herself not to cringe. "Look, I ain't got time to put in fancy furniture and clean up. It's not like I've had much time these last few months."

"Dee-Ann, a couple of crates does not true furniture make." He hit the switch for the lights—lights that didn't come on. "Is the Group not paying you enough?"

Dee cringed. This was getting worse by the second. "Of course, they are. You are. I just haven't been back here for a while and I haven't had time to set up the apartment bills to be automatically paid online. It's not a big deal. I'll take care of it tomorrow."

"It's roasting in here. The middle of summer. No electricity, no AC. You'll overheat."

"I'll pant."

"You'll be like a dog locked in some idiot's car." He took several steps farther in. "And you're still living out of your bags?" He faced her, his eyes naturally reflecting the light coming from a streetlamp outside her apartment window, which had no curtains or blinds. "How long have you had this place?"

Months, but she wasn't about to admit that. "It'll be fine."

She walked past him to her window. Her eyes narrowed and she opened the window, leaned out, and gave one of her vicious snarling-barks at the males circling around Van Holtz's car. They took off running and Dee turned around to find Ric . . . cleaning her floor?

"What in hell are you doin'?"

"You're not staying here. I am not letting you stay here."

He wasn't cleaning her floor, he was shoving the few clothes she had here back into her duffle bag. Dee rolled her eyes in an attempt to hide her mortification at this current situation.

"That's real sweet of you, Ric," although she had to work hard not to sound bitter, "but I don't need you to . . . what are you looking at?"

Still crouched on the floor next to her bag, he was staring off in a dark corner near her barely used closet. Standing, he walked over, spun around, and came right back, picking up her duffle bag.

"We're out of here."

"What is it?"

"Vermin. You have vermin." He looked at her duffle bag, flung it to the floor. "I'll buy you new clothes."

"Darlin', this is New York City. There's vermin everywhere. They were just circling your car."

"I'm not talking human vermin, Dee-Ann. I can handle human vermin. *This* kind of vermin . . . I can't handle."

Surprised a wolf would openly act so freaked out about a god-damn rat, Dee-Ann walked over to her closet to show Van Holtz how a *Smith* handled a little ol' vermin problem.

Ric stood by the door, foot tapping impatiently, his entire body coiled and ready to make a crazed sprint out the window and to the safety of the unsafe street below. But, as much as he might want to, he would never leave Dee-Ann alone to face that . . . that *thing* she had living in her closet.

It was a known fact around the world that there were two things the Van Holtzes hated universally, whether it was the American Van Holtzes, the German, the Italian—whatever. And those universally hated things? Roaches and *rats,* the bane of any restaurant's existence.

For the Van Holtz Pack the hatred went far deeper than that. It wasn't unexpected that one of their restaurants would be shut down for weeks if there was *any* sign of vermin. Even the health department's more scummy inspectors, willing to take a payoff to overlook things, didn't bother to try to elicit bribes from any Van Holtz. What was the point when the whole group reacted to any sign of mold, fungus, or vermin with an intense violence rivaled only by actual house cats? In fact, a few Van Holtzes, including Ric, were known to hire feline line cooks *just* so they could deal with any rodent problems. But there could be no *playing* with the vermin, as some felines liked to do—especially those mountain lions and leopards—they were there to kill, kill, kill. One of Ric's favorite grill men was an Ecuadorian cheetah who went after vermin with an almost psychotic glee. When he finally left the restaurant to run his own kitchen—Ric cried a little.

Sighing dramatically, Dee ambled across the room to see the horror that lay in wait. He knew what she was going to do. Or what she'd try to do—show Ric what a big wuss he was being. Well, *let her try*, he thought, seconds before she fled back to his side, panting, eyes wide in fear.

"It hissed at me," she said, her voice a tad higher than he'd ever heard it before.

"Let's get out of here."

"Are rats supposed to hiss?"

"It's not a farm rat, Dee. It's a Manhattan rat."

"It's the size of my cousin's dog!"

"And has a nest it's protecting, so I suggest we just get the hell—"

It came skidding out into the middle of the room, all long and ripped like it had been on steroids for years. It hissed at the pair again, beady eyes red and pulsating with rage. And, going on instinct alone rather than rational thought, the two wolves made a crazed run for it, right out the door and into the hall, Ric slamming the door shut behind them. They stood with their backs against it, their shoulders pressed together, both of them panting, even shaking a little.

On the other side, that thing slammed its entire body against the wood, small claws viciously digging. The pair jumped and

Dee, the She-wolf who had faced the meanest predators in this country and others, grabbed Ric's hand and yanked him away and down the stairs, jumping over trash and drunks until they reached his car, which he was glad to see was still there.

He unlocked the doors with his remote and yanked the driver's side door open. That's when Ric looked up, sensing they were being watched. He'd give anything to see some terrifying human standing there, maybe with a high-powered rifle, ready to shoot them both dead. But it wasn't some terrifying human.

"Dee . . ."

Slowly, Dee looked over her shoulder and up. The rat—a female with babes to protect—stood on the sill of that open window, glaring down at them with those beady rat eyes. Then it hissed again, showing a mouthful of fangs.

They both scrambled into the car.

"Go!" Dee yelled. "Go, go, go!"

He did, starting the car, and tearing out of that spot, grateful that the German car gods had created his car so that it went from zero to sixty in six seconds flat.

Ric didn't stop driving until he was forced to by traffic and a red light several blocks away.

Still panting, he gripped the wheel. "You're never going back there," he told her, unconcerned that he was ordering her around about her personal life, a line he rarely ever crossed with anyone. Yet he simply didn't *care*. "That rat and her family *own* that apartment now. We'll find you something else. Something nicer."

Dropping back against the seat, Dee nodded and said, "Okay." And left it at that.

The light changed and Ric headed back to his place, where there was furniture, electricity, and absolutely, unequivocally, *no vermin.*

Chapter 9

"I'm not dirty."

She couldn't even look at him she was so mortified. Mortified and embarrassed.

"Sorry?" Van Holtz said, all politeness. But she knew what he must be thinking. What she'd be thinking if the tables were turned.

"I said I'm not dirty," Dee-Ann repeated. "I know that's what you must be thinking after seeing that . . . *thing* in my apartment, but it's not true."

"Why must I be thinking that?"

"Gee, I don't know. 'Cause there was a colony of rats in my place?"

"I'd probably be more concerned if you actually lived there, Dee-Ann. But you clearly haven't been." He stepped next to her and placed a plate in front of her. It was filled with a hunk of that angel food cake with white icing that he had at his restaurant. A cake that had become her all-time favorite. So did Ric just happen to have her favorite cake lying around? He preferred German chocolate cake from what she could tell.

"Except for the few clothes and your bag," he went on, "your scent had faded. I didn't see any weapons and Christ knows you'd have needed them in that place. So I'm in no way assuming you are some filthy rat-meister who breeds rats for your vicious army that will one day take over the world. Milk?"

Dee blinked, snorted a little. He'd made her laugh. At this moment, no less. For that alone, she might just love him a little. "I would like some milk. Thank you very kindly."

Ric walked to the fridge and brought over an unopened carton of whole milk. "You can sleep in the room Lock used to use when he didn't have his apartment yet. It's got a bear-size king." He filled a tall glass with milk, but left the carton. Dee knew she drank milk like a growing fourteen-year-old on the junior high football team, and Ric always seemed to make sure to have several fresh cartons in his apartment for when she dropped by to talk business. "And you can wear one of my T-shirts."

"I sleep naked."

She saw him swallow.

"And feel free to keep doing so."

She laughed again. "All this fuss isn't necessary. I don't need to stay here."

"I have tons of room."

Yeah, he had tons of room all right. His place was huge, with high ceilings and extremely wide rooms. It was a place he'd bought himself and he only lived on the top floor. He leased out the rest of the building and made a fortune doing it. And not once, since Dee began showing up at all hours to meet with Ric about the Group, had she ever felt like she belonged here.

"I can crash at my cousin Bobby Ray's place."

"With the wild dogs?"

He had a point. "I can stay with Sissy Mae. She's rarely there anyway."

"But when she is, Mitch Shaw is with her and you'll get the joy of dealing daily with a demanding lion male."

Damn him, but he was right. More than once Dee had wondered how Sissy put up with Mitch Shaw and had often found herself daydreaming about all the ways she could tear pieces of him off his body without actually killing him.

"Guess it'll be Rory then." Great. More females she'd have to kick out on a daily basis, no matter how many times the man promised the latest one-night stand was the last. "He won't mind."

"I bet he won't," Van Holtz muttered, slamming his own plate of cake down as he sat cattycorner from her.

"Is there a problem?" she asked.

"No. Not at all. Crash at Reed's, if that's what you want. Hope you two are very happy together."

"Just because I'm crashing at Rory's place don't mean we're doing anything together . . . and why am I explaining this to you?"

He stared at her and asked, "Why do you think?"

Dee thought about it a minute. "You're interested in Rory Lee?"

Ric lowered his head, his eyes shifting from human to wolf. They were blue when wolf. Like an Arctic wolf's. "You cannot be that clueless, Dee-Ann."

"Depends on who you ask."

"You know what? Forget I said anything." He pointed at the cake she hadn't touched yet. "Are you going to eat that?"

"When I feel like it."

"You don't have to get snippy. I brought the cake from work for you."

"Did I ask you to?" she snipped at him.

"Fine. Don't eat the cake. I'll eat it myself." He reached for it and Dee, feeling really difficult, shoved it out of his way.

"Didn't say I wouldn't eat the cake, Van Holtz."

"Then eat the damn cake and call me Ric."

"I'll do what I want."

"And what is that exactly? Do you even have a clue?"

"Yeah. I have a clue."

"Then for God's sake, do it already!"

Pissed off more than she could remember, Dee did exactly what Van Holtz suggested and "did it already" by wrapping her hand around the back of his neck, yanking him forward, and kissing him dead on the mouth.

*   *   *

Ric didn't know what was happening. One second he was blindingly jealous of some oversized wolf who seemed to live his entire life being referred to as "one of the Reed boys" while wearing a myriad of baseball caps. And the next second . . .

He felt the anger in Dee's kiss but Ric simply didn't care. He'd been waiting way too long to kiss this She-wolf. Way too long to find out the depth and dimensions of this mouth, the heat. And to be quite blunt, Ric had grown tired of waiting.

With their mouths still fused together, Ric slid off the kitchen stool and caught hold of Dee around the waist with both hands, yanking her up and off her chair, pulling her in tight against his body. She groaned a little, her body jerking in surprise when Ric's tongue dove in to her mouth.

God, she tasted perfect. Perfect for him.

The wolf inside him responded immediately, having already decided that Dee was the one for Ric as soon as they'd seen her amble into Lock's hallway. Dirty, loose-fitting jeans hanging low on her hips, boots scuffing Lock's hardwood floor, worn jacket that had seen better days hanging off a strong, powerful body.

Yet Ric fought the wolf's need to make Dee-Ann his forever. He fought it because while his wolf ran on instinct and need, the man ran on logic and sense. Dee-Ann was not some female sitting around, waiting for her mate to show up. She was a wolf who didn't like boundaries or limitations. She didn't like feeling, to quote her, "hemmed in." He knew that she didn't automatically feel that a mate of her own meant she was trapped for eternity, but she did feel that she had to find the *right* mate. She had to find the one who understood that sometimes she'd wander off for no reason other than she needed some air. That she might disappear for days or weeks either to handle a job or because she needed to roam the forests and woods of the closest hunting ground. That she might stop talking for a few hours or days for no other reason than that she had absolutely nothing to say.

Any male who wanted to claim Dee-Ann as his own would have to understand these things—and Ric did. He understood these things about Dee-Ann and loved her more because of them. But he also knew she wasn't ready to believe that Ric was the one for her. She wasn't ready to grasp the depth of their connection yet.

In other words, she was going to be difficult to *get*. Not in his bed, but permanently in his life.

Faced with that realization, Ric quickly analyzed the situation, coming up with a big-picture question that would need to be answered. The question? How did a nice wolf-next-door lure the most dangerous She-wolf alive into his life for good? Astounding sex was the most immediate answer and, based on this kiss alone, Ric had no doubt that would be obtained with little effort on either of their parts.

Perhaps romantic declarations of love? Expensive gifts that sparkled? A whirlwind romance filled with exotic locals and high-end hotels complete with staff?

Heh. If Ric weren't busy finding out how talented Dee was with her tongue, he'd laugh at that. All of it. Because none of those things mattered to Dee-Ann Smith. Words, money, glamour—to Dee, he might as well be speaking Cantonese. In fact, Ric was pretty sure doing any of that would only make his She-wolf run from him faster than a gazelle from a cheetah.

While his mind turned, he thought about the woman currently in his arms. This woman, this *female*, was a predator. A hardened predator that appreciated a meal more when it put up a fight. And that was true about Dee-Ann in every other facet of her life. She'd accept the easy meal, the half-eaten carcass lying in her path, waiting to be devoured. But that wasn't nearly as fun as the moose calf hiding behind its pissed off mother.

No, if Ric merely bent Dee over the stainless-steel island in the middle of his kitchen, took her from behind, and told her she was his and they would be together forever, she'd laugh, take her orgasm, and go. He'd never see her again, even if he marked her with every fang in his head. He knew that with the same certainty as he knew how to breathe.

And that left only one option for the first phase of making

Dee-Ann a permanent part of Ric's life. A risky option Ric really didn't want to take, but he had no choice. He wanted Dee forever, not just now, for tonight.

So Ric did the last thing he ever wanted to do.

He pulled away.

"Dee," he forced himself to say around all that panting and a cock that was so hard it hurt and made it almost impossible to think straight. "We really shouldn't be doing this."

Yellow, predatory eyes watched him for a moment, her brain trying to wrap itself around the idea of a male, any male, stepping away from what she'd clearly been offering. First, it was confusion he saw in her eyes. Then, it was realization. But it wasn't until those cold eyes narrowed the slightest bit, her gaze locking on Ric with an intensity that took his breath away that he understood something very important . . .

He was now running away simply so he could be caught.

CHAPTER 10

D ee had to admit she was damned confused. What was Ric doing? He was panting, had a hard-on, and looked ready to eat her alive. So why was he pulling away? Someone else might guess he didn't want the good Van Holtz name sullied by having a Smith in his bed, but she knew that was not Ric's way of thinking. This had nothing to do with money or lack of money or fancy names or any other prestige bullshit. Besides, who had to ever know? They were two people in this apartment, alone, and horny. It all seemed perfect to her but still . . . here was Ric, pulling away.

If she thought for a second he simply didn't want her, she wouldn't worry about it. She'd head off to bed and quietly masturbate. In her estimation it was one of the reason's the Lord gave them all fingers—just for this scenario.

But he *did* want her.

So maybe he was shy? She'd known him quite a few months now and although he spent a lot of his time around other females, from what Dee could tell, he hadn't put a move on any of them. Good, ol' friendly Ric. Kind of funny since a good chunk of these women went after Van Holtz like a wild dog went after a tennis ball. Canines, felines, full-humans—they all went after Ric and that perfectly sculpted face. They all wanted him but none had been able to get him.

This was usually where Dee would assume that maybe Ric was gay. With a father like he had, she could totally understand the man hiding it. Yet that didn't make sense either because more than once she'd looked over at him and found him peering at her like she was a piece of Japanese beef begging to be sautéed in one of his pans.

No. She felt pretty certain that being gay wasn't the issue. Neither was Dee's miniscule bank account and less-than-reputable family name.

So then . . . what?

Dee decided to ask. "We shouldn't do this—why?"

Ric took a step back. "We work together, Dee." Yet he was always trying to talk her into getting naked. Damn it, the man was confusing!

Dee took a step forward. "We'll be discrete."

He cleared his throat, took another step back. "I'm your supervisor. It would be grossly inappropriate of me to take advantage of our situation."

She took another step forward. "We're not full-humans who don't understand boundaries, Ric. We both know we would never ruin our working relationship over sex. And that's all this is . . . just sex." Really hot, sweaty sex, she was betting. Something that she hadn't realized until this moment she needed a good dose of.

"Right," he said, taking another step back, and slamming his perfect ass into the counter behind him. "Just sex. That's great. Just sex," he rambled on. "It's just that—"

Dee slammed her hands against the counter behind him on either side of his hips, caging him in with her arms and body. "It's just . . . what?"

"I'm more a . . . uh . . . relationship kind of guy."

Dee almost rolled her eyes. Was that it? He wanted a "relationship"? Well, they already had a relationship, right? They were friendly . . . damn near friends some would say. And that was good enough, wasn't it? It had to be, because when she stepped in closer, pressing her groin into his, and she felt the length and width of the steel pipe waiting for her behind that zipper . . . she knew it would damn well *have* to be good enough.

"We're friends, Ric."

"I'm friends with Lock, but we've never—"

"Right." Lord, the man could be literal. "But we're . . . *special* friends." She leaned in a little closer. "And that's the best kind of friends of all."

Don't laugh, he told himself. *Do not laugh.*

How she came up with "special friends" he didn't know, but man was it lame.

But Ric didn't care. In less than five minutes he had Dee-Ann Smith stalking him around his kitchen and putting moves on him he'd only seen in documentaries on animal-mating rituals.

Even better, she was leaning in and sniffing him. Considering he hadn't showered, she should be kind of turned off, but she looked to be about seconds from rubbing her body all over his.

"Special friends?" he repeated back to her. "Is that like special needs?"

"Look," she snapped when she opened her eyes and glared at him. "Let's not make this complicated."

"But it is complicated, Dee-Ann. We work together, we're friends—and," he added in a moment of sheer brilliance, "I can't handle another morning waking up all alone after some female has had her way with me. Only calling me when she needs me to service her—like some stud bull."

Dee focused her gaze over to the refrigerator, taking a moment to squeeze her eyes shut, her entire body shuddering a bit as she let that sink into her stubborn brain.

When she seemed to be calm, her gaze returning to his, Ric added, "I just don't want to be used anymore."

"Okay, okay!" Dee paused, the look on her face telling him her mind was racing, trying to convince him this was the best idea ever. God, he was good. Uncle Van would be proud. "You . . .

won't be used anymore. We'll simply take this slow. Keep it between us, but . . . um . . ." Her gaze focused on his mouth. "You
know, it'll be like a . . ."

"Relationship?"

"Yeah. Sure. Why not?"

"You'll be here when I wake up tomorrow, and you'll let me
feed you?"

"Uh-huh. Sure."

Ric brought his hand up and used his fingertip to trace the
lines of her mouth. "You promise, Dee-Ann?"

Her panting worse, she said, "I promise. Promise, promise,
promise."

"All right then," Ric said, his finger gliding across her jaw to
her ear, until his hand slid into her hair and gripped it hard,
pulling her head back a little so he would have a better angle on
her mouth.

"As long as you promise," he whispered, before he took her
mouth and made it his.

Wait. Hold it. When did she lose control here?

She had no clue, but when both his hands held her head and
he kissed her with that much intensity, she stopped caring. Instead, she let him kiss her like that, her body pulled tight into his.

His tongue swirled around hers, teasing, engaging until he
pulled back slightly.

"I have to take a shower," he said, his lips brushing against
hers with each word.

"A shower?" *Now?*

"I didn't get a chance after practice."

"Yeah, but—"

"You'll join me." He grabbed hold of her hand and stepped
away from the counter, pulling her behind him as he walked out
of the kitchen. "Two birds, one stone."

Together they walked down the long hallway until they entered his big bedroom with the astoundingly big bed.

"Is that the bear-sized queen?" she finally asked, seeing as she'd always wondered.

"Yes. I thought about going for the bear-sized king, but I was afraid I'd end up in the middle and get lost forever."

She chuckled as he led her to the ultra-bright and clean bathroom.

Still holding her hand, Ric pressed a button beside the enclosed shower and five of the seven heads inside burst to life, a little digital readout next to the button stating that the temperature was a warm seventy-eight degrees.

The man certainly did like his luxuries.

He turned toward her and finally released her hand, but that's when he started stripping her naked. He slid her jacket off her shoulders and untucked her T-shirt from her jeans. He stepped in closer, eyes locked on hers, and reached around her, removing the sheathe that held her bowie knife and the holster that held her gun. He placed those carefully on the counter and returned to her. He gripped the bottom of her T-shirt and lifted it up and over her head, letting it drop to the floor. With his finger he unhitched the front clasp of her bra and used both hands to push the cups aside.

Ric stared at her for a long moment, his eyes feasting on her before he slowly brought his hands up and palmed her breasts, stopping to squeeze.

Dee's eyes closed, her toes curling inside her boots. He squeezed again and Dee's panting began to fill the enormous bathroom along with the sound of the running shower.

"I'm sorry," he said politely before moving his hands away from her breasts and down to her waist. "I simply can't wait." Then he leaned over and caught one of her nipples in his mouth. Dee's panting turned to groaning, her head falling back, her hands reaching over and gripping his shoulders.

He sucked and toyed at the hard bud with his lips and tongue, his fingers digging into her flesh. Her hips began to move, slowly tipping forward in time with each tug and suck of her nipple.

Ric released the one he was working on and moved to the other while one of his hands moved away from her waist and went to the button of her jeans. He opened it and unzipped the fly. He pulled her closer with the hand still on her waist and tugged at her jeans until they dropped to her feet. His hand slid between her legs and cupped her pussy, one finger teasing her clit through her black cotton panties.

Now Dee's groaning became little yelps, her hips moving against his hand, her mind completely overwhelmed by the mouth on her breast.

She was moments from coming. She knew it, he knew it. That's why he pressed his thumb hard against her clit and made little circular motions until Dee's grip on Ric's shoulders nearly took flesh off.

"God," she panted out, not caring she was blaspheming. "God, yes! Right . . . right there . . ."

That orgasm ripped through her, her claws unleashing and imbedding into Ric's shoulders, her body shaking with the force of it.

She kept coming, the power of it rolling through her in a non-stop wave. "*Yes!*"

Okay, Dee would never say she actually blacked out there for a minute, but she would say that maybe she had a few seconds of . . . um . . . severe lack of consciousness?

Claws tearing into his shoulders had never felt so good before.

Dee's body went slack in his arms, her claws sliding out of his skin. Ric lifted his head, releasing her nipple as he did, watching her eyes flutter open. She looked around the bathroom until her gaze slowly settled on his.

Ric smiled, feeling a tremendous moment of connection. A moment that Dee didn't seem to appreciate very much as her hand wrapped around his throat and cut off his ability to breathe. She pulled him up until they were eye to eye.

"You really think you're cute, don't you?"

He tried to tell her that yes, he did think he was quite cute.

Adorable, even! But she was gripping his throat in such a way as to ensure maximum loss of breathing, swallowing, and speaking. It was a technique taught at the Group but Dee had come in with the skill already learned.

Her muscles bunching and tensing, Dee shoved Ric into the wall. His back slammed hard, but he kept his head from hitting anything that would cause permanent damage or coma. He coughed and rubbed his throat, bending over a little at the waist.

Now that he could speak, he said, "You're being unreason—"

She stood in front of him now completely naked, the rest of her clothes pulled off and kicked all around his bathroom.

"Do you really think you can handle me?" she demanded, grabbing a fistful of his T-shirt and twisting. "Are you so sure you wanna try?"

Did it make him weird that he was quite sure? That he had no doubts? Even with her looking like she was about to snap his neck and then dismember his body in the running shower where she wouldn't have to worry about all the blood?

"Give me your best shot," he heard himself say, and he briefly wondered when he'd lost his ability to reason. Especially when he was always so reasonable. Or perhaps he'd lost his will to live. Had he begun to think that living was overrated? Maybe. On a bad day.

The truth was, however, he knew he couldn't back down now, nor did he want to. The idea was to lure Dee-Ann Smith with the chase, then go toe-to-toe with her.

"Just look at the brave little rich boy," she murmured.

"Well, I do have excellent medical care and doctors willing to make house calls so I can afford to be brave."

"That's good," she said, unleashing her claws. " 'Cause by the time I'm done, I'm guessin' you'll need all that."

Dee shredded Van Holtz's T-shirt until she had nothing between her and all that hard, muscled flesh. He didn't have many scars on his chest. Barely any. All his scars were on his hands from years of working in one of the many Van Holtz kitchens and training since he could breathe on how to use those fancy knives to cut up animals into pretty little pieces.

And, honestly, Dee kind of liked that lack of imperfection. She liked how smooth his hard body was. A very nice counterpoint to her own. To all the scars she'd picked up over the years from those trying to kill her—or those who'd fought back when she'd tried to kill them.

She placed her hands flat on his chest, right at the center, his heartbeat strong and healthy beneath her fingers.

Lord, she'd have to be careful with this one. Because she could get used to all this. The nice bathroom. This amazing body at her disposal. The way he smiled when he looked at her. It was such a sweet smile, like she delighted him somehow.

Dee leaned in and pressed her mouth against his throat while she lightly dragged claws across his chest. Van Holtz groaned, his hands reaching for her. She tongued her way up his throat, pressing her breasts into his chest, her hands gripping his shoulders.

"I want you," she told him plain. "Here. Now."

Laughing and groaning at the same time, he half-heartedly pointed at the shower. "It's not even five feet away."

"Later." Because she had to have him *now*.

Dee pulled at his jeans, trying to get them off, about to release her claws to do to his jeans what she'd already done to his T-shirt. But Ric caught her hands with one of his own and used the other to press against her forehead.

"What are you doing?"

"Checking for the fever." It was the way their bodies sometimes healed, but Dee knew she'd already bounced back from the cut on her arm and the loss of blood. In fact, she felt great! And horny!

"That little faith in yourself, Van Holtz?" she had to tease.

"I just wanted to be sure. I do not want any complaints in the morning."

"Do I pass inspection?" she asked when he pulled his hand away from her forehead.

"You do. So please"—he gestured to the lower half of his body—"continue removing my jeans."

She held her hand up, unleashed her claws.

"Okay, okay," he said, stepping away from the wall. "I'll remove them myself. So impatient," he muttered.

Dee watched Ric push his jeans down before kicking them and his sneakers and socks off. When he stood tall, she was right behind him, her groin pressing into his ass. She wrapped her arm around his neck, her lips against his nape, her free hand smoothing around his hip until she could reach his cock. She grasped it in her hand, fingers tightening until he gasped, his head turning, his mouth meeting hers.

She stroked him, running her thumb over the head until he pulled away from her. "Get on the floor," he ordered her. Then he stopped, squeezed his eyes shut, and added, "Please."

Unable to keep from laughing, Dee stretched out on the floor, watching as Ric tore through the cabinet under his sink. "They're in here," he promised. "I swear. They're in here."

He was halfway inside the damn thing when she heard him cheer, "Yes!" That was also when he tried to stand before he was out of the cabinet, his head colliding with the sink pipe. "Ow!"

Ric muttered what may have been cuss words as he crawled back out, but he held a box of condoms.

"Give me that," Dee said, sitting up and snatching it from his hand. "Don't want to take the chance you'll damage these, too."

"I'm usually smoother than this," he told her, his hand rubbing the back of his poor head. "Usually."

"Yeah. And sometimes I can be downright chatty." She opened the box of condoms and pulled one out. She ripped open the packaging and caught hold of Ric's cock with her hand. It was already hard, so she didn't have to worry about that. Instead she focused on getting the condom on him and his cock inside her. That's the only thing she wanted at the moment—and she'd be damned if she didn't get it.

*   *   *

Ric watched Dee-Ann roll the condom down his cock. Once she did that, she looked at him and smiled. "See?" she asked. "That wasn't so hard, now was it?"

And that's when Ric basically . . . well . . . lost it.

All that culture and breeding and education meant very little when faced with the sexiest woman in the world. A woman who wanted him.

Ric caught hold of Dee's face between his hands and kissed her while the rest of his body forced hers to the floor. She opened her thighs to him and he was between them and inside of her in seconds, the feel of her wet heat wrapping around his cock nearly killing him, it was so intense.

He froze, his body overwhelmed by the woman he was in. The woman he loved. And she had no idea. To her this was fun times with a good buddy, but to Ric this meant everything. And to find out being inside her was even better than he'd dreamed. . . .

"What's wrong?" Dee asked. "Why'd ya stop?"

"I'm trying for some Zen-like control here, Dee-Ann. You're not helping."

"Fuck control, darlin'." She brushed her forehead against his chin. "Fuck rules and supervisors and what's right and what's wrong. Fuck it all." She pressed her lips against a little spot right under his ear. "But right now, with that big cock of yours takin' up all that room inside my pussy, it's time for you to fuck me."

Then she bit him. Not enough to break skin, not enough to mark him. But enough.

Ric caught hold of her wrists and slammed her hands to the floor, his body rising up over Dee's. She grinned up at him, ripping away his last bit of control.

No matter how much they might try to hide it, a wolf was a wolf was a wolf. And Ulrich Van Holtz was a wolf. She'd known that long before now, but this just confirmed it. Because no fancy rich boy could fuck her the way Van Holtz was fucking her, his body powering into hers, over and over. Dee's arms were pinned by her head, unable to move as Ric took what he wanted from her.

Dee-Ann closed her eyes and let the delicious feeling of Ric being inside her take over.

He brought his lips down to her breast, grasping a nipple and sucking it into his mouth, tugging at it. She writhed from the pressure, trying to pull her hands away from his grasp, but unable to manage.

He moved to her other breast, this time grazing his fangs against the tip. Dee shuddered from the contact, her hips rocking up to meet each of Van Holtz's thrusts.

Another orgasm tore through her, making her toes curl, her fangs burst from her gums, her claws unleash. Her body shuddered and shook beneath Ric's, a low snarl slipping past her lips.

Ric followed right behind her, groaning into Dee's neck, his body jerking from each ejaculation.

When he finally crashed on top of her, his breath coming out in hard pants, his hands unable to hold her wrists any longer, Dee said, "See? *Now* we can take that shower."

And she laughed when Ric's only reply was, "Quiet, Dee-Ann. Just . . . quiet."

Chapter 11

Dee-Ann woke up when she felt the stitches in her arm being tugged out.

It was Ric doing the tugging. Naked except for a sheet, he was trying to carefully and quietly remove the stitches so as not to wake her.

Dang, but he was cute. She'd never realized before. She'd noticed he was pretty, sure, but not so . . . *cute*. With his polite, fussy ways, and insistence on feeding her.

"What are you doing?" she asked.

He flinched. "Damn." Brown eyes looked at her. "I was trying not to wake you."

"You're removing a foreign material from my skin. How could you not wake me?"

"I thought I could at least try. Your skin was starting to grow over so I couldn't leave it any longer."

Dee sat up in the enormous bed and pulled her arm away from Van Holtz. Using her fangs, she methodically tore out each stitch, spitting the material into her free hand, until she was done.

Ric, staring at her, observed, "You've done that before, haven't you?"

"A time or two." Of course, when she'd done it before, she'd been knee-deep in some jungle or African grassland, waiting for hunters to take the bait and move into her line of sight. She'd definitely not done it while lying in a big, comfortable bed with a handsome wolf grinning at her.

"Got a trash can?" she asked, raising her hand with the stitches.

Reaching over his side of the bed, Ric lifted up a small stainless-steel trashcan and held it out for her to toss the evidence of her recent knife-fighting incident away.

"What time is it?"

He returned the trash can to the spot on the floor and glanced at the clock by the bed. "Six. I overslept."

"Need to be at the restaurant?"

"No, I have dinner service tonight. I was going to try and get in some practice at the rink so that idiot would lay off."

"Y'all sure don't like that boy, do you?" Neither Ric nor MacRyrie had a nice word to say about Bo Novikov. She found it kind of funny simply because they were normally so damn nice.

"No. We don't. But Blayne loves him so there's not much we can say." He reached out, his finger tracing the line of her jaw to her throat, to her collarbone. "You need to eat."

"I'm fine."

"It wasn't a question, Dee-Ann. Or an offer." He leaned in and pressed his lips to her throat.

Dee's eyes closed, her left hand sliding up his bicep to his shoulder.

"You don't always have to feed me, Van Holtz. I can find food on my own."

"You find crap on your own." He moved in closer, nipped at her jaw and Dee's nipples hardened, her pussy getting wet. "You need a healthy meal so you can face the day."

He was pushing her back on the bed. She wasn't trying to stop him. "And what do I have to face today?" she asked, both hands gripping his shoulders now, holding him tight against her.

"Worry about it later," he told her—so she did.

* * *

Dee came out of the bathroom, her body again freshly scrubbed clean. She wrapped one towel around herself and used another to roughly dry her hair. As she stepped from the bathroom to the bedroom, she had to pause and stare at the bed. It was so *big*. It made sense since it was built specifically for bears but . . . good Lord. Not only was the bear-sized queen mattress more than double the size of a regular king, the frame was made of extra-thick steel. Sometimes even titanium for those who could afford it. *In case the bear cubs decide to jump up and down?*

Shaking her head, she walked into the hallway and instantly scented a foreign wolf in the vicinity. She followed the scent to the guest bedroom and saw some scraggly looking homeless wolf going through the extra clothes there.

Standing behind the wolf, arms resting at her sides, fingers twitching just a little . . . she waited.

Stein Van Holtz, family black sheep and all-around recent loser, dug through his cousin's extra clothes drawer. How low he'd fallen. How low.

It still dazed him sometimes to think about how far and how fast he'd crashed back to earth after so long at the top. Where did his luck go? He still had skills, but everything had gone wrong. In three years he'd gone from top of the heap to absolutely nothing. And through all of that, he'd lost his family and his Pack. If he had one or the other, he'd be okay, but he'd lost both.

So, when he'd needed help, he'd ended up approaching the last person he'd wanted to go to with his hand out, but he'd had no choice. Honestly, he'd thought the one cousin who'd toss him out on his ass would be Ric, but he hadn't. And that's why Stein had probably come to him because he knew Ric was the one blood relation who would help him.

The realization tore at him because it had been Ric that Stein had fucked over the worst. But still, it didn't mean that—

Stein's head lifted, the hackles on his neck rising up, his fangs sliding out. He shot around to face whatever was behind him, but the She-wolf had him by the throat before he could blink and, one handed, slammed him up against the wall, his feet not quite touching the ground—and they were about the same height.

"Stealin', boy?" she asked in an accent he found a tad off-putting. Especially when she was choking the shit out of him. "That's just rude."

He tried to tell her he was a Van Holtz, that he knew Ric, that he could be here, but she wouldn't loosen up her grip enough to allow him to say much of anything. Her towel slipped off and she stood brazen and naked, still holding him. She wasn't exactly pretty or anything and her body had tons of scars, a few long and angry looking but mostly a bunch of little ones all over. But it was her eyes . . . Christ, her eyes. Cold, bright yellow wolf eyes gazed up at him with no remorse, no doubt, no pity.

This wasn't some average wolf, trying to scare him by shifting only her eyes. No, this was a warrior wolf. The kind Stein used to hear about from his grandfather, who loved talking of the times when Van Holtzes were only Holtzes and had faced down legions of Roman soldiers. This female would have been on the front line, a banshee if he'd ever seen one.

"Did you find something to wear?" Ric asked, walking into the room while mixing up batter for pancakes. He stopped in the doorway, took in the scene, and said, "Oh. Sorry. Didn't realize you were busy." And walked away!

Stein tried to call him back. Tried to beg him to get his ass back here and help his poor, baby cousin! What was he playing at? He had a pitbull loose in his apartment but he didn't have voice control?

The female sized him up again. "You know him?" she asked and Stein didn't know why she was asking him questions when she gripped his throat so tight he still couldn't speak.

"Yeah," Ric replied, coming back into the room. He leaned against the doorjamb, still mixing that batter as if his cousin wasn't in mortal danger. "He's my cousin."

"Invited?"

"Yes. Invited."

Her fingers tightened once more, convincing Stein she was going to snap his neck anyway. Then she released him, letting him drop to the floor.

Bent over at the waist, Stein took in big gulps of air, wheezing while he rubbed at his throat. He looked up to see the She-wolf pick up the towel and wrap it around her body. She walked past Ric and he watched her with a territorial gleam that Stein had never seen from his cousin when it came to a female.

"Dee, your clothes were cleaned last night and I put them on the bed. Or you can borrow something of mine if you'd prefer."

"Thanks."

"Breakfast will be ready in a few minutes."

"I should go," she called back.

"You need to eat, Dee-Ann. You're skin and bones." Skin, *muscles,* and bones. Did the man not see those muscles? Was he blind to the size of that woman? Did he not see the way she'd tossed his baby cousin around his guest bedroom like one of those bouncing chew toys?

"You didn't seem to mind last night."

"Only because I knew I'd be feeding you this morning. Don't argue with me on this," Ric said, walking out of the room. "You're eating before you go anywhere. You wouldn't want me to get cranky, now would you?"

Stein got to his feet, feeling shaky all over. He didn't know what to make of his cousin with that She-wolf, but it was none of his concern, now was it? Stepping back to the drawer, Stein pulled out a T-shirt and sweatpants. He'd go commando before he'd wear someone else's boxers, though.

He was digging for some socks when he found a wad of bills tucked into a corner. The wad was thick, at least four or five grand. Stein's fingers brushed across the cash, his mind whirling with the possibilities of what he could do with that much cash. A few rounds at a card table and he could win enough to pay everyone back and . . . and . . .

Make things worse. He'd make things worse.

Curling back his fingers, Stein grabbed a pair of white sweat socks and quickly closed the drawer. Trying to ignore what had become second nature to him was definitely the hardest part of this, but he was determined not to fuck up this time.

He left Ric's bedroom and found another bathroom with a shower he could use. By the time he'd showered, shaved, and put on clean clothes—his first in months that hadn't been hand washed in a dirty sink—the She-wolf was gone and his cousin was sitting at the counter staring blankly at the morning edition of *The Wall Street Journal.*

Stein didn't think Ric would notice he was in the room, but without looking up he pointed at the stove. "There's batter left for you. I already made the bacon. Eggs are in the refrigerator. You remember the basics, don't you, cousin?"

"Yeah. Sure." Stein walked to the stove and, man, but did it feel good to be back at one.

As Stein got to work, he asked his cousin, "Are you all right, Ric?"

"Yes. I'm fine." Ric sighed, placed his elbow on the table, and his chin on his raised fist. "Just in love."

Remembering clearly the cold wolf eyes that had gazed up at him as if he were some sort of bug she'd trapped in a jar and the grip that female had had on his throat, Stein didn't have any response to his cousin's statement other than the tried and true, "Oh. Good for you."

Because really . . . what could a man say to his cousin after that?

CHAPTER 12

R ic sat at his desk. He was completely alone in his apartment now. His cousin was gone and so was Dee-Ann. Her scent still lingered in his place, though, and he liked it. Probably more than he should since he had no idea what would come of all this. But he was willing to fight for her. She might not realize she was perfect for him, but he knew she was. They just fit together like a really odd puzzle no one could figure out.

But he could think about that later. Right now, he had to focus on something else.

Getting out several pencils and a notepad from his desk drawer, Ric opened the package his Uncle Van had sent him to review and got to work. And the deeper he got into the Van Holtz books, the worse it got.

Dee-Ann stopped by the Group office first and checked in. She also looked in on the young hybrids that currently called the Group office their home. Every day the hybrid pups, cubs, and kits she'd found and brought in received all sorts of training, from basic hand-to-hand combat techniques to learning how to manage their bodies when they shifted. A challenge for a few of them whose DNA mix created something brand new and different. When they weren't getting training, they were in classes that would hopefully let most, if not all, of them get their high school diplomas. The only one who'd already graduated high school was Hannah, but whether she'd end up going to college or not, Dee didn't know. The girl didn't talk much.

And then there was little Abby. How many months had she been part of the Group and she still refused to shift from her animal form to her human one? They only found out her name because they discovered it written on the girls' bathroom mirror. And in the beginning, because she had a tendency to be destructive, Dee had placed her with the Kuznetsov wild dog Pack. Jessie Ann was her cousin-in-law and her dog Pack was tolerant of mixed breeds. It had worked out well, but then Abby started showing up at the Group's office, still in her animal form, roaming the halls, begging for food, generally pretending to be the office mascot. It was weird. Then again, so was Abby.

Yet it was all working out, and Dee was just glad to have these kids off the streets. They deserved better than to be going through trash and sleeping under overpasses. Of course, every kid deserved that, but she could only do what she could do. And what she could do was help her own.

"Everything all right here?" she asked Charlene. The fox liked to check in on the hybrids throughout the day and Dee appreciated that.

"Pretty much. They're getting used to being here, I think. A few have started talking about what to do after they graduate from high school or get their GED. I think most of them will stay on when they hit eighteen." She glanced at Dee. "They kind of worship you."

Startled, Dee could only manage a, "Huh?"

"Gonna play that game, eh? Okay. Fine."

Ignoring those comments, Dee asked, "Hannah?"

Charlene blew out a breath. "Yeah . . . Hannah."

They'd rescued the pretty but scarred bear-canine hybrid with the brown eyes, brown hair with black tips, and nearly six-three height at one of the illegal fight training centers they'd shut down outside of Ursus County. Dee had wanted to put Hannah down then and there. She'd seemed so . . . empty. The pitbull no one trusted because she'd been in one too many fights. But Teacup had begged and pleaded and all the other shit she liked to do to make Dee-Ann's life hell. Now they had Hannah here and no one would go near her, even the Unit vets who'd seen it all.

Dee grimaced. "That bad?"

"It's not like she does anything, ya know? She doesn't get into fights or threaten anyone. Not like you."

Dee briefly pursed her lips. "Thanks."

"But she scares everybody. She's a scowler. A silent scowler."

"Yeah, but . . . so am I."

"It's different. We know you'll kill if you have to and you'll do it without remorse. But so will half the breeds in the Group. But Hannah . . . I think she's fighting so hard not to be who and what she is—she's so afraid of it—that she comes off as just downright terrifying. Because you never know what's going to finally set her off. What's going to really make her snap her bolt."

"I don't know what will either. But I'm not ready to give up on her yet."

"Because you think she can change? Or because you don't want to hear Blayne Thorpe's hysterical crying . . . again?"

"I'm leaving," Dee said.

"You mean running away from the conversation because you refuse to admit you kind of like Blayne?"

Dee stopped and glared at the bite-sized fox.

"Just kidding," Charlene said, backing away. "Just kidding."

Dee left the office and walked into the diner down the street. She spotted Malone and Desiree at a table in the back. They were both eating breakfast. Desiree had a newspaper folded up for easy reading while she ate an egg white omelet. Malone was reading a full-human hockey magazine and downing waffles, toast, bacon, ham, and eggs. They weren't speaking to each other and didn't look up when Dee sat down.

"Sorry I'm late."

"No problem. We haven't been here long." Desiree pushed a coffee cup and a carafe over to her. "You want breakfast?"

"Nah. Already ate." Dee poured herself a hot cup of coffee

and took a sip. It was definitely what she needed. "What's the plan?"

Desiree shrugged. "We could investigate a few more of the property owners."

"Yeah," Malone said, "but I really think that's going to be a waste of time. Why would the ones who own the property put themselves at risk by having the fights there? So far, all the properties have been owned by those who haven't touched them in some time."

Desiree poured herself more coffee. "You know what it feels like to me? A real F-U to us. To the ones trying to stop this. And to the ones who own the property."

"What makes you think that?"

"Well, it reminds me of the time right after we were married when Mace got his sister to let us use her summer house in the Hamptons. She kept saying we had free rein of the house—but we weren't allowed to go in her bedroom. Stay away from her bedroom because it was her private sanctuary, even though she only stayed there for a few weeks in the summer with her entire Pride."

Malone grinned. "You fucked on that woman's bed, didn't you?"

"Like bunnies. Because the more she said 'don't,' the more we did. And that's what using these properties says to me. 'F-U 'cause I can do what I want.' "

"We need to find the money," Dee repeated the words of the NYPD sow who'd put them on this. "They have to be getting the money somewhere."

"Yeah," Malone said, "but does it really take that much start-up money to run a dogfight?"

"This ain't no dogfight, Malone. They've gotta transport these people, house them, feed 'em, and it ain't like feeding some pit you keep in your backyard. Plus, you didn't see the office we took down back in February when they went after Blayne. It rivaled Group offices. *That's* serious money. And that's what we need to find."

"Then we need to find a fight."

"I don't know about y'all, but the last three we got a line on were closed down by the time we got there."

Malone and Desiree nodded, silently agreeing they'd had the same problem.

"So someone's warning them when to get out."

"You think our people—"

"No, no." Dee shook her head. "I'm not saying we've got anyone on our teams rattin' us out. But there's always chatter. One of us talks to another to another . . . until it ends up in someone's lap."

Malone leaned in a little closer. "But you do think the money is coming from our kind?"

"Don't you? And something tells me KZS thinks either some if not all of that money is cat money. Otherwise, why else would y'all get involved?"

"You haven't changed, Smith. You'd love to put this on us," Malone accused.

"I'd love to put this on the ones doing it. I don't expect much from the full-humans—no offense, Desiree"—Desiree shrugged, ate more toast—"but I do expect a lot from my own. If it's one of us behind this, I wanna know. I don't care what species or breed."

Malone nodded. "I feel the same way. So does my boss."

"Good. So we need to track down a fight and we need to be quiet about it. We keep it among the three of us, pull a team at the last minute, and no one says anything to anybody until we're done. Sound good?"

"So how do we find a fight?"

"I've got a contact." Desiree pulled out her cell phone. "He works with the ASPCA." When Dee and Malone only frowned, she added, "His thing is shutting down regular dogfights. But I'm guessing he's got a line on one of the other types without even realizing it."

*　*　*

Ric dropped into a chair in his Aunt Adelle's kitchen and announced with little preamble, "I am so screwed."

Adelle, who'd left the setting up for lunch service in the hands of her sous-chef so she could "get up when I damn well feel like it," placed a cup of coffee in front of Ric and kissed the top of his head. "All right, darling cousin. Tell me what's going on."

"I don't think I can."

Adelle sat down at the wood table that Lock had built for her a couple of years ago and studied the small pile of cinnamon buns she had on a plate in front of her. "Is this about your father?"

"Maybe."

"Because he's stealing from the business?"

Ric gaped at his aunt. "You know?"

"Who do you think told Van?" She sipped her coffee. "You might as well accept the fact that your father's a scumbag."

"Adelle!"

"What? Am I lying?"

Ric put his head on the table and sighed into it, "No."

"Why are you so upset?"

"He's my father."

"Only genetically."

Ric looked up at his older cousin.

"Look," she argued, "we all realized a long time ago that you were an at-risk pup. So Van and my brothers all decided to quietly raise you themselves. You were such a smart child, we knew your father would feel threatened."

"Dad always said you guys babied me."

Adelle placed her cup down on the table—hard. "First off, we never babied you. Not killing you while you slept is not babying you, Ulrich. No matter what your father may have told you. We, as a Pack, decided to raise you. Properly. And, as a humble She-wolf, I'm happy to say that we did a wonderful job."

Laughing, Ric sat up. "Unbelievably humble. The world is filled with humble chefs."

"Exactly. Now"—she picked up a cinnamon bun, waved it in the air—"you've got two choices, young man."

"Two choices about what?"

"Spending July Fourth weekend with your father and the Pack at the Macon River Falls house or—"

"I could set myself on fire."

"That is *not* the second option."

"Well, anything but go to another disastrous holiday weekend with my father."

"If you don't go," she teased, "who will apologize for your father's fuck-ups? You can't expect *me* to do it."

"Second option, Adelle?" Ric pushed.

"You attend the children's hospital charity ball after the Fourth as the Van Holtz representative. I think Van donated something like forty thousand this year."

Ric hated charity events, but he realized he could invite Dee as his date—then he just as quickly realized she'd turn him down. But still, anything was better than ruining his holiday weekend by spending it with his father. He'd rather sit home alone, watching the fireworks on TV.

"Charity ball."

Adelle nodded. "That's what I thought. I'll let Van know."

Ric watched her bite into her cinnamon bun and admitted, "Mom came to me the other day . . . asking for money for Dad."

"You better have said no."

"I did," he confessed. "I did . . . but maybe I should have—"

"No, Ric."

"But—"

"No."

"But maybe if I invest in this ridiculous restaurant idea he has, I can . . ."

"What? Undo your father's decision to steal from his own Pack? Do you really think that by giving that man money, you'll be changing *anything*?"

Ric shrugged, because he really didn't know the answer to that question. Or did he?

"It won't," Adelle told him flatly. "And you know that, Ric. Without me telling you."

"Yes," he forced himself to admit. "I know. But I'll go over the books one more time before I say anything to Uncle Van. Make sure I didn't miss anything."

"You didn't."

"I want to make sure."

"Fine. But it won't change anything, Ric. You simply can't rescue everybody." She eyed him. "And that includes idiot young pups who thought they'd be high rollers in Vegas."

"Atlantic City," he corrected her, knowing she was complaining about seeing Stein washing dishes at the restaurant.

"Whatever. I can't believe you gave that brat a job."

"You didn't see what the bears did to him."

"I don't care what the bears did to him."

"Adelle."

"He probably deserved it."

"Adelle."

"He gave me the finger when he left. I should have taken that finger and shoved it up his—"

"Adelle!"

"What do you mean no?"

Halfway through her lunch burger, Dee looked up from her plate and across the diner booth to her cousin Sissy Mae and Sissy Mae's second in command, Ronnie Lee. While Sissy stared at her, Dee continued to chew her food and stare back.

"Well?" Sissy pushed.

Dee swallowed her food, wiped her mouth, and replied, "What do I mean no about what?"

"About July Fourth weekend."

"What about it?"

"We're all going to Bren's house in Macon River Falls."

"Yeah?"

"And I invited you to come."

"Yeah?"

"And you said no."

"Well, Sissy Mae, that's the beauty of the invite—you can turn it down."

Her cousin's eyes narrowed and Dee could already see this was not going to be an easy conversation, which she found mighty irritating since she'd gotten off early. With Desiree, Malone, and Dee using their contacts to track down a hybrid fight, there was nothing to do but wait. Desiree had headed home to her son, Malone back to the KZS office that was in some secret location no one was supposed to know about—they were in Queens and had been for the last forty years—and Dee had wanted a nice, quiet lunch at her favorite diner with nothing but a burger, extra crispy fries, and one of her favorite Agatha Christie books. She liked ol' Aggie. True, the mysteries and the scandalous activities of some of the characters may seem tame by today's standards, but Dee enjoyed the simplicity and straightforwardness of the stories. She got enough bloodbaths from her daily work, she didn't need it in her leisure reading.

"That's true," her cousin said, "you can turn down my generous offer—"

"How is it *your* generous offer when it's Brendon's house?"

"—but you *shouldn't* turn it down."

"Why?"

Sissy sighed, long and loud. Like the weight of the world rested on those big She-wolf shoulders. "Dee-Ann, darlin', I am trying to make you more part of the Pack."

"I am part of the Pack."

"True, but you don't act like you're part of the Pack."

"I'm there when you need me. What more do you want?" Dee caught the wrist of the She-wolf reaching from behind her to grab a fry off her plate. "Do you wanna keep this hand, Dolly Mae?"

Her young cousin, a new recruit to the New York Pack, said, "I just wanted a fry, Dee-Ann."

"I just wanted to eat in peace. Don't look like that's gonna happen either."

"Can't you share?" Sissy asked her.

"No." She released her cousin's wrist, ignoring her when she began to rub it. *These weak sub-adults. Grow a spine already.* "Look, when I became part of this Pack, Bobby Ray promised me that I wouldn't be hemmed in." She glanced around at the group of She-wolves now surrounding her. Some in the booth behind Sissy and Ronnie, some standing next to the table, and some in the booth behind her. Like Dolly Mae . . . who was still trying to get her fries. "I'm feelin' hemmed."

"No one's trying to hem you in," Sissy argued. "God forbid anyone try and hem in Dee-Ann Smith. But you can't bond with your Pack if you're not part of it."

"I'm part of it. You need me, I'm there. Otherwise, don't bother me."

"Dee-Ann . . ." Sissy began. But, sick of Dolly Mae and her sneaky fingers, Dee caught hold of her hand and gripped it until she heard bones crack . . . and break. The She-wolf whimpered, sounding all sorts of pitiful until Dee flung her hand away.

Slowly, she looked back at her cousin. "You were sayin', Sissy Mae?"

Another dramatic sigh, accompanied with a sad head shake. "See?" she asked. "You need my help more than you ever realize."

Dee picked up her book. "Actually, what I need is for you to fuck—"

"Lunch!" Ronnie Lee cut in. "We haven't had lunch yet." She motioned to the waitress. "Let's get lunch since we're already here. You don't mind if we join you, do you, Dee-Ann?"

"Well—"

"Good!"

One of Ronnie Lee's cousins snatched Dee's book from her hand. "Watcha readin'?"

"Reading's boring," another cousin complained. "Why read it when you can just watch it on TV?"

Dee crossed her eyes and resigned herself to "Pack time" as her momma always liked to call it. Of course, when she would say "Pack time," Dee's daddy would follow that up with a walk to his favorite shotgun followed by his favorite saying, "Guess it's time to start the killin'."

If only . . .

Ric walked into his kitchen an hour after lunch service had ended. Adelle was finishing out her shift and laughing at something Stein said while the kid pulled a couple of sizzling steaks from the grill. Standing behind him, arms crossed over his chest, Ric waited until the kid turned around—and fell back against the ovens.

"Uh . . . Ric. Hi. Uh . . . I was just . . . uh . . . making something to eat for Adelle." Ric stared at Stein, but didn't say anything. It was a trick he learned from Dee-Ann and he'd found it was quite effective. Kind of like now.

"She said it was okay . . . and I thought she needed something to eat after all that time working. . . . It was so busy in here . . . and everyone did a great job . . . and . . . and . . ." Stein winced. "My head's hot."

Ric finally spoke, "Because it's resting against one of the oven doors."

Stein stood tall, pulling his head away and shaking it. Good thing the door wasn't open—he'd probably have fallen in. "Oh. Right."

Ric glanced at the still-sizzling steaks on that single long plate. "That's all for Adelle?"

Stein looked at the plate and back up at Ric. "Yeah. Sure. All for Adelle."

"Then give it to her and get back to work. Those dishes won't clean themselves."

"Right. Absolutely." He put the plate on the counter and scurried back to his sink full of dishes.

Going over the tickets from the lunch run, Adelle shook her head and laughed a little. "You're being awfully hard on him."

"I know." Ric grabbed two forks and two steak knives and

maneuvered the plate between them. "You said yourself he deserves worse."

"From me. You're the nice one." She put her paperwork aside and took the fork and knife handed to her. They both cut off a piece of steak and took a bite. They chewed and gazed at each other.

Finally, Adelle announced, "That's amazing."

"Ssssh. Don't tell him."

"I mean . . . *amazing*."

"Keep your voice down. I'm not done with him yet. No matter"—he took another bite of steak and groaned—"how damn good this is."

They continued to eat in silence for several more minutes until Adelle asked, "So explain to me why you had a naked Dee-Ann Smith running around your apartment this morning?"

Ric somehow managed to swallow his food without choking on it and answered, "Uh . . . no reason?"

"What is it with you and Van and the weird-eyed girls?"

"Dee's eyes aren't weird. They gorgeous. I call them canine gold."

"You always were an odd but self-contained child, Ulrich."

"I love her," he admitted. "I have since I met her."

"I'm not even going to argue with you about this because the Van Holtz men have the most disturbing taste in women since our first known ancestor, Eberulf the Goat Killer married Himiltrud the Hideous. And clearly you're no different."

Ric thought on that a moment and then asked, "Our first ancestor was a *goat* killer?"

"Ulrich . . . the man had to eat."

Dee spit the liquid back in the bottle and glared at Rory Lee. "What is this?"

"Non-alcoholic beer."

"You *dare* give this to me?"

"That's all they have." Rory sat back in the booth of the karaoke bar they were in and asked, "Why are you here again?"

"Because my cousin's torturing me."

"Sometimes you have to pretend to be part of the Pack, darlin'. So when you're old and grey, they won't rip your throat out because you're toothless."

"That's lovely. Thank you."

He leaned in a bit and sniffed her. "You've got strange wolf on you." His eyes narrowed. "Who you been fuckin'?"

"Rory Lee Reed! You speak to me proper!"

"All right." He lowered his voice several octaves and said, "Who you been fuckin'?"

Dee grinned. "Ric Van Holtz."

"Really?"

"Yeah, but don't tell."

"Why? You ashamed?"

"Nope. Just seems more dirty that way."

"You and your dirty fetish."

"Can't help it . . . turns me on."

"Ew."

"Besides," Dee went on, "you can't tell anyone because once Ronnie Lee knows everyone will know."

"Including your daddy."

"And Ric is just so damn pretty, it would be a right shame to see him all . . ."

"Eviscerated?"

She sighed. "You do know how Daddy likes to eviscerate."

"He does have a skill."

"A man has to know his strengths."

"So do you like him?"

Frowning, "I love Daddy."

"Not him. Van Holtz. Do you like Van Holtz?"

"Oh." Dee thought a moment, then answered, "Yep."

"And?" he pushed.

"And what?"

"Ain't ya gonna gush about him or somethin'?"

"Gush? Who the hell do you think you're talking to?"

"Sorry. For a minute there I thought you were a girl, but then I remembered that you're just sleeping with one."

"Don't be jealous 'cause you don't look like a supermodel, too. Not everybody can be that pretty."

They focused on the stage and Dee demanded, "What in hell are we listening to?"

"A lion male singing 'Sweet Home Alabama.' "

"Ya see?" she asked her friend. "Daddy was right."

And together they said, "Time to start the killin'."

CHAPTER 13

Ric sat at his kitchen table, working on ideas for the next day's menu based on what product he knew would be coming into the restaurant that morning and what they had left over that was still fresh. He enjoyed doing this, coming up with new ideas, pulling out old ones, turning them into a cohesive whole that worked with their standard cuts of meat. So focused on his menu, he didn't know he wasn't alone until Dee slammed down a plate of angel food cake onto the table and dropped into the chair beside him.

"Hello."

"Hey," she replied while . . . well, while pouting.

"Something wrong?"

"Just tired."

"No more problems with Malone?"

"Not today. Tomorrow, of course, is another story."

"Make it work, Dee-Ann."

"Yeah, yeah." She glanced at him. "What's wrong with you?"

"Nothing."

She snorted. "You're a bad liar."

"And you're not just tired."

Dee toyed with her dessert plate. "Do you ever wonder sometimes what it would be like to be a nice, solitary cat, without all the Pack fuss?"

"Not really." Ric picked up her fork and lifted a piece of cake to her mouth. "All those hairballs and obsession with yarn. Plus, I just don't know how to do that thing they do."

"What thing?" she asked before opening her mouth so he could feed her the cake.

"That arch look of disdain they all have about absolutely *everything*. Let's be honest, Dee. It's a skill canines simply lack."

She could tell something was bothering him, but she wouldn't push him if he didn't want to talk about it. Nothing irritated her more than people pushing her when she wasn't in the mood to be pushed. Instead, she ate the cake he fed her.

"I'm glad you came back," Ric told her, lifting another forkful to her mouth.

"So am I." She grinned. "Because you're lookin' *sexy*."

"I'm not a whore, Dee-Ann. You can't just come here to use and abuse me before going on your merry way. Unless, of course, you're naked."

"Still not bored with that yet?"

"Never."

"Most males are scared off by my scars."

"Even wolves?"

"There's a difference between survival scars and 'I kill for a living' scars. And wolves with half a brain can tell them apart." She took the fork from him and proceeded to feed him several pieces of cake.

"Does your father have a lot of scars?" he asked between bites.

"Not as many as mine. Daddy was not one for the close-up kill unless you really pissed him off."

"But you enjoy more . . . direct engagement?"

"I can kill from a distance like anyone else with my training, but that don't always feel right to me. I'd rather know when my end is coming. I'd rather look it in the eye. Tell it 'How do ya do?' To those who deserve it, I try and do the same thing. For those who don't . . . they get whatever's comin'." She suddenly smirked a little at the expression on his face. "Am I making you nervous, Van Holtz?"

Ric shook his head. "Not really." He took the fork from her fingers and placed it on the table. Then he gently gripped her hand and lowered it to his groin, pressing it against the bulge he had eagerly pulsating against his zipper.

Dee swallowed and admitted, "You're a strange boy, Ulrich Van Holtz."

"Am I making *you* nervous now?"

Her hand turned so she could more easily grip his groin with her fingers, the denim between them making it more erotic. "Nah. You are making things a bit more interesting, though. Fancy boy like you, gettin' all turned on by a hard-hearted bitch like me."

His hands slipped into her hair, fingertips massaging her scalp. He stared into her face and said, "Your heart isn't hard, Dee-Ann. It's strong and maybe encased in a ribcage made of granite, but it's not hard. Far from it."

"You think you know me so well, do ya?"

His lips were inches from hers now and all she wanted was a kiss from those sweet lips, especially with that bit of cake icing waiting to be licked off. "Every day I learn something new about you. And every day I like you more and more."

"Yep," she teased. "Strange." Then she kissed him and realized that every day, she was growing to like this wolf more and more, too.

Kissing Dee-Ann was becoming addictive. And not just because she tasted like Jean-Louis's angel food cake, but because she *was* addictive. And delicious. And amazing. She had a way of soothing him without even trying, her presence alone easing him . . . even when she grabbed his T-shirt and hauled him out of the chair. She was always a little rough with him—and he liked it. Because it told Ric how hungry she was for him. How much she wanted him.

It was Dee's coldness that scared others. The way she could

snap a human spine without raising her heart rate was what made her such a dangerous female. But for Ric it was the knowledge that he was seeing the warm-blooded side of his She-wolf. He knew he confused her, sometimes irritated her, sometimes made her smile, but being able to turn her on absolutely made his day.

Dee stepped away and quickly removed the holsters for her gun and knife, placing them on the kitchen counter. She pulled off her T-shirt, unhooked her bra, tossing them aside while walking backward out of the kitchen, her eyes on him. She crooked her finger at him and Ric followed her, yanking his T-shirt over his head and throwing it over his shoulder while she went to his bedroom. By the time he walked in, she had stripped herself naked, pressing her body against his. Their arms encircled each other, their mouths meeting, tongues seeking.

Ric lifted Dee up, carrying her over to the bed. He lowered her to the mattress, kissing her neck, her collarbone. Once they were on the bed, she shoved him onto his back, straddling his waist with her strong and deliciously long legs. Licking her lips, she pressed her mouth to his chest, kissing her way down his body until she reached his jeans. She unzipped them, stepping off the bed long enough to tug them down and pull them off. Then Dee's hands were brushing up the inside of his thighs. Ric groaned when her mouth followed, her tongue easing against his flesh, fangs scraping against his muscles. By the time her mouth wrapped around his cock, Ric had dug his hands into her hair, his back arching off the bed.

So many nights he'd dreamed about this, prayed for it even, but to have Dee-Ann Smith deep-throating his cock was more than he could have hoped for. Especially when she seemed to enjoy the giving as much as the taking.

Dee heard the catch in Ric's throat, the way his fingers tensed in her hair, the way every one of his muscles tightened under her body. His reaction made her body hot, made her slip two fingers inside her pussy, and start stroking herself in time with each suck of Ric's cock. When he came, she came with him, her fingers buried deep inside her.

Ric lifted her head, his hands shaking. She only had a moment to give a little gasp before Ric was kissing her hard, his fingers digging deep into her scalp. She felt his desperation in that kiss, the taste of him still on her lips, in her mouth. He didn't seem to care.

Lord, she'd never had a man react to her like this. Like he couldn't get enough of her. It was strange and delightful and almost cruel because how could this go on? This was just for fun, wasn't it? Just a diversion while Dee dealt with a tough job. Nothing more, nothing less. But . . . but who was she kidding?

She was stupidly falling for a Van Holtz. The enemy wolf of her Pack. Her daddy hated Van Holtzes the way Dee hated the taste of zebra. Since she could crawl he'd been warning her about staying away from them, never trusting them, and outright killing them if they got too close.

Well . . . how could the man be any closer? He'd pushed her onto the bed and had buried his face into her pussy, licking and sucking his way into her heart. Turning her inside out, making her come again.

It just wasn't fair. How was she supposed to fight this? And, as she came all over his face, her entire body writhing on his giant bear-sized bed, she wasn't real sure anymore she wanted to fight this.

Because, in the end, the man did make a hell of a waffle. . . .

"Thought you were sleeping," she complained when he bent her knees up and to the side, and took his time entering her, groaning at the heat that wrapped around him, shuddering at the muscles that squeezed him.

"I woke up," he said into her neck. "And you didn't look busy."

"Such a horny wolf," she growled, her arms reaching out for him.

"I am, but that's your fault."

"Yeah. Sure."

She didn't believe him, but she should. Because no female he'd been with had ever managed to make him wake up every few hours with an intense need to be back inside her, taking her like he was taking Dee now. It was hard to believe she didn't see it or feel it. The intensity between them. And even when she griped with that annoyed-sounding "Again?" she still responded to his touch, to his cock, to him. She panted beneath him, sweat glistening on her body as if the air conditioning wasn't going full blast all around them.

Dee turned her face toward him and he took her mouth, kissing her hard, enjoying every moment he was inside her.

Reaching between her legs and stroking her until Dee came again, Ric followed her over.

Afterward, as they lay there, Ric's arms wrapped around her and holding her close, he asked, "If I asked you to a charity dance thing, you'd immediately turn me down, wouldn't you?"

"Faster than you can say, 'Dee-Ann . . . what are you doin' with that gun?' "

They both laughed, Ric kissing the back of her neck. "What about the July Fourth weekend then? I'm purposely avoiding the yearly family event since I usually spend the aftermath apologizing for something my father said or did. I'd much rather spend the time with you."

"Can't," she said, rubbing his arm. "If I'm not working, I'll be dealing with the kin. A few Pack events throughout the year usually keeps 'em off my back the rest of the time and Sissy made it clear she wanted me at this one." She glanced at him. "But if it makes you feel better, I'd much rather spend that weekend with you, too."

"That does make me feel better." He kissed her cheek. "We'll have to pick another weekend then. I want you to see the new house I bought out on the Island."

"How much property do you have anyway?"

"Enough so that if I'm ever forced out of the Pack, I'll have ample places to stay."

"Your Pack do that a lot to its own?"

"The Pack as a whole . . . no. My father?" He shrugged, not really wanting to talk about him when he was having the time of his life with Dee. Although, he'd never felt safer talking about the man except with Lock.

"Don't worry," she teased. "If you ever need a place to stay, there's this apartment you can share with a lovely family I know. If you don't mind beady red eyes."

He glared down at her. "That's not funny, Dee-Ann," he said while she laughed. "Vermin is *never* funny."

CHAPTER 14

"Someone just got laid."

Dee froze in her tracks, her hand on the plain front door that led into the Group office. Slowly, she turned and faced Malone and Desiree.

"She appears freshly laid to me," Desiree said, grinning. "It's the walk."

"The 'I just got laid walk.'" Malone nodded. "Yep. Saw that, too."

Dee-Ann moved away from the door and over to the two females she was currently forced to work with. "Is there a reason y'all are here?" she asked.

"Avoidance," Desiree observed. "Must be kind of serious."

"So are we getting a name, Smith? Or is it just some poor loser wolf from whatever backwoods coughed you up?"

Dee was in Malone's face, the two snarling at each other, but without fangs since they were on the street in the full view of God and everybody.

"Cut it out," Desiree sighed. "We've got a line on a fight. And I don't mean you two."

Stepping back, Dee gave one last bark at Malone before focusing on Desiree. "Where and when?" she asked, already looking forward to hurting some people who deserved it. Not that Malone didn't deserve a good beating, but Dee couldn't really get away with it at the moment, so beating someone else would have to do . . . for now.

Ric was busy changing into his black sweats, black T-shirt, and black chef's coat when his cousin Arden entered the employee locker room.

She smiled at the others getting changed for the dinner service and she walked up to Ric. She placed her hand on his shoulder and he came down a bit so she could whisper in his ear. "Did you know your father's here?" she asked.

Ric briefly closed his eyes. "No. Did he ask for me?"

"No. Just went to the manager's office and started going through the papers there. Do you want me to get Adelle?"

"Don't." She'd only make it worse in her attempt to protect Ric. "I'll go see him."

"Okay. Dell is with him."

That made Ric snarl. Wendell. Ric's brother. He liked to be called Dell because he hated his name—which meant that Ric called him Wendell at every given opportunity.

Ric finished changing, wrapped a black bandana around his hair since he felt the same way about chef hats as he felt about chef clogs, and headed to the general manager's office.

His father sat at the small desk, scanning papers, his small round glasses perched on the end of his nose. At the four-drawer file cabinet stood his older brother, Wendell, searching through all the folders. What they were looking for, Ric could only guess.

"Dad," Ric said to his father and to his brother, "Wendell."

His brother scowled. "It's Dell."

Ric closed the door behind him and leaned against it. "What can I do for you two?"

His father glanced at him over his glasses. He was a singularly fussy wolf, with his receding hairline, pinched features, and too-small eyes. Blayne called those eyes beady and she was right.

Among the American Van Holtzes, there were two kinds of wolves: The fussy, smaller East Coast wolves who kept their territories safe by being extremely sneaky and devious with absolutely no regard for what the long-term effects of their actions might be; and the bigger, more direct, but much meaner West Coast wolves that kept their territories by tearing apart anything that tried to take what they believed belonged to the Pack.

Yet Ric represented neither side, taking after his mother who hailed from a small Pack located in the Colorado Rockies. He got what his father referred to as his "pretty girl" looks and "weak nature" from "*that* side of the bloodline."

Ric, however, didn't believe he had a weak nature. Having a soul didn't make one weak and he felt his father knew this because he only pushed his son but so far. Then again, that could have a lot to do with his Uncle Van. Because Adelle had been right. Niles Van Holtz had always done his best to protect his young cousin from Alder. For every attempt his father made to break Ric down, Uncle Van was right there to build Ric right back up. It had meant a lot to him growing up and both men knew now that if push ever came to shove, Ric's loyalty would always be with his Uncle Van. Always.

Something else his father resented Ric for, but really, what did the man expect?

"You're paying Fortelli too much for the fish." He raised a recent invoice and slammed it on the desk. Pulled out another invoice. "And the seal meat."

Ric didn't reply. He simply did that thing he did when his father got like this. He "went away." He just thought of something else. Something more pleasant or more interesting or more anything than the old bastard muttering at him in that fussy tone about something Ric didn't control—that's why they had a general manager—and knew wasn't true anyway.

Instead, he thought about Dee. Gorgeous, sexy Dee. She wouldn't be easy to make his own. Dee-Ann Smith would be a challenge for any wolf, but for Ric especially because he was a Van Holtz. It was rumored that Smiths warned their pups away from Van Holtzes from birth and something told Ric that Dee's father had definitely been one of those. Of course, that wouldn't stop Ric from trying. Just because the bone he wanted was on the other side of the fence didn't mean he would ever stop trying to get over, around, or under that fence until he got what he wanted.

A rather antiquated reference to the well-known Van Holtz determination, but still true today.

"What are you smiling at?"

Ric looked up and realized his father was standing in front of him, Wendell on his right. Not the best position for any wolf to be in.

"Nothing. Is there anything else?"

His father stepped closer, studying him from behind those small round glasses. "Are you sure there's nothing you want to tell me about . . . *son?*"

Ric shook his head. "No, sir."

Another step closer, Wendell moving in from the other side. "Really?" Another step. "Not even about what I saw washing the dishes not more than twenty minutes ago?"

Damn. So concerned over those bloody books, Ric had completely forgotten about Stein.

"I don't see what there is to discuss."

"Is that right?"

"I have full discretion on whom I hire and whom I don't."

"Have you forgotten what he did? Why he was removed from the Pack? From the family?"

Christ, his father made it sound like they'd had a tumor surgically removed before it got too big. Stein was a lot of things, but not something to be coldly and callously excised from those he knew and loved. And not only that, but talk about the pot calling out the kettle. At least Stein had his youth as an excuse to stealing from his Pack. What was Alder's excuse?

"I've forgotten nothing," Ric replied simply.

"And?" his father pushed.

Ric shrugged. He wouldn't elaborate. He wouldn't argue this any further. There was no point. Besides, it was when Ric was trying to defend himself that Alder Van Holtz went in for the kill. He could do with words what many could do with knives or claws. Even Uncle Van didn't go toe-to-toe with Alder when it came to words. In fact, the only one among them brave enough? Van's wife, Aunt Irene. One of the many reasons Ric adored her like the moon.

"And nothing."

By now, Alder was only a few inches from his youngest offspring. "Do you really think," he whispered, "that your precious Uncle Van will keep running to your rescue, boy? You're not a pup anymore."

"No. I'm not. And that's why I'm telling you to get the hell out of my restaurant."

His father smiled, seeing some opening that Ric was unaware of. Mind scrambling, Ric tried to figure out what he could have missed, what he could have said that gave the bastard a way in for the kill. While he did, he prepared himself for the blow. Not a physical one. That he could handle and if it came, it would be from his brother. No. This would not be physical, but it would do much worse damage.

"Listen to me, Ulrich," his father said, still smiling, "I—"

The door swung open, slamming into the back of Alder's head and pushing him into Ric's arms.

"Ric, you in here? We need to talk, supermodel."

Dee-Ann stepped into the room, her eyes catching sight of Wendell. "Are you supposed to be in here?" she demanded.

"Are you?" Wendell shot back.

"Yeah."

The comeback was so calm and simple that Wendell had absolutely no response. It was amazing.

"Dee-Ann?"

She looked around the door. "There you are."

Ric helped his father back to a standing position. Not because he wanted to, but because he wanted the man out of his arms.

"You remember my father?" Ric asked.

Dee looked at the door and at the older wolf glowering at her. "Oh." She looked at the door again. Then Ric's father. "Oh, Lord."

* * *

Although Dee didn't like Ric's father, she still didn't want to go beating him up with doors. That was rude and her momma would expect more from her. Especially when Dee was sleeping with the man's son.

"Mr. Van Holtz, I'm very—"

Before she could finish her apology, the wolf stormed past her, practically shoving her into the door she'd battered him with.

She leaned out into the hallway, calling after him, "I'm real sorry. I can assure you it was an accident."

"Like your birth?"

That came from Wen-*dell*—she always made sure to enunciate the last part of his name since it seemed to piss him off so much. But as she turned to tell him exactly what she thought of his birth, she saw that there was no point. Because she didn't have the chance.

Ric had reached out and caught his brother by the throat with his left hand, yanking him forward, and took hold of Wendell's arm with his right, pulling it back. "Apologize," Ric told him, looking more pissed off than Dee had ever seen him. Even the time he threw that zebra hoof at her—*long story*—he didn't look that angry.

"Fuck yo—"

Ric unleashed his claws, burying them in his brother's throat, blood dripping over his hand and onto the floor. "Apologize," the wolf told his brother calmly. "And do it *nicely.*"

"Sorry!" Wendell managed to get out. Then Ric shoved him forward and right into the hallway. The wolf slammed into the opposite wall, his head leaving a dent in the drywall.

"Get out of my restaurant," Ric told him, his voice even, not raised at all. "You can return when you've learned some manners."

Ric turned away and walked toward the desk. So he missed his brother unleashing his own claws and coming for him from behind like some untrustworthy feline. But Dee silently stepped in front of Wendell, her bowie knife out. She waved it once and softly said, "Uh-uh."

The worthless wolf pulled back. Maybe he was willing to take his brother on, but not her. Then again, Dee was doing him a favor. This pissed off, Ric would tear the idiot's throat out, but that wouldn't sit right with him. He'd never forgive himself and Dee wasn't going to have that.

She motioned Wendell away with a tilt of her head. He went, shoving aside the crew members who'd come into the hall to watch Ric slap him around. Nope. Wendell wouldn't be forgiving this bit of embarrassment anytime soon.

Hearing Ric moving behind her, she quickly slid her blade back in its sheath and turned.

He was just facing her. "Sorry about that," he said and she had to laugh.

"Darlin', that's Thanksgiving dinner over at my Uncle Bubba's house."

"I know you need to talk to me, but can you give me five minutes?"

"Sure." She started to step out but he walked past her and into the hallway. She went back into the office, rested her butt on the desk, and waited.

Arden got the quick scoop from her Aunt Adelle, who'd heard it from the sous-chef, who'd gotten it from the garde-manger, who'd seen it himself! And Arden had to say she was entertained and immensely proud of her cousin! Mostly because as much as she adored Ric, she loathed her cousin Wendell in equal parts. He was more weasel than wolf, in her opinion.

Tragically, she couldn't stay around and gossip more about the whole thing. She had to get to class unless she wanted to spend her life showing people their tables and taking complaints. Although it was a great way for a twenty-year-old to make sixty grand a year, get her tuition for her Ivy League tech school paid in full, *and* have flexible hours, so she wouldn't bitch about it too much.

She charged around a corner, her arm reaching out to hail a cab, when someone caught her and yanked her back.

"Hey!" she screeched, ready to fight like a full-human first, then unleash claws if necessary. But it wasn't anything to be worried about. Just Wendell.

"If this is about Ric—" she began, trying not to giggle at the claw marks on his neck.

"I don't give a shit about him. I want to know about Stein."

"What about him?"

"Why is he back?"

"I don't know." She tried to walk off, but Wendell yanked her back again. "Hey! Get off me!"

"Then answer my question."

"Why do you think? He owes money to somebody."

"From Vegas?"

"Atlantic City. There. Happy now?"

"Ecstatic." He pushed her away. "Let me know when you grow tits, cuz. Maybe I'll hook you up with one of my boys then."

"Like you actually have friends, dickwad." Then Arden caught her cab and headed to class.

CHAPTER 15

When Ric wasn't back in five minutes, Dee went looking for him. She actually had somewhere to be and she was only giving him a heads-up on what she, Malone, and Desiree were doing.

Dee stuck her head in the kitchen. "Where's Ric?" she asked the room.

"In the alley," one of the cooks told her.

Dee headed to the door that led to the alley and stepped outside. Ric was at the far end of the alley where it was blocked off by a brick wall that was attached to the restaurant and the deli next door. He had his back to her, his body hunched over.

Dee moved up silently behind him, curious to see what he was doing all huddled into a corner like that. When she stood right behind him, she went up on her toes a bit and peeked over his shoulder. A brow went up and she relaxed back to the flat feet she was born with—and waited. Because she knew she wouldn't have to wait too long.

Ric froze, knowing she was right behind him. Knowing she was watching him do what he hadn't done in two and a half years. But after those six months of patches and nicotine-tinged chewing gum until he'd gone cold turkey for two years—Ric was right back where he'd been.

He clenched the cigarette he'd bummed off a full-human from the deli next door tight between his lips, the engraved gold lighter he hadn't used in more than two years clutched between his hands as he tried to get the goddamn thing to light. Knowing he couldn't avoid her forever, Ric slowly turned and faced Dee-Ann. She had her arms folded over her chest, a smirk on those perfect lips, and one brow raised while she waited for him to say something.

"Look," he immediately began to argue around the precious, precious stick of death he had gripped between his lips. "I'm not going to sit here and explain why I need this. I . . . I just need this, okay?"

"Uh-huh."

Since she didn't say anything else, he tried again to get his lighter to work. He shook it a few times, praying there was a little lighter fluid left at the bottom. Finally, he had flame and he brought it close to the cigarette. His mistake was looking again at Dee-Ann. Her expression hadn't changed. She wasn't shaking her head or "tsk-tsking" him. She wasn't trying to grab the cigarette out of his mouth, or bursting into tears, or telling him how disappointed she was in him. But she wasn't walking away either, or telling him to "do as ya like," or pretending he wasn't smoking and getting on with whatever it was she needed to discuss with him.

No. Dee-Ann didn't do any of that. She simply watched, smirked, and waited.

Waited for him to realize he was making a huge mistake.

Although Ric knew all the reasons it was bad to smoke, he'd given it up two and half years ago for one reason and one reason only—it fucked with his taste buds. Something that, as a chef, he couldn't afford. He also knew if he started again now, he'd probably never stop. Quitting was too painful a process, too time consuming, and the reason for why he'd begun smoking in the first place would never go away. At least not anytime soon.

He'd been fifteen when he started, somehow managing to keep it a secret among scent-prone wolf shifters until, when he was seventeen, his mother found his pack when she'd picked up his school jacket to hang it in the closet. He remembered how angry she'd been, how hurt, but he knew she kind of understood it, too. At the time, it was the only way Ric had of dealing with his father. The tobacco soothed his nerves, cleared his mind, settled his spirit, and allowed him to make it through nightly dinners with Alder and Wendell. Ric had only stopped when he knew it was putting his cooking career at risk and, more importantly, he was no longer living with his father and brother.

Ric closed the lighter and pulled the cigarette out of his mouth.

"I hate you," he muttered.

"I know." She took the cigarette from his hand. "A non-filtered wolf, I see."

"I took whatever Joey at the deli had. I was desperate."

"Is this about Wendell?"

"Hardly. He was rude. He's lucky Adelle didn't hear him. She would have torn his hair out."

"Then it's the old wolf. Why was he here?"

"I have no idea."

"Okay then."

"It isn't that he was here that's the problem, Dee."

"It's his presence on this planet?"

Ric finally smiled. "Well . . . yes. Plus some other stuff that I can't get into."

"Understood. We're from enemy Packs, so you can't go around telling me your precious enemy Pack secrets."

"Now you're making me feel stupid."

Dee chuckled. "Not my intent." She glanced back at the door. "This doesn't have to do with that scruffy, homeless wolf you had roaming your apartment the other morning?"

"He's not homeless . . . anymore. He's sleeping on the couch of my saucier. And although I doubt Stein has anything to do with what happened today, I'm sure my father will use him against me somehow."

"His name's *Stein*?"

"At least it's just *one* name."

She grinned. "Look at you trying to sweet talk me."

Ric flinched. "Sorry. Unnecessary roughness."

"Not where I come from."

"Stein's my cousin. I hired him to mop the floors and wash dishes."

"What's wrong with that? You're supposed to watch out for your kin."

"Not when your kin has been shoved out of the Pack. And it's not like the kid didn't deserve that shove. He did."

She stepped closer. "How bad could this get for you?"

"That depends. If Stein never screws up again, takes this opportunity to become the best chef that has ever walked the earth, and he manages to make this world a better place for everyone throughout the universe—*maybe* my father will let this go before he's on his deathbed. If the kid screws up even once . . ." Ric shrugged. "Well, I've always wanted to open up a little bistro in Soho. Now this could be my chance."

"Seems a lot of trouble to let a kid wash dishes."

"He needs the work, Dee. Really needs it. And from what I can tell, he can't drop any lower at this point. Not without some real effort. I can't just turn him away. I at least have to give him one more chance to ruin everything for both of us."

"Now see?" she asked and Ric realized that they were so close that all Ric had to do was lean in another inch or so and he'd be kissing her. "What am I supposed to do with a wolf that's just so dang nice?"

"Get naked with me in the office? General manager won't be in for a couple of hours."

"You have no idea how much I *really* want to, but I can't. I only came here to give you a heads-up what I've got going on tonight with Desiree and Malone."

"You and your damn work ethic."

"It's a flaw. I know." She petted his cheek, stepping into him until their bodies were flush. "You gonna be all right?"

"After seeing you slam my father's head with that door?"

"*That* was an accident . . . so maybe you shouldn't smile about it."

"Can't help it." He kissed her, feeling nothing but hope at the way her body kind of melted into his. When they finally stopped, Ric pressed his forehead against hers and closed his eyes. The She-wolf let him stay that way for several minutes until his soul had calmed, his desire to shift and run until he hit Jersey throttling down to a tolerable hum of awareness.

"Come back to my place when you're done," he told her.

"All right."

He stepped away from her, knowing he had to let her go. "Come inside and tell me what's going on first and I'll give you a set of keys for my apartment." Something he'd forgotten to do earlier.

She smirked. "Keys? What do I need keys for?"

"So you can at least *pretend* you're not breaking and entering?"

"If you're going to be particular about it."

Laughing, Ric headed to the alley door. "Come on."

"Yeah. Give me a minute."

"Sure."

Ric reached for the door but stopped and faced Dee again. He returned to her side and stared at her.

She blinked. "What?"

"Dee-Ann," he told her, "it's me."

"What's that supposed to mean?"

"Do I really need to call your mother about this?"

She snarled at him. "Sometimes you are just *mean!*" She slapped the cigarette back into his hand. "How did you know anyway?"

"I could see it in your eyes when I came back over. This cigarette was going down. How long?" he asked and she knew what he meant.

"Since I got home from the Marines and Momma caught me

smoking behind the barn. She slapped that cigarette from my hand and threatened bodily harm on her only child—all while crying."

"It was the crying, wasn't it?"

"Of course it was the crying. There's some things I simply can't tolerate. Wild dog howling, zebra, Teacup"—Ric threw his hands up at that—"and seeing my momma cry."

"Since my mother also would be destroyed by her youngest taking up smoking again, we'll make a deal." Ric crumpled the cigarette in his hands until it was nothing but bits of paper and tobacco. "If we think about starting up again, we'll call each other."

"And chat about it like girlfriends?"

"Only after we talk about what Prada is coming out with in their latest fall shoe line." When she only stared at him, Ric quickly added, "I'm kidding. I'm kidding. I don't wear Prada. They make my ankles look fat."

She turned away from him, walking to the door.

"I saw that smile, Dee-Ann. You can't hide it from me."

CHAPTER 16

They'd handpicked their teams. Three from each group, the people they most trusted when it came to skill set and the ability to keep their mouths shut. Plus, the order was they were to call *no one*. Not their mate, their best friend, their mom. No one.

Only the three supervisors who'd put the team together knew anything and they weren't telling even their own bosses.

Using a tip from Desiree's ASPCA contact, they'd come to this warehouse out in an industrial area on Long Island, not far from Malone's home off the Meadowbrook State Parkway. Something that annoyed the She-tiger immensely.

It was nearly ten by the time they parked their vehicles and made their way down the street, keeping to the shadows. The felines took to the roofs; the grizzly, wolf, and coyote that Dee brought stayed close to her; and the three cops—two wolves and a fox because she was such a dog person—Desiree had rounded up circled behind the warehouse to come in the back way.

Dee, Malone, and Desiree went toward the front. Dee would admit she'd been a little worried about bringing Desiree along. She was the only full-human among them, but once she had her bulletproof vest on and more weapons than seemed authorized by the NYPD, Dee stopped worrying. The girl was a Marine down to her toes and that's all Dee needed to know.

Using hand signals, Dee motioned for Desiree to head left, Malone right. She went straight for the front door, still using the shadows. She could hear the cheers and yelling coming from the other side, but it didn't block out the howls, roars, and whimpers. She was a few feet from the building when the door opened.

Dee dashed off to the side as a man walked out, already reaching for his zipper so he could unleash and piss in the first bush or open car window he could find. Dee waited until he'd passed her before she grabbed him from behind, twisting his head and snapping his neck. She pulled the body back and dropped him off to the side. She went back into the shadows and inched up to one of the windows, working hard to peer through all the dirt. She saw about fifty full-humans making up the bloodthirsty viewing crowd and another fifteen armed men, keeping everyone in control. They all surrounded a makeshift pit where a fight raged between what appeared to be a feline hybrid and a canine mix.

Standing by a set of stairs that led to the roof were two more men. One was counting the entry money and another was watching him, smoking a cigar. And she knew that was the one she wanted.

Deciding she'd seen enough, Dee crouched low and indicated with hand signals what they were about to face. Both females nodded, and Dee moved in front of the door. It opened again, an armed male coming out this time. She caught him by the face, shoving him back into the building. She raised her automatic weapon and shot through him. Most of the audience bolted for the back door—where Desiree's team waited. So Dee wished them good luck on that.

Using the man in her arms as a shield for the bullets coming at her, Dee pulled back a few feet until she could drop the corpse and dive behind a bench. She cleared out the empty clip and slammed in a fresh one. She heard more gunfire and knew Malone and Desiree had made it into the room. Taking a breath, she came up, firing the entire way.

The money man and cigar guy grabbed the cash and ran up the stairs.

"Malone!" Dee yelled, catching a fist that was swinging at her face and twisting until the arm attached to it broke in several places, the full-human going down screaming. "Stairs! Go!"

Malone moved and Dee slammed her booted foot into the face of the male at her feet just to stop all that damn screaming. The fact that she'd probably killed him in the process didn't worry her much. Not after seeing all the hybrid bodies piled in a corner.

"Dee!" Desiree called out. "Back up Malone! Go!"

Dee ran for the stairs, ducking as shots flashed past her. She hit the bottom step and charged up. When she got to the second floor, there were more men coming toward her. She fired and kept running, jumping over their bodies and hitting the next set of stairs. It was quieter on this floor, but she scented the presence of full-humans as she headed to the next flight of stairs. She had her foot on the bottom step when a hand caught her from behind. She turned and slashed down and across with her knife, cutting through skull, an eye, nose, lips, straight through a jaw. Then she was away and up the stairs. She saw a door that led out to the roof and Dee yanked it open and went through.

The felines were holding their own against another group of men, one of them going fist to fist with Malone. *Honestly . . . Malone and the brawling.*

Dee stepped out onto the roof, raising her weapon to start shooting anyone who didn't naturally have fangs when she realized someone was behind her. She spun and a brawny hand caught her weapon, lifting it up. The other hand punched her in the face a few times, forcing her up against the wall. Her automatic weapon was snatched from her hands and her face was hit again. She blinked, shaking her head, ignoring her broken nose and possibly readjusted cheekbones.

The full-human male, clearly a steroid user, tossed aside her weapon and came back to batter her face a little more. Dee blocked his fists with her arms and kicked at his leg. But she missed his knee, hitting his overdeveloped thigh. It hurt him, but only enough to piss him off. He backhanded her across the face, sending her flipping across the roof. When she managed to get to her hands and feet, he was there, kicking her in the gut. Dee rolled with it, but realized too late she was near the edge of the roof. She landed on the ledge, half of her dangling into nothing.

The man reached for her, grabbing hold of her vest and lifting her up. Dee unleashed her claws and ripped them into the man's head. He screamed and she dug in deeper, then outward, trying to tear his face off.

He fought her, swinging at her, and finally flinging her away and over the side, but Dee still clung to him. He screamed, trying to pull her claws from his face while she dangled several floors off the ground.

Dee held on but the blood was making it easier for him to pull her away from his irreparably damaged flesh, his hands gripping her wrists. He was almost free, her claws nearly out, when Malone landed on the man's back, her own military issue knife ramming into the base of his neck, again and again.

Whatever steroid this asshole was taking, he wasn't going down easy. Even spouting blood from a major artery, he still fought two She-predators like a demon, holding on to one of Dee's wrists with one hand and reaching back for Malone with the other. He flipped Malone over and out. But after releasing her own blade, Malone grabbed a healthy amount of the bastard's hair and held on.

Dee now had at least one arm free and she grabbed hold of her bowie, sticking it into the man's neck and yanking it from ear to ear. His eyes glazed over and he lurched forward.

Still holding her knife, Dee caught hold of the ledge while Malone scrambled back over the man's body and onto the roof. The man spilled forward and went sailing—but he still had a death grip on Dee's other wrist. She screamed when the weight of the big bastard nearly tore her arm out of its socket.

Malone snatched the knife from Dee and reached over, sawing

at the man's hand until she'd cut through flesh, muscle, sinew, and bone. His body dropped and Malone reached for her, but as she lowered her body to get a good grip on Dee's waist, Dee saw another man behind the feline, his gun raised. One of Malone's team was near, but she'd never reach the man before he got a shot off. With her right arm unusable at the moment since it wasn't in its socket, and the other the only thing holding her onto the ledge, Dee did the one thing she could think of. She grabbed Malone around the back of her neck with her fangs and yanked her off the ledge like a momma-wolf would her cub.

Roaring, Malone dangled from Dee's mouth, unaware of the gunshots that had nearly blown the back of her head off.

Malone slapped one of those big tiger claws against Dee's throat and was seconds from ripping in and down when big bear arms reached over and caught hold of them both. With a good pull, he dragged both She-predators back over the ledge and then got between them when the fists began to fly.

"Aren't you both too old for this?" he asked as only a twenty-something male could stupidly ask two fighting females sliding down the dark edge of thirty-five.

"Ow!" he yelped. "*What are you hitting me for?*"

Dez MacDermot put her gun away and caught hold of the man Dee-Ann had told her was probably the one in charge.

She yanked him up and into a chair and handcuffed him to it.

"I want a lawyer," he said and Dez could only laugh at him.

"Oh, baby. Don't you realize you're past lawyers?" She let out a sigh. "I've had to adjust a lot of my beliefs in order to do this job, but it's the price I pay to take care of those I love. Now it's the price you'll pay."

"You trying to scare me, cop? You trying to convince me you're gonna actually *do* something to me?"

"Me? Probably not. I don't have the stomach for that. But my partners do."

Dez walked to the door and opened it, letting in the woman Dee had asked for help. A woman Dez loathed—and to be honest, feared. But Dez was beginning to realize more and more that they were all in this together. Yes, even with the hyena whose Clan had once tried to kill her.

"I'd like to introduce you to Gina Brutale." Dez motioned to the giggling females behind her. "These are her cousins. At least . . . some of them. Now, you can tell me what I want to know or I can let Gina have some fun."

"Is that supposed to scare me?" He looked Gina over. She was her usual big-haired, gum-popping self in too-tight designer clothes, so he didn't seem too impressed. But Dez had learned the day Mace Llewellyn walked back into her life never to let someone's looks fool her.

"It should," Dez told him honestly. "And if it doesn't, it will." She stepped back and let Gina walk up to him. She kneeled in front of him, between his spread legs.

"Hi. I'm Gina. I'm here to hurt you until you tell the cop what she wants to know. I'm not here because I owe anybody anything or because I am doing this for high moral reasons. To be honest, I could give a shit what happens to hybrids. But I will do this . . . for fun." She laid her hands on his thighs and leaned in, sniffing him like a good meal. "I like to have fun. My Clan calls me the fun-time girl."

She moved in closer, brushing her head against his chin. "Let me show you how much fun I can be."

When it started, Dez focused on the floor. Too bad she couldn't block out the screaming.

"Are you sure?" Cella asked the leopard she'd handpicked for this gig tonight. "I mean really *really* sure."

"I'm sure. Barb is sure. We all saw it."

"Great." Letting out a sigh, Cella walked over to Smith. She was pressed up against one of the trucks, the young grizzly trying to find the right way to put her arm back in its socket.

Unable to watch a second more of the bear fumbling along, Cella pushed him aside and took Smith's arm.

"The team told me," she said, feeling around Smith's shoulder, "you saved my ass back there."

Wincing from the pain, Smith said, "You saved mine."

"Yeah, but I'm better than you."

The She-wolf grinned. "Is that what your lord god Satan tells you during your feline rituals?"

Cella sneered, but forced herself to say, "Anyway . . . thank you."

"Same here."

"Ready?"

"As ready as I'll—*goddamnitmotherfuckerbastardgoddamnit!*"

Cella grinned. "Now . . . that wasn't so bad, was it?"

"Bitch."

"Whore."

The door to the warehouse opened and MacDermot walked out.

"Well?" Smith asked.

MacDermot held up a slip of paper. "Names. Two. I have addresses and—"

"Let's hit 'em tonight," Cella suggested, taking the paper from the full-human. "It's not even eleven yet."

"Or we could get back to it tomorrow," MacDermot tried.

"Or we can get it done tonight." Cella motioned to Smith. "She's up for it."

"She's a machine," MacDermot countered. "Besides, I'm sure these people will be there tomorrow."

"Tonight," Cella pushed, not wanting to take the chance. "We do this tonight. Just the three of us, and we'll be done in no time."

"All right. But first we're getting coffee from that diner we passed." MacDermot went off to release her team and Cella faced Smith. She was still rubbing her shoulder. "You are up for this, right?"

"I'm a machine."

"I'm sure MacDermot didn't mean that literally."

"Thanks." Smith held her hand out and Cella put the paper with the names on it in her palm.

"Anyone you know?"

"Nope."

"Good. Makes it a little easier when they're not friends." Cella motioned to the warehouse. "Do you want me to call in a cleanup team for this?"

"Nah. Brutale's Clan will take care of it."

Cella shook her head and walked around the truck to the driver's door. "Hyenas. They'll just eat *anything* won't they?"

"That's what's great about them."

CHAPTER 17

R ic woke up at his desk. He'd come home from the restaurant
and had dived right back into the books Uncle Van had sent
him. He continued to check and double-check numbers but he
knew it was a waste, and he was only putting off the inevitable
call to his cousin, but he was desperate. Hoping to find *anything*
that could turn this around.

Packing up all the paperwork, he put it in his standing safe.
Yawning and scratching his head, he headed to his bedroom but
stopped outside the guest room. He sniffed the door before easing it open. He didn't know when she'd come in, but he was glad
to see her back and safe, even if she wasn't in his bed.

Knowing Dee, she probably assumed it was rude to get into
his bed without receiving a direct invitation. He'd have to let her
know she had a standing invite from now until forever.

Gazing at her stretched out facedown and naked on the bed,
he could easily see what she'd been through that night. Bruises
and cuts littered her body, the worst bruising on her shoulder. All
those angry reds, purples, and blacks against pale white skin
suggested that particular area had been through hell and back.

Ric stripped naked and got on the bed with her. He wrapped
his arms around her waist and pulled her in tight against him,
making sure to avoid her damaged shoulder. She snarled at him
in her sleep anyway, but he kissed her neck and said, "It's Ric."

Dee settled down then and slept comfortably in his arms while Ric stared at the wall across the room and tried to figure out what he'd do next about his father. Because he honestly had no idea.

Dee-Ann woke up alone, although Ric's scent still surrounded her. Rubbing her eyes with her fists, she sat up and stretched long and hard. Her body still hurt some, but nothing she couldn't tolerate. Especially after those first few minutes of dawn when she'd felt Ric gently kissing her scars and stroking her bruises. The horniest wolf she knew, but she didn't mind because he always made her feel so damn good.

Leaving the bedroom, she headed to the kitchen. In the stove, she found a plate filled with bacon, ham, eggs, and toast. With a small smile, she reached for it, until she heard a noise coming from the opposite hallway.

Still naked, she followed the sound and ended up in front of Ric's home office. Head tilting to the side, she watched his brother, Wen-*dell,* trying to open the safe there. A safe he wouldn't get open anytime soon, if he knew about safes. Dammont safes were developed and built by wolves out of East Texas. No one was getting into that safe without the combination or a small thermonuclear device. Whether Wen-*dell* simply didn't know safes or he was so desperate he had to try, Dee-Ann simply didn't care.

All she knew was that he was trying to steal from his own brother and that's all she had to know. There were some lines one just didn't cross with family. At least not with her around.

She stood behind him, watching him fumble with the lock, getting more and more frustrated, for at least five minutes before he finally realized that she—or someone—stood right behind him.

The wolf spun around, fangs and claws unleashed, and Dee punched him in the face. His body slammed back into the safe and she moved in, punching him in the gut and kidneys until he was bent over at the waist. That's when she kneed him in the jaw.

Once he was out cold, Dee caught him by the hair and dragged him out of the office, down the hallway, to the front door. It opened while she was reaching for the knob. An older She-wolf stood there, eyes wide in surprise.

"Uh . . . you must be Dee-Ann," she said.

"Yes'm."

"I'm Mrs. Marshall. Ulrich's housekeeper."

"Mrs. Marshall. Nice to meet you."

"Um . . . he told me you might be here until you get a place of your own. I'm not . . . uh . . . interrupting anything, am I?"

"No, ma'am. Just taking out some trash."

"Ah. Mr. Dell. Yes. You're right." She pointed at the end of the hallway beside the elevator. "The garbage chute is right down there. You might have to push a bit to get his shoulders through, but you look strong enough."

"Thank you kindly."

Dee walked past the She-wolf and dragged the just-waking wolf down the hallway. By the time his eyes opened fully, Dee had most of his body in the chute.

"Wait—" he began, but Dee slapped her hand against his forehead and gave one last shove, sending him screaming down to the pits of hell—or more likely a Dumpster.

Wiping her hands against each other, she walked back into the apartment, closing the door.

"Clothes, missy," Mrs. Marshall told her. "You can't walk around a kitchen naked. It's tacky."

"Yes'm."

"And you better wash those hands, too, before you eat."

"Yes'm."

"And you can call me Mrs. M. like Ulrich does."

Or . . . just ma'am. Whatever worked. "Yes'm."

"Well, don't just stand there, girl. Move like you have purpose."

Dee ambled off to the bedroom to get a fresh set of clothes.

* * *

Lock MacRyrie opened his eyes when he caught the first whiff of coffee. He snarled at the wolf grinning down at him.

"Good morning, sunshine."

"Where's Gwen?"

"Work. I saw her on the way out. She wanted me to give you her love. Would you like the kiss, too?"

Lock turned over and pulled the covers over his head. No matter how many times he changed the locks on his door, getting stronger and more expensive models, nothing seemed to stop the wolves from getting into his apartment when they felt like it.

"Up. Up," Ric coaxed. "Time to face the day."

"Go away or I'm killing you."

"I need advice, old friend. There's my French toast in it for you."

"I don't want French toast. I want sleep."

"Bacon? Eggs? All fresh and made by loving hands."

"Shut up." He pulled the covers back and glared at his child-hood friend. "You're getting so weird these days."

"You have no idea."

And something in Ric's voice had Lock dragging his exhausted ass out of bed and into the shower.

By the time he walked out of his bedroom in a pair of jeans, the table was set and Ric was putting out his plate of food. The man's timing had always been impeccable.

Sitting down at the table, Lock reached for a slice of bacon. "So what's up? And this better not be more crazy shit about Dee-Ann."

"No. It's not about Dee-Ann."

"Good."

"We're sleeping together, but that's not why I'm here."

Lock threw the half-eaten strip of bacon onto his plate. "You're sleeping with her?"

"Figuratively and literally. But that's not why I'm here."

"I don't care that's not why you're here. You can't sleep with Dee."

"Too late."

"And when she's done, you'll let her go or are you going to do that annoying wolf thing you guys do? Where you keep trying to get them to be yours with flowers, chocolates, deer carcasses, and all that goddamn howling outside their window? Kind of like stalking but less threatening because you're only partially human. Because I know for a fact that Dee hates when guys of any breed or species does stuff like that and she doesn't respond to it well."

"I'll worry about that when we stop sleeping together."

"You're an idiot," Lock snarled, picking up another piece of bacon.

"So you enjoy telling me when it comes to Dee-Ann. Now can I get on with it?"

"What could be worse than you *stupidly* sleeping with Dee-Ann Smith?"

"My father stealing money from the Pack?"

Lock raised his gaze to his friend's, the pair staring at each other. Finally, Lock admitted, "Yep . . . that wins."

"Morning, Dee!"

Dee stopped mid pull-up, gritting her teeth.

"Aren't you going to say 'hi' back?"

Dee let out a breath and lowered her legs, releasing her grip on the pull-up bar and dropping to the ground. She came to the Group's in-house gym so she could work out in peace. So she could get in tune with her body while letting her mind work other issues out in the quiet and sanctity of the one place everyone knew she'd kill them as soon as look at them if they got on her dang nerves—a fail-safe she simply didn't have at the bigger but busier gym at the sports center.

Unfortunately, there was one part-time employee of the Group who didn't seem to understand the word "boundaries."

With a sigh, she faced the wolfdog. "Morning, Teacup."

A few months back they'd given Blayne a part-time job at the

Group. She had two roles: help the young hybrids that Dee had picked up off the streets to acclimate to life in a normal society, and teach them how to fight with knives. Because as much as the wolfdog irritated her last nerve, Dee had to admit the truth—the girl had some skills. Plus, she talked the language of the hybrid, which could be frighteningly off-kilter. Just like Blayne.

Teacup held out a sheaf of papers. "Evaluations."

Dee took the files and quickly flipped through them. "Well?"

"What we've both been saying. Most are doing well, but a few . . ."

"Hannah?"

Teacup grimaced. "Okay. She's a little resistant to . . . everyone. I'm working with her, though," she added quickly.

"I know, Blayne." Dee always used the woman's real name when they discussed business. It was proper. "But she makes the higher-ups nervous."

"Why? Because she's broody and stares and snarls and snaps when anyone gets too close?" Her nose crinkled a little. "Now that I think about it . . . that might make me nervous, too." She shook her head and stood tall. "Nope. Not ready to give up on her yet. Hannah's young. Lots of potential. And, oh, my God, she's so smart!"

"She can also rip a man's heart out of his chest with her bare hands."

"Well, who can't do that?"

Dee shoved the papers back at Blayne. "You want her to stay, you deal with her."

"I was thinking, though . . . it might be good if *you* stepped in as her mentor."

"Why?"

She blinked. "What do you mean why?"

"I mean why."

"Shouldn't you just feel, like, honored that I'm asking you?"

"No."

"Asking you to take her under your wing and—"

"No."

"But—"

"I let her live. That means my good-deed job is done."

"Please, Dee-Ann."

"Forget it."

The wolfdog's bottom lip began to tremble, her eyes welling with tears, but those tears seemed to be a siren song for bears because as soon as Teacup turned them on, every bear from miles around came to her aid. This time it was a grizzly, polar, and a sloth. And they were all glaring at Dee. She hadn't even lunged at Blayne yet.

Yet.

"Problem, Blayne?" the polar asked, brown eyes glaring at Dee from under one giant white uni-brow.

Bursting into hysterical sobs, Blayne turned and buried her face in the seven-nine polar's . . . well, stomach since she didn't reach his chest.

"Jesus Christ, Dee-Ann! What did you do to her now?" the polar demanded.

"Well, I started off by minding my own business. You should try it."

The grizzly sow pushed her shoulder. "Why are you so mean to her?" she wanted to know.

" 'Cause it makes me smile. And if you touch me again, I'll destroy every nerve that allows you to walk upright."

"Touch you again? You mean like this?"

The sow reached for her but a hand caught hold of the sow's wrist and bent it back.

"Now, now. No need for everyone to get testy."

Malone released the sow and stepped next to Dee, Desiree on the other side of her. It had been a long time since Dee had felt she had some backup during these day-to-day office dramas. It was nice.

"Problem, Dee?" Desiree asked, folding her arms across her

chest so her light jacket opened up enough that everyone could see the .45 she had holstered on her hip.

"No, no," Blayne said quickly, suddenly able to get control of her torrent of tears. "It's no problem. Everything is fine."

"You sure, Blayne?" the polar asked.

"Positive. Thanks, guys."

With a little jaw popping in warning, the bears walked off and Blayne faced Dee again. "This is so not over. I will bend you to my will."

"Sometimes I look at you," Dee stated flatly, "and I just want to pull your little head off and play basketball with it."

"You are so *mean*," Teacup snapped, storming off before Dee could bother *not* arguing with her.

"You are kind of mean, Smith," Malone told Dee.

"There's no 'kind of' about it. I just am."

Desiree grinned. "And yet you sound so proud."

"Girl's gotta know her strengths." Dee cracked her neck. "What's on the schedule?" Although the previous evening's raid had gone well and they'd dug up a little more info from the ones they'd gone to see right after, they still had a ways to go until they tracked down the money and the ones truly responsible.

"We're on hold for a few hours."

Malone looked around the training room. "Since we are, you up for a little training session, canine?"

"What kind of train—"

Dee's words were cut off by Malone's fist slamming into her face.

Desiree stepped back. "On that note, I think I'm going to go take a nap in the sleep room you guys have. You two have fun. Let me know when it's time to go."

Dee touched her nose. "You never know how to act, do ya, Malone?"

The She-tiger shrugged. "It depends on who you talk to."

"Do you really think your father would steal from his Pack to open his own restaurant?"

"I think he'd steal from a sleeping baby to open his own restaurant."

"Why?"

"He wants to prove he's better than Uncle Van, which is stupid. Because no one is better than Uncle Van."

"You still have that six-year-old's love of him, don't you?"

"He taught me how to butcher my first gazelle, how to pick
up chicks that are way dumb compared to Aunt Irene, and how
to not get beaten by the French chef you're working for. These
are things that I can never forget."

"You going to tell him?"

"I can do that. Adelle thinks I should do that. Or I can just
give my father the money so he won't need the Pack's money, or
I can replace the money he stole."

"Because you suddenly owe your father *any* of that?"

"Maybe I'm a son desperate for his father's love."

"You don't even like your father."

Ric grimaced. "I know. I really don't. I really don't like him at
all. That makes me a bad person, doesn't it?"

"No. It means you've got good wolf instincts. And to be really
honest with you, Ric, no one likes your dad. I don't think your
dad likes your dad."

Leaning back in his chair, Ric admitted, "I have to tell Uncle
Van, don't I?"

"Let me ask you this . . . do you feel you have to tell Van because you're afraid of what will happen to you if you don't? Or
do you have to tell him because you love and respect the man
and your Pack?"

"I've never been afraid of Uncle Van." But, when he was
younger and weaker, he had been afraid of his father. And as
much as he wanted to love him, he didn't.

"Then you know what you have to do. And you'll be doing it
because it's the right thing. No matter what your father will ac-
cuse you of—you'll be doing what's right."

Feeling a weight lift, Ric said, "Thanks, man. That really helps."

"I'm a bear, tiny wolf man. We're all about the wisdom."

"Really? Then tell me how to make Dee-Ann Smith mine forever."

"Dude," Lock laughed, "that's never going to happen."

"Thank you, wise bear."

The grizzly shrugged. "Just trying to help."

Chapter 18

R ic walked into the Group office. He felt better after getting Lock's perspective and now he needed to get some office work done before he made that call, using the three-hour time difference between New York and the West Coast as an excuse to delay the inevitable.

"Morning, Charlene." He stopped by the front desk and took the mail from the perky fox admin, who always had a smile. "Everything going all right?"

"Yep. We have visitors, though. Detective MacDermot and Marcella Malone of KZS."

"Any problems?"

"Don't think so. They're in one of the training rooms."

"Good. Thanks."

Knowing that Dee-Ann hated to be interrupted during her workout, Ric headed straight for his office. As soon as he stepped inside, he knew that the She-wolf had been there. Her scent still lingered and she'd left a report on his desk, along with a note.

We need to talk.—Dee

Vividly remembering the last twenty minutes of his conversation with Lock: *Let's face it, you'll never hold on to Dee, so when she dumps you—which will be way sooner than later—just accept it. You'll be better off and live longer,* Ric couldn't shake the feeling he had, in fact, been dumped. Already. Talk about not giving a guy a chance.

Annoyed and with no intention of listening to the bear's advice on this particular subject, Ric crumpled up the note and tossed it into the trash can. That's when he saw little Abby Vega dancing outside his office, her little wolfdog or wolf-coyote—to be honest, they hadn't been able to tell specifically what she was and no one could get close enough to find out by scent or blood tests—feet prancing.

"Hi, Abby. You okay?" Did she need a walk? God, he hoped not. That would just be beyond the realm of weird.

She barked, ran away, charged back, barked.

He remembered to have patience and decided not to tell her to cut the crap, shift already, and *tell* him what she wanted him to know. "Do you need me to see something?" he asked, tempted to add "Lassie" to the end of that.

She nodded and started off again.

Ric followed Abby down several hallways until they reached the room with the training ring where Group members practiced hand-to-hand combat.

Unfortunately, Ric couldn't really see what was going on. It seemed that *everyone* in the Group had stuffed themselves inside or at the big windows that looked in.

Abby crouched down and crawled on the floor, but Ric wasn't about to do that. He had his dignity. Instead, he pushed his way in, ignoring the snarls, growls, and nips that followed.

The fist slammed into Dee's throat and she dropped to her knees. Malone moved on her, swinging at her again, but Dee caught her arm, yanked the She-tiger in, and turned her, dropping her to the mat. She then pushed her knee into Malone's chest and twisted her arm up and away from her body.

While Dee was trying to get Malone to submit, she heard a soft throat clear and looked up into pretty brown eyes glaring at her from under scowling brows.

Shit.

Her grip loosened on Malone's arm and the She-tiger brought up her leg and slammed her knee into the upper part of Dee's back, sending her crashing into the ropes of the ring, which had her flying back and right into Malone's waiting fist.

That was pretty much the last thing Dee remembered for quite a bit until Malone slapped her and yelled, "Wake up, Smith!"

Dee opened her eyes. "Thank you very much," she snapped.

"You let that pretty face distract you. Mistake number one." She handed Dee a damp cloth to wipe the blood off. "Would it make you feel better if I said you *almost* had me?"

Taking her time, Dee sat up. When she felt stable, she reached out and cuffed the side of Malone's head.

"Hey!"

"Help me up."

Malone gripped her arm and yanked Dee to her feet.

"Can you stand on your own?"

"Yeah."

Malone released her and Dee immediately held up a finger. "Don't hit me again."

Malone lowered her fist and grinned. "I'm glad to see you're still the toughest canine I've ever met. Still not feline, though. Ya gotta work on your finesse, Smith."

"Here's your finesse," she offered, raising her middle finger while she searched the thinning crowd now that the fight was over. She didn't see Ric, so she went between the ropes and jumped down.

"Hey," Malone called out. "You want me to come along and help you smooth things over with your boss?"

"He's my supervisor and I can't blame you for everything if you're standing right beside me, now can I?"

"Excellent point." Malone, still in the mood to tussle, held out her arms. "Anybody else up for a little—"

A male tiger leaped into the ring and Malone shook her head. "Forget it."

"Oh, come on. You and me, let's go for it."

Still wiping her face with the cloth, Dee made her way to Ric's office. She found him behind his desk, seething.

"I know what you're thinking—" she began.

"What part of 'make this work' were you not clear on?" he asked, sitting back in his fancy office chair, fingers interlacing over his flat stomach.

Dee walked up to the desk. "It's not what you think."

"You two *weren't* beating the hell out of each other in the ring on *Group* territory?"

"All right, it *is* what you think, but it wasn't done viciously or anything. We're actually getting along. Wouldn't say we're friends, but after I fell off that building last night she—"

Ric held his hand up. "You fell off a building?"

"Sorta rolled off the ledge, but I didn't hit the ground or anything 'cause I had hold of—"

"Stop." The wolf shook his head. "If I don't know exactly what you do to get done what you do, I can't be freaked out by it, now can I?"

"That's how my momma gets through the day."

"Then that's what we'll do."

Dee frowned. "*Is* something else wrong?"

"No." He gazed at her. "Do *you* think there's something wrong?"

"Other than you acting weird? No."

"Then I guess nothing's wrong." He focused on his computer and she got the feeling she'd just been dismissed.

Deciding it would be better to talk to Ric when he wasn't being such a snobby prick about a friendly little brawl in the middle of the office, Dee stepped away from the desk, but she caught sight of a single crumpled paper in the otherwise empty trash can. She reached in and pulled it out when she realized it was the note she'd left for him.

"You're throwing out my notes now?"

"I have a wonderfully intact mind," he told her, not looking away from his computer screen. "I would have remembered to discuss whatever issues you may have at a later date. When it was convenient for me."

Shocked, Dee demanded, "What is your problem, Van Holtz?"

"I don't have a problem," he said while typing on his keyboard. "I simply thought we were going to keep personal issues out of the office."

"Yeah, but I thought you'd want to know right quick if I found your brother trying to break into that big ol' safe you've got in your office."

Ric spun his chair around to face her. "Wait. What?"

"I caught your brother trying to get into your safe. Since he didn't seem to have the combination, I'm assuming he was breaking in."

Van Holtz blinked. "Oh. Oh. Oh!" He sat up, arms on his desk, back straight. "Oh. Right. You're absolutely right. He shouldn't have been anywhere near my apartment. In fact, I banned him from there because he insulted Lock. So . . . good job."

Dee studied him. "That was a lot of 'ohs,' Van Holtz."

"No. Just . . . you know."

Dee looked at her note, straightening out the crumpled paper. She read it again and raised her eyes to the wolf. She'd never been one to write wordy notes but this one, if taken out of context . . . "Did you think I was—"

"No."

He answered so quick, she knew. "You did, didn't you?"

"Okay, I misread it. Can we let it go?"

"Not really." Not when he was blushing and just twenty dang levels of cute!

"Look, I made a mistake. Okay? It happens. Let's just not talk about it."

"Like it'll be that easy." Dee slammed his office door and locked it, then faced him.

"What are you doing?"

"I think we need to clear some things up," she said, ambling back over to his desk.

"Not necessary. Nothing to clarify. I say we forget it ever happened. Can't we forget?"

Dee moved around the desk and over to Ric, straddling his thighs with her legs until she dropped right into his lap.

"Nah."

He squirmed a little in the chair. "Well, can you do this while *not* sitting on my lap?"

She gazed down at his lap. "You gettin' hard, Ulrich?"

"You're sitting in my lap, Dee-Ann. Smelling all sweaty and bloody—of course, I'm getting hard."

"Then I'll make this quick, just so we're clear. I don't end things with people by leaving notes, sending texts, or shootin' someone an e-mail. Instead I—"

"Shoot them once in the back of the head?"

"You've been talking to MacRyrie, I see, and it was a paintball gun I used on that cheetah. He survived."

This wasn't remotely fair. She wore only a sports bra, workout shorts, and sneakers. Her hands had been taped up for the fight and still had Malone's blood on them. Her hair was drenched in sweat and her multitude of scars were shiny bright and silver against her damp flesh.

Honestly . . . he could only handle so much!

And Dee-Ann Smith knew it, too. She knew what she was doing to him, pressing her hands against his shoulders and kind of pinning him against the chair, making him feel all vulnerable and helpless.

Evil sex sorceress!

"Trust me, darlin'," she said low, "when this thing is over between us, I'll let you know, in person. Like a woman. Not like some frightened little girl leaving bullshit little notes. And if you're not sure . . . ask me."

"If I ask, are you positive you won't run?"

"I only run when police are involved . . . or I'm out of ammo."

"That's perfectly fair."

"Glad you think so," she murmured, then slowly leaned in and sniffed his neck. "Lord, you smell good."

Ric groaned. "Dee, we can't do this here."

"Why not?"

"It's the office and we're two highly trained professionals who don't screw in the office."

"You were all ready to screw me in your restaurant office."

"The restaurant is mine. This place belongs to the Group. Plus, I don't have condoms just lying around for impromptu chair sex with horny, sweaty She-wolves who are driving me wild."

She pressed her lips against his neck, her tongue making little figure eights against his skin. "Guess we'll have to come up with something else to do as highly trained professionals."

Forcing himself to put his hands on her shoulders, Ric pushed her back—and God, it had to be the hardest thing he'd *ever* done—and said, "We'll have to come up with something else *tonight*. Not here."

"You don't want anyone to know about us?"

"I really don't care who knows. But there's such a thing as decorum and standard operating procedure, which I'm pretty sure doesn't include sex on my desk."

"What about in your kitchen?"

"*Never* in my restaurant kitchen. Hygiene. But all bets are off at my house. We just have to make sure to clean up before Mrs. M. shows up for work."

"Okay. Okay. I got it." She stood and if his cock had hands, it would have wrung his neck by now for letting her get away.

While Dee walked to the door and he tried to get control of his baser urges, Ric said, "Wait. When you caught Wendell . . . what did he say to you?"

Dee stopped in front of his desk and slowly faced him. "Nothing," she said after a long moment, which worried him.

"Dee-Ann . . . what happened?" If his brother had touched her . . .

"I, uh . . . kind of beat the hell out of him."

"Pardon?"

"Look," she explained, "among the Smiths, there are just some things you don't do to your own kin. You don't steal a wolf's 'shine, his vehicle, his She-wolf, unless she ain't marked proper and she wants to go, or his money. I figured that's what he was trying to get to so I . . . punched him a few times and kicked him in the face and, uh . . ." She cleared her throat. "I shoved him down the garbage chute. Your Mrs. M. showed me where it was."

"Just tell me one thing, Dee-Ann"—Ric's hand gripped his desk—"were you . . . naked?"

Now it was Dee's turn to feel embarrassed. Lord, her cheeks were hot! She wasn't sure she'd ever blushed before. Then again, she was willing to bet that rich, cultured Ulrich Van Holtz had never had one of his overnight guests shove his brother down a garbage chute. She could only hope her momma never heard of it.

"Lord love you, Dee-Ann," her mother would exclaim. "Must you be so much like your daddy?"

"Were you, Dee-Ann?" Ric pushed.

"Well . . . you know I ain't one for puttin' on clothes first thing. I was hungry so I got up and—"

He was up and around his desk like a shot. When he caught hold of her arm, she thought for sure he was going to toss her out and tell her he didn't want to see her again. But instead he grabbed her other arm and pushed her until her ass hit his desk. Taking his hand he swiped everything off except his computer and shoved her back against the polished wood.

"Uh . . . Ric?"

Busy pulling down her shorts, he stopped and asked, "You locked the office door, right?"

"Yeah, but—"

"Good."

Her shorts and panties went flying and suddenly Dee had a tongue between her legs.

"I thought"—her eyes crossed—"no foolin' around in the office?"

His tongue danced across her clit before he lifted his head and answered, "Do you know how often I've daydreamed about shoving my brother down that garbage chute? I've also thought about throwing him into a moving plane propeller, but I know that would be really wrong."

"And first-degree murder."

"Right. But you . . . you shoved him down the chute. And you did it for me."

"Because he shouldn't steal from his kin."

Ric laughed and there was a touch of bitterness to it. "He doesn't have a great role model for that. But I was lucky enough to have Uncle Van." The bitterness faded and the grin returned. "And now I'm lucky enough to have you."

"Hope you're not thinking about making this permanent, Van Holtz," she warned.

"Is this where you tell me you don't do permanent?"

"No. This is where I tell you that I like you too much to think of you being buried in a shallow grave behind my momma's house. Because that's what's going to happen if my daddy finds out a Van Holtz is messin' with his only baby girl."

Big hands with incredibly talented fingers stroked down her thighs. "Guess it's too bad I think you're worth the risk."

"You go up against my daddy, Van Holtz, you won't win."

"I know." He slid his arms under her legs and dragged her to the edge of the desk, spreading her thighs wide. "That's why I'm going to have to be a little . . ."

Her eyes narrowed. "Wily?"

"Like I said, Uncle Van's *my* role model—and the man is good at wily."

Then his grin disappeared between her legs and Dee didn't have the strength to stop a superbly talented tongue from giving her the best head ever.

*   *   *

Dez sat at the red light, waiting for it to change so they could head into Jersey. Malone sat in the passenger seat and Dee-Ann was in the back. Janis Joplin's "Me and Bobby McGee" was playing on the radio while the sun began to set for the night.

At first, Dez thought Cella was humming along with the radio. She had a nice voice, too, throaty and mellow. She usually sang along with all the old rock songs. Anything from the sixties and up.

But when Cella turned her head and looked at her, Dez realized Cella wasn't the one humming along to "Me and Bobby McGee."

Dee-Ann had her long legs stretched out across the backseat of the black SUV; the blade she kept on her at all times held casually in her hand, her gaze focused out the window—and she hummed along with Janis.

The light changed and Dez moved forward, heading to their job for the night, and wondering what could make someone like Dee-Ann Smith hum.

CHAPTER 19

Dan Phillips of South Jersey was nearly asleep when he felt that weight pressing down on his chest, that blade against his throat.

His eyes shot open and in the blackness of the night, he could see nothing but those shiny eyes. The eyes of an animal.

He opened his mouth to scream but a soft "Hush, now," stopped the words in his throat.

Beside him lay his wife, sleeping peacefully, blissfully unaware that something was on top of him with a knife to his throat.

It leaned in close and whispered against Dan's ear. "The only reason I haven't killed you yet is because you don't really know what you're helping to fund. So I'm going to give you one chance to save your life and keep what seems to be a happy family from mourning the loss of their daddy. Understand?"

He nodded.

"The name of the client that provides money to the Connecticut Animal Rescue Foundation?"

That's what *it* wanted to know? About the goddamn animal rescue that a bunch of rich do-gooders invested money in?

He gave the name and he felt whatever was on top of him stiffen in surprise. Then it said, "Thank you kindly" and was gone.

It didn't need to tell him not to say anything to anyone or not to call the police. It didn't have to. He knew if he ever said a word to anyone, it would be back—and he'd be dead.

Cella was stretched out on the hood of the SUV, staring up at the stars. "Are you sure you heard him correctly?"

"There ain't nothin' wrong with my hearing, Malone. I know what I heard."

Fuck, this was bad. Very bad. And the two females resting against the SUV knew that already.

"Well?" Smith demanded. "Anyone have any bright ideas?"

MacDermot walked a few steps away from the SUV and suddenly yelled out, "Fuck! *Fuck!*"

Cella sat up. "Let's all calm the hell down."

"How do you expect me to calm down?" MacDermot asked. "I mean, seriously? This is bad."

"For all of us," Cella reminded her. "With what I found out and Smith . . . this is bad for all of us. But we knew some serious money had to be behind this."

"Yeah," Smith said, "but *this*? Did you know?"

Cella scowled at the wolf. "What are you accusing *me* for?"

"Stop," MacDermot ordered them. "We're not going to turn on each other now."

"So what do we do?"

Smith pushed away from the SUV. "I'll handle it."

"No—" But Smith was already moving toward the back of the SUV.

Cella and MacDermot went after her. "You can't do this without authorization," MacDermot reminded her.

"Fuck authorization."

She unlocked the trunk, but Cella slammed her hand over it. "You're not doing this, Dee-Ann. Not without authorization."

"And you really think we're going to get that?"

Cella nodded. "Yeah. I think we'll get it. But only if we handle this right."

"And what's the right way to handle this?"

"To let our bosses do it. Not us."

"Why not us?"

She decided to be honest. "You"—she pointed at Dee-Ann— "kill at the slightest provocation. I hit for no other reason than I feel like it. And MacDermot is rude and abrasive." Cella put her arms around each woman's shoulders and hugged them in tight. "Oh, my God! I just realized. I love you guys!"

"You're touchin' me," Dee-Ann complained.

"Yeah, but at least this time it's not 'cause I'm hitting you."

"Only 'cause my back's not turned."

MacDermot laughed. "She's got a point, Malone."

CHAPTER 20

D ee decided to walk in the front door of Ric's building, rather than skulking around the back until she found a way in. As she approached the big glass doors, the doorman rushed to open it.

"Good evening, Miss Smith," he said, tipping his hat.

Dee froze, her body tensing. She scowled at the full-human, but he only smiled and waited for her to walk through the door. She did and entered the elevator, taking it to the penthouse.

Going against everything she practiced on a daily basis, she used the set of keys Ric had given her and opened the front door. She pulled off her jacket, hung it up in the closet, and walked down the hallway. She still felt like she was skulking, sticking to the shadows of the dimly lit apartment. Deciding she didn't want to skulk around the man's apartment any more than she wanted to skulk around his building, she stepped more into the middle of the hallway and headed toward the kitchen. The one place he always seemed to be.

"Ric?" she called out, assuming people who didn't skulk made noise. They always did in movies and on TV. She pushed open the swinging door and stepped in to the kitchen. "Ric? Are you here?" That always seemed like a stupid question coming from shifters since she *knew* the man was somewhere in the apartment. Her nose picked up his scent, her ears could hear him moving around, and she could feel his presence. But it was a normal question and she could do normal in short, controlled bursts. Like gunfire.

A low growl came at her from the darkness and Dee stepped out of the kitchen, letting the door swing closed behind her. The growl moved closer, and eyes reflected the light from the few lamps that were lit.

Smiling a little, despite the problems she and her team had walked into, Dee moved away from the kitchen door and more into the hallway.

"Now what do you think you're doing, Mr. Van Holtz? To some poor little gal all alone in the middle of your big ol' apartment. Defenseless."

Big paws padded softly against the marble flooring, the wolf circling around Dee-Ann, staying hidden in the shadows, but she knew where he was at every second.

Thinking that play should wait, Dee-Ann said, "We need to talk, Van Holtz." But he snarled at that. "I know what you'd rather be doing but that's not the point. We should talk. About business. Like two professionals."

He stepped out of the darkness, all rippling muscle and power passed down from ancestors hundreds of years gone. He lowered his head, bright blue gaze locked on her face.

Dee stepped back and shook her head. "This ain't professional, Ulrich."

And that's when he charged her.

Dez walked into the Brooklyn home she shared with her husband and mate. Her two purebred Rottweilers met her at the front door, greeting her with wet kisses and excited tail wags. She'd refused to dock their tails like some owners and she was glad she hadn't. Nothing drove Mace crazier than when her dogs knocked shit down with their tails.

She petted them and scratched the spot where their tails met their rumps until they were nothing more than wiggling dog flesh on the floor. Standing up, she pulled off her jacket and placed it over the banister. Her backpack dropped at the front door, Dez walked toward the kitchen, but before she got too far, the door opened and the most important thing in her life charged straight at her. Dez fell to her knees and opened her arms wide, laughing as the hyperkinetic bundle slammed into her body, knocking both of them to the ground.

She showered Marcus with kisses, knowing that everything she did during these long days and many nights was to ensure that one day he'd be able to roll around on the floor with his own son or daughter or both and all their dogs—because her son would have dogs. Even if he was a cat. Because what was a life without dogs?

"What is this on your face?" she asked him, realizing it was probably all over her face now, too.

"Okay," Blayne Thorpe told her, barreling through the kitchen door. "It was just a slight mishap with the brownie mix. No reason to panic!"

Except Blayne appeared worse off than Marcus. Christ, the kid was covered. Did they actually *bake* any brownies?

"But I called in the heavy artillery," Blayne went on, "to get this place spic and span."

Dez got to her feet, lifting Marcus up until he wrapped his arms around her neck. "You called your boyfriend in to clean my apartment?"

"Someone had to do it," came a voice from behind the kitchen door.

"Any other problems?" Dez asked, turning toward the front door as it opened and her husband walked in, *his* dog beside him. Apparently the mixed Rottie rescue was too good to stay at the house among Dez's average, run-of-the-mill purebreds. Instead, she had to go into the city with Mace to help him endure the work day and keep Smitty's dog, Shit-starter, from bothering him.

The little whore.

"Sorry I'm late," Mace said. "Job ran long."

"No problem," Blayne chirped. She was perhaps the chirpiest

person Dez had ever known. Marcus adored her and Mace . . . tolerated her more than most. And that said a lot. "No derby practice tonight."

"My son," Mace said, pulling Marcus out of Dez's arms without an invitation and holding him high above his head. "Future of my bloodline."

Dez shook her head in disgust, Blayne giggled.

Marcus scowled down at his father, pulled back his arm, and slashed at Mace's handsome face with nonexistent claws.

"Viper child!" Mace snarled.

Holding out her arms, Dez ordered, "Give me my son, Llewellyn."

"Momma's boy. That's what you've turned him into." He shoved his son back into Dez's arms. "An ungrateful momma's boy. I allow you to live, boy! Don't you forget it!"

"Thank you, Blayne," Dez said over all the bellowing and her son's giggling. "Are you sure we can't pay you?"

"Absolutely not!"

"Yeah, because everything should be for free," Bo Novikov complained from the kitchen. "So we can live in a Blayne-like utopia."

Blayne smiled and said, "Excuse me a moment."

Dee waited until Blayne had gone back into the kitchen before she faced her husband. "We need to talk."

"What did I do now?"

"Nothing."

"Because whatever it was, I'm sure I didn't mean to do it."

"You're not helping yourself, Captain Ego."

"And if I want to help a friend," Blayne bellowed from behind the kitchen door, "I'll do it! And you're not going to give me any shit over it, you oversized Visigoth!"

" 'They're such a cute couple,' " Mace imitated back to Dez from a recent wild dog party where she'd had a tad too many margaritas.

"They *are* a cute, if unstable couple."

"He's more bear than lion."

"Which means what? That his head's not as big as yours?"

"Okay." Blayne came back through the door, her hand gripping Novikov's forearm. Dez would never say it out loud, but the size of that man was . . . off-putting. To her anyway. Mace was only a nice, relatively normal six-four, but getting into the seven feet and over range just freaked Dez out. What was it like to fuck someone that size? Could you be smothered? Especially when he wasn't some skinny basketball player type but nearly four hundred pounds of muscle. God, what if he died on top of her? Would Blayne be able to drag herself out?

Mace bumped her with his hip and Dez realized she was staring at Novikov again. She probably had what Mace called her "look of abject horror" expression. She had to work on that.

"Thank you both," she said to hide the fear.

"No problem," Blayne kissed Marcus on the forehead as the boy tried to latch on to Blayne with one arm while still holding on to his mother.

"You'll need to buy more cleaning products," Novikov told her, scowling down at her like he might bite her head off at any second. "I had enough to clean the kitchen but that was it." He glanced around. "Although you really need someone to clean the whole house. It's kind of a sty."

"Okay!" Blayne began to charge toward the front door, dragging Novikov behind her. "Anytime, Dez. You need me, you call, and I'll be there! 'Night!"

" 'Night, Blayne."

The door slammed shut behind the couple and Mace headed to the kitchen, shaking his head. "I think our house is clean enough, thanks. What a freak."

He disappeared behind the door.

"Let me put Marcus to bed," Dez said, "and then we can—"

The kitchen door slammed open again, Mace standing there, his eyes wide. "Dez, you have to see this kitchen. It's like something from a freakin' Lysol ad."

Cella disconnected her call with her boss and tossed the phone onto the old kitchen table. It was one of the few things her mother hadn't replaced as she'd done with almost all the other furniture in the Malone Long Island family home Cella had grown up in.

She knew that now she was back in New York, she'd have to get her own place. Probably a place in the city, but at the moment she was enjoying living with her family. One of the rare tiger families that had a male involved who wasn't a son. Most She-tigers couldn't stand having a tiger male around once they'd gotten pregnant, but her parents had met each other in grade school and had been together ever since. That was her parents, though. Cella had gone about things a little differently.

"You just getting home?" her seventeen-year-old daughter asked, closing the door to the basement that had been her bedroom since her mother had joined the Marines and left her in her grandparents' care.

"Yep. Busy night."

"Busy couple of days. There's some leftover lasagna from dinner. You want me to put some in the microwave?" Her daughter always phrased such things as a question even while she was already cutting up the leftover lasagna, putting it on a plate, and dropping it into the microwave.

"Sure. Thanks, baby."

"No problem."

Cella stood, heading toward the stairs to her room. "I'm going to change clothes. I'll be right back."

"Okay. But Uncle Kevin spent the night so—"

Before her daughter could even finish, Cella was tackled from behind, her younger-by-four-years brother slamming her to the floor.

"Your skills are weak!" he told her like he told her every time he did this. "As always, I am the stronger sib—owww! Damn, Cella! Why do you always hit so hard? I'm telling Ma!"

Dee's naked body collided with the wall, Ric buried deep inside her, his face pressed against her neck. He slid his hand under her thigh and lifted her leg, his condom-covered cock tapping some delicious new angle that had her panting hard and gripping his shoulders.

"I thought you'd never get home," he gasped, nipping the tendons along her neck.

"Working," she said, yipping when his fingers tugged at her nipples, his hips grinding against her.

"I have to give you better hours."

"Ric—" But he kissed her before she could finish, his tongue plunging into her mouth. She kissed him back, unable not to. He had the sweetest-tasting mouth.

His body kept her pinned to the wall, his hands moving off her breasts so that he could force her arms against the wall.

"We have to talk," she tried again when their mouths separated.

"Later," he told her, now fucking her with powerful strokes. "Tell me all about it later."

"Okay," she squeaked.

Mace Llewellyn pushed the dark chocolate ice cream he'd scooped out for himself and Dez away, shaking his head at her words. "That can't be right. They're lying."

"They have no reason to lie."

He paced away from the stainless-steel kitchen counter and back again, the dog he'd made his own right by his side, sensing her master's mood.

"The information has to be wrong, Dez."

She came out from behind the counter and put her arms around his waist, understanding how hard this was for him. "But it's not. You know it's not."

Dez held Mace tight, relieved when she felt his arms wrap around her body and hold her.

"We'll fix it," she said. "I promise."

"There's only one way this will get fixed," he said, and buried his face against her neck.

And she knew he was right.

* * *

Ric sat up in the middle of his hallway floor and gazed at Dee-Ann.

"Missy Llewellyn? Mace Llewellyn's sister?"

"That's where the money leads."

"Are you sure? We have to be sure."

"I'm sure that the information I have is right."

He scratched his head, unable to wrap his mind around this. "It can't be Missy, Dee-Ann. It can't be coming from her."

"Why not? Because she's too rich?"

"No," he argued. "Because she's too damn lazy." He laughed, resting his arms on his knees. "I've known Missy for a lot of years. We run in the same society circles and although she's not a fan of hybrids, Missy isn't a fan of *anyone*. She hates equally across the board. But to invest this kind of money and risk, you'd have to really hate hybrids with a passion. Missy doesn't do anything with passion except complain. My God, can she complain."

Dee-Ann sat up and Ric forced himself to focus on her face. If he looked any lower, he'd be all over her again rather than focusing on the bigger issue.

"Then what do you think's going on?"

"I don't know. Unless she's being set up. By hyenas, maybe?"

"Hyenas ain't puttin' money out for hybrid fights. They hoard their cash."

"Very true." Ric grimaced. "There's a Llewellyn on the Board, you know." The Board had come into existence in the late 1800s to handle territory disputes that had turned ugly. Representatives from the bigger Prides, Packs, and Clans now met twice a year to discuss any issues or concerns, but would meet more often if there were problems that couldn't be resolved easily and quickly through phone calls or e-mails. "Matilda Llewellyn. So we'll have to be careful how we handle this."

"Yeah. Wouldn't want to insult the rich felines who're maybe killing their own kind."

"That's not what I meant. So feel free not to put words in my mouth. And why are we arguing when we're both naked?"

"Let's face it, Ric, to put together an organization like this, to run it right—there has to be some serious money involved."

"The Van Holtzes have money like that. The Magnus Pack. The Löwes. And that's what Missy is going to say, and she'd have a valid argument. What about her brother, Mace?"

"Forget it." Dee shook her head. "I can go on and on about Mace Llewellyn and why he'd never in a million years be involved in something like this, but most important is that he's never had direct access to pride money. Not ever."

"Can he be trusted if we go to him?"

"Absolutely."

"Let me talk to Uncle Van. He deals with Matilda, so maybe he has some ideas."

"Malone's people may deal with it."

"If they do, I might end up feeling a little sorry for Missy."

"Oh?"

"Felines are *mean*, Dee-Ann," he said, standing up. "Just . . . mean. At least you'd be in and out quick."

"True enough."

Ric started to walk away to get his phone, but he came back, crouching in front of her.

"You said you need to call your Uncle Van."

"I know. I just wanted another kiss."

"We start kissin', you're not going to call your uncle."

"Cousin."

"Whatever."

Ric leaned in. "Kiss me anyway. So we can make up for arguing while naked. We should never argue while naked."

"Lord, once you set your mind to something—"

"—like a wolf with a bone," he finished on a whisper.

CHAPTER 21

Dee had been right. He never made it to the phone, but it didn't matter because KZS got in touch with Van themselves. And, at four a.m., a conference call came in for Ric involving Van, the head of the KZS Victoria Löwe, and the sow who ran the NYPD shifter unit, Lynsey Gentry. It was a two-hour conversation that basically ended with his cousin telling them all to, "Take the weekend. We'll discuss on Tuesday."

At first, Ric didn't know why Tuesday, then he remembered that it was July Fourth weekend in another day. And that his father was throwing that big Pack get-together at the Macon River Falls house. An event Ric had already told his mother he wouldn't be attending. These days she didn't even bother to argue—she knew his not attending was for the best. Now, though, he was doubly grateful he wasn't going after he finally called Van earlier in the day and not only confirmed what Van and the other cousins already knew, but he also revealed how much deeper Alder's thieving actually went. It would, eventually, get back to Alder about Ric's involvement in his exposure as a thief and betrayer of his Pack, and Ric knew that would be a dark day indeed.

And because of all that, Ric did make sure to call his Uncle Van back after the conference call ended and give him the heads-up that Dee-Ann had found Wendell trying to break into his safe, probably trying to find out how much Ric knew. Van's response to that information had been . . . surprising.

"Dee-Ann Smith was in your apartment?"

"She's always in my apartment. She comes and goes as she likes."

"And she just happened to be there in the early morning?"

"Well, she's been staying here until she gets a new place to live."

"Uh-huh."

Ric mentally shrugged. "Okay. Fine. I'm sleeping with her."

"Have you lost your mind?"

"No." And then, just to irritate, "But I have lost my heart."

"You idiot."

"I love you, too, Uncle Van."

"She's a Smith."

"She's amazing. And cute."

"There is nothing cute about Dee-Ann Smith. What is wrong with you?"

"What can I say? There's just something about her. I think she's—"

"Don't say it."

"—the one."

"Christ, you said it. What is wrong with my people? You're all running around, looking for 'the one.' "

"I wasn't looking for her. She just sort of appeared. In Lock's hallway. I knew then. And you said Aunt Irene is 'the one.' "

"That was luck on her part. That she found me."

"Then I guess I'm lucky."

"Okay." He could imagine his cousin trying to find a different way to approach this. "And what does she say?"

"She mentioned something about her father and a shallow grave with me in it but . . . I think I can win him over, too."

"You cannot win over Eggie Smith. There is no winning over Eggie Smith."

"But you told me yourself that I'm charming."

"You're also an idiot."

Ric grinned. "But a charming idiot."

His cousin hung up on him then, never having patience for his in-love brethren, and Ric finally returned to his bed.

He smiled, seeing Dee-Ann in it. She—and the gun and knife she had under her pillow—fit in perfectly. Ric just didn't know why no one else seemed to see it. Except Blayne. Blayne saw it, but she seemed to be the only one. Not that it mattered, though. The only one who mattered was Dee-Ann and he was more than willing to work with her on this.

Ric eased into the bed and across it—it was a really big bed—until he was able to snuggle up close to Dee-Ann. He put his arms around her and held her tight.

His eyes were closing, moments from falling asleep when the bear-sized queen bed with its titanium frame—possibly one of the heaviest beds in the world—briefly went up, then crashed back to the floor. Both Ric and Dee pulled their guns, Ric's from a holster he'd had built directly into the mattress for easy access; and Dee's from under her pillow. They aimed directly at the foot of the bed, their fingers on the triggers, rounds already in the chambers.

Yet the bear-lion hybrid at the end of the bed showed no fear. He gazed at them as only "The Marauder" Novikov could and said, "I need to borrow a house."

Did the mutt have any idea how close he'd been to getting shot? Dee had armor-piercing rounds in her gun that were strong enough to go through bear hide.

"You want what?" Ric asked. Poor thing. He'd been up for hours and had just gotten back into bed a few minutes ago. And her exhaustion must have been bone deep for her not to have scented Novikov before he even got into the house. That was definitely not like her at all.

"I need to borrow a house. I know you have several locally."

"What do you want a house for?"

"Why do you care?"

Dee's finger tightened on the trigger, her lips pulling back over her fangs. But Ric made her lower the gun, his hand firm against hers, pressing it down onto the bed.

"You have your own houses," Ric argued. "One with a seal farm."

"Not around here. And Blayne wants a party."

"What's wrong with your apartment? It's massive."

"And?"

"Do it there," Ric reasoned.

"I don't want people around my stuff."

"But you want them around mine?"

"I don't care about yours."

Dee was reaching for her bowie knife then when Ric pinned her to the bed with his body.

"Why don't I make this easy for both of us? Instead of turning my home over to you, I'll just pull something together for all of us."

"Here?" Novikov looked around the bedroom. "It's kind of boring here."

Dee had nearly gotten free of Ric's grasp by that point, but he caught her in his arms and held her tight. The fact that they were both naked, Dee's fangs bared and her claws out, while these two strange idiots were still talking like they were having tea and cakes did fascinate the part of her brain not busy trying to kill Bo Novikov.

"It wouldn't be here. I have my own place out on the Island. Near the beach."

"Shifter friendly or do I have to keep my fangs in?"

"Shifter friendly, but very exclusive. Lots of room in the house, too, so we'll all be quite comfortable. There's even a park and beach nearby. I also have an Olympic-sized pool right in my back—"

"That'll work." And Dee had a feeling the hybrid would never leave the pool once he got there.

"Excellent. I'll get everything organized from my end and e-mail you later in the day." Ric motioned to the door with his chin.

"Now go away. And if you took the door off the hinges to get in here—put it back."

"You're not training this morning?" Novikov asked.

Ric yanked Dee back to his lap before she could bury her knife in the hybrid's throat and snapped, "Novikov!"

"It was just a question."

Novikov lumbered out as silently as he'd appeared and Dee relaxed back into Ric's chest. "You should have let me kill him."

"I need him for the team. It's the price I'm forced to pay." Ric brushed the hair off her neck and kissed her throat. "It would make this weekend tolerable if you came with me."

"I'll probably have work."

"Doubtful. And I'll make sure you don't get anything thrown at you at the eleventh hour."

"That don't seem fair."

"I don't care about fair. I care about you relaxing with me on Long Island."

"With Teacup and Mr. Fussy Pants?"

Ric laughed. "Can I call Novikov that forever?"

"Be my guest."

"Plus Lock and Gwen will be there."

"Gwen hates me," she reminded him.

"Don't be narcissistic. She hates everyone."

"You have a point."

"Besides, when was the last time you had a little vacation from killing stuff?"

"When I left the Marines and before I got this job."

"But you were staying with your parents—so is that really a vacation?"

Dee shrugged. "I enjoyed it."

Ric held her tighter. "Come with me."

Feeling real regret, Dee admitted, "You know I can't. I gotta be with the Pack."

"You're going to Tennessee?"

"Nah. Just to the Shaw house, with the Shaw brothers, my

cousins, the New York Smith Pack, and the Kuznetsov Pack. It'll be hell on earth but . . . it's family."

Still holding Dee, Ric moved them both closer to the side of the bed until he could reach his cell phone. He speed dialed someone and smiled at her while he waited for the other end to pick up.

"Morning, Jessica." He'd called Bobby Ray's mate and Alpha of the Kuznetsov wild dog Pack? Good Lord, but the man played dirty. "It's Ric. How are you? Great. Great. Listen, I know this is last minute, but how would you like to come out to my house on the Island for the July Fourth weekend? Uh-huh. Well, you can bring anyone you'd like. I understand, though, if you'd rather spend the weekend with the Shaw brothers. Watching them eat . . . and sleep. That is when they're not ordering everyone around because it's their property or they're snoring while you try to get the baby to sl—oh? Really. Are you sure? That will be wonderful. Blayne, Lock, and Gwen will be there, too. Yes. And the lunkhead, but I'm sure he'll practically live in the pool, so it's not like you'll have to communicate with him in any way. I'm not being mean. I thought everyone called him lunkhead. It's so fitting," he finished on a murmur. "All right. Yes. Bring anyone who wants to come. There's more than enough room. Just send me a list later today so I can get enough food. Great. See you then."

Ric disconnected the call and grinned at her. "See? Now no excuses."

She pressed her hand against his forearm and looked into his eyes. "Exactly how big is this house you bought?"

He kissed her shoulder before replying, "Pretty big."

Holding his son in his arms, Mace Llewellyn tried to stop scowling when Ulrich Van Holtz opened his front door. Of course, anytime Missy was involved, scowling always seemed to be involved.

The wolf waved him in with his hand before covering the

mouthpiece of the phone he had to his ear with his fingers. "Give me a moment, Mace. I'm ordering meat."

Okay. "No problem."

"No," Van Holtz said into his phone. "I'll need more sea lion than that. Do you have the steaks?" He pointed down the hallway. "Go on into the living room. I won't be long."

Mace walked down the hallway and into the living room, stopping short right at the entrance when he spotted Dee-Ann Smith sitting on the floor in cutoff shorts and a tank top, cleaning her guns. He knew Dee-Ann worked for Van Holtz and the Group but . . . she seemed awfully comfortable.

"Dee-Ann?"

"Hey, Mace," she said, not looking up from methodically using a chamber brush to clean the barrel of a .45.

"What are you doing?"

"Cleaning my guns."

Mace had forgotten that he was dealing with Dee-Ann. One of the more literal females he'd known over the years. "I mean, what are you doing in Ulrich Van Holtz's apartment?"

"Cleaning my guns."

At that point he decided to let it go. It took too much energy to care.

"Watcha got there, Llewellyn?" Dee-Ann asked, squinting up at Marcus and smiling.

"A spoiled brat who clearly needs more time around males. Or you know . . . you."

Dee chuckled and got to her feet, wiping her hands off on a cloth. "How would this spoiled brat like some ice cream?"

Marcus hissed at Mace and swatted at him, trying to get him to let go. "Stop doing that!"

"You male cats. Ornery ain't even the word for it." She took Marcus from Mace. "Come on, handsome. Let's get you some fancy, overpriced ice cream." She walked out of the room as Van Holtz walked in.

"I'll have you know, Miss Smith, that *gelato* is superb."

"Overpriced!" she shot back.

Van Holtz motioned for Mace to sit on one of the couches, but he stopped when he walked around them, seeing the pile of guns spread out on a rather thin cloth laid over his rug.

"Isn't that the rug you picked up at the charity auction a couple of years ago?" Mace asked.

"Yes."

"The one for six figures?"

"It's a one-of-kind original from the eighteenth century."

"Then you definitely want gun oil on it."

"I'd yell and throw my hands up dramatically, but she'll just tell me I paid too much."

Mace sat down on a couch. "My sister."

Van Holtz nodded and sat across from him. "Nothing's been decided yet."

"You can't believe my sister had anything to do with this. This is Missy Llewellyn we're talking about."

"I made sure to point that out. And I can assure you that we're going to investigate this thoroughly before we make any final decisions." Van Holtz leaned back on the couch, raising his foot and resting it on the opposite knee. Mace didn't think he'd ever seen the rich wolf looking so casual except when he was cooking. Worn jeans, bare feet, and a Cathedral High School Lacrosse T-shirt. They'd gone to the same school, although Mace had been a few years ahead of him. He remembered Van Holtz's older brother, though. What an asshole that guy was, and he hadn't changed much. But they didn't seem alike at all.

"Just promise me you won't . . . do anything until you talk to me."

"If she's done this, Mace—"

"She hasn't. But if she's caught up in it somehow—just talk to me. My sister is a lot of things, but she's my sister. Understand?"

"I do. And you are married to one of our top people on the case."

Mace gave a little snort. "Considering how well they got along in school . . . you better be the one to give me a heads-up."

"I will. I'll also ask that you not discuss this with the other members of your Pride."

"They're not my Pride. Haven't been since I turned eighteen and refused to be bartered off like cheap garbage. But Missy is still blood. She's still Marcus's aunt. I can't forget that."

"I won't either. You have my word."

"Thanks." Mace got to his feet and walked into the hallway, where Dee-Ann and Marcus almost collided with him. He gazed at the pair and finally asked, "Was there a problem?"

Dee-Ann shook her head. "No. Why?"

"No reason." He took his son, making sure to keep the child's face far away from him since he didn't want to be covered in chocolate gelato the way Dee was. The kid had to be the sloppiest eater on the planet and yet every female, including Desiree, let him get away with it.

Mace took the cone Marcus held—ignoring the way his son latched on to his arm like it was a chicken bone, tiny teeth trying to dig into human flesh—and headed to the door.

"Have a good weekend," Van Holtz told him.

"You, too." The door closed behind him and Mace headed to the elevator. Once inside, he held the cone up for his son so he would unleash his hold on him and lick the cone instead.

"I don't know what allure you have for women," Mace told the little brat, "but I'm guessing it has a lot to do with the mini-mane you've got going on."

"Cute kid," Dee-Ann told Ric when the door closed. "I like the hair."

"He likes you."

"I'm guessing that like his father, he likes anything with tits."

Ric stepped closer and licked the melted chocolate gelato off Dee-Ann's nose. "Yum."

"Was Mace here about Missy?"

"Of course. She's his sister."

"True, but she doesn't deserve it. Don't even think she wrote him when he was stationed overseas and he spent most holidays in Smithtown with Bobby Ray."

"It's still his sister and that's all that matters to him." Ric slipped his arm around her waist. "Are you packed?"

"Packed?"

"For the weekend away. You're still coming?"

"Not much choice now that *everyone* in the New York Pack is coming. They all want to see your house."

"I got the list from Jess. I had to up my zebra and gazelle meat since the lion males are coming as well. But *you're* still coming, aren't you?"

"If you're still sure."

"Why wouldn't I be?"

"Sissy and Ronnie are going to be there. They'll see us together. Trust me when I say records will be broken gettin' that information back to Tennessee."

"So?"

She petted his cheek. "I'll miss you when you're gone."

"You know, your father might actually like me."

And Ric tried not to take it personally when she burst out laughing and went back to cleaning her guns on his expensive, eighteenth-century rug.

CHAPTER 22

"So what do you think?" Ric asked her.

Studying Ric's "recent purchase," Dee could only say, "Seems more a . . . resort than a house."

"Why would you say that? Because of the guest houses?"

"And the multiple tennis courts, the nearby lake. All you're missing is a gift shop and one of your restaurants."

"It's a Pack house. Where a large number of wolves can relax and enjoy a weekend away from the bustling city. Or, as in our case, a large number of random shifters who should probably never be in the same place at the same time, getting on each other's nerves for an entire weekend until someone ends up mauled and whining."

To prove that point, MacRyrie lumbered up to them, the grizzly grinning. "This place is great, Ric."

"Thanks."

"I brought you a house-warming gift."

Ric glanced down. "Cats?"

"Huh?"

"Your hands, my friend."

MacRyrie looked down at his big hands. "Oh, gosh! I did it again. Sorry, guys." He dropped Brendon and Mitchell Shaw, the two lions slamming hard to the ground. "Let me show you what I made you."

The grizzly went back to his truck and returned with a coffee table made entirely of wood, created by MacRyrie himself. Dee knew the man had some skills but damn . . . he was really good.

He plopped the table down, forcing the lions on the ground to flatten themselves to the grass so that they weren't hit on the head.

"What do you think?"

"It's gorgeous, Lock. Thank you."

"It's nothing." But the bear's wide smile told Dee he'd put a lot of work into it.

"I think it will look perfect in the main living room," Ric added.

"There's a *main* living room?" Dee asked.

"Don't judge."

"I'll take it in." The grizzly picked it up and headed into the house, carrying the table under one arm.

Dee glanced at Ric. "That thing weighs about a hundred pounds, doesn't it?"

"Probably more. I have him place the furniture he gives me and then I never touch it again. I don't want to strain my back."

More cars, SUVs, and trucks pulled up into the long winding road that led up to the Long Island property.

"Guess I better get inside." He kissed Dee's cheek. It was a sweet kiss, but still managed to make her heart beat just a little faster. "I hope you'll relax this weekend."

"Do I have to wear shoes?" she asked.

Ric shook his head. "Not if you don't want to."

"Then relaxing should be easy enough."

"Good." Ric walked inside his home, and Dee watched him, thinking about following him. Maybe dragging him into the nearest bedroom for a few minutes before everybody showed up.

But Ric had barely stepped inside the big house before Sissy Mae and Ronnie Lee were standing beside her.

"You and Van Holtz?" Sissy asked.

"Yeah." Dee-Ann faced her younger cousin and Alpha Female. "And?"

"Nothing. Ulrich Van Holtz just seems . . ."

"Out of my league?"

"I was gonna say he just seems smaller than what you usually go for. And much more pleasant."

"At least he's not dragging himself off the ground after getting slapped around by a grizzly."

Brushing dirt off his T-shirt and shorts as he got to his feet, Mitch Shaw snapped, "He didn't slap us around. That bear's dangerous and unstable. And shouldn't be around my delicate baby sister!" he yelled as Gwen walked past with her duffle bag.

"Let it go already," she shot back.

Dee reached around and grabbed Ronnie Lee's hand—the hand holding the phone—and squeezed.

"Ow!" Ronnie Lee yelped. "Ow, ow, ow, ow, ow, ow, ow, *ow-ow-ow!*"

"Who you callin', Ronnie Lee?"

"No one!"

Dee squeezed tighter. "Who you callin', Ronnie Lee?"

"Just my momma. To say hi!"

"Let's not do that, okay?" Dee waited until she heard metal bend and some bones crack before she released Ronnie's hand. "That all right with you, Sissy Mae?"

"A day not talking to my mother is like a day of sunshine and sweet tea."

"Good." Dee faced Ronnie. "That all right with you, Ronnie Lee?" The wolf glared up at her from the spot on the ground where Ronnie had dropped to her knees.

"Yes," the She-wolf hissed. "But you could have just *told* me not to call."

"I could have also twisted your arms outta their sockets. Figured this was friendlier. Now y'all have yourselves a great time." Dee went into Ric's SUV and grabbed one of the cases of over-priced wine he'd brought with him and headed into the house.

Ric rubbed his forehead with both hands. When Novikov had said he was going to be arriving at the house a few hours before anyone else, Ric simply assumed the man was going to get in some pool time before he had to fight the swamp-cat lions for space. But he was realizing that Bold Novikov was much more diabolical than that.

The seven-one hybrid stood proudly in front of the chart he'd written out on several giant Post-Its that he'd stuck to the wall. The wall Ric had designated for the Jackson Pollack he'd purchased a few years back. He briefly wondered whether Novikov would have still put his precious chart up there if the Pollack had already been in place.

"Now," the hybrid went on, "as you see, I've assigned rooms to everyone on your attendance list, keeping the Smith wolves in close proximity to the dogs, with Bobby Ray Smith and Jessica Ward-Smith in the room set up between them. Plus, this one also had an attached room they could put their baby in." He'd written out each person's name on smaller pieces of sticky paper and carefully placed them in the rooms he'd meticulously drawn out. To be honest, Ric hadn't seen house specifications so expertly drawn outside a set of government-official blueprints.

"I was really thinking people could just pick their own rooms," Ric tried to suggest.

Blue eyes narrowed. "But I have a chart."

"Yes. You do. With colored legend and arrows and, of course, illustrations of each breed."

"I always feel that visuals help." He held up a stack of sheets. "I also made accompanying flyers for everyone."

Ric's hands curled into fists. "Yet the idea is that everyone can come here and just relax. Unburdened by rules and regulations as long as everyone keeps the Viking-like pillaging to a minimum."

Novikov pointed at the wall. "But I have a chart."

"And a lovely chart it is. Truly. Beautiful. But it seems like a lot of work for you. Wouldn't you rather lounge in the pool for . . . you know . . . ever?"

"I have schedules for pool use." Novikov stuck another giant Post-It onto the wall. "That way we can all get a proper amount

of pool time without actually infringing on each other's space."
Then Novikov added. "You don't have to thank me for that."

Before Ric could tell the man how much he *wasn't* going to
thank him for that, Lock walked up to him. "Your cousin's
here."

"Specifics, Lachlan." Since he had *hundreds* of cousins world-
wide.

"Stein."

Finally! "Stein!" Ric yelled out.

His younger cousin walked into the room, looking comfortable and summer-ready in baggy swim shorts, an Hawaiian shirt,
and a ridiculous straw hat.

"Cousin! Man, this weekend is just what I need." He slapped
Ric on the back. "Thanks so much for inviting me."

Ric stared at him, just gazed until the kid finally got it.

"I'm here as slave labor, aren't I?"

"Kitchen. Meat. Chicken. Clean, strip, debone, season. Now."

"But can't I—"

"Move!"

Shoulders slumping, the kid wandered off to find the kitchen.

"What fantasy world is he living in?" Ric wanted to know.

Lock motioned to Novikov's charts and schedules. "What is
this?"

"These are the sleeping arrangements. As you can see, I placed
you here in room 4B."

"The rooms are numbered?"

"They are now. White duct tape."

Ric gritted his teeth. "You put white duct tape on my ma-
hogany, hand-crafted doors?"

"This place is huge, Van Holtz. You don't want your guests
getting lost."

Ric went for Novikov's throat but Lock held him in place
with an arm around his shoulders. "What's that?" Lock asked
the hybrid.

"That's the pool schedule. I also have a tennis court schedule
and basketball court schedule."

"Pool schedule?" Lock laughed. "You don't think that's going to work, do you?"

"Of course, it will. I wrote it out. In pen."

But to prove the ineffectiveness of his theory, two lion males tore down the stairs, made a mad dash through the house, tearing off clothes as they went, and crashing into each other, Ric's furniture, and the walls, screaming, "Pooooooool!"

"Wait!" Novikov yelled, running after them. "There's a schedule! Your time isn't for another three hours!"

And like that, Ric's anger vanished, replaced by laughter.

"Come on," he said to Lock. "Let's go torture Stein by telling him he's doing everything wrong even when he's not."

"Excellent plan."

Lock walked off and Ric began to follow, but stopped long enough to return to the chart and move Novikov's precisely placed people all over the place, separating couples from each other, their children, and spreading them out randomly so breeds and species were all sorts of mixed.

Laughing harder, he headed toward the kitchen, already deciding he didn't like the way Stein deboned those damn chickens.

Yeah. It was going to be a great weekend!

Dee headed into the house from a side door after spending a couple of hours in the pool with her Pack and kin. As she passed through, she saw that the Shaw brothers had moved from lounging next to the pool to lounging in the living room, both of them sprawled over Van Holtz's furniture like the big, lazy beasts they were. In fact, Mitchell might actually be drooling. Shaking her head, disgusted, she walked down the hallway toward the kitchen.

"Dee," she heard behind her, but Dee kept walking. "Dee. Dee-Ann. Dee-Ann. *Deeeeeeee-Annnnnnnn.*"

Eyes closed, Dee stopped, took a breath, before she faced Teacup. "Yeah?" Dee gritted her teeth when the wolfdog hugged her. "Why are you touching me?"

"Because you're really a wonderful person and maybe the world thinks you're just a heartless killer, but I think you're the best. The best!"

Dee looked over the wolfdog's head at the small group of hybrid pups and cubs that she'd invited to come here this weekend. The rest of the Group's hybrid kids had plans with their foster families, but this bunch, including Hannah, had no one. So, yeah, Dee had invited them all to attend after talking it over with Ric. It wasn't a big deal. Why did Teacup insist on making everything a goshdarn big deal?

"Get her off me," she told Hannah.

"Why me?"

"Get her *off*."

Sighing, the bear-canine hybrid took hold of Blayne's waist and pulled until she'd finally released Dee.

"Go find rooms," she told them all. "Anything that doesn't already have someone's bags in it. I don't want to hear any damn arguing over it either."

The kids took off, running up the stairs, someone yelling, "But did you look at the chart?" from somewhere in the house. Dee didn't know who and she didn't care.

"You want to play tennis with me?" Blayne asked.

Good Lord, the woman had so much energy. Dee had seen her taking a run around the property, disappearing for several hours. She'd probably run ten, maybe even twenty miles, and now, standing in Van Holtz's marble hallway, sweat pouring from every pore onto the man's floor, she didn't want to shower and pass out like the cats. She wanted to play tennis. *Freak.*

"Nope," Dee told her, turning away. "Don't want to play tennis."

Blayne cut in front of her. "How about a swim? Or basketball? There's a basketball court, too."

Dee caught hold of Blayne's nose between the knuckles of two of her fingers. "What is it I just said?"

"You said no. You said no! Ow! Let me go, you Amazon!"

Twisting the nose she held a little more, Dee pushed Blayne down the hallway until they reached the kitchen. Using Blayne's body, Dee shoved open the large swinging door and stalked in.

The wild dogs sitting around the kitchen table, eating more chocolate than was probably good for them, looked up at her, eyes wide.

"What did I tell you people when you arrived? What did I say to you? My exact words?"

"Keep the wolfdog away from me," they all repeated back to her. All except Jessie Ann, who was too busy giggling around a mouthful of dark chocolate brownies. At least Dee guessed the brownies were dark chocolate. Bobby Ray's woman had a real thing for dark chocolate. It couldn't be normal.

"And yet what is she doing?"

"Annoying you?" one of the wild dogs asked.

"Yes. Annoying me." She shoved Teacup away from her. "Don't annoy me!"

"But I just wanted to show you how much we love and care and—"

Ric appeared beside Blayne and shoved a piece of chocolate cake into her mouth. "Isn't that delicious, Blayne? Enjoy." He grabbed Dee's wrist and dragged her toward the back of the house, stopping long enough to glare at a busy Stein, who'd stopped butchering something to wipe his forehead.

"What?"

"Get to work."

"I was just—"

"Don't argue!" Ric pulled her out of the kitchen, through the mud room, and out the back door.

"Why do you keep torturing that poor boy?"

Ric stopped and faced her. "You ask me that after you had Blayne's nose in a Dee-lock?"

"She's *annoying*. Stein is working his ass off."

"And he'll continue to do so. There's no easy way back into the Van Holtz Pack. And if I'm going to make a good case to get him back in, he'll need to prove to *me* that he deserves it."

Dee smirked. "Look at you, Van Holtz. Trying to sweet talk me."

MacRyrie walked out of the house, carrying a baseball bat.

"Is that for Novikov?" Ric asked, sounding way too hopeful.

"No. Wanted to see if anyone was up for a little softball game."

Dee folded her arms over her chest. "You? Playing softball? This isn't your idea, is it, MacRyrie?"

Because MacRyrie was a lousy liar, he looked past Dee and asked, "Why would you ask me that?"

Dee glanced over at the kitchen window and saw Blayne and the wild dogs duck for cover. Snarling, Dee snapped, "Teacup!"

"Oh, come on, Dee," Ric argued teasingly. "How bad could a little game of softball between friends be?"

CHAPTER 23

"**I** don't see what the problem is!" Blayne yelled at Mitch Shaw while they stood on the pitcher's mound. "*You're* playing for the Smiths!"

"I'm mated to a Smith, in case you hadn't noticed. You, however, are *not* mated to anyone in the Kuznetsov Pack. You are, point of fact, Pack-less."

"Oh, Lord," Ric heard Dee-Ann sigh next to him. "And here we go."

And, sure enough, Ric's beloved but "sensitive Sally" Blayne burst into tears, the entire Kuznetsov Pack rushing the field to give her a big hug while yelling at Mitch.

"Oh, come on!" Mitch yelled, arms thrown out dramatically. "You're not buying this, are you?"

"Does he mean Blayne's performance," Ric quietly asked Dee, "or his own?"

"Probably both."

Jess stormed onto the field after shoving her daughter into a laughing Smitty's arms, and slammed her finger into Mitch's chest.

"I'll have you know, Mitchell Shaw, that Blayne *and* Ric are part of the Kuznetsov Pack. As is Gwenie and Lachlan MacRyrie of the Clan MacRyrie. So if they want to play on our team, they can!"

"You're kidding, right?" Mitch felt the need to argue, as always refusing to accept that he'd never win this fight. Not against a female predator. Not without backup—and Mitch's brother Brendon Shaw didn't appear ready to be anyone's backup. "At least Blayne is half wolf. But Gwenie? Hello? Feline. MacRyrie? Bear. And Van Holtz has his own Pack!"

"Well," Jess said, stepping into Shaw, "now he has *two!* And you, ungrateful kitty, will apologize to Blayne Thorpe right this second!"

"I will not! You can't make me."

Ric winced. "Yes. She can."

Jess did, too. By taking away the one thing Mitch Shaw cherished with all his lion male heart—besides his food, need for sleep, and high-end hair products.

"*No more karaoke for you!*" Jess screamed in his face and Shaw stepped back, stunned.

"Jessica!"

"Apologize or you're out!"

"But . . . but you love me!"

"And we'll learn to live without you, too." Her brown eyes narrowed. "Unless you apologize."

Shaw rolled his eyes. "Sorry, Blayne," he mumbled, sounding like the twelve-year-old brat Ric often compared him to.

"Do you mean it, Mitchy?" Blayne asked, making sure to sniffle and wipe her eyes.

The lion snarled a little but Jess added, "No more power ballads, Mitchell. No more Frank Sinatra. No more Mariah Carey."

Frowning, Ric looked at Dee who, frowning herself, was already looking at him. They both shuddered and silently agreed never to speak of it again.

"Fine!" Shaw yelled. "Yes, Blayne. I mean it. I'm sorry. Have whoever you want on the team."

"Yay!" Blayne cheered, clapping her hands together. She ran back over to Ric and Dee. "You're up, Ric." Then with tears abruptly gone, her voice and attitude strong, she added in a whisper, "Pop it low and right at Brendon Shaw. He's so fuckin' lazy, he'll never dive for it."

Making sure not to laugh, Ric nodded. "You've got it."

"Isn't this fun?" Blayne demanded of Dee. In answer, Dee slammed her catcher's mask down in front of her face. "I think so, too!" Blayne happily squealed before running off, oblivious as always.

"Why do we not only let Teacup make these stupid suggestions, but follow them?" Dee asked him, smelling delightfully of She-wolf and sweat and sun protector.

"Because even you can't ignore the tears of a wolfdog."

"Only 'cause she started making those snot balls with her nose. I hate those."

It was true, though. Having wolves playing against dogs in this heat was really a recipe for disaster, and he'd be much more annoyed and fed up—if he weren't really enjoying himself so damn much.

Then again, Ric always did find entertainment in the strangest places.

"All I gotta say, Ric, is those ribs you and your cousin are planning to barbecue for tonight better be damn fantastic."

"When aren't they?" he demanded, insulted she'd once again questioned his culinary expertise. "When aren't my ribs perfect?"

The corners of Dee's lips turned up into one of her smiles. "Don't take it personally, supermodel. I'm just sayin' that you better cook as good as you look. Because after a day like today, I'm going to be hungry and cranky. You'll need to satisfy one and appease the other."

His desire to say, "Marry me," nearly choked him, but Ric fought it off and he promised, "The meat is seasoned. The corn shucked and wrapped in foil, ready to be grilled." He smiled at her. "I know how you like your corn."

Her smile grew a little more. "Love corn."

"Are you two done staring longingly in each other's eyes or should we just take a break?"

Now scowling, Dee turned her head and focused on the only idiot really taking the game seriously.

Mitch took a step back, grabbing his brother and yanking him in front of his body. "Take him, Dee. Take him!"

"You bastard!" Brendon yelped.

"Can we just get on with this?" Novikov demanded. They'd chosen him to be umpire since no one thought it would be fair that he should play on *any* team because he'd only cause serious bloodshed in his quest to win. Plus, he was such a dictator about sports, he wouldn't give anyone an unfair point.

Ric stepped up to the plate, watching as Mitch did his little pitcher's dance before he pitched the damn ball. Dee, the catcher, crouched low behind him, her mitt raised.

"And don't try distracting me, Dee-Ann," Ric warned her. "I'm focused."

"Wouldn't bother," Dee said.

Mitch nodded at whatever hand signal Dee had given him, checked the bases one more time, then pitched.

Ric readjusted his stance, pulled back his bat, and waited for the perfect moment to knock the softball right into Brendon Shaw, who was now back at first base.

And that was when Dee whispered, "You are going to *love* the tiny black bikini I'm wearing after the game, Van Holtz."

It was the last thing he remembered for a good three minutes after that softball slammed into the back of his head.

A bag of ice in her hand, Dee ignored the glares and low growls of the wild dogs and their friends and sat down next to Ric on the bench.

"Don't talk to me, evil She-wolf." He rested the left side of his body against the metal fence that was behind the bench, his arms crossed in front of his chest. "You're not welcome here."

"Don't be that way, Ric." She grabbed hold of Ric's T-shirt and pulled him over until his weight rested against her. She placed her hand against the back of his neck and lowered his head, placing it against her chest. Using her fingers, she eased around and found the swelling knot at the base of his skull and carefully placed the bag of ice there. "Doesn't that feel better?"

He grunted a little, his arms now wrapping around her waist, his face burrowing deep against her breast. After a moment, he settled and said, "Now it does."

Dee rolled her eyes in disgust. Honestly, wolves took any advantage they could get. At their core—they were all the same.

Horny, pathetic, and cute.

With one hand, she adjusted the ice pack, making sure that the entire area was covered. With the other hand, she stroked Ric's hair.

"What are you doing?" Bobby Ray, Smitty to his friends, asked her.

"She's coddling me. Mind not ruining it?" Ric asked, snuggling in closer.

Dee shrugged at her cousin's confusion. "Someone has to do it."

"Yeah, but . . . *you're* doing it."

"What's that mean?"

"You're not exactly a coddler, Dee-Ann. You're very far from a coddler."

"Now you're just pissing me off, Bobby Ray."

"No need to snarl."

Bobby Ray headed over to Rory and Reece Reed. The three of them stood there, watching her.

Blayne came over with another ice pack, exchanging it for the nearly melted one.

"What's wrong?" she asked and, for some unknown reason, Dee told her.

"Seems my kin's being a bit judgmental about who I allow to rest on my tits."

"Oh?" She followed Dee's gaze, nodded. "I'll take care of it."

Dee watched Blayne—Teacup!—walk over to the three much bigger wolves. She started off nice enough, but when she didn't seem to get an answer she liked—and Bobby Ray started to walk away—she unleashed a rant that had Ric lifting his head from

Dee's chest so he could watch, all the other shifters turning away from whatever they were doing to watch the finger-pointing, profanity-laden tirade.

Dee couldn't make out much of it, other than the cussing and something about "Project Wolf-Wolf" and "I'll be damned if I let you ruin what I've worked so hard for!" Whatever any of that meant. Of course, this was Teacup. She didn't have to make sense.

When she was done, Bobby Ray threw his hands up and that seemed to be the answer Teacup wanted. She came back over to Dee and Ric. "All fixed." She grinned. "Now let's get this going. We still have, like, a ton more innings!"

Perky as all hell, Blayne skipped off—were shifters supposed to skip?—and Dee shook her head, reaching for her bat. "Did I mention that the reason I hate baseball or any of its variations is because it never seems to *end*?"

"Be grateful," Ric told her. "Lock says she wanted to play dodgeball. Which, as former runts, both Lock and I consider a form of government-approved torture."

"Guess I shouldn't mention then that I rocked at dodgeball, huh?"

Ric sniffed. "I wouldn't."

Ric got another fresh bag of ice and stood outside the metal fence, looking in. He held the ice to his head, the swelling already going down, and watched the two teams argue about something new. This time, however, Blayne didn't involve herself in the fight, but came out to stand by Ric.

She tucked her arm around his and asked, "How's your head?"

"Much better. That lion throws like a girl."

Blayne giggled and rested her head against Ric's shoulder. "I'm so happy for you, my friend."

"It's not a done deal yet, Blayne."

"No, but I think you're close." She leaned in and whispered, "When you're not looking, she gazes at you lovingly."

"You sure she's not trying to think of the best way to bury my body when she's done with me?"

"No way. She's given me *that* particular look a ton of times, and the one she's giving you is totally different."

Laughing, Ric put his arm around Blayne's shoulders and kissed her forehead. "You're the best, Blayne. Did you know that?"

"I am aware. I'm just waiting for the universe and Dee-Ann Smith to catch up to this knowledge."

"Speaking of which, how did you get Smitty to back off anyway?"

"Easy. I reminded him that I would often be babysitting his beautiful daughter and I could either teach her to be a rational, *logical* wolfdog—or I could teach her to be like me. His choice."

"Ruthless."

"When I have to be."

Ric stopped talking, his head turning, ears perking up. He watched little Abby charging out of the trees. She'd followed Hannah, who had no desire to play baseball for any team, out into the park. But now Abby was back and on her own.

"Damn," he said before following the panicked dog, with Blayne right beside him.

They finally made it into a nearby clearing and stopped, Ric's arm shooting out to halt Blayne. It was hyenas—and they had Hannah surrounded.

"You're up, Dee-Ann," Sissy called out. "Let's go!"

Dee stepped forward, the wood bat in her hand. She didn't like those aluminum ones. She hated the sound they made when they collided with the ball.

Dee walked up to the plate, wincing when she saw who the pitcher was for this inning. It was one of Jess's best friends and one of the wild dog captains, Phil. For kind of a girly wild dog, he'd turned out to be a hell of a ballplayer.

His mate, and the one Mitch called "the Russian hottie,"

Sabina, crouched behind Dee, catcher mask pulled down to cover her face. "Don't worry, big She-wolf. I bet he send ball over plate nice and slow for you," she taunted in that damn Russian accent, which only made what she said sound even meaner. "You are one of his favorite people. After stalking and tagging our poor Blayne like animal in wild."

Ignoring the dog, Dee faced Phil and raised her bat. Signals were passed between the pitcher and catcher and after a few seconds, Phil nodded and readied his pitch. Dee dug her feet in, pulled the bat back a little more and—

"Strike one!"

Dee blinked, looked around, and saw that Sabina had the ball in her mitt.

"You never even saw it, did you, She-wolf with shoulders like man?" She threw the ball back to her mate. "He is so fast that one. But not in bed. There he takes time. Like good vodka take to develop."

Damn wild dogs and their "ringers."

Dee raised her bat again, dug her feet in, and—

"Strike two!"

"Mother fucker!" Dee yelled out. If she hadn't felt the wind of the ball going by her, she'd have sworn the damn wild dog hadn't pitched anything and that Sabina had just hidden extra balls on her somewhere.

"Awww," Sabina said. "Poor, freakishly sized She-wolf. She not so good at softball. Perhaps she should try something more in line with the width of her shoulders. Like pro football or security for zoo."

Fed up, Dee pivoted on her foot, facing Sabina, the tip of her bat pressing against the wild dog's mask.

"What will you do, manly She-wolf?" Sabina asked, the grin behind her mask practically begging for a fight. "What will you do to Sabina to make her cut you into long ribbons? Like meat for sub sandwich."

Dee was about to show the little bitch exactly what she'd do when Sabina gripped the end of the bat and slowly stood. Her head tilted, ears twitching. Her wild dog hearing was picking up something.

Sabina snapped her fingers and pointed at the wild dog pups running loose. As one controlled unit, the wild dogs grabbed their children and Dee knew.

"Hyenas," Sabina said, pointing toward the trees. "In there."

Dee quickly looked around. She'd seen Ric and Teacup wander off into the woods, but no one else had. She hadn't thought much about it either until now.

Tossing off the baseball helmet but gripping the bat tighter, Dee charged toward the trees, tracking Ric's scent deeper into the park.

She caught up to him quickly. He'd shifted to his wolf form, Blayne by his side. Her large wild dog ears were plastered back against her head while she bared her fangs and went after any hyena that got too close. Ric circled around, catching a retreating male by the leg and dragging him back.

At first, Dee thought the hyenas were going after Blayne. It wouldn't be the first time bored hyenas had gone after the wolf-dog but this time . . . it wasn't her. Or little Abby, who'd leaped onto the back of one large female, digging her claws into the hyena's backside.

No, it was Hannah they were after—and she wasn't moving. She sat with her back against a tree, her arms wrapped around her raised knees. She was still in her human form, her gaze locked on a distance far away. She wasn't reacting at all to what was going on around her. There was no crying, no whimpering, no trying to get away. If Dee didn't see everything that was going on, based on Hannah's reaction, she'd think it was a quiet day in the park.

Cranky now, Dee stepped into the fray, swinging the bat she held, enjoying how it felt when she made contact with hyena bone and flesh. She sent the cackling bastards flying, knocking them out of the way until she reached Hannah's side.

Catching the kid's arm, Dee hauled Hannah to her feet. One of the hyenas shifted to human. A female, brown eyes raging. "Is she with you?" the hyena demanded, blood pouring from a gash on her head, her lip swelling.

Dee didn't answer. Instead, she kept her grip tight on Hannah's arm, trying to find the best way to pull her out of the battle.

"Keep that freak away from us. We've got cubs with us."

The fact that the hyenas were doing exactly what Dee's Pack would have done had one of the hyenas gotten too close didn't change the fact that the wording still pissed her off. She pulled the bat back and the female shifted to her hyena form, turning to get away. But before Dee could follow through with her swing, Hannah caught the bat and easily held it, stopping Dee from doing anything with it.

"Let her go."

"Were you just going to sit there?" Dee demanded. "Just going to let them beat the shit out of you?"

Without a reply, Hannah walked off, going deeper into the park. Dee threw down her bat and followed.

"You're just leaving your friends? They're fighting for you."

"I didn't ask them to."

Knowing that no other species would be happy to have Hannah around or near their territory, Dee caught the girl's arm and pulled her up short. "Stop."

Hannah stopped. It appeared she wouldn't fight Dee either.

"Is this it for you?" Dee asked her. "Is this how you plan to go through life?"

"I plan to mind my own business."

"That's great, but you can mind your own business on Van Holtz's territory."

Finally fed up, Hannah yanked her arm away from Dee. "I'm not a kid. I can leave when I want."

"You go wandering around here, some other Pack, Pride, or Clan is going to rip you apart. Van Holtz won't stand for that, so he'll run in to rescue you—again. But I won't let him get hurt because you're too full of self-pity to protect yourself. Now move your ass back to the house, 'cause you are gettin' on my last Confederate nerve."

CHAPTER 24

The hyenas were sent packing once the Shaw brothers joined the fray. Lion males always loving a good hyena slap-fest. The rest of the softball game went off without a hitch, the Kuznetsov Pack eking out a win, and the group returned to the house relatively unscathed, considering.

Hannah, still pissed off, had headed right to her room, slamming her door behind her. Abby trotted after her. Dee could hear her scratching at Hannah's door until she was grudgingly let in. Dee guessed it was grudging by the annoyed sigh that she heard before the door slammed shut again. Honestly, Abby really was more canine than human based on the level of abuse she was willing to take.

Ric had left the game before the last inning even got underway, and when they all finally made their way back to his house, he already had the barbecue pits going and poor Stein pulling together side dishes for dinner in a few hours.

Yet as soon as everyone was back, they all split off again. Sissy and Bobby Ray took a chunk of the Pack off for some hunting; a large group of the wild dogs slathered sunscreen on their pups and took them down to the beach for a few hours before dinner; Mitch and Brendon Shaw passed out in lounge chairs by Ric's pool, under big protective umbrellas, snoring away; Blayne went running because "I have so much panicked energy after that hyena fight, I have to do *something*!"; Novikov did lap after lap in the pool; Gwen and Lock took a nap in their room . . . with the door closed (didn't really sound like they were napping, though); and Dee-Ann wandered around Ric's house being nosey.

She simply couldn't help herself, though. Dee had never been inside a place like this before. Well, she'd never been *invited* inside a place like this in the daytime . . . without a weapon, a target, and specially designed night-vision eyewear that prevented her eyes from being seen in the dark.

Moving through the house, Dee marveled at all the space. So much room to get lost in for a social predator. Personally, Dee didn't need all this indoor space. She didn't need square footage. She needed acres. The three-bedroom house her parents lived in was more than enough for Dee because the house was surrounded by thirty or so acres of land. Acres that were part of a bigger Smith territory that Dee was free to run and hunt on as well.

And God help her, but some days she missed that territory more than she had a right.

Still, it was so strange being an actual invited guest in a place like this. Dee didn't get invited to much unless her family was throwing the party, but Ric treated her like an honored guest. It made her feel special.

Taking her time, Dee explored the entire house. Funny, it was Ric's first time staying at the place and yet the entire house had been furnished. Even his bookshelves were filled, and each of the large, flat-screen TVs had collections of DVDs nearby for random viewing. She thought of her pitiful apartment with no furniture and the growing family of steroid-using vermin and she wondered how Van Holtz managed to be so put together.

Dee headed up the stairs and down the long hallway. She could hear laughter and chatter coming from behind the doors and she smiled. She might not always feel comfortable being part of all that, but she did enjoy having it around, knowing that the people she cared for were happy and relaxed.

She passed a set of wide double doors, stumbling to a stop when one of them opened.

"Hey," Ric said.

"Hey. Thought you were downstairs torturing your cousin."

"That got boring. What are you doing?"

"Wandering around, being nosey."

"Did that get boring yet?"

"Well—"

"Good."

He caught hold of her forearm and yanked her into the bedroom, slamming the door behind them.

"Honestly," she said when he pulled her into his arms and began walking her over to the big bed, "you have to be one of the horniest wolves I've ever known."

"I can't help myself. I've been waiting months to get you into my bed. Now that I've got you here, I'm not in the mood to let you go."

"Don't you have some cooking to do?"

"I don't need to start working the grill for another hour." He dropped them both to the bed, Ric on top of her.

Dee looped her arms around his neck. "A whole hour, huh? Now what do you think we can do for a whole hour?"

Ric jerked awake when he heard the banging on the door. "What?"

"Are we doing this or not?"

"Doing what?"

He could hear Stein sighing on the other side of the door. "Cooking food for these hungry, whining people."

Ric glanced at the clock next to his bed. "But we still have— damn!" He sat up quickly, not realizing that Dee had been asleep on top of him until she rolled off and hit the floor.

"Dee!"

"I'm all right." She sat up, scratching her head. "I love getting tossed out of bed like that. Makes it seem all dirty and wrong."

"I'm sorry." Ric slipped out of bed and helped her to her feet.

Not that she needed the help, but he loved touching her. "I've got to get dinner on—"

"I know." She began picking up her clothes. "Go on. I'll be fine."

"Are you sure?"

"Not spun glass, Van Holtz."

"All right. All right. No need to get that tone."

Ric dashed into the shower, scrubbed himself clean, and quickly put on clean jeans and a T-shirt. He kissed Dee before racing out of the bedroom and heading to the kitchen. He wrapped one of the white bandanas he kept in the kitchen drawer around his head and got to work. Somehow he managed to ignore the knocking at the window and the lion males whining about how hungry they were.

Absolutely the one breed of cat Ric couldn't stand cooking for.

Dee got out of the shower, dried off, and slipped on a pair of cutoffs and a T-shirt. She was heading down the stairs when Reece Reed met her halfway. "Could you not keep the man busy when we're all so damn hungry?"

Dee caught Reece's T-shirt and lobbed him over the banister, enjoying the sound of him hitting the floor and whining about "the pain! My God, the pain!" She passed Rory sitting on the last steps, reading the local newspaper. "I tried to tell him not to bother you."

"He was never a bright boy, your brother."

"Nah. Never real bright."

"You both do know I can hear you? I'm lying right here!"

Dee left the Reed brothers and walked into the kitchen.

"Gun?" she asked.

Without looking away from his work, Ric pointed at one of the high kitchen cabinets. "It's buried in the back."

"Thanks." Dee went up on her toes and opened the cabinet, searching around until she found a .9 mm. "Bullets?"

"The third cabinet to the left in the teapot."

Dee retrieved the magazine and popped it into the gun. She put a round in the chamber, walked over to the kitchen window, and aimed it at the two cats who stood on the other side of the glass, constantly roaring in an effort to get Ric to move faster. The Shaw brothers dove for cover and Dee put the safety back on the weapon and returned the gun and the magazine to their original hiding places.

"Thanks," Ric said.

"No problem."

Ric was slicing potatoes for his last-minute decision to make his potatoes au gratin when Blayne ran in. His knife paused in mid-cut, his eyes narrowing on her.

"What are *those?*" he demanded.

Panting and sweating from her workout, Blayne frowned and looked behind her. "Oh! Strays." She smiled. "They started running with me."

"Get them out of my kitchen."

"But—"

"Out!"

Blayne's smile turned into a pout. "You are so mean!"

"And they're filthy. Remove them or I'm adding them to the menu."

Gasping in indignation, Blayne walked out the back hallway, the stray dogs following. Ric returned to his work but listened for the back door to open and close. A few minutes later, Blayne returned.

"Happy now?"

"I'll be happier when you get out, too."

Blayne gasped again. "*Me?*"

"You're sweating all over my floor, and I don't want you anywhere near the food until you take a shower." He gestured to the swinging kitchen door that led to the front hallway. "Now go. *Schnel!*"

"Don't bark at me in German! I hate when you bark at me in German!"

She stormed out—again—and Ric went back to work.

"What can I help you with?" Dee asked him.

"Help?"

"You know. As in assisting."

"Uh . . . I don't really know what you can help with. Unlike me, you haven't been trained since birth to handle yourself in a Van Holtz kitchen. What if you crack under the pressure?"

"Do you want my help or not, Van Holtz?"

Chuckling, Ric admitted, "Stein might need you more at the grill."

"Okay."

"Hey. Come here."

"Why?"

Ric faced her. "Move that cute butt, Smith."

She walked over to him and he kissed her. "Don't let my cousin smooth-talk you into doing all the work or try to take you away from me. Understand?"

"I enjoy how you think I'd let anyone *but you* get away with half the shit you try."

"As long as we understand each other."

"We do." She kissed him again, their arms slipping around each other, their mouths and tongues exploring.

Until . . .

"Are you two at it again?" Stein demanded. "I'm drowning out there! And if those cats don't get away from me . . ."

Dee-Ann pulled away, laughing as she did. "I'll handle it," she told Ric. "You just keep making your potatoes au gratin."

"What makes you think I'm making that?"

"Because you'd better be."

She turned away from him and headed toward Stein. "Let's go, kid. I'll help you out."

Stein plastered himself against the wall, blue eyes focusing on Ric's She-wolf. "You?" he asked. "You . . . you're going to help me?"

Dee stepped in close, her arms crossed over her chest. "Is that gonna be a problem, hoss?"

"No. No, sir . . . er . . . ma'am. No, *ma'am*."

He eased away from her, his back pressed into the wall until he hit the doorway, then he sprinted for freedom.

"I do have a way with the young ones, don't I?" Dee asked before she followed Stein.

"Sure, you do," Ric muttered to himself. "Just like parole officers and wardens."

"I heard that, Van Holtz," she called back.

And Ric laughed, enjoying this weekend way more than he'd ever thought he could.

CHAPTER 25

Dee woke up on Fourth of July morning alone. But on the pillow next to her was a note and a granola bar.

Had to run into town with Stein for more breakfast food—damn lions! We'll be back soon. Please eat this until I return. I'm afraid you'll start feeding on your own muscle mass if you don't get some food in you.

Chuckling, Dee sat up and ate her granola bar. She was nearly done when she heard the howling from beneath her window.

"What?" she asked her cousin once she'd opened the window. "Couldn't you put on a T-shirt or something?"

"It's not like you haven't seen my tits before, Sissy Mae."

"That's not the point. There's a time and place!"

"When did you become Sally Etiquette?"

"Just get your suit on. We're hittin' the beach."

"I just woke up and—"

"Not a request. Just move your ass, cousin."

"Fine."

"I know it's fine. In fact, it better be goddamn fine!"

"Heifer."

"Rich man's whore!"

"At least mine can cook the food he eats. And replaces it, too."

"Now see, Dee-Ann Smith. That was just *mean!*"

Ric adored farmer's markets. Fresh produce and dairy and rel-atively friendly people, and a healthy mix of full-humans and shifters. It was perfect. Even his cousin's constant complaints couldn't bring him down.

"Do you think Dee's more a roses kind of girl? Or lilies?" he asked.

Stein stared at him. "Honestly? I think a machine gun and ample ammo is more your scary girlfriend's speed, cousin."

"See how you are?" Ric shook his head. "She keeps telling me I shouldn't be so tough on you, and here you are, talking shit about her."

"I wasn't talking shit about her. God, please don't tell that woman I was talking shit about her. She's liable to cut my head off and wear it on her jacket as a brooch. And you *are* being too tough on me. I haven't had a moment to relax or enjoy the pool, get in a little tennis, nothing, since I've become your indentured servant."

"You owe me, Stein. Don't forget what you owe me."

"How can I? You won't let me."

"Is it so impossible for you to realize that you have to work your way back up? That you're still not going to get a kitchen when you haven't been trained?"

"How is washing dishes and scrubbing floors training?"

"My best cooks started off washing dishes and scrubbing floors."

"They're also not blood relations and they're mostly immi-grants."

Ric faced his cousin, but didn't say anything. He let Abby do the talking for him. She'd tagged along with them for the trip since she'd been up bright and early, eating food she'd dug out of the trash. Why she felt the need to do that when she had an en-tire refrigerator of fresh food at her disposal, Ric had no idea.

Although they were low on things because of the cats, they still had food.

Abby snarled and snapped at Stein, nipping at his feet and forcing him to back up several steps.

"This is Abby Vega," Ric told his cousin. "I'm thinking right now she does not like you."

"Great," Stein sighed. "I'm stuck on the politically correct team."

"Does it ever occur to you that sometimes you shouldn't speak?" Hannah asked Stein, standing off to the side. She'd come along because she seemed to fear she'd have to, in her words, "talk to Dee" at some point today. Ric wasn't sure what Hannah was so worried about. If she was afraid she'd have to have some big, psychological discussion with Dee-Ann Smith about her inability to shift to her hybrid form when seriously threatened by hyenas, she was wasting her time. Dee didn't have big, psychological discussions. That's what Ric liked about her. His friends talked to him all the time about their problems, and although he didn't mind, he enjoyed Dee's lack of complaining. Besides, it was fun trying to figure out what had pissed her off at any given moment and how he could fix it.

"I didn't know you were capable of creating a sentence, sub-adult," Stein shot back. "I thought you could only brood and glare. Ow! Motherfu—"

"Stein," Ric warned.

"She's eating my leg!"

Abby had latched on to Stein's leg, and was doing her best to rip out his calf muscle.

"Then maybe you should be nicer."

"You really hate me, don't you?"

"If I hated you, cousin, I would have let Dee-Ann tear your colon out when she had the chance."

"What about bread?"

Ric and Stein looked over at Hannah, surprised by her sudden question.

"What about it? Ow! Get off me, crazed female!"

"Are you going to provide bread? Because if you think any is left after those cats wake up, you're delusional."

"She's right," Ric agreed. "But I don't have time to make bread this morning."

"They're selling fresh French bread right over at that stall."

"*Bought* bread?"

"You act like I just suggested roach-infested bread from Satan's bakery."

"I do fresh or I don't do bread." All right, kind of a lie, but she didn't need to know that.

Trying desperately to shake Abby off his leg, Stein prompted, "He wants you to make the bread, Hannah. He's under the happy-go-lucky delusion that being able to bake will make you feel better."

"Actually, I don't think that way"—much—"but if you want Blayne to think you're involving yourself in this weekend's festivities—even if you're off in a corner by yourself, pounding dough—this is the way. It'll get Blayne off Dee's back about your mental health, which will get Dee off your back about pretending your mental health is fine so that Blayne will leave her alone. Trust me, Hannah, it's a win-win. So make the damn bread."

"Whatever," she sighed, wandering off to get what she needed.

"See?" Ric asked his cousin. "It's all about how you talk to people."

"That's great, but could you just get this crazed bitch off my leg?"

"What did I just say about how you talk to people?"

Dee put on more sunscreen and adjusted the big umbrella so that her entire body was in the shade. She didn't plan to spend a moment of this weekend recovering from sunburn.

"So I'm thinking about breeding," Ronnie Lee suddenly announced to their small group. "With Brendon, of course."

And Dee gave the only answer she could think of. "So?"

"Could you at least pretend to be happy for me?"

"I'm not unhappy for you. I guess I just don't care one way or the other."

"What is wrong with you?" Ronnie demanded.

"Nothin'. Why?"

"Sissy was happy for me! I got a hug and tears. What do I get from you? A 'so.' "

"Sissy's your best friend."

"And what are you?"

"Your Packmate. On more occasions than seems right, your drinking buddy."

"That's it? That's how you see me?"

"I don't know why you're so upset."

"Because we're friends, and friends are happy for each other."

"When did we become friends?"

Frowning, Ronnie asked, "We're not friends?"

Dee thought about it a moment and finally answered, "No."

At this point, Sissy Mae was lying on her side, hysterically laughing, her arms around her stomach.

"How could you say we're not friends?"

"We're not enemies."

"I don't understand you sometimes."

"Thereby proving we're not friends."

"Stop!" Sissy begged. "Stop! You two are killing me!"

"I don't think it's funny, Sissy Mae."

"Is this where you tell me I hurt your feelings?" Dee asked.

"Yes!"

"Sorry. Not my intent."

"Are you like this with Ric?" Ronnie Lee demanded.

"No. 'Cause with him I'm usually naked when we're having these kinds of conversations, which makes them a lot less painful."

"This is not funny, Sissy Mae!" Ronnie bellowed.

"The hysterical snorting and feet kicking would suggest she feels different on that."

"Shut up, Dee-Ann."

Dee shrugged. "I would, but you keep talking to me."

* * *

Stein ended up cleaning out the dairy farmer's supply of milk and eggs. But the man was a local bear and once Stein explained he was feeding two male lions at their house party, he completely understood. While the farmer's sons took Stein's purchases to the SUV, Stein checked out the asparagus in the next stall.

"Sir?" the girl behind the counter asked.

"Uh-huh."

"Did you know you have a dog attached to your leg?"

"Yep. I choose not to discuss it." He smiled at the full-human girl. "So . . . what's your name?" *And age. And breast size.* "Ow!" He glared down at the hybrid. "What is *wrong* with you?"

"Is it your dog?"

"Hardly."

"Animal Control is out today, despite the holiday. If you want, you can turn it over to them." The girl frowned. "What kind of dog is that anyway?"

"The annoying kind."

Stein purchased several bags full of asparagus and headed back to the car without bothering to get the girl's phone number. It wasn't like he could hook up with her today anyway, not with his cousin watching his every move like a hawk. He was trying really hard not to be resentful over spending an entire Fourth cooking and cleaning up after ungrateful shifters who weren't even in his Pack, but Stein knew Ric was right. If he ever hoped to make it back into the family, he'd have to suck up the pain and get the job done. That was what one did when one was a Van Holtz. And though his uncle may have pushed him out of the Pack, Stein's bloodline would never change. Ric realized that and took care of his own like always.

Stein reached the SUV and unlocked the trunk. He found a spot to place the asparagus and quickly counted what they had. Another shipment of meat would be arriving at the house within the hour—only Ric was able to get that kind of personal service on a holiday—and that should get them through today and to-morrow morning. It was a good thing they were leaving before noon, though. The way those cats ate, the cousins would be back to the market for more supplies if they were staying any longer.

The hybrid finally released him and Stein let out a breath. "Finally! Thank—"

A big hand rammed Stein's head into the side of the SUV, black dots swirling through his vision. But when his sight cleared, he stared up—way up—at three polar bears. Dave Smolinski and his two brothers.

"Hiya, Steiny," Dave said. "We've been looking just *everywhere* for you."

Ric and Hannah were nearly back at the SUV when Abby gripped the back of Ric's jeans and held on. It seemed as if she was trying to drag him back to the market, but he had no idea why.

He stopped and gazed down at her. "Do you know what she's doing?" he asked Hannah.

"Why would I know?"

"You seem to spend the most time with her."

"She won't leave me alone. It's not like I invite her anywhere."

"Well, if you had to guess."

"She doesn't want you to walk over to the SUV."

"Why?"

"This would be much simpler if she would just shift to human."

"Except there'd be a sixteen-year-old naked girl biting at my jeans. I'm almost positive that would only go badly for me."

"That's a valid point."

Ric lifted his nose, sniffed the air. "Bears."

"That's probably me."

He turned his head, took another sniff from her neck. "No. Not you."

"All I have to say is . . . that was kind of weird."

"You'll get used to it." He sniffed the air again. "Polar bears." And fear. He smelled Stein's fear, and his rage. Yet something didn't seem right to Ric. Why were the bears lingering around? Did they want Ric to pay since they couldn't get their money from Stein? Maybe, but still . . .

"Go back to the market, Hannah. Take Abby with you."

"Why?"

Ric added the bags he held to the bunch Hannah had. "Don't question. Just do."

Hannah nodded and returned to the market, Abby following behind her, but stopping every few feet to look back at Ric.

"It's all right, Abby. Go."

Once she and Hannah were gone, Ric crouched down and pulled the gun he kept holstered on his ankle. He stuck it into the back of his jeans and covered it with his T-shirt. Taking a breath, he headed back to the SUV, easing around the front of the vehicle. But he stopped short when he found nothing. No bears. No Stein.

Ric casted for the scent again, locked on, and followed. He tracked them to a row of stores closed due to the holiday and around to the back. There were two of them battering Stein around. The poor kid hit the ground, blood pouring from gashes on his face and neck. When he saw Ric, he shook his head. "Go, Ric. Go. It's not me they—"

A tugboat of a foot slammed into Stein's gut, cutting off the rest of his words.

"That won't be necessary," Ric explained, knowing that unlike some other species, bears could be quite rational when one didn't startle them into unnecessary violence. "I can get you your money if you'd only allow me to—" Ric abruptly spun, catching the hand holding the gun that was about to be placed against the back of his head and slamming his foot into the weak spot on the third bear's kneecap, fracturing it.

"I've spent months," Ric explained over the screaming of the bear at his feet, "learning to sense the presence of the most lethal She-wolf in the world. So your tiptoeing sounds more like an elephant stomping through dry brush to me."

He pressed the bear's gun to the back of its owner's head. The safety was already off and Ric had the feeling that his death was their intent, not merely getting money from Stein.

"Why are you here?" he asked. The bears stared at each other, the other two still holding on tight to Ric's cousin.

When no one answered, Ric pointed the gun at the taller bear across from him and pulled the trigger. Another kneecap damaged, the bear went down screaming.

"I'll ask again because I really have to get back and make breakfast for my guests. Why are you here?"

"Why do you think?" the one he held replied, his voice thick with pain while he lay on his side.

"The kid's debt was bought," the uninjured one volunteered. "But we were offered an extra fifty grand on top of that."

"As payment for killing me?"

"Ain't killin' nobody for fifty K, but we'll mess you up good. Good enough that you won't be gettin' up again for a while."

Ric knew he should feel pain. Acute, ripping pain deep into his soul at such a betrayal—but he felt nothing. Not pain or surprise—not even fear.

"Thank you for the information, gentlemen. I'll assume I won't be hearing from you again."

"You're not really worth the trouble—and we've already gotten the money for what he owed us."

"Let's go, Stein."

Stein picked himself up off the ground and limped his way over to Ric's side, following as Ric headed back onto the deserted street. All the activity was on the other side of the small town where they'd had a parade and set up a carnival with rides for the locals and tourists.

"Who was he talking about?" Stein asked him. "Who bought the debt? Who would do this to you?"

Ric stopped and faced his cousin. "Who do you think?" He shrugged a little. "My father."

CHAPTER 26

D ee walked into the kitchen from the back door. She had sand between her toes and in her bathing suit and she couldn't wait to rinse it all off. But she immediately stopped and watched the wild dog females and Blayne busy cleaning up a battered Stein.

"What happened?" she asked, wondering if Ric had met up with those hyenas again. Hannah had gone with him and was now quietly making dough—*why is she making dough?*—in a small corner in the kitchen while the rest of the females fawned over Stein.

"Nothing," Stein lied. "Everything is cool."

"Where's Ric?"

"Went upstairs to get more bandages." He glanced around at the other females. "I should go to the bathroom. Ric will have a fit if I get blood on his kitchen floor."

Dee-Ann headed out into the hall and to the stairs. Ric was coming down with a first aid kit and they met at the last step.

"Are you all right?"

"I'm fine." He kissed her cheek and she smelled gun powder on him. "But glad I'm home."

"What happened?"

"Nothing. Just Stein's past catching up to him. Don't worry." He smiled and she didn't believe it for a second. "I handled it and his debt's taken care of. They won't be bothering him any-more." He headed toward his kitchen. "Let me get the kid out of my kitchen and patched up and I'll make you breakfast."

"Sounds good."

Dee went upstairs to the bedroom she shared with Ric and tracked down the gun he'd used. It was a tacky, gold-plated one that Van Holtz would never buy on his own. She returned the weapon to its hiding place and took a quick shower to get all that sand off. Slipping on the bikini she'd told Ric about and a pair of cutoff shorts as well, she headed back downstairs. Stop-ping briefly to gape at a first-floor bathroom filled with fe-males—now including her cousins and Ronnie Lee—and one young Van Holtz, all trying to wipe up a little blood and put ice on a few bruises, Dee returned to the kitchen. Ric was busy at the sink with his back turned to Dee, so Dee paused briefly and gazed at Hannah until the sub-adult female looked up from what she was doing. Once Dee had her attention, she left the kitchen, went out the back, and over to the far side of the house out of Ric's line of vision from the kitchen windows.

She found a bench to sit on and waited—she was very good at waiting—until Hannah found her and sat down beside her.

"Well?"

Hannah's flour-covered hands twisted in her lap, flecks of bis-cuit dough still clinging to the tips of her fingers. She also wore one of Ric's bandanas wrapped around her dark brown hair with the black tips.

"We got back to the SUV after shopping and Stein was gone. Ric sent me and Abby back to the farmer's market." Abby ap-peared in front of them, sitting back on her haunches and pa-tiently watching them. "I remembered what you said about not helping and he'd been pleasant enough to me without all that pressure to be happy I get from Blayne." She took a breath. "So Abby and I followed from the roofs. And we saw that Stein had been grabbed by some bears. Polars, I think." She shrugged. "I'm still learning all the breeds and everything. The people who raised me before I was snatched are full-human." She rubbed her forehead with the back of her hand. "Ric handled himself really well. Really put a hurt on those guys. Shot one in the kneecaps when he wouldn't talk. I didn't think he would. He was so polite the whole time."

Dee kept her smile to herself, real proud of Ric at this moment, and waited for Hannah to continue.

"There was something about Stein owing them money. I didn't understand much of that. But someone bought out the debt and then paid more so that they'd hurt Ric. Hurt him bad."

"Kill him?"

"No. Just hurt him. A lot."

Dee nodded, understanding. "Anything else?"

"No."

Abby barked and Hannah added, "Well, Ric said something to Stein about his father."

Dee turned her head away, briefly closed her eyes.

"I'm not sure I understood all that, either. And he seemed so calm or whatever. I don't know how true it was."

"Thank you, Hannah. I appreciate you telling me."

"Like I said, Ric's been nice to me without the pressure."

Dee did smile at that. "I know exactly what you mean."

"I thought he'd tell you all this himself, though. You two seem kind of . . . close, or whatever."

"We are, but Ric didn't want me to use one of my father's favorite expressions. 'Time to start the killin'.' "

Hannah nodded. "Yeah. I don't see Mr. Van Holtz being much of a 'killin'' type of guy. He was so polite during the whole thing. Never once raised his voice."

"Yeah. That's Ric." She motioned Hannah back to the house. "Go on now. And no one needs to know about this conversation. Understand?"

"Yeah. Sure." She walked off and Dee looked at Abby. "Get me a phone, would you, Abby?"

Abby barked and ran off. A few minutes later she returned with a phone, dropping it into Dee's lap. Dee quickly punched in a number and waited for the connection.

*   *   *

After what became a brunch had been devoured and the guests went off to do their own things until dinner time, Ric went back to his kitchen and got to work on the just-delivered meats. Stein stayed out of his way, mostly working outside getting the industrial-grade equipment scrubbed clean and set up for the next bout of summer grilling.

Ric didn't know why his cousin was avoiding him. For once the problem had very little to do with Stein, even if the means of getting to Ric had come through him. It was simply too easy to blame the kid, for the fact remained that if his father hadn't used those polars, he'd have found something else. Something with more skill at getting to Ric. In a way, Ric was grateful to Stein. His father could have easily found himself a Dee-Ann type who'd have left Ric disabled and bleeding to death behind a closed Long Island dress shop.

Deciding to put it out of his mind for the moment, because he refused to let his father do what he did so well—ruin his holiday weekends—Ric finished seasoning the turkey legs he hadn't ordered but thought he might have fun experimenting with and turned toward the four stoves he'd had built into his kitchen when he'd purchased the house. He debated whether he wanted to roast the turkey legs or grill them or—ooh!—fry them, when he realized Dee-Ann was with him in the kitchen, cleaning and preparing the vegetables. And, it occurred to him, she had been there for a while. She even wore one of the bandanas over her hair, knowing how he'd have lost his mind if her hair was swinging free in his hair-free-zone kitchen.

She looked up from the green beans and blinked. "What?"

Ric shrugged. "Just glad you're here."

She returned his smile. "Me, too."

"I'm especially glad you're wearing that bikini." He stepped closer and tugged at the cutoffs she wore over her bikini bottoms. "Although these aren't really necessary." And yet Dee still managed to wear them the sexiest way possible, the top button undone, the zipper halfway down to give him a peek at those black bikini bottoms. As Stein had remarked to Ric at one point the day before while he'd watched Smith She-wolves walk past his grill and head toward the pool, "There's definitely a benefit to having Southern sensibilities around, cousin."

Very true.

"There are children around. Don't want to ruin 'em for all other females."

"Good point."

She took hold of his T-shirt and tugged him closer. Ric pressed his mouth against hers but he didn't manage to get very far.

"I'm hungry," a cat whined, standing on the other side of the kitchen island. "Dinner ready yet?"

Ric glared at Mitch Shaw. "I just fed you a couple of hours ago."

"Why do you wolves always say that to me like it's supposed to mean something?"

"Is there more food?" Brendon Shaw yelled from outside.

"No!" Mitch yelled back. "He's in here making out with Dee instead of feeding us!"

And if Ric had been a half-second slower, Mitch Shaw would have been *wearing* that eight-inch chef's knife Dee had aimed at his face.

Dee had to admit she was impressed by how Ric ran these mass barbecues with lots of breeds and personalities involved. Several barbecue pits worth of meat could lead to all sorts of trouble when dealing with so many predators, but he had been smart from the beginning and drafted Lock, Novikov, and Bobby Ray to manage the food. Then he let the wild dogs feed their kids first, ignoring the whining and roaring from the lions who had woken from their deathlike slumber as soon as someone yelled out, "Food's on!"

Once the kids were taken care of, he set up lines for the buffet, but had already pulled out a couple of slabs of ribs just for Mitch and Brendon. While the pair downed that, the rest of them were able to get their food without much of a fuss. Something Dee was sure all concerned appreciated.

Two hours later, there was barely any food left and the pool area was filled with well-fed shifters enjoying the night as small lights automatically popped on around the property.

Like her mother and her mother's mother, Dee-Ann had made sure everyone else had eaten before she went back to the buffet to get her own. There wasn't much left to choose from and she sighed a little, picking up one of the few clean plates stacked at the corner of the table.

"Your food is inside, Dee," Jessie Ann told her, taking the plate away while a group of wild dogs and Blayne helped clean up.

"Sorry?"

"Ric made you a plate. It's in the kitchen somewhere."

"Probably in the oven," Blayne piped in, expertly stacking up dirty plates and platters.

"All right. Thanks." Dee started to walk off, heading back to the kitchen, but she stopped and asked, "You know where Ric went?"

"Check the roof," Blayne told her.

Dee went to the kitchen. Stein sat at the kitchen table with his head resting on his arms. The poor thing had had a hell of day, hadn't he? Beaten up by polars and made to cook for demanding lions. He'd come through it like a trooper, though.

"You all right?" Dee asked while she found her plate of food right where Blayne had told her it would be.

"I'm all right. Just exhausted."

"You did a nice job this weekend. Taking care of all these people. And the food was great."

"That was mostly Ric. He's an amazing chef."

"You will be, too."

Stein slowly sat up. "How do you know that?"

"I know that because I know your cousin. He wouldn't bother pushing you like he does if he didn't think you had the talent to back it up."

"Really?"

"Really."

"Thanks."

She shrugged and gathered together a fork, knife, and cloth napkin.

"And if you have any more problems with those bears, you let me know. All right?"

"Sure."

"But no more gambling, or I'm liable to get ornery. Understand?"

"I understand, but it's not that easy."

"Make it that easy. Because you won't like it if I get ornery, son."

"I'm sensing that."

"Keep sensin' it."

Dee tucked a bottle of imported beer into the back pocket of her jean shorts and took her plate up several flights of stairs until she reached the stairway and small door that led to the roof.

Van Holtz sat Indian–style on the roof's balcony, an empty plate next to his crossed legs, a bottle of wine and a half-empty wineglass near his knee. A small insulated bag sat behind him. He was mid-yawn when she stepped out and she debated going back out again to give him some much needed peace but he saw her first—and smiled. Moving over a bit, he patted the empty space next to him.

Feeling more welcome than she ever had before, and with only a simple gesture, Dee sat in the spot he indicated. She placed her plate down and pulled the bottle of beer out of her back pocket. She suddenly wished she'd brought a bottle opener since using her front fangs seemed the height of tacky, something her mother had always told her and something Dee had always ignored.

"Let me see that," Ric said, spotting her dilemma. He took the bottle and popped off the top using his claws. "Adelle taught me that." He handed the bottle back to her. "She worked a few summers in the hardcore seafood restaurants out here."

"Thanks," Dee said, retrieving the bottle from him and taking a quick sip. "And why would she do that?"

"Experience. A lot of us worked in different restaurants when we were younger, to get a feel for not being in a Van Holtz kitchen."

"Was it tough?"

"Not really. You keep taking jobs at restaurants with the worst reputations in the city or state, thinking there has to be somewhere more abusive than working with your own family—then you find out you're wrong. You'll never work any place tougher than a Van Holtz kitchen."

Dee took her first bite of a beef rib, the meat falling off the bone, the tenderness of it literally melting in her mouth, and she could only reply, "Shut up, suffer, and learn from your kin, Van Holtz, 'cause this is amazing."

Ric laughed. "I'm glad you like it. Your beans were a big hit, by the way. Who knew you could sauté?"

"Told you I wasn't helpless in the kitchen."

"Everyone says that. Then they end up crying in a corner."

Ric sat back with his wine and let Dee finish her food. Like most predators, she ate quickly, always worried someone was going to steal her meat from her and drag it up a tree out of her reach. But when she leaned back, licking the last remnants of barbecue seasoning off her fingers rather than using her napkin, he knew he'd made a damn good meal.

"You do have a way with meat," she finally said, leaning back with her palms flat behind her, her long legs stretched out and crossed at the ankles.

"I know that's a compliment, but it still sounds . . . weird."

She smiled and Ric felt himself melting.

No. Not melting. There could be no melting around Dee-Ann Smith. Especially when he should be angry with her because she couldn't keep her damn mouth shut.

"Uncle Van called me."

"Did he?" She laughed when Ric scowled at her. "What, Ric?

Did you think I wouldn't find out? That I wouldn't tell him what I knew? You could have gotten killed today." Then she softly added, "I could have also handled this myself, but I didn't."

"You could have at least waited until after the holiday before you told him."

"Could do lots of things—often don't."

"I don't know what that means, but I'm heading to Washington tomorrow to meet with him."

"Good."

"You're coming with me."

"Can't. Got some killin' to do."

"If you mean my father—no," he said simply. "If you mean Missy Llewellyn—no."

"You're ruining all my fun."

"I'm cruel that way. We wait until we talk to Uncle Van."

"He ain't my Alpha."

"No. He's just the man who signs your checks. *He's* your boss. And mine."

"Fine. We're not flying coach, though, are we?" She hated being stuck in those tiny seats with nowhere for her long legs to go.

Ric gawked at her, making her think she'd started speaking in tongues like old Great Aunt Delilah used to do during church services.

"A commercial plane? Me?"

Dee laughed outright. "Foolish me. Thinking we might have to sully ourselves on a commercial flight like all those normal people."

"That's an insane way of thinking, Dee-Ann, and completely unacceptable when you're with me."

"I'll keep that in mind." She glanced around at the empty plates. "You ready to head back down?"

"And miss the best part?"

"Best part?" She figured he meant to get her naked up here—

not that she'd complain if he did—but off in the distance near the park they'd been at the day before, explosions sounded and fireworks exploded in the sky overhead.

The guests below reacted with cheers and applause—although some of the dogs yipped nervously and the pups squealed.

"See?" Ric asked, grinning at her. "Best part."

"Absolutely. Although if I'd known there'd be a show, I'd have brought us some dessert so we could eat something sweet and watch."

"Ye of little faith, Miss Smith." Ric reached into the small insulated bag he'd brought with him. He pulled out small plates, placing one beside her and the other in front of himself. On each he placed four graham crackers and two very large marshmallows.

"Aren't we supposed to melt these?" she asked, more tickled than she'd ever been before.

"I've always loathed the idea of picking up random sticks that were in the dirt and sticking them through clean food. Besides, I'm relatively certain I don't want to build a fire up here. So no melting."

Lord, the man was just so logical. And it was just so . . . cute.

"And the best part . . ." He reached back into the bag and pulled out two bars of Hershey milk chocolate. She appreciated the fact that he didn't try to use that expensive, snooty chocolate the wild dogs preferred. He'd gone with an all-American favorite and since it was Fourth of July with all that "rockets' red glare" overhead, it only seemed right.

He handed her the still-wrapped candy and she took it, her fingers grazing against his—and that's when they both froze, the immediate recognition sending a shiver of absolute pleasure down Dee's spine.

She looked into his eyes, eyes that were suddenly more familiar than they'd been only an hour ago and she saw the same thing there that she felt.

"Thank you kindly," she whispered and they smiled at the same time.

"I told Uncle Van I'd be the one to feed you," Ric sighed out.

"Pardon?"

"Nothing." Ric's hand slipped behind the back of her neck and pulled her closer. "Nothing at all." He kissed her, the fireworks display completely forgotten, and Dee knew in that moment that her daddy would finally have to accept a few things: She'd never be a doctor or lawyer, chances were that killing was as much a family business as her momma's pie shops, and that his only baby girl would forever be in love with a Van Holtz.

CHAPTER 27

Van opened his front door and let out a little sigh. "Dee-Ann."

"Mr. Van Holtz."

"How are you?"

"Feelin' pretty fine."

"Is Ric with you?"

"He's around." They gazed at each other and Van knew what he saw: that the cold, bloodthirsty, *deadly* spawn of Eggie Ray Smith loved Van's favorite cousin.

Why, oh, why, did these things happen to *him?*

"Would you like to come in?" he finally—and grudgingly—asked.

"Thank you kindly."

She stepped inside, those dog-yellow eyes taking everything in. "Nice digs."

He nearly shuddered. "Thank you."

Ric stepped through the doorway, carrying two small duffle bags.

"Uncle Van!"

Grinning, feeling pure joy at seeing his cousin alive and well, Van hugged the kid right off his feet.

"I'm so glad to see you, Ric."

"I'm glad to see you, too."

Van released him and took a step back. "You're all right?"

Ric's gaze moved across the hallway floor to the She-wolf wandering along, studying the pictures on the walls. "I'm doing great."

Van's eyes crossed. "You're such an idiot."

Ric grinned. "I love you, too, Uncle Van."

Dee went around a corner, wondering if there was a bathroom nearby, and came face-to-face with a full-human female. She had ice blue eyes and curly dark brown hair that had streaks of grey throughout. The hair was thick and she wore it on top of her head in a loose ponytail. They gazed at each other for several long seconds until the female asked, "Are you doing that on purpose? With your eyes?"

"No, ma'am. Born this way. Just like my daddy."

"Really? Fascinating. And your height? Is that normal for your kind or are you freakishly built?"

"*Irene*," Niles Van Holtz said from behind Dee.

"What? I didn't ask for a blood sample this time."

"Dee-Ann Smith, this is my wife, Irene Conridge-Van Holtz."

"Ma'am."

"You're a Smith?" She studied Dee a little more. "I thought they were to be killed on sight," she said to her husband.

"*Irene*."

"Why do I keep hearing that tone?" She looked at Dee. "Was I offensive to you?"

"Not so's I'd notice."

"See?" she smirked. "Not *so's* she'd notice." Dee chuckled and watched the female move around her. "Ulrich?"

"Hi, Aunt Irene."

The full-human opened her arms to Ric and he swept her up, hugging her tight. "I'm so glad to see you."

"And you."

He placed her carefully on her feet, kissed her cheek.

"You look very good," she told him. "Your excellent bone

structure will help ensure that you're extremely attractive well into your sixties. Perhaps even your seventies."

He winked at Dee. "Did you hear that?"

"I'm standing right here."

"Oh," the full-human said. "Are you two sexually involved?"

"And we're done," Niles Van Holtz announced, catching the hand of his mate and pulling her to his side. "Ric, why don't you show Dee-Ann your room . . . since I guess you two will be sharing. And meet me in my office after you get settled."

"Okay." Ric took Dee's hand, openly claiming her in front of the Alpha of her Pack's fiercest enemies, and pulled her toward a big set of marble stairs. They walked up the steps and met an older teenage female coming down. She was pretty, had her daddy's face but her momma's eyes. Cold like her momma's eyes, too.

"Ulrich."

"Ulva." He kissed the girl's cheek. "How are you doing?"

"Well. I head to Oxford in the fall."

"Oxford? No restaurant time for you then, huh?"

"Not necessary. I received a full scholarship." She glanced at Dee and Ric introduced them.

"Nice to meet'cha," Dee said.

"Yes," the girl replied.

"Uncle Ric!" Dee heard young boys scream down the second-floor hallway and Ric ran up the stairs to meet them, leaving Dee alone with Niles Van Holtz's only daughter.

They stared at each other until Dee finally warned her, "You ain't ready for me yet, little girl."

"I believe you're right," she admitted. "But from what I've heard about you, I'm surmising I should endeavor to have you as an ally rather than an enemy."

"Ain't you a little young to be so . . . conniving?"

The girl gave a little half smile and continued on her way, but Dee heard her when she replied, "Not in this family."

Dee headed up the stairs and found Van Holtz rolling on the floor with three boys who were slightly younger than their sister.

They all stopped and gazed at her.

"That your girlfriend, Uncle Ric?" one of them asked.

"It is. Isn't she pretty?"

"Gorgeous," one of them sighed and all Dee could do was shake her head. Because something was just plain wrong with all the Van Holtz men.

Before involving Dee-Ann, Van wanted to speak with Ric alone.

"Your father," he said by way of introduction to the subject.

"Yes, sir."

"Dee-Ann said he didn't want you dead."

"No, he didn't." Although Ric wasn't sure if Alder would have minded if it accidentally happened anyway.

"Does he really think that we don't already know he's been stealing from the Tri-State restaurants? That we don't already know what he and Wendell have been doing?"

"I think my father hoped that the distraction of my injuries would have allowed him time to replace what he'd taken. Especially if being incapacitated gave him direct access to all my money. Because once the money was back, he could claim he'd only borrowed it due to an emergency of some kind and he could use any additional cash to help open his restaurant."

"And Stein?"

"Convenient. Alder has no use for him anyway, so if something had happened to him, it wouldn't have mattered."

"It would have mattered to me," Van said. "The kid needed a wake-up call but he's still a Van Holtz. He still has our protection."

"I know."

"Your father needs to go, Ric."

"You can't kill him, Uncle Van. I'm not sure my mother would ever recover from it, and that I can't allow."

"You'd fight me on this?"

"If I had to. This is her mate and her firstborn son we're talking about."

"I adore your mother, but—"

"Let her move back to Colorado. To be with her Pack. She'd love that and you can explain to Alder and Wendell that they have no choice but to go with her."

"And what about you?"

Ric frowned. "You're going to make me move to Colorado?"

"No." Van chuckled. "I mean, who's going to take over the Van Holtz Pack in New York once your father's out?"

"Anyone but me?"

"You're the most logical choice."

Ric admitted the ugly truth. "I'd rather set myself on fire and let pit bulls tear my carcass to pieces than be an Alpha."

"You know, Ulrich, most people just say no."

Irene sat back and watched her sons watch Dee-Ann Smith make them something as foreign to them as Ancient Egypt—a peanut butter and jelly sandwich.

Berg, her youngest, observed, "But you didn't even cut off the crusts."

"Why would I?"

"And that peanut butter," Carl pointed out, "it's the kind we use to get our pet dog to take his pills when he's sick."

"What was I supposed to use? That organic crap y'all got?"

"Yes," all Irene's sons answered. So much like their father, she already pitied the poor women who'd eventually fall in love with them.

"Shouldn't you use the homemade jam we make each season?" her middle son Finn asked. "Rather than that store-bought grape jelly?"

"P.B. and J. ain't supposed to be fancy, boys. It's supposed to be delicious."

The abnormally large female cut the sandwich into four pieces and gave one to each before taking one for herself. They all took a bite and she grinned at their appreciative groans. "See?" she said around a mouthful of peanut butter and jelly. "Isn't that good?"

"And so decadent," Berg sighed. "I feel like I'm eating evil. Pure, unadulterated evil."

"But good evil," Finn added. "The finest evil ever."

"Come!" Carl, the unabashed history fan and future historical "re-creator" of the lot—an activity Irene had always thought was an incredible waste of time for any human being with a brain—cried out, "Let us tell the others of this glory and what we have learned here today from the enemy She-wolf!"

"Huzzah!" they all cheered and ran out the kitchen back door.

The female turned to her and said, "Bless their hearts."

Irene had the distinct feeling that wasn't necessarily an actual blessing, but she couldn't prove it and she didn't want to get into a discussion about religion.

"So you're in love with our Ulrich?" Irene asked, always one to cut right to the heart of the matter rather than dance around it.

"I reckon."

"You reckon? Is that . . . some form of agreement?"

"Yep."

"Where are you from exactly?"

"Tennessee."

"Well, the Southern states are known for their colloquialisms."

The She-wolf took out more bread and made two more sandwiches, giving one to Irene. She handed it over on a paper towel, turning the sandwich into decadently relaxed dining. Something Irene hadn't experienced since the eighties when Holtz, her personal nickname for her husband, had made it absolutely clear that peanut butter and crackers—her favorite "work" food— was no longer accepted in his house. It hadn't stopped her from eating her favorite delicacy, but she often did it when he was out of town on business and there was less chance of her being caught in the act of "betrayal" to his cooking, as he insisted on calling it.

The Van Holtzes took their food very seriously and Irene had come to terms with that. It seemed only fair since Holtz had come to terms with the fact that nine-point-three times out of ten, Irene would insult or completely terrify his friends, Pack-mates, family members, and business associates. Not on purpose, but still . . .

Irene bit into the sandwich made with average white bread—not sour dough baked fresh that day, but white bread Dee-Ann Smith had brought with her from the nearby 7-11—and relished the taste of generic grape jelly and peanut butter. She ate while Miss Smith found tall water glasses, and took out fresh milk from the refrigerator. She poured them both a glass and joined Irene in eating.

And as Irene neared her last bite, Holtz stepped through the kitchen door, coming to an abrupt halt when he spotted her, his eyes wide.

"What are you eating?" he asked. He made it sound like he'd found her fellating one of his teenage male cousins.

Irene tried to reply around the sticky substance tacked to the roof of her mouth, but it took too long and the enemy She-wolf answered for them both.

"Made a couple of P.B. and J.s for your boys and wife. You want one?"

"Demoness!" Holtz exploded. "Out of my kitchen!"

"Are you trying to sweet talk me?" the female asked and Irene almost choked on her sandwich.

"Ulrich!"

Ulrich rushed into the kitchen. "What is it? What's wrong?"

"Look what she's doing . . . in *my* kitchen."

Holtz's young cousin sighed and shook his head sadly. "Oh, Dee-Ann."

"What? We were hungry. Ain't that right, Irene?"

"Starving," Irene finally managed, enjoying the way her husband's face turned all red like that. Of course, that could be due to the words the She-wolf was speaking or the fact that she'd sullied up his kitchen counter with jelly and peanut-butter-covered utensils that she hadn't wiped up as she'd gone along.

Irene secretly admitted that his clear OCD issues surrounding his kitchen still amused her after all these years.

"And we had no clear idea how long you would be in congress with your cousin," Irene added.

"Then you come get me, woman! You don't let this She-wolf feed my young, defenseless pups crap!"

Those strange yellow eyes that Irene simply couldn't get enough of because they were so fascinatingly strange narrowed a bit. "I'm hearing a nasty tone I'm not a fan of."

"First you seduce my young, hopeless, pathetic cousin," Holtz accused.

Ulrich glanced up at the ceiling in confusion. "Wait . . . what?"

"And now you come here to seduce the rest of my family with your unhealthy food products?"

"Good Lord, man, it's a sandwich not some Satanistic ritual callin' up dark demons . . . which I wasn't planning to do until midnight or so." She glanced at Irene and added, "The witchin' hour."

Irene laughed and Holtz's aghast expression had her clearing her throat and honestly admitting, "I find her amusing. But I'm laughing with you," she told the She-wolf. "Not *at* you. That's rare for me."

"Out of my kitchen!" Holtz ordered. "Everyone out of my kitchen!"

Ulrich went around the kitchen counter and grabbed the She-wolf's arm, pulling her out of the room. "See everyone at dinner!" he said before the door closed behind him.

"I like her," Irene told Holtz and when he barked at her in outrage, she did her very best not to let more laughter trickle out. He was—as was she—getting older and she didn't want him to suffer a stroke from the strain.

Missy Llewellyn lifted her gaze from the paperwork in front of her and blinked in surprise at the sight of her brother standing in her office doorway . . . glaring at her.

She relaxed back in her chair and asked, "What did I say to your precious wife this time to insult her?"

"You haven't spoken to Dez since the wedding," he shot back.

"Then I don't know why you're standing there—scowling at me."

"I was going to wait to see how this worked out but I need to ask you something and you need to be straight with me or we're going to have some real problems."

Not understanding what in the holy hell her brother was talking about, Missy shrugged and said, "Ask." So that he could leave more quickly.

He stepped farther into the room. "Have you been financially backing an organization that's been trapping and using hybrids as fight dogs?"

Missy gazed at her sibling. "What?"

"You heard me."

"Yes, but I believe I must have had an aneurysm while you were speaking because your words made no sense."

"Don't fuck around with me on this, Missy. Seriously."

"And, seriously, I think you've lost your mind. Just like our father, apparently."

"Answer me."

"No. I have not. It's true that I don't want mutts dirtying up the Llewellyn gene pool and I'm at least grateful for the fact that your bride is trash but full-human trash so that my nephew is pure Llewellyn. But other than those issues, I haven't actively bothered with anyone. I have things to do. This Pride is not easy to run and I don't have the time to chase around after genetic mistakes."

"Amazing," her brother said. "You managed to insult an entire group of people with your open hatred, while at the same time proving that you are, in fact, too lazy to kill off what you term 'genetic mistakes.' "

"And your point?"

"My point is that you have a problem. Because someone is

using your name and, more importantly, your bank account to fund this little operation."

"That's impossible, Mason. You know how I am about *my* money. And because this Pride belongs to me, it's all my money. There is no way that I would not notice if . . ."

When she stopped speaking, Mace moved closer to her desk. "What?"

Missy shook her head, refusing to believe that what she was thinking could remotely be possible. "Nothing."

"Like hell it's nothing . . . what?"

"No . . . it's . . . it can't . . . it's not possible."

"What's not possible? Talk to me, Missy."

"No. We will not discuss this further."

"You don't seem to understand the situation you're in."

"What do you mean?"

"If it's proven that you're involved in this, one night you're going to go to sleep and you won't wake up again."

Missy sat up straight in her chair. "And you'd allow them to do that to me? Your own sister?"

"No. But the people who handle this sort of thing know how to bypass people like me and Smitty. So if you know something, you need to tell me. *Now.*"

"There's only one other person who has unlimited access to Pride accounts. *All* Pride accounts."

He briefly closed his eyes. "Please don't tell me it's Allie or Serita." Their younger sisters.

"No, no. Of course not. Like me, they're much too *lazy* to do such a thing. But . . ." She swallowed.

"Who?" Mason pushed. "Spit it out already."

"Our grandmother. As former head of the Pride, she has complete access and unlimited usage of all our funds."

Mason dropped into the chair across from her. "Oh, my God."

"This can't be right, though, Mason. It can't. It's our grandmother. Matilda Llewellyn. Blue blood, actively involved in some of the most prestigious local charities, on the Getty and MOMA board of directors—"

"And one-time Nazi supporter!"

"That was never proven!"

They stared at each other again and then burst out simultaneously, "Oh, my God!"

"Okay, okay," Mason said. "We can't panic."

"But what are we going to do?"

"What can we do if she's involved in this?"

"Mason, she's our grandmother."

"And a sociopath!"

Missy pressed her hand to her mouth. "Could she really?" she asked around her fingers. "*Would* she really?"

"I don't know."

They were silent for several minutes until Missy finally said, "Do whatever you have to, Mason. I will not be a party to this."

He let out a relieved sigh. "The first sensible thing you've said in quite a while."

"Well, of course. I can't allow the taint of our grandmother's involvement in the wiping out of those genetic misdeeds bring down the Llewellyn Pride name if it gets out what that old sow has been up to."

Mason threw up his hands. "Oh! Well as long as we have our fuckin' priorities straight!"

"Don't you dare curse at me, you motherfucker!"

CHAPTER 28

R ic found Dee by the lake on his cousin's territory. She'd taken down a small deer, but she'd only gnawed on the remains a bit. She'd had a big early dinner cooked to perfection by Uncle Van, who seemed to feel the need to prove something, but Ric knew Dee wouldn't miss the chance to do a little free-range hunting. She could have hunted with the Pack, Ric's presence ensuring she'd be accepted at least for the few hours they planned to stay, but that wasn't something she wanted to do. Like her father, Dee enjoyed hunting alone.

He dropped to the ground near her and waited. She lifted her head from her snack, tongue hanging out, blood covering her muzzle.

"Enjoying yourself?" he asked, constantly entertained by this woman. There was just something about her. And Aunt Irene liked her! Aunt Irene didn't like anyone. It was like evidence of God or something!

Dee rolled to her back, paws in the air, her wolf grin wide. Ric laughed and watched her roll back over and make a sloppy leap into the lake. She came out, shook off her coat, and trotted up to him. But by the time she sat down at his side, she was human again.

Ric took his sweatshirt off and helped Dee put it on. Even in July, the evenings were still cool in Washington state.

"That felt so good," she sighed, snuggling up next to him.

"You don't get to hunt enough."

"There are few who'd say that."

"This kind of hunting, I mean." He studied her. "You're glowing, Dee-Ann."

"Am I?" She rested her head on his shoulder. "Maybe I am."

Ric took her hand in his. "Talked to Van."

"And?"

"He wasn't too crazy about the idea of letting my father off to move to Colorado."

"Neither am I." She squeezed his hand. "But I do understand it."

Ric cleared his throat. "He also wanted me to take over as Alpha."

"And you said no."

"I don't want to be Alpha, Dee."

"That's your choice. It's gotta be something you really want 'cause there will be a whole lot of kin more than happy to snatch it away from you if you don't."

"He was disappointed, though."

"I'm sure, but he'll understand. You gotta do what's right for you. Being a chef, playing hockey, aligning yourself with the strangest people—that's what gets you up in the morning. You take the Alpha position just because it'll make your cousin happy and you won't hold it for six months. And it's hard coming back from that, darlin'. Even with family."

"I know. Still, it was hard to tell a man I love so much 'no.' "

"But he respects you as much as he does because you have your own mind and do what's right for you, what's right for your Pack, your friends, and the Group. Don't doubt that now because you didn't tell him what he wanted to hear."

"What about you?" Ric asked.

"What about me?"

"Are you disappointed?" Many She-wolves grew up dreaming that their mates would be Alphas one day. But since he and Dee-

Ann had never discussed it before, Ric didn't know if that had once been her dream, too.

"Do you think *I* want to be an Alpha?" Dee *was* an Alpha; she just didn't run a Pack.

"Your view never changes if you're not head of the line."

"We're using quotes from T-shirts now?"

"When you include the visual of sled dogs . . . it works for this instance."

She laughed, shook her head. "You can't be Alpha when everybody's damn near terrified of you. Not respectfully scared, mind, but terrified. Besides . . . I just don't care. I care about me and mine. Anything else is merely a reason to 'Start the killin'.' "

"Does your father have any other sayings?"

"None I like as much."

Ric laughed, kissed her cheek. It had taken a lot out of her not to loudly thank the Good Lord that Ric didn't take that Alpha position. There was always so much bullshit to worry about when you ran a Pack and Dee liked being the one called in when there was trouble, but otherwise was left alone to do what she liked to do. It was a relief to find out that Ric definitely had the same philosophy because he could very well be Alpha of the Van Holtz Pack—if that was what he wanted. He was wicked smart, excessively charming, and wily. Damn wily. And, of course, ruthless when he had to be.

She really liked the ruthless side of him.

She looked down at the sweatshirt he'd put on her. "I think this is the first time you've ever insisted I put on clothes."

"Don't want you to catch the sniffles, my spun-glass princess."

Grinning, Dee got to her knees and crawled into Ric's lap.

"Dee-Ann, you're not planning to take advantage of me out here . . . in the open?"

"Of course, I am. I'm a Smith. We're tacky like that."

"Not tacky . . . inventive."

She kissed him, stroking her hands down his bare shoulders and chest. She really didn't know if she'd ever get tired of the taste of him. Like one of his New York strip steaks with that peppercorn sauce he made, the man simply tasted good. What did those chefs always say? "Simple, fresh ingredients make the best meals"? Yeah, that was Ulrich Van Holtz. Simple, fresh, and the best meal a girl could have if she was lucky. And apparently Dee-Ann was damn lucky.

She reached for the waistband of Ric's jeans. "Lord, please tell me that you remembered to bring condoms with you."

"I actually didn't remember, but when I told Uncle Van I was coming out here to find you, he forced a handful on me and said, 'For the love of all that's holy do this for me!' " Ric nipped at Dee's neck, licked her collar bone. "I'm not sure what he meant, though."

"I don't care what he meant." Dee gripped Ric's shoulders and shoved him to the ground. "Although I appreciate his ability to plan for the inevitable."

Dee got Ric's jeans unzipped and he'd kicked off his sneakers. She lifted her weight off him enough for him to pull the worn denim and his boxer briefs down to his knees. When he'd done that, she dropped back on top of him and let him yank the sweatshirt over her head.

Big, talented hands stroked her flesh while Dee took his mouth with her own. She pressed her hips against him, her pussy becoming wet and desperate. The two of them writhing, groaning.

Ric suddenly pushed her up. "Get that condom on me, Dee-Ann. Now."

She snatched the condom he'd pulled from the back pocket of his jeans and tore it open. She rolled it down his cock and gripped the solid piece of hot flesh. She lifted her hips and put him inside her, allowing her weight to drop down hard, his thick cock slamming into her. They both gasped, Dee's body shaking, her nipples tingling.

Ric reached up to her, his hands stroking her face, her neck. "I love you, Dee," he told her. "Ever since the very first time I saw you, I've loved you."

And that's when she gripped his neck with her hand, fingers pressed against major arteries, her claws ready to unleash at any moment.

Yet Ric kept his gaze steady, never backing away from what she could do to him. "I love you," he said again. And that's when Dee leaned down, unleashed her fangs, and tore into Ulrich Van Holtz's throat.

Ric barely stopped himself from coming the minute Dee's fangs dug into his flesh.

Barely.

But he held on for her. Clutching her hips with his hands, he thrust his cock up inside her, taking what was his while she claimed what was hers.

When she unhinged her jaw and her fangs slid from his skin, Ric flipped her over onto her back and bit into a spot above her right breast. A scar-free space that he'd been eyeing to claim as his own ever since the first time he saw her in a low-cut tank top. She cried out, the sound bouncing off trees, nearby hunting wolf kin howling back at another Van Holtz male marking his female.

Ric lifted his head, Dee's blood running down his chin, and continued to thrust hard inside her, until her body shuddered and seized around him, her pussy clamping down on his cock so hard he saw stars.

He kissed Dee-Ann, their blood, like their lives, mingling.

And when he finally came, knowing as only a wolf can know, that he'd found the female who was the perfect fit for him, who would be by his side from now until their lives on this physical plane ended, Ric didn't think he could ever be happier.

They held each other, the world around them getting darker, but the moon all wolves loved shining down on them like it was blessing their union.

Then Dee, who rarely got "caught up in the moment" as some She-wolves were known to do, realized something.

"Oh, Lord," she sighed, pushing Ric onto his back again and stroking his hair. "How in the world am I gonna tell my daddy?"

Ric kissed her throat before looking her in the eye. "We'll tell him together."

"Because you don't think he'll kill you right in front of me?"

"That's a big part of it."

"Jesus Christ!" Niles Van Holtz snarled, stumbling to a stop when he caught sight of them. "First off," he snarled, pointing a damning finger. "Outside fucking isn't done until after ten o'clock p.m. When all the Van Holtz pups have gone to bed."

"Then you shouldn't have given Ric the condoms," Dee kindly explained.

"But I told him not to use them until *after* ten o'clock!"

"True," Ric agreed, "but that would have ruined the mood."

"Get in the house," the older wolf ordered. "We've had something come up."

Dee sat up and Ric's cousin turned away from her. "What came up?"

"Can we talk about this inside while you're wearing some clothes?"

"No."

He let out a sigh. "Just got a call from Mace Llewellyn. It seems Missy isn't our problem, but Matilda Llewellyn is. Their grandmother."

"Sure he's not just trying to protect his sister?"

"Yes. I'm sure. Now can we discuss this inside?"

"What's there to discuss? I'll head back to the city and kill the old bitch and—"

"No. You're not handling this. I'm going to bring somebody else in for this job."

"Why?"

"Isn't Mace Llewellyn a friend of yours?" the older wolf demanded.

"We're friend*ly*."

"You're not handling this, Dee-Ann."

"Still waitin' for a why."

"Because I said so," Niles Van Holtz spit out between tightly gritted teeth.

"Look at you treatin' me like family," she teased.

"That's it! Both of you get into the house, get washed up. You're heading back to New York so you can handle something for me."

"I'm killing somebody else?"

She watched the wolf take a deep breath, his cousin still buried deep inside her, Ric's hands behind his head while he grinned up at her, Dee's breasts still hanging out to God and everybody.

Honestly, she was having the best day.

Until Ric's cousin looked at her and smiled in what was less than a friendly way. "In fact, Miss Smith, what you'll be doing is extremely far from actual killing. But something tells me that it's really going to hurt anyway."

Nope. She didn't like the gleam in the man's eyes. But, to be honest, what concerned her more . . . if she or Malone weren't doing this job—she just assumed they'd never ask Desiree to take it on—then who was?

Darla sat on her porch and stitched the pillow she was making for her Dee-Ann. It was too humid a night to sit in the house until she was ready to go to bed and it kept her busy. She needed to be busy at the moment because something was going on. Eggie had gotten a call on that cell phone of his that he never used and then he'd walked out of the house and gone hunting. That was a couple of hours ago and he hadn't been back.

So Darla stitched and she waited.

Finally, she saw her mate lope toward the house, half a deer carcass in his mouth. He'd eaten the other half, but he always made sure to bring a little something home for her. Of course, she had a freezer full of perfectly good cow, but the gesture still meant something after all these years.

Eggie dropped the deer at the base of the porch and came up the steps. He stopped, turned, shifted to human and, naked, sat down on the top step. Darla didn't start asking him questions because she knew he'd get around to telling her when he was good and ready.

After a few minutes, he started talking. "Need to go to New York."

"All right."

He scratched his knee and Darla peeked through her lashes at her mate. He was no longer the young wolf who'd sat outside her window night after night, howling at her, being run off by her daddy, brothers, and cousins, only to come back and start the whole thing over again. Strange, Darla hadn't thought she'd ever end up with a Smith male. They were more her sisters' speed. Lots of drama and arguing and getting each other jealous. Darla didn't have the patience for all that foolishness. She liked things calm and quiet. It never occurred to her at the time that a wolf who had become universally feared, not only by his own Pack but by nearly every other, would be her mate. Especially one nicknamed Eggie. But he'd been the one and still was. And, even better, he'd managed to keep that delicious physique she'd learned to love all those years ago. The body was older, had a lot more scars, but still . . . damn.

"Like you to come with me," he grumbled.

That made Darla miss a stitch, something that over the years she'd taught herself not to do when Eggie and her baby girl were around and she never knew what they'd do or say next.

"Pardon?"

He shrugged. "I need you to come with me."

"Whatever for?" Not once, in all the years they'd been together had Eggie Smith ever asked her to come out on a job with him. Not ever. And Darla never thought he would. Then why was he now?

"You need me to come with you? Why?" she pushed when he didn't answer her first question.

"I need you to talk some sense into our dang daughter, that's why."

"About what?"

Eggie grumbled, cussed under his breath, grumbled some more, and finally snarled, "She's just gone and fallen for the bull- shit of some damn Van Holtz."

"Oh." Darla felt her heart leap, but she kept her face pur- posely blank. The thought that her daughter might have found herself a mate, that she wouldn't end up old, alone, wandering these Tennessee hills with no pups to call her own had worried Darla something fierce. Wolves simply weren't meant to be alone and Dee-Ann was more wolf than nearly anybody Darla knew except Eggie.

"Which one?" There were *so* many Van Holtzes.

"That supervisor of hers. Taking advantage is what I say. It's inappropriate work place somethin' or other."

"I see." Because their baby girl was such a frail, easily manip- ulated little female, of course. Darla picked up her stitching, al- ready daydreaming about having little grandbabies she could stitch things for and holidays when they'd come to visit.

"A Van Holtz," Eggie growled. "Heard she's already living with him in some fancy penthouse. My little girl. And you know Bubba Ray's gonna have a fit over this."

"Probably." Darla stitched a little more and added, "But I'm sure he thinks Dee-Ann's just desperate to get herself a man now that Sissy Mae has one. Figures she's settled on the first one who showed her any interest, so maybe he won't take this all so badly."

Eggie looked at her, annoyance pulling his heavy brows down practically to his nose. "That's a load of bull. My baby girl don't have to settle for nobody."

"I know. But you know how Bubba can be."

"He can damn well keep his mouth shut. At least my Sugar Bug has picked someone in the same damn species, even if it is a Van Holtz. And if a Van Holtz is what she wants, she'll damn well get one."

"I guess." Darla put her stitching back into the wicker basket she kept by her rocking chair and headed into the house. "Guess I better go pack." She'd only gotten to the stairs of their cozy home when she quickly returned to the back porch and yelled out, "Egbert Ray Smith! You get your butt back here right this second! You can deal with your brother later!"

Chapter 29

"**M**e," Dee-Ann said again, looking as if she was on the verge of tears. "Going to a charity auction *dance*. I feel like an idiot!"

"You look like one, too," Rory told her, shaking his head while he sat and watched her try on dress after dress. None of them fitting her right. Rory would admit, Dee-Ann was the only female in the world he'd take time out of his day to come to this high-end, shifter-friendly store to help find a damn dress for a damn dance. A dance she'd be attending with Ulrich Van Holtz of all people. He knew Dee liked the little runt, but he'd had no idea they'd gotten so . . . close. Then she'd gone off to Washington after the Fourth of July weekend and had come home marked, mated, and forced to go to dances.

It was like the world was off its axis!

"I think this dress is quite complimentary," the sales girl told them and Rory could tell his friend was real close to beating that cute little fox to death for being such a big, fat liar.

"You can't be serious," he argued.

The sales girl glared at Rory. "I'm *trying* to help."

"You're *trying* to get a commission, but you're not going to do it by making my friend look like an idiot."

"Well, I don't know what you want me to do about it," the sales girl snapped. "I'm not a miracle worker!"

Rory shot off the couch and yanked the fox out of the way of Dee-Ann's slashing claws and snapping fangs.

"Dee-Ann!"

"She started it!"

Rory sent the sales girl off and attempted to help Dee on his own. "Maybe we should get you something shorter. You do have decent legs."

"Thanks, Rory. That means a lot."

"I'm trying to help."

"Try harder!"

Rory heard a delicate throat clear and he looked over at a dark-haired Latina beauty that he was ready to give up everything he had or would ever have just for one night with her.

"Well, hello, darlin'." He started to walk over to her, but Dee caught him by the hair and yanked him back. "Damn it, Dee-Ann!"

"Do not piss me off, Rory Lee Reed. And do not leave me to go on a pussy hunt."

"If you're interested," the beauty answered, seemingly unaware of their tusslin', "I can make a suggestion."

"Are you actually trying to help me," Dee asked, "or just torture me like the rest of them?"

"Don't know you well enough to want to torture you." She smiled at Rory. "I usually save that for my friends."

"So, darlin'," Rory began, "are you new in town?"

"Rory Reed!" Dee snapped.

"Sorry, sorry." It was a hard habit to break. Beautiful woman with long legs and a curvy body and Rory was a lost wolf.

"I'm desperate," Dee admitted to the female Rory now realized was a full-human. Surprising. There was something so predatory about her he'd just assumed she was feline.

"Don't panic." The beauty walked up behind Dee and studied her in the mirror. "It's your shoulders. They're huge."

"Because I need more bitchy comments about my body."

"Just an observation. You've gotta work with what you've

got." She went to one of the racks and pulled out a sleeveless floor-length blue thing and handed it to Dee. "Try this on."

Dee looked at the price tag, her eyes wide. "Have you lost your damn mind?"

"Look, hillbilly," the woman snapped, "it costs money to make someone clearly raised in a holler look good. Now get your skinny ass in that room and try the damn thing on before I get testy."

Dee stormed away from them and the beauty faced Rory. He grinned. "How you doin', darlin'?"

"I come to Manhattan and yet the hillbillies still manage to find me," she announced to the air.

God, she was so mean. He loved mean.

"And get that look out of your eye, redneck. I'm taken."

Man, but was she taken. The scent of the cat who'd claimed her covered her from freshly done hair to freshly painted toes. It was like the feline had rubbed himself all over her before he'd let her out the door.

"You don't think I'm afraid of a little ol' cat, do ya?" Rory asked.

She smiled and Rory felt his nuts tighten. "Actually, sport," she leaned in and finished on a whisper, "you should probably be more afraid of me."

She winked and stepped away from him. Rory was ready to fight the cat to the death for this woman when his best friend of the last thirty-five years walked out of the dressing room. Stunned, he stepped back.

"God, Dee-Ann."

"That bad?"

He shook his head but the beauty answered, "No. I think it's that good. See what a few extra dollars will buy you?" She nodded, clearly appreciating her own skill. "You look much less frightening. My God, I'm good." She looked Dee over, but stopped at her head. "You'll have to do something about that mop on your head, though." Dee snarled and the woman laughed at her. "Don't bare your fangs at me, hillbilly." She took a card out of her tiny handbag. "Here. Call this salon, tell them Angelina sent you. They'll take care of you."

She glanced at the diamond-studded watch on her wrist. "Must fly. I have to go to this stupid charity auction tonight."

Rory pointed at Dee. "Dee's probably going to the same thing."

"Then I'm glad I helped, otherwise I would have been forced to mock her relentlessly if she'd worn that other dress. Oh." She pointed at Rory. "Pick out some shoes you think are sexy. Something with a heel."

"A heel?" Dee yelped.

"Thankfully, the dress is long enough to cover up the actual size of those feet, but I'm sure your boyfriend will like them."

She walked off. "Nice meeting you both."

"Hot," Rory sighed, watching the woman's ass sashay away from him. "So very fuckin' hot."

Without a word, Dee headed back to her dressing room.

"Where are you going, Dee?"

"Going to change so I can beat the fuck out of you without worrying about getting blood on this overpriced dress!"

"But," Rory complained, "I haven't picked out the shoes yet!"

Ric pulled out his tux, shoes, shirt, and tie in preparation for that evening's dance. Normally he limited his attendance to this sort of thing. He didn't mind giving money or volunteering to help on a grassroots level, but dressing up in a tux and mingling with the rich and powerful was not something he enjoyed doing very often. But he'd attend this event at his uncle's request as a representative of the Van Holtz family and also because he'd need a good alibi. Because tonight was the night that the Group would deal with Matilda Llewellyn and the betrayal of her kind.

It should be something that Ric or one of the other supervisors handled themselves, but his uncle had taken it and Ric was just fine with that. Because Matilda Llewellyn was top of the food chain politically and had been around for a very long time, Van didn't want any of those involved in this to also be involved in her death. Prides could be very fussy about that sort of thing.

Besides Matilda would not be easy to take down, no matter her age. So Ric would do what his cousin told him to do and go to a charity dance. It shouldn't be too bad, though. Lock and Gwen were going to attend and, more importantly, so would Dee. It would be their first time out as an official couple and he couldn't wait to show her off.

"Hey."

Smiling, he stood and faced the woman he'd just been thinking about. "Hey." Ric blinked. "Did you do something to your hair?"

She shrugged, appearing completely distraught. "They tried, but apparently my hair is too unruly and they didn't know how to hide the damage to my ear from when Teacup shot me. Eventually the hairstylist just said, and I'm quoting here, 'Fuck it.' That's what she said. About my hair. 'Fuck it.' "

"I hope you didn't tip her."

"After what I paid for this goddamn dress, you're damn right I didn't tip her."

"You bought a dress?"

She dropped the shopping bags she had in her hands. "What do you think I have in here?"

"I never thought it would be a dress."

"I don't want you embarrassed when you have to go to these things."

"I wouldn't be. No matter what you were wearing."

"You say that now—"

"Dee-Ann, I don't care if you come in your jeans and boots . . . as long as you're comfortable and happy."

She grunted at him, which was kind of new. She'd grunted at others, but never him.

"Whatever you do, don't get used to it," she went on. "It's too expensive, the sales people hate me, and apparently I have freak-ishly large shoulders that can't be fitted correctly in clothes so strangers feel the need to come up and give me fashion advice. I never wanna go through this again!"

Ric rushed to her side and placed his hands on her shoulders. "Never again. I promise. Let's do this thing tonight to appease my cousin and then that's it."

"Will we have to get married?"

Sensing an oncoming panic attack because that question had come out of left field, Ric calmly told her, "That's a decision we can make ourselves at another time."

"Rory Reed says we'll have to get married because all Van Holtzes get married, but marriages are just a waste of money. Especially for wolves."

Damn that Rory Reed!

"First off, you'll never have to worry about money again." And when her eyes narrowed to angry slits, he quickly added, "Not because you'll be living off me but because you already have so much of your own money and your career has nowhere to go but up!"

Her eyes un-narrowed a bit. *Nicely handled, Van Holtz. Nicely handled.*

"And, when we get this whole thing with Matilda Llewellyn resolved and everything has calmed down, we'll discuss what we want to do and what we don't. But not tonight and not right now."

She let out a breath. "Okay."

"You sure?"

"Yeah. I'm sure."

He pulled her into his arms and hugged her. "We're in this together, Dee. Don't ever forget that."

"I won't," she whispered, hugging him back.

"I'm sorry, Ulrich," Mrs. M. said from behind them.

"It's all right, Mrs. M." He kissed Dee's neck before stepping away from her. "What is it?"

Mrs. M. frowned a bit. "Your mother's here to see you."

Not exactly what he was ready to hear, but probably for the best. He'd have to see her sometime. But before he could get good and worried about it, Dee slipped her hand into his. "Come on." She smiled at him. "It's time I got a proper introduction to your momma."

Dee immediately saw where Ric got his looks from, even with the tears streaming down his mother's face and her eyes blue instead of brown. He was clearly his mother's son and in more ways than one, considering how upset she was.

"I'm so sorry, son. I'm so, so sorry."

"You didn't do anything wrong," Ric told her, hugging his mother tight.

Maybe not, but the She-wolf hadn't actually protected him either.

Of course, Dee tried hard not to judge other She-wolves. The Lewis and Smith Pack females were tough mothers, never letting their pups get away with anything. But they were also well-known as notoriously dangerous females when it came to protecting their pups, hunting down anyone who got too close or harmed their pups even slightly. And if you harmed their pups more than slightly? You'd be lucky if anyone found *pieces* of you, much less whole parts.

Even worse, though, was that Ric went out of his way to protect his mother. He hadn't planned to tell her about any of what his father had done, and his cousin Van had promised to say nothing as well. But they should have made Irene promise the same thing, because once she'd found out that neither male had said a word, she'd picked up the phone and called Jennifer Van Holtz herself, telling her everything. About the money that was stolen, the attack on Ric and Stein, and what would now happen to her, her eldest son, and her idiot husband. Irene had held nothing back, proving once and for all that Dee liked that strange full-human woman more than she could say.

"I don't want you to worry about anything," Jennifer told her son. "We're going back to Colorado. We've already discussed it with my parents and the Alphas and it's done."

Dee didn't know if it would be that easy. She didn't see some-

one like Alder Van Holtz happily slinking off into the mist because he was told to by the cousin he loathed and the mate he
didn't take seriously.

Honestly, the wolf should be grateful that he wasn't a Smith.
The Pack either would have run him off by now or just tossed
him into the lake with Ralph the alligator and let them fight it
out.

Dee chuckled at the thought and both mother and son looked
over at her.

"Sorry. Just thinkin'."

Forcing a laugh, Jennifer wiped tears from her eyes. "My, my.
You must think I'm such a mess, Dee-Ann."

"Not at all, ma'am."

"Please. Call me Jennifer." She petted her son's arm. "I'm not
staying. I just . . . wanted to see you."

"When are you heading to Colorado, Mom?"

"Soon. Before . . ." She cleared her throat "Well, it looks like
your Uncle Leo will be taking over the Pack. At least for now."

Dee blinked and asked, "You have an Uncle Leo?"

"It's short for Leonard."

"*Leo*? As in—"

"Yes. My grandfather had a sense of humor."

"Clearly."

"Well, as you know," Jennifer went on, "Uncle Leo and your
father do not get along. So, I decided to get us moved out sooner
rather than later."

"I'll see you before you go."

"And you'll come to visit, won't you?" And Dee's heart broke
a little at the need in the woman's voice.

"You know I will."

"And you'll bring your Dee-Ann." She took Dee's hand and
gave that brave, pathetic smile. "Both of you will come, yes?"

"Absolutely," Dee told her, because there was no way in hell
she'd let "her" Ric go to Colorado on his own. Not without Dee
there watching his back. And maybe she'd bring Rory . . . and
Sissy . . . and Bobby Ray. Maybe her daddy, too.

Just as a precaution, of course.

Dee waited while Ric escorted his mother to the door. When he came back, she asked, "You all right?"

"I will be."

She walked over to him and wrapped her arms around his shoulders. "In this together," she reminded him. "Don't ever forget that."

CHAPTER 30

Mace Llewellyn gazed at the two youngsters that Blayne Thorpe had brought with her to "help" her babysit Mace's son so that he and Dez could likely spend less than five minutes at some ridiculous charity dance. He would normally never go, but Niles Van Holtz had suggested their attendance. Mace didn't want to think too much on why the Van Holtz Alpha would suggest that, because he already knew why.

So that he and his sisters, who would also be attending, would have an acceptable alibi—just in case.

"So I hope it's okay that I brought them," Blayne rambled on. Cute girl but she could go and go with the talking. "They're very reliable and good with kids!" She grinned and Mace nearly sneered back at her. A mutt who wouldn't shift to her human form and a bear-hybrid female that glowered like she might kill everyone at any minute. In fact, she'd managed to put Dez's dogs under the couch with little more than that glower, even his sweet little pup was hiding under there. Dez's dogs hadn't had that re-action to anyone since Mace had first walked into this house. So, yeah, not sure he was buying the "great with kids" line but, whatever. He knew Blayne would take great care of Marcus and that's all that mattered on these nights when his cheetah nanny was off.

"No Novikov?" he asked, trying to keep the conversation going while simultaneously trying to will his wife to appear.

"Practice tonight." And she launched into more talking that Mace really wasn't listening to. Eventually, his wife rushed down the stairs, Marcus in her arms.

"Sorry, sorry." She handed their son over to Blayne and Marcus hugged her tight, kissing Blayne on the cheeks and nose. So young and yet already exhibiting his father's smooth moves.

"Stop looking so proud," Dez warned him as she dragged the dogs out from under the couch and put them in their individual kennels in the office. A good idea since Mace didn't want to come home later that evening and clean their piss off the floor because the bear hybrid made them panic.

Dee quickly returned and grabbed a silk wrap while putting Blayne through her usual coplike gauntlet. "You have all my numbers, plus the direct contacts to the precinct, Marc's doctor—Oh! And where's your phone, Blayne? You always leave your phone buried somewhere."

"It's in my bag."

"Which bag? You brought three."

"The black one."

"They're all black."

"No. One's a dark grey and the other's granite."

"You're making me mental, Blayne."

She giggled. "You sound like Bo."

"Dez," Mace sighed. "Can we go, please?"

"Okay, okay. But you have to drop me off at Ulrich Van Holtz's apartment and I'll catch up with you at the hotel."

"Why?"

Dez's lips grew tight and he got the feeling she was trying not to laugh.

"All right, woman, what's going on?"

"Uh . . . it's Dee-Ann. She's—" Dez snorted. "She asked me and Malone to come over and help her with the dress she's wearing tonight."

"Dee's wearing a dress?"

"I think she wants to look good for Ric."

"Ric who?"

"Ric? Ric Van Holtz?" Mace stared at her. "You talked to him about your sister? Just a few days ago?"

"That sounds vaguely familiar."

"Forget it."

"No!" Blayne yelped. She'd been trying to look like she wasn't eavesdropping when that was exactly what she was doing. "Don't forget. Tell. Tell!"

Dez laughed. "Tell you what?"

"Why does Dee want to look good for Ric?"

"Because he's a hot supermodel type?"

"Dez!"

"I'm not positive but me and Malone think they may have made the leap."

Blayne squealed, the hybrid dog barked, and the scary hybrid sow and Mace snarled in annoyance at the sound.

"I knew it!" Blayne crowed. "I knew it! Project Wolf-Wolf is a success!"

Mace opened his mouth to respond to that but Dez cut him off with one raised hand. "No."

"Anything else?" Blayne pushed.

"Dee is also wearing heels."

"See," Mace said to his wife, "now you're just making it up. You went too far. I will now no longer believe anything you ever say to me again."

"Whatever. Blayne get your phone and keep it handy this time." Dez kissed their son's forehead. "Now come on, Captain Ego." Dez moved toward the door. "I better get over there before Dee-Ann starts killing everyone in a thirty-mile radius."

She had a point, but really, all Mace could think about was the ending to this evening. Because once the evening was over— so was his agonizing over what had to be done tonight.

* * *

After checking into that overpriced flea trap in the middle of this horrid city, Eggie Smith had left his mate in the hands of his niece Sissy Mae and that idiot lion of hers. Although the boy could play ball, so that made up for a lot of his worst attributes and made it worth feeding him.

Once he'd done that, Eggie stole a car from outside a bar and drove over to one of the Llewellyn Pride's homes right outside Greenwich, Connecticut.

Parking a healthy distance from the property, Eggie made his way to the lion territory, moving as quick and quiet as his old bones would let him. He found a good place to take up position, managing to get himself safely ensconced among the leaves and branches of a large oak right outside the Pride house. He checked the distance with his scope and, satisfied he had a good eye line to his target, he opened the backpack he'd brought with him and quickly put together his rifle. Once he'd done that, he sat and waited for it to get dark. These long summer days made this sort of thing take much longer than usual. But it would only be a little bit longer and Eggie could wait.

While he sat and waited, he worried about his daughter. Worried she'd made a mistake choosing that damn Van Holtz, but Darla had been real adamant about letting Dee make this decision on her own.

"Lord, Eggie. She's grown. You can't make these decisions for her anymore." As if he'd made any decisions for Dee-Ann Smith once she'd grown out of her diapers. That little girl always had her own way of doing things and none of that had changed. He doubted it ever would. And as long as this Van Holtz fella understood that, Eggie would have no problems with him. But if he ever lost sight of that . . .

Eggie saw some activity inside the house and he raised his weapon so he could use the scope to get a better look. The target was on her phone and, because it was always a good idea to keep up on the skills the government had been so keen to teach him, he entertained himself by reading her lips. And Lord, but could that woman complain. Even the air seemed to annoy her. Typical cat. Pouncing on dust balls and biting at lint.

Then the tone of the She-lion's conversation changed. She was talking to someone else and Eggie could feel his fangs slip out of his gums because the female managed to go farther—or maybe it was lower—than any of them had given her credit for. She was willing to cross a line that even Eggie would never cross. Not in this lifetime.

Lowering his weapon, Eggie took apart the rifle and put it back into his bag. He dug out the holster with his sidearm and attached it to the waistband of his jeans. He headed down the tree and ran toward the She-lion's home, moving quickly before it was too late.

Ric stood outside one of the Kingston Arms Hotel's luxurious ballrooms and patiently waited for Lock and Gwen to arrive. He'd admit he was nervous. Word of his relationship with Dee was spreading through the shifter community like wildfire. He didn't mind but he wanted to be the one to shock Lachlan MacRyrie into pure bafflement. It was fun!

Of course, he'd been planning to be standing here with Dee-Ann at his side, but she'd told him to go on without her and he had. It wasn't that he intended to regularly torture her with these kinds of events, but tonight was different. Tonight was the night that Matilda Llewellyn would meet her end for the crimes she'd committed against her own kind. To limit backlash, not only among the shifter community but any full-human legal entities as well, those who might normally be suspected of the crime would be making an appearance at this event. Including, but not limited to, Mace Llewellyn and his sisters, Dee-Ann, Cella Malone, Dez MacDermot-Llewellyn, and Ric.

Although dealing with Matilda probably wouldn't stop the hybrid fights completely, it would definitely put a dent in their well-funded and well-oiled fighting machine. Things like that needed money to survive and those who weren't making money often walked away to find other illegal activities that would. Not that any of that made Ric feel better, but he could only help one disenfranchised group at a time.

Eventually Lock walked up to the ballroom with his arm around Gwen's waist.

"You look gorgeous," Ric told her, leaning down to kiss her cheek.

"Thanks. Although, I gotta admit. I hate this shit."

"I know. But I appreciate you being here. You can be my alibi."

"Because that's always fun," Lock told him. "So how did it go with Van?"

"Great. Until he found out I'd marked Dee. Then he went a little hysterical."

The pair gawked at him, eyes wide and mouths open. Then Gwen laughed. "Holy shit, Ric, you actually pulled it off."

"You and . . ." Lock shook his head. "She didn't mind?"

"Lock!" Gwen squeaked.

"No," Ric told him with a smile. "She didn't mind."

"And what about her father?"

"After this gets done, we'll head down to Tennessee and tell him together."

"Do you really think her presence will stop that man from killing you?"

Ric admitted, "I'm hoping."

"Tell me," Dee pushed. "Do I look stupid?"

"No." And Malone seemed kind of surprised by that. "You look great."

Dee again fussed with the deep blue, full-length gown with swaths of material that wrapped around her shoulders. It wasn't really sleeveless, which wouldn't work for her upper-body type, but it didn't really have sleeves either.

"Honestly, you look great," Desiree told her again.

Dee turned back to the mirror. If they really thought so . . . "You don't think he'll want this sort of thing too often, do you?" she asked Malone and Desiree. Because the damn dress alone had cost as much as the casket Dee knew she'd one day be buried in.

"Doubt it." Desiree took another sip of the coffee she'd brought with her. "He's usually too busy for these charity things. He mostly just gives money and makes his excuses."

Thank the Lord for some small favors.

"Let's get out of here so we can get this over with," Malone said, picking up her purse.

Dee grabbed a few extra clips from the top drawer where she now kept her underwear and dropped them into her purse. She already had her .45 holstered to one thigh under her dress and her bowie knife holstered to the other thigh. The fact that she could easily hide weapons under this dress did make it more tolerable that she'd been forced to spend so much money on it.

"Do you think you have enough ammo?" Malone asked her.

Dee shrugged. "A girl can never be too prepared."

"What are you doing here, Mitch?" Gwen demanded, and Ric quickly faced the cats in the extremely juvenile hope that he'd get to see his best friend toss the lion male around before he had to go inside the ballroom and deal with all that boring politeness the richer shifters insisted upon. "You better not start anything," Gwen warned.

"This isn't about you, O' Narcissistic One."

Ric glanced at Lock. "House. Stone. Glass. Throwing."

Lock chuckled and Mitch Shaw pointed at Ric. "I'm here for the puppy."

"Why? To perhaps thank me for the wonderful weekend I provided you?"

"Hardly. Not enough food. But I'm sure you'll fix that for next time."

Horrified, Ric asked, "Next time?"

But Mitch didn't answer, he simply stepped to the side and Ric saw that Sissy Mae was standing behind him with an older She-wolf.

"Ric," Sissy said, "I'd like you to meet Darla Lewis. Dee-Ann's momma."

Ric stepped forward, took the She-wolf's hand. "Miss Lewis. It's an honor."

"Darla," she said sweetly.

"Miss Darla," Sissy corrected. "So's not to get yourself slapped around by some cranky wolves I call Daddy and my uncles."

"Of course."

The She-wolf leaned forward and pressed her hand against Ric's cheek. She closed her eyes, silent for a long moment. When she opened her eyes again, she announced, "As pretty on the inside as he is on the outside. My Sugar Bug chose well."

Mitch snickered. "Sugar Bug."

Lips pursed, a gesture that was all Dee-Ann, Miss Darla asked the lion, "Do you still want that key lime pie I brought for you, Mitchell Shaw?"

Mitch ducked his head. "Yes'm."

"Then you be nice."

"Does Dee know you're here?" Ric asked.

"Not yet. But she will." She turned to Lock and opened her arms. "Lachlan MacRyrie."

Lock went in for the hug, squeezing the She-wolf tight but gently. "I'm so glad to see you, Miss Darla."

"You never come to visit like you used to."

"My schedule's no longer aligned with Dee's and coming to Smithtown on my own—even for the honey cream pie—seems a tad foolish. Even for me." He pulled Gwen around. "This is my fiancée, Miss Darla. Gwen O'Neill."

"My goodness, ain't you just the prettiest little thing."

Gwen actually blushed a little. "Thank you . . . uh . . . ma'am."

"Why are you here, Miss Darla?" Lock asked.

"I'm here with Eggie."

All eyes focused on Ric and he suddenly felt like he'd just been handed a speedy death sentence.

"Not for that!" Miss Darla gasped, then added with a firm nod. "Don't you worry one bit, Ulrich. I made Eggie fill in that shallow grave before we drove up here."

Lock grimaced and Ric swallowed. "Thank you?"

Mace Llewellyn walked up to the group, golden lion eyes narrowing. "Why are you all standing out here? I'm not going in there alone."

"Mace Llewellyn," Miss Darla chided. "Is that how you say hello?"

"Miss Darla?" Smiling with what seemed to be true welcome, the large male bent down, kissed her on the cheek, and hugged her. "How are you?"

"I'm doing just fine. And you look wonderful."

"Thank you." He frowned a bit, shook his head. "What are you doing here?"

"She came with Eggie," Ric explained.

"Oh," Mace said. Then he blinked. "Oh." He thought another moment and, flinching the slightest bit, "Oh."

"Not sure it could possibly get any more awkward," Mitch muttered, earning a punch to the ribs from Sissy.

They left the bedroom, Malone stopping long enough to gaze at the bed Dee now permanently shared with Van Holtz.

"Dee . . . this bed."

"Bear-sized queen."

"Frightening."

Dee chuckled, reaching into her purse and pulling out her phone, answering it. "Yeah?"

"It's Ric. When are you getting here?"

"We're on our way." They headed down the hallway.

"Heads-up," he warned her. "Your mother's here."

"Good Lord, why?" Considering the She-wolf referred to

Manhattan as "that den of true evil where my Sugar Bug is forced to keep everyone in line."

"She came with your father." Ric's voice dropped to a whisper. "She says he's not here for me."

If Eggie Smith had been, Dee would be burying Ric at this moment, not chatting about her father's arrival.

"Don't worry. We'll be there in a few—"

"Dee-Ann?"

Dee stopped in front of Ric's pitch-black living room, her eyes searching the shadows. Her mouth dropped open a little. "Daddy?"

"Sugar Bug. You look mighty pretty."

"Thank you." She motioned to Malone. "Daddy, this is Marcella Malone."

Her father sneered a little. "Feline."

"Daddy," Dee warned before gesturing to Desiree with her hand. "And this is Desiree MacDermott-Llewellyn. You remember Mace? This is his wife."

Her daddy stared at Desiree so long that Dee could feel the woman itching to reach for the gun she also had stashed under her clothes.

"Daddy? What's wrong?"

He reached into the darkness behind him and yanked something out, tossing it at their feet.

White hair and claws were the first thing Dee saw before that head lifted and—

"Holy shit," Desiree murmured. "It's Matilda Llewellyn."

The She-lion, her face bloody and her dress-covered body bruised in all the visible places, hissed and roared at them, backing away until Dee's father planted his big foot against Matilda's back, halting her progress.

"Daddy," Dee snapped, stepping forward. "What in all of heaven or hell are you doing?" She worried that her father had finally lost his mind; that what he'd done for so many years had finally gotten to him. Because *this* was not discreet. This was not the Smith way of handling things.

"Tell them," he snarled at Matilda. "Tell them," he pushed when the old bitch's hissing turned to wheezing laughter.

"Kill me," she told them all, but specifically Desiree, "and you, whore, and my betraying bastard of a grandson will *never* see your boy again."

Chapter 31

Dee hit the gas and maneuvered Ric's SUV around slow Friday night traffic. Her father sat in the backseat, quiet, staring out the window. Malone was beside him, loading up the weapons they'd quickly grabbed on the way out the door. Desiree was in the passenger seat, her gaze steady on her phone as she continued to redial her house phone and Blayne's cell. But typical Blayne, her phone was probably buried in that endless pit she called a bag and who knew what was going on with the house phone.

Then again, none of them ever saw this coming. Not only sending out full-humans to kidnap her grandson so that, according to the old bitch, "I can have him raised correctly as a Llewellyn Breeding Male." But using the boy as leverage to keep her worthless hide alive. Yet once they'd all heard the plan, like the well-trained team they'd become, the three females moved with purpose, Eggie willingly taking orders from his baby girl, while Malone had KZS sending in choppers to monitor the house and follow if the full-humans managed to get Marcus out.

Although Dee knew that wouldn't be easy. Not with Blayne there. But they had to move quickly because Blayne and two untrained sub-adults could only do so much.

Ric, who'd still been on the phone when they'd discovered what was going on was already heading over to Llewellyn's

Brooklyn home with Mace, Sissy Mae, Mitch, and Lock. Bobby Ray and Rory were heading over from a job in the Bronx. But Dee had a feeling that none of them would get there any faster than herself. Not the way she was driving. Even the teams converging together from the Group, KZS, and NYPD wouldn't beat her because she had the boy's mother sitting next to her. Deadly quiet and ready to kill anyone who tried to harm her child.

Hannah, unable to help herself, smiled at the little boy. He had such an infectious grin that she couldn't imagine anyone not smiling back at him. And his smile managed to do the impossible. Make her feel relatively comfortable. The last thing she'd wanted to do was leave the safety and quiet of the Group's headquarters—especially since she was still recovering from that long weekend with all those people—but Blayne had begged and pleaded with some whining thrown in to really test Hannah's nerves.

Eventually, Hannah had agreed. So here she was in Brooklyn, in a stranger's home, with two annoying canines—Blayne and Abby—and the cutest little kid she'd ever seen in her entire life. Then again, if the kid grew up looking anything like his father, then he'd probably end up the cutest *adult,* too.

Blayne charged down the stairs and stopped. "I can't find Abby anywhere."

Hannah looked away from the kid and pointed at the dining table. Blayne crouched down and gazed under the table.

"What's she doing under there?"

"Why does everyone seem to think I can read her mind?"

"Because you're friends. I can totally read Gwenie's mind. I know when she's about to House Cat somebody or when she's about to go Irish on their ass."

Nope. Hannah would not be suckered into asking what "House Catting" someone entailed. She honestly didn't want to know.

"Come here, Abby. Come here, girl." When Abby refused to

come out, Blayne stood. "Dez has to have Milk Bones or something around here."

"Wait. You're actually going to try and coax her out from under that table with *Milk Bones?*"

"You think I should use peanut butter?"

And that's what Hannah got for being suckered in. Again!

"Or maybe some steak," Blayne went on. "Dez is living with a lion male so she has to have some meat around here, don'tcha think? And my God what is that noise?"

"Your phone."

"My phone's been ringing? Why didn't you get it?"

"I'm not going in your bag."

"You couldn't call me and tell me that my phone was ringing?"

"How's that my job?"

"How can I help you, Hannah, if you won't help me?"

"Help you by fetching your phone? I'm only half dog, Blayne."

"I didn't mean . . ." Blayne frowned, thinking. "Wait a minute. *I'm* half dog!" Blayne stomped her foot. "It was easier talking to you when you didn't respond." She picked up her backpack from the floor and placed it on a chair. She began digging through it while demanding to know "And what is *that* noise?"

"The house phone."

Her head snapped up. "You didn't answer the house phone?"

Hannah shrugged. "It's not my house."

"Goddamnit, Hannah! That's probably Dez and she's going to flip the fuck out because I didn't answer the phone . . . again. And this is what I'm talking about! How can you hope to make any friends if you're always so bitchy? I mean, maybe if you were feline you could get away with it, but they never take bitchy from canines or bears. Our feet and shoulders are just too big for that. Although not mine. I have cute, dainty feet. And something else," she went on while digging deep for the stupid phone. Abby pressed up against Hannah's leg, and that's when Blayne suddenly stopped talking. Since she never stopped talking of her own volition, Hannah immediately knew something was wrong.

Hannah stood. "What—"

She didn't get to finish her question, Blayne silencing her with a raised hand. Then she pointed at Marcus.

Hannah was just reaching for him when they kicked in the front door.

"Run, Marcus!" Blayne yelled and the kid took off running, heading for the back of the house, Hannah and Abby right behind him.

It was Abby's first instinct to run away and never look back. As long as she could remember, she'd always made sure to look out for herself and only herself. But as she watched Hannah— unfriendly, could-care-less-about-anyone Hannah—go after little Marcus like he was her own and Blayne taking the knife she kept on her all the time these days to the first guy who came through the door, cutting his throat, and immediately going to work on the others—*many* others—Abby knew she couldn't run for it. She couldn't leave them.

Instead, she ran after Hannah and Marcus. Hannah swept the boy up into her arms and hard charged for the back door in the kitchen. But before she reached it, they kicked that door in, too, the dogs that Mace and Dez had kindly put in their kennels losing their minds as they tried to get out and protect Marcus, but no one pulled their weapons.

Abby dived over Hannah and ripped into the first guy she could get her paws on, forcing him back and into his friends. She flipped him over the back stairs and into the yard, tearing his throat out until he stopped screaming.

Hannah barreled down the stairs, holding on to Marcus. Men from all sides came at her. Abby knew they didn't want to hurt the boy, because one man grabbed the screaming child and pulled while the others battered Hannah with fists and knees, trying to get her to release Marcus.

Blayne ran out of the back door and jumped into the middle of it. A male backhanded her, sending Blayne flying. She hit a tree, bounced off it, and ran forward again. Another male caught her around the waist and they both went down. Blayne brought her blade up, but he caught her hand and turned the blade back on her, shoving it into Blayne's side.

She howled in pain and Abby rushed forward as they finally pried an hysterical Marcus from Hannah, fists flying as they beat the sow to the ground.

Abby ran up to the man holding Marcus and, when she was only a few feet away, she shifted to human. Startled, the man stumbled back and Abby laid him out with a right cross, yanking Marcus into her arms and dashing for one of the trees. Using the power of her legs, she leaped onto the closest branch and scrambled up.

"Get that bitch!" someone screamed. "Kill her if you have to!"

Dee hit the brakes and the car stopped right in front of Desiree's house. NYPD had already arrived and Dee had them secure the area, keeping the neighbors out of their business and the non-shifter NYPD away from all this. Lord knew, they'd only make it worse in their attempts to help.

Dee and the others moved toward the house, their weapons drawn. The front door had already been kicked in and they went through it.

Guns raised, they entered the house. They heard yelling and Desiree sprinted toward the back.

"Malone!" Dee called out, following Desiree. "Side of the house! Daddy, take the top floor!"

They went through the kitchen door and Dee only had a moment to spot movement before she caught Dez by her dress and yanked her back and out of the kitchen, dropping them both to the floor as bullets riddled the door.

"No!" Desiree screamed out, trying to get out of Dee's arms. But Dee knew they wouldn't risk hurting the boy. Matilda, who'd they'd left duct-taped in Van Holtz's closet, with her complaints of Mace's "betrayal," would never allow damage to a Llewellyn male cub. Not when she still had use for him.

Yet, explaining that to a panicked mother would be ineffectual and a waste of her breath. So Dee held on and waited until the gunfire stopped.

Eggie heard the gunfire below, but he didn't let it directly affect what he was doing. He had no doubt that his daughter knew how to handle herself and this situation.

Silently stepping onto the roof, Eggie pulled his knife and eased up behind the two full-humans who'd been placed there. He slit the throat of one, and when the other turned to him, he buried the knife in his eye.

He yanked the blade out and pushed the body out of his way. He settled down in a good spot on the roof and put his rifle together. Once he was set up, he looked through the scope, picking out good targets who were nowhere near the boy or the hybrids trying to protect him, and did what he did best—he started the killin'.

Ric saw that the front door had already been kicked in so he, Lock, and Mace went around the house to the back. He had Sissy Mae and Mitch, who were unarmed, wait for the teams that were only seconds behind them to tell them what was going on. If there were extra weapons they wanted to use, they were more than welcome to join.

Ric saw Cella crouching near the corner of the house. He snarled a little and she looked at them over her shoulder. Using hand signals, she told them how many men were back there—a lot—and the distance they were away from them. She also mouthed, *Eggie,* and pointed up, meaning he was in one of his more comfortable positions—sniper.

Nodding he understood, Ric mouthed, *Marcus?*

She took another look, glanced back at them and shook her head, shrugged.

Ric put his hand on Mace's shoulder. "We'll get him," he whispered next to Mace's ear. Because the last thing he needed was for this lion to flip a switch and get himself, his wife, and their son killed. But, thankfully, years of Navy training had Mace Llewellyn nodding and ready to finish this.

Taking off his tux jacket, removing the bowtie from around his throat, and loosening his collar, Ric pulled his gun and nodded to Mace and Lock. They began to inch forward when Cella suddenly stood. "Shit!" she yelped and bolted forward.

Deciding stealth would have to wait, they all followed.

Hannah lay in a fetal position, fists and the butts of rifles battering her. Now that she no longer had Marcus in her arms, she was sure they'd kill her, but they quickly lost interest. Instead, assuming she was out or too hurt to move, they went after Abby.

Hannah lifted her head, looking around. That's when she saw Blayne lying a few feet away from her, her knife sticking out of her side. She looked into Hannah's eyes and held her hand out. "Marcus," she said. "Please. Get Marcus."

Tears clouded Hannah's sight as she slowly, painfully pushed herself to her feet. Not tears of self-pity or sadness, but tears of rage.

The men who'd turned their attention to tracking down Abby and Marcus seemed to sense that Hannah was right behind them. Slowly, they faced her, a few raising their weapons, some of them laughing at her.

"Good God," one joked. "She's fucking crying."

But they didn't understand, did they? They'd never understand that they'd managed to spark the one thing Hannah had been fighting so hard to avoid all these months—her temper.

She roared, and a few of the men dropped their weapons in sheer terror from that powerful sound alone. Several of the windows in Dez's house broke and Hannah bolted toward the men, shifting from her human form to the form that had brought in the big money on the fight circuit. Some men screamed and tried to run, some just stared and lost control of their bowels or bladders but Hannah didn't stop, hurtling forward before any of them could ever hope to move. And using her six-inch claws, four-inch fangs, and not a bit of rational thought, Hannah began to rip and tear human males apart.

Desiree grabbed Dee's arm when they heard the roar and glass breaking. "Jesus Christ, Dee? What is that?"

Clueless, Dee stood. But before she could head back into the kitchen, human males sped through it, making a crazed dash for the front door.

Which was where her team and KZS caught up with them.

Dee and Desiree ran into the kitchen. They came face to face with more men and Dee used her knife to cut throats while Desiree sidestepped around the falling bodies. They tore through the room and out the back door, but both stopped at the top of the stairs where they had an amazing view of what was happening in Desiree's backyard.

"What is that thing?" Desiree asked.

"That's . . ." Dee almost laughed. "Darlin', that's Hannah."

Desiree only had a moment of surprise before both females had to duck as what was left of someone's leg winged past their heads.

From the roof, Dee's daddy methodically took out scumbag after scumbag with his sniper rifle, not letting anything distract him from what he was doing, which was good. Because so much was going on.

Malone ran past the bottom of the stairs and Dee watched her, panic setting in when she saw Malone drop to her knees by Blayne.

"Shit!" Dee jumped over the banister, easily landing and rushing to Blayne's side.

"Marcus," Blayne kept saying. "Get Marcus."

"Where is he, Blayne?" Dee asked and Blayne pointed over at Hannah who was in the middle of separating a man's body from his head.

"Blayne!" Ric and Lock ran to her side, Ric examining the wound.

"Get the medical team over here," he told Malone.

"Marcus," Blayne kept insisting.

"I'll get him, Blayne," Dee promised.

She stood, ready to battle her way over to Hannah's side and, hopefully, to Marcus. But she could quickly see that there was no need to battle anywhere. Between her daddy and Hannah—there was nothing left to fight.

Lowering her gun and knife, Dee headed toward a heaving, blood and gore-covered Hannah.

Dee stood in front of her, holstering her weapon and slipping her blade back in its sheath. "Where's Marcus, Hannah?"

Still in what could only be described as an interesting mix of grizzly and dog form, Hannah walked over to a big tree and pressed her claws into the base of it.

Dee, Desiree, and Mace stood behind her, waiting.

That's when a female head peeked out from under all the leaves. Big brown eyes gazed at them and she let out a relieved breath. "Thank God."

She disappeared again, leaves rustling, and when she jumped down, she held a sobbing but healthy Marcus in her arms.

Seeing his mother, Marcus screamed, arms outstretched. "*Maaaaaaaaaaaaa!*"

Desiree rushed forward, grabbing her son away from the naked female, and holding the boy against her body.

Shaking, Mace put his arms around his wife and son, held them close and Dee looked at the female who'd helped keep Marcus safe. After a moment, she asked in disbelief, "Abby?"

Abby gave a little wave. "Hiya, Dee."

CHAPTER 32

R ic watched as Blayne Thorpe slowly opened her eyes and looked around the hospital room she was in. She gazed at Gwen, Ric, Dee, Lock, her father, Ezra Thorpe, and, eventually, her gaze returned to Gwen. That's when Blayne wailed, "*I'm dead!*"

They all jerked a little and Gwen snapped, "No you're not!"

"Then why are *you* here? In a hospital? In what you so lovingly call a 'death trap'?" Blayne demanded. "And how can you even hear me if I'm on another plane of existence?"

"Plane of . . ." Gwen snarled and claws sporting the Philadelphia Eagle's team colors extended from her hands. "You idiot, you are *not* dead. You're recovering from a stab wound to the side—but you're not dead!"

"Don't yell at me when I'm the one who's dead! Who had so much to live for!"

"You are not dead, Blayne, but I can easily change that fact."

"If you're my spirit guide to the next world . . . you're not very good at it. Perhaps you should seek another line of work. Like Angel of Death or something." Blayne looked at her father and waved. " 'Bye, Daddy. I'll miss you so."

Ric glanced over at the wolf and all Ezra Thorpe could do was shrug and admit, "I adored her mother and she made me promise to always take care of her. No matter how idiotic she may be acting."

"Now what's *that* supposed to mean?" Blayne demanded.

"Sir!" one of the nurses called from outside the hospital room. "I'm sorry but you can't go in there. There are too many people already. Sir!"

Bo Novikov, ignoring the nurses trying to stop him, stomped into the room. He still had on his training gear without the skates or helmet. They'd asked Eggie to go get him because they'd rightly assumed he was the one male completely unafraid of the Neanderthal.

Novikov pushed Ric and Lock apart and stepped up to Blayne's side.

He glared down at Blayne as if *she'd* done something wrong, and Ric wanted to grab her and make a run for it. That she managed to get past the glare some players still woke up screaming from was a testament to Blayne's capacity to love just about *anything*.

"Are you my new spirit guide?" Blayne demanded of Novikov. "Because I'm not real impressed with the last one they sent me."

"Spirit guide?" Novikov asked.

"To lead me to the next plane of existence."

"And I'd need to do that because . . ."

"I'm *dead*. Don't you people get paperwork on this sort of thing?"

With his hands still covered in his hockey gloves, Novikov poked Blayne on her wounded side.

"Owwww!" she screeched.

"Did that hurt?" Novikov asked.

"Yes!"

"Then you're not dead."

With her hand resting over her now-agitated wound, Blayne looked around at everyone and finally asked, "Well, why didn't anyone tell me?"

That's when Gwen tried to get her hands around Blayne's

throat and Lock was forced to lift the hissing feline up and away
while Novikov held Blayne down by pressing his hand against
her forehead. The wolfdog swung her arms wildly, trying to slap-
fight her best friend. Fortunately, the need for IV drugs to help
speed Blayne's recovery had been unnecessary since Blayne had
begun to heal even before they'd left Desiree and Mace's house.
So there was no abuse of IV bags or lines when the fight broke
out.

Chuckling, Ric turned to say something to Dee when something strong grabbed his shoulder and yanked him out of the
room.

Dee wandered out of Teacup's room, already bored by all the
fighting—did these people not know how to simply be grateful
they were alive? She walked over to Desiree and Mace, Marcus
asleep on his momma's lap.

"Y'all all right?" Dee asked. "Want me to get you something?"

"No," Desiree answered for them all. "We're fine. How's
Blayne?"

"Arguing over something ridiculous with her freak-necked
friend Gwen—so I'm going to guess she's just fine."

"I owe her so much," Desiree said and Dee shook her head.

"Please, Desiree. No more tears. I can't handle any more."

"Look, bitch," Desiree snapped. "If I wanna be fuckin' grateful for you people protecting my son, I'm going to be mother-
fuckin' grateful."

"My delicate flower," Mace muttered.

"Shut up."

He grinned, winked at Dee. Yeah. Some couples were just
meant to be together.

"You seen Malone?"

"Yeah. She's down there talking to Abby and Hannah." At
the mention of the two young shifters, it looked like Desiree was
tearing up again, so Dee quickly escaped to a spot next to Malone.

"MacDermot still crying?" Malone murmured.

"Lord, yes."

"Give her some time."

Dee understood. It was hard to come so close to losing the most important thing in your world and not feel it.

Focusing on the two girls, Dee said to Abby, "You going to spend a little more time being human from now on?"

She shrugged, tugging at the loose-fitting hospital scrubs the nurses had given her when she'd come in naked, unwilling to leave Blayne or Marcus yet. "Maybe."

"Well, just so you know . . . you're not ugly."

Malone snorted and Hannah raised a brow.

"That was the bet in the office. That you wouldn't shift because you were ugly. But you're not. You're cute enough."

Malone pressed her hand to her mouth, but the snorts of laughter slid past her fingers.

"Gee. Thanks."

"Welcome." Dee looked at Hannah.

"You going to tell me I'm cute enough, too?"

"No. I'm going to tell you that I better not see even a moment of you looking ashamed for what you did tonight. Not in front of me. Not unless you want to get punched in the face a few more times. Understand me?"

"Yeah."

"Oh, my God," Malone laughed, unable to contain it anymore. "Is this your rallying pep talk?"

"Yep. What do you think?"

"Don't quit your day job," the three females told her in unison.

"That was kind of rude." Dee turned, thinking she could use a soda from the machine when she saw Mitch and Sissy Mae standing there, staring at her. "What's wrong?"

"We thought . . ." Sissy Mae and Mitch glanced at each other, Mitch grimacing and looking away.

"Sissy, what is it?"

"We just saw your daddy walking off with Ric and—the other stairs, Dee!" Sissy yelled after her. "He took the other stairs!"

Ric shook Eggie Smith's hand and nodded. "Thank you, sir."

But before he could pull his hand away, Dee-Ann charged into the basement parking lot and, except for the blood and powder burns, she looked absolutely gorgeous in that dress.

"Hey," he said.

She eyed the males closely. "Hey. Everything all right?"

"Yes." Ric smiled at Dee's father. "See you for dinner tomorrow?"

"If I have to."

Dee's eyes widened. "You're staying, Daddy?"

"That a problem?"

"No, no. Of course not."

"Your momma deserves a vacation." He looked back and forth between the pair, then said, " 'Night." Got into a car and drove off.

"Why were you shaking my daddy's hand?"

"He gave me his blessing."

"There's no call for lyin', Ric Van Holtz."

"I'm not lying. He said it. I think he meant it."

"Are you sure?"

"Pretty sure. I mean, he didn't stuff me in his trunk and drive me out of here. So I take that as a good sign. Don't you?"

"Yeah." Still . . .

"I met your mother, too. She's really amazing, Dee."

"Did you say that to my daddy? In that same way?"

"Yes, but she is," he argued. "There's just something about her."

"You did it," Dee told him.

"I did what?"

"Found the way to my daddy's heart despite your tragic birth into the Van Holtz family. And that is to go through my momma's heart first."

"Oh."

"No call to look so cocky, though."

"Fair enough. Now, come here," Ric told her and she eagerly went into his arms, the pair hugging each other tight after such an incredibly bad day. But it had ended well, and that's all that mattered in the long run.

"When we have kids," Dee told him, "we're getting Blayne, Abby, and Hannah to babysit."

Ric laughed. "Absolutely." He hugged her once more. "You ready to head home?"

"Not yet. Not quite done for the night."

"Funny, that's what your father said."

"Hmmm," she replied, but that was it.

Holding hands, they headed back to the elevator, but Dee suddenly stopped and looked into his eyes. "Love ya," she said.

Ric grinned. "I love you, too, Dee."

She nodded and together they returned to Blayne's hospital room and what had turned into a very nice mini-brawl.

Together, the three females dressed in designer gowns hauled the duct-taped, white-haired female from the back of the old Chevy one of them had stolen and dumped her into a dirt hole in the middle of a Staten Island landfill.

The She-wolf reached down and yanked the duct tape off her mouth. "Got anything to say?"

"Do you really think you've changed anything?" the white-haired woman demanded. "Do you think you've done any real good here? Or that you'll do any good by killing me?"

"I think," the She-tiger replied, "that your mistake was fucking with the wrong mother."

The only full-human among the small group stepped forward, raised the .45 she held and squeezed the trigger—once.

Afterward and together, they filled in the hole and cheerfully chatted about big dinner plans for the following day.

CHAPTER 33

Dee-Ann hugged her mother, smiling when Darla said, "Oh, my little Sugar Bug. I'm so glad to see you."

"I'm glad to see you, too, Momma."

Darla stepped back but held her daughter's hands. Her eyes filled with tears. "Look at you, Dee-Ann. So beautiful."

"Momma, don't cry."

"I've just missed you so."

"I visited back in May."

"I know but that don't mean I can't miss my little girl every day."

Darla held her hand out and Ric grasped it, moving around Dee to hug her mother.

"I'm so glad you're both all right after all that ruckus last night."

"We're both fine, Momma. Where's Daddy?"

"In the bedroom. Go on in and see him."

Dee walked through the Kingston Arms hotel room. Mitch had upgraded their room to a suite after everything that had happened. Dee offered to pay and for a brief moment, she feared that the cat would hit her, he was so dang insulted.

And, as she expected, her daddy looked mighty uncomfortable with all this luxury. Where most people would be ordering room service and getting massages, since absolutely everything was being comped, her daddy was staring out the big picture window at the bright morning sky like a poor dog trapped in its kennel. She gave him another day, maybe two, until he'd have to go home again. Until he was running free on his beloved Smith-town hills.

"Hey, Daddy." She put her arm around his waist.

"Hey, Sugar Bug." He kissed her forehead. "You all right?"

"I'm fine. Momma started to cry."

"Your momma cries at those sappy Christmas card commercials, so I wouldn't worry too much."

"Are you all right?"

"Knowing that my baby girl is going to be able to handle anything that comes her way? I'm just fine."

"You were worried?"

"A father's always going to worry. You're my heart, Sugar Bug."

"Then what's Momma?"

She heard him give a low chuckle. "My soul."

"Would you like to order some breakfast, Ulrich?" Darla asked after showing him around their fancy suite with a living room and three whole bedrooms! They stood in one of those bedrooms now, the morning light shining in on Ulrich Van Holtz and, good Lord, he certainly was a handsome man. She'd seen for herself over the years that many of the Van Holtz males were handsome, but this one . . . whew!

"Actually, I was thinking I'd like to take you and Mr. Smith back to our apartment and I'd make you breakfast instead, Miss Darla. I have a car waiting for us downstairs."

Mated only a few days and he was already so comfortable making Dee-Ann part of his life without missing a beat. How long had he loved her? Probably longer than Dee-Ann would ever realize.

"That sounds lovely. If you wouldn't mind, with all the cooking you have to do and everything."

"Not at all. I love cooking. It's what I do. And I don't know if Mr. Smith mentioned it to you, but I'm also closing the restaurant down tonight and having a little party, very casual, for some friends and associates. It would be wonderful if you would both come."

She smirked. "He neglected to mention that." Damn Smith males. You had to be dang Matlock to know what was going on with any of 'em. "I'll definitely be there, Ulrich, and I'll see if I can talk Eggie into it."

"Talk me into what?"

Darla jumped, then turned and slapped at her mate's arm. "Don't do that!"

"All these years and you still can't tell when I'm right behind you? How's that my fault?"

"That's it," she snapped. "We're going to dinner tonight at Ulrich's restaurant."

"Not paying all that money for a dang steak, Darla Mae."

"It's a casual get-together," Ulrich clarified. "On me."

She saw her mate sneer a little. "Get-together? Is that girly speak for—"

"*Eggie.*"

"Fine. We'll be there."

"Excellent," Ulrich stated, ignoring the fact that Eggie was being dang difficult.

Darla knew her mate liked the young wolf, but he'd never make it easy on him. It was a Smith male thing and she refused to worry about it.

"But first . . . breakfast. At our place," Ric said.

"Can't we just eat here?"

"Must you be so difficult?" Darla demanded.

Dee-Ann whispered something to her father. Honestly, the pair of them. Thick as thieves. Just like Darla had been with her daddy all those years ago.

"Waffles, huh?" Eggie grumbled.

"With blueberries," Ulrich added.

"Canned?" Eggie asked and Darla adored the brave and annoyed snarl that comment brought out from the young wolf.

"Did you say something to him?" Ulrich demanded of his mate and the way Dee was laughing, Darla would bet that she had.

"Not a word," Dee-Ann replied. *The little liar.*

"Not canned," Ulrich informed Eggie with a sudden stiffness. "Fresh and only fresh."

"Fine then."

Lord, the man acted like he was being forced to eat dog food from a bowl.

"I have a car waiting for us outside."

"A car?"

"Eggie."

"Fine." Muttering, he stormed to the door. "Don't see the point payin' money for a car that you're only going to use for five minutes. Maybe ten. Seems like a dang waste to me."

Dee-Ann followed her father, not even bothering to hold her laughter in. As she passed young Ulrich, Darla watched the boy watch her daughter. His eyes lit up and the warmest love flowed right through him. Darla could see it the way she could look out the window and see the morning sun.

In fact, the young wolf looked the way Darla had always felt once she'd realized she loved Eggie Smith. She almost felt sorry for Ulrich in a way. To love someone so much who would never be easy to love.

"You just adore her, don't you, son?" she asked him softly.

And, without even a pause, "Like my next breath."

"I used to worry, you know? Worry that she'd never find someone who understands her. Who would try and tame her. She's so much like her daddy. . . ."

"The only thing I want, Miss Darla, is to love her and feed her. She's too skinny," he whispered. "After all she does in a day, she needs to come home to a good, solid meal. Made by me."

Yep, she liked the boy more and more. But he needed to be clear. He needed to understand. "She ain't no socialite, Ulrich. She'll always have that damn bowie knife on her and the willingness to use it. She'll wander off on you sometimes and if something moves by her too fast, she's liable to look at it like prey. She'll make a great mother, but Lord help anyone who crosses her child. And it'll probably be best that you go to any parent-teacher conferences because she'll just disturb the parents and teachers. You do understand all that?"

"I understand that I can't imagine my life without her." He shrugged. "Or without her big bowie knife."

The boy had a sense of humor. Thank goodness! That was a necessary part of getting through any day when dealing with Eggie Smith or Eggie Smith's little girl.

"Are you two comin'?" Eggie barked from the next room. "Or are me and my Sugar Bug going to just starve out here waitin' on y'all?"

Ulrich tucked Darla's arm around his own and together they headed toward the front door.

"Sugar bug?" Ulrich softly asked.

"There are some things you don't question, Ulrich. But instead, you simply accept it. Sugar Bug is one of those things."

"I will keep that in mind, Miss Darla."

She patted his shoulder. "Good man."

Alder Van Holtz was having trouble sleeping. He was so angry, he could barely see straight and he had been this angry since he'd gotten word from his cousin Niles that he was to be packed and out of Manhattan in the next two days. He and his eldest son. Apparently, they were being dumped on his wife's relatives in the middle of nowhere Colorado.

As if Alder would ever let that happen. As if he'd allow his cousin to steam roll over him. His wife, who'd stopped speaking to him after she'd gotten a call from his cousin's bitch wife, had already started

packing up the apartment. His son had already made arrangements
to move his own wife and pups out in the next week. They were just
accepting all this. Alder would never accept it. Not ever.

Raging now, Alder went to toss and turn—hoping to annoy
and wake up his wife and force her to talk to him—but something, he abruptly realized, was resting on his chest. He opened
his eyes and saw shiny, bright yellow eyes staring down at him.

He opened his mouth to yell, but something sharp and pointy
pressed against his jugular.

"Uh-uh, hoss," a gravelly voice told him. "One warning:
You're out and on your way to your new home day after tomor-
row or the last thing you'll see"—he leaned in close and now
Alder could see the wolf's face clearly in the dark—"will be *me*."

A Smith. It was bad enough his idiot son had mated with one,
but now he had her white trash relatives making appearances in
his bedroom in the middle of the night.

"Understand me, *boy?*"

Alder wanted to argue, but the blade pressed in deeper and he
felt blood trickling down the side of his throat. It was something
he could tolerate, something he would normally not care about.
But what scared him, what had him wanting to reach for his wife
to shake her awake so that she'd call the police or one of their
Pack for help, was the way the wolf watched what he was doing.
It was like Alder was something to play with. A bug to be tor-
tured under a magnifying glass on a sunny day. Killing him
would mean nothing to this wolf. Honestly, Alder got the feeling
all the bastard wanted to do was kill him. To cut his throat and
let him bleed out while Jennifer continued to sleep beside him.
Or maybe the wolf would drag Alder out and kill him somewhere else and get rid of the body so he was never found.

Unwilling to risk either of those scenarios, Alder nodded.
"Understood."

"Thank you kindly," the wolf told him before the weight on
Alder's chest vanished, those freakish yellow eyes with it. And although Alder heard no footsteps, no doors or windows opening

or closing, he knew the wolf was gone. Disappearing into the shadows that he'd eased from.

Suddenly Alder didn't think he could get out of Manhattan fast enough.

Van parked his rental car in front of his Fifth Avenue restaurant, closed down for the night due to a big dinner party that involved all those who'd worked on shutting down this particular case, including KZS and NYPD. There would be others who would try to use hybrids, thinking they were dispensable, but this was a good start. A very good one.

He glanced over at the wolf sitting beside him. They hadn't spoken since the wolf slipped into his car and Van had headed here. They were already an hour late.

"So everything is settled with my cousin?"

"Yep."

Eggie Smith—chatty as always.

"Good. And I guess you're aware of what's happened between Ric and your daughter."

"You didn't see that coming twenty-five years ago?"

"I was hoping I was wrong."

"You always were kind of stupid."

Van glared at him. "Get out of my car."

"As ya like."

Van knew he'd really have to watch his kids from now on, especially his sons, to make sure they didn't fall into the same Smith seduction trap that his poor, defenseless, *clueless* cousin had.

"Poor, poor Ric," Van sighed, before he headed inside the restaurant to find his family.

Dee-Ann put her arm around Ric's waist and laid her head on his shoulder. She'd left a very tolerable get-together to track down her mate, locating him at the mouth of the alley, leaning against the side of the building.

Blayne, fully recovered from her wounds and subsequent slap-fight with Gwen, was working the room in her skates, showing off her faint knife scar. Desiree, Mace, and Marcus were sitting at the table with Bobby Ray and the wild dogs, having the best time, considering all that they'd been through. Although when Desiree thought no one was looking, she'd hug her son tight. Novikov had managed to only insult two or three people so far. Abby had lasted in human form for a good hour before she couldn't stand it anymore and shifted back to her animal form and had begun to go from table to table, begging for scraps. Hannah sat in a corner, quietly glowering at everyone in the room. Stein continued to complain loudly from the kitchen that he was not slave labor. Malone had shown up with her entire family including a grown daughter Dee had known nothing about, three brothers, her superstar father, and her mother. Their table was right next to Sissy's table because it's always a good idea to seat wolves and the lions they love next to tigers who loath both breeds equally.

Yep, just another day in New York City.

"Everything all right, darlin'?" she asked.

Ric's eyes narrowed a bit, his gaze on the valet in front of his restaurant. "Can you explain to me what possible reason my Uncle Van and your father would have getting out of the same car together?"

"I could—but you sure you want to hear that response?"

Putting his arm around Dee's shoulders, Ric admitted, "As always you have made an excellent point."

"I try."

"I'd better get back inside," he said, turning around and putting both his arms around her. "Make sure that food is getting out to the ravening, blood-thirsty hordes."

"Or," Dee said, hugging the man she loved, "you can just call 'em family."

"Makes sense. We're stuck with them anyway. Just like blood relations."

"Such a positive viewpoint."

"I do my best."

Arms around each other's waists, they headed back to the side door of the restaurant.

"I never got to say," Ric told her, "how amazing you looked yesterday in that dress."

She smiled, feeling intense pleasure at his praise. "Thank you."

Ric held the door open for her. "Although I have to admit, Dee, that in the end, I still prefer you naked."

Laughing, Dee walked into the restaurant. "And I still say— like a wolf with a bone, Van Holtz."

If you liked this book, you've got to try
DEMON HUNTING IN DIXIE,
the debut from Lexi George, out this month!

A ddy shot off the couch like she'd been bitten. The sword-carrying, creature-of-darkness-fighting dude from the park gazed down at her without expression. In the semi-darkness he'd been handsome. In the bright light of her living room he was devastating, a god, a wet dream on steroids. Tall and powerfully built, with wide shoulders and a broad chest that tapered down to a lean waist and hips, he was the most handsome man Addy had ever seen. His long, muscular legs were encased in tight-fitting black breeches, and he carried a sword in a sheath across his back. He was also a stranger, a very big stranger, and he stood in her living room.

"Who the hell are you?"

"I am Brand." He spoke without inflection. "I am a Dalvahni warrior. I hunt the djegrali."

"Of course you do." Hoo boy, the guy was obviously a nut case. Real movie star material, with his shoulder-length black hair and disturbing green eyes, but a whack job nonetheless. Addy grabbed the back of the couch for support as a wave of dizziness assailed her. "That would explain the flaming sword and the me-dieval get-up you're wearing. Nice meeting you, Mr. . . . uh . . . Brand." She flapped her hand in the general direction of the door. "If you don't mind, I'm a little freaked out. I'd like you to leave."

"I cannot leave. The djegrali that attacked you will return."

Addy clung to the couch for dear life as the room began to spin. "Look, I appreciate the thought, but I'll be fine. Really." She closed her eyes briefly and opened them again. "Dooley will protect me."

He crossed his arms on his chest, his expression impassive. "Dooley? You refer, I presume, to the animal that led me to this dwelling?"

This guy was unbelievable. His superior attitude was starting to tick her off.

"The 'animal' is a dog and, yeah, I mean her."

"This I cannot allow." He spoke with the same irritating calm. Dooley, the traitor, ambled across the room and sat at the man's feet, gazing up at him in adoration. "She would not be able to defend you against the djegrali."

"Cannot allow—" Addy stopped and took a deep breath. She was dealing with a lunatic. He wouldn't leave and she couldn't run. She was too woozy to make it to the door. Best to remain calm and not set the guy off. Besides, the spike in her blood pressure made the dizziness worse. "Okay, I'll bite. What exactly is this juh-whats-a-doodle thing you keep talking about?"

"The djegrali are demons." He raised his brows when she gave him a blank stare. "Evil spirits. Creatures of dark—"

"I know what a demon is." The guy thought he was a demon chaser, for Pete's sake. "Okay, just for grins, let's say this demon business is for real. What's it got to do with me?"

"The demon has marked you. He will return. He will be unable to resist."

"Oh, great, so now I'm irresistible. Just my luck he's the wrong kind of guy. Don't worry, I've got a .38, and like a good Southern girl I know how to use it, so you can leave." She waved her hand toward the door again. "I'll be fine. If this demon fellow shows up, I'll blow his raggedy butt to kingdom come."

The corner of his lips twitched, and for a moment she thought he might smile.

"You cannot kill a djegrali with a mortal weapon."

"I'll rush out first thing tomorrow morning and get me one of those flamey sword things, I promise."

Again with the lip twitch. "That will not be necessary. I will protect you."

"Oh, no, you won't!" Addy straightened with an effort. Her chest still hurt like a son-of-a-bitch. "I'd never be able to explain you to my mama."

"This mama you speak of, she is the female vessel who bore you?"

"Yeah, but I wouldn't call her a vessel to her face, if I were you."

"You fear her?"

Addy rolled her eyes. "Are you kidding? The woman scares the crap out of me. *Thirty-two hours of labor, and don't you ever forget it,*" she mimicked. "*You owe me. Big time.*"

The eye-rolling thing was a mistake, because the room started to spin again.

"The mama will not be a problem," he said.

"You're darn tootin' the mama won't be a problem, 'cause you're not going to be here!"

She stepped way from the couch and her knees buckled.

One moment he was across the room, his shoulder against the wall, the picture of aloof boredom, and the next she was in his arms. She closed her eyes and swallowed a sigh as she was lifted against his hard chest. The man sure had muscles, she'd give him that.

"You will recline, at once." His tone was stern.

Okay, muscles and a few control issues.

She opened her eyes as he lowered her to the couch, and saw a grimace of pain flash across his features. It was the first expression of any kind she'd seen on his face, unless you counted the lip twitch thing. The man could give a marble statue lessons in being stoic.

She caught his arm as he started to rise. "That thing hurt you!"

He stilled, his gaze on her fingers wrapped around his wrist.

"You are mistaken. The djegrali did not injure me. It is your touch that disturbs me."

Addy stiffened and drew back. "Well, excuse the hell out of me."

He caught her by the hand. "You misunderstand. You do not repulse me."

He knelt down beside her. He put his fingers under her chin and tilted her face with gentle fingers. Addy stifled a gasp. Who was this guy? The merest touch from him and her breasts tingled and she felt all hot and wobbly inside. What was the matter with her?

"Look at me," he commanded.

Sweet Sister Ruth, he had a voice like whiskey and smoke. She shivered and raised her eyes to his. He stroked her cheek with his thumb, a rapt expression on his face. His thumb drifted lower to brush her bottom lip. "You must be patient with me, Adara Jean Corwin. The Dalvahni do not experience emotion. It would be superfluous. We exist for one purpose and one purpose alone: to hunt the djegrali. For ten thousand years, this has been my objective, until now."

"Ten thousand years, huh?" With an effort, she squelched the sudden urge to scrape the pad of his thumb with her teeth. No doubt about it, she was in hormonal meltdown. "Sounds boring. You need to get a new hobby, expand your horizons."

"Earth is but one of the realms where the Dalvahni hunt the djegrali."

Oh, brother, too bad. He was paying a visit to schizoid-land again. Then the impact of his words percolated through the fog of lust that set her brain and her body on fire.

"Hey, wait a minute, I didn't tell you my name!"

"The animal you call Dooley informed me of many things, including how to find this dwelling."

"You don't say? Funny, she's never said a thing to me in four years."

He put his hand on her shoulder as she tried to sit up. "You will not rise," he said with annoying calm.

"Oh, yeah? That's what you think, bub."

She pushed at his arm, an exercise in futility. The man was built like a proverbial brick outhouse.

His hand slid over her abdomen and down her running shorts to her legs. She froze. His hand felt hot against her bare skin.

"Dooley, come here," he said.

The dog rose and trotted over to the couch.

Brand traced an intricate pattern with his fingers along the skin of her inner thigh. Addy began to shake. What was happening to her? This was so unlike her. All her life she'd struggled to rein in her reckless nature, the wild streak that made her mama wring her hands in despair. Self-control was her hard-earned mantra. Think first and feel later. But this guy . . . this guy really got her going, made her want to throw caution to the wind. She wanted to arch her hips against his hand, a *stranger's* hand.

"Speak, Dooley," Brand said with his gaze on Addy's face.

"DOOLEY LOVE ADDY. LOVE, LOVE, LOVE," the Lab said in the growly voice of a three-pack-a-day smoker. Flinging up a back paw, she scratched her ear. "CAN DOOLEY HAVE CHICKEN LEG IN COLD BOX? CAN DOOLEY?" Her head snapped around. "OH, LOOK, A BUG!"

There was a long moment of silence as Addy gaped at her dog in shock. Slowly, she raised her eyes to Brand's.

"Who *are* you?"

A slight crease appeared between Brand's brow. The expression in his eyes grew puzzled. "Until tonight, I thought I knew."

Lowering his dark head, he kissed her.

Don't miss Mia Marlowe's newest,
TOUCH OF A THIEF,
available now . . .

Only once more, Viola vowed silently. Though, like the Shakespearean heroine for whom she was named, she'd miss wearing men's trousers from time to time. They were ever so much more comfortable than a corset and hoops.

From somewhere deep in the elegant row house came a low creak. Viola held her breath. The longcase clock in the main hall ticked. When she heard nothing else, she realized it was only the sigh of an older home squatting down on its foundations for the night.

The room she'd broken into still held the stale scents of cigar smoke and brandy from the dinner party of the previous evening. But there were no fresh smells, which meant Lieutenant Quinn had taken Lord Montjoy up on his offer to introduce him at his club this evening.

Probably visiting a brothel instead. No matter. The house was empty and why made no difference at all.

She cat-footed up the main stairs, on the watch for the help. The lieutenant hadn't fully staffed his home yet, but he'd brought a native servant back with him from India. During the dinner party, Viola had noticed the turbaned fellow in the shadows, directing the borrowed footmen and giving quiet commands to the temporary serving girls.

The Indian servant would most likely be in residence.

So long as I steer clear of the kitchen or the garret, I'll be fine, Viola told herself.

Besides, the stones would be in Lieutenant Quinn's chamber. Her fence had a friend in the brick mason's guild who, for a pretty price, happily revealed the location of the *ton*'s secret stashes. Townhouses on this fashionable London street were all equipped with identical wall safes in the master's chamber. The newfangled tumbler lock would open without protest under Viola's deft touch.

She had a gift. Two, actually, but she didn't enjoy the other one half so much.

Slowly, she opened the bedchamber door. *Good.* It had been oiled recently. She heard only the faint scrape of hinges.

The heavy damask curtains were drawn, so Viola stood still, waiting for her eyes to adjust to the deeper darkness. There! A landscape in a gilt frame on the south wall marked the location of the safe.

Viola padded across the room and inched the painting's hanging wires along the picture rail, careful not to let the hooks near the ceiling slide off. She'd have the devil's own time reattaching them if they did. With any luck at all, she'd slide the painting right back and it might be days before Lieutenant Quinn discovered the stones were missing. After moving the frame over about a foot, she found the safe right where Willie's friend said it would be.

Viola put her ear to the lock and closed her eyes, the better to concentrate. When she heard a click or felt a slight hitch beneath her touch she knew she'd discovered part of the combination. After only a few tries and errors, the final tumbler fell into place and Viola opened the safe.

The dark void was empty. She reached in to trace the edges of the iron box with her fingertips.

"Looking for something?" A masculine voice rumbled from a shadowy corner.

Blast! Viola bolted for the door, but it slammed shut. The Indian servant stepped from his place of concealment behind it.

"Please do not make to flee or I am sorry to say I shall have to shoot you." The Hindu's melodious accent belied his serious threat.

Viola ran toward the window, hoping it was open behind the curtain. And that there was a friendly bush below to break her fall.

Lieutenant Quinn grabbed her before she reached it. He crushed her spine to his chest, his large hand splayed over one of her unbound breasts.

"Bloody hell! It's a woman. Turn up the gas lamp, Sanjay."

The yellow light of the wall sconce flooded the room. Viola blinked against the sudden brightness. Then she stomped down on her captor's instep as hard as she could.

Quinn grunted, but didn't release his hold. Instead, he whipped her around to face him. His brows shot up in surprise when he recognized her. "Lady Viola, you can't be the Mayfair Jewel Thief."

"Of course, I can." She might be a thief, but she was no liar. "I'd appreciate it, sir, if you'd remove your hands from my person."

"I bet you would." The lieutenant's mouth turned down in a grim frown and he kept his grip on her upper arms. His Indian servant didn't lower the revolver's muzzle one jot.

"Did I not tell you, *sahib*? When she looked at the countess's emeralds, her eyes glowed green." The servant no longer wore his turban, his coal-black hair falling in ropey strands past his shoulders. "She is a devil, this one."

"Perhaps." One of Quinn's dark brows lifted. "But if that's the case, my old vicar was right. The devil does know how to assume pleasing shapes."

That was a back-handed compliment if Viola ever heard one. She hadn't really considered Lieutenant Quinn closely during the dinner party. She made little time for men and the trouble they bring a woman. Once burned and all that. Besides, she'd been too intent on Lady Henson's emeralds at the time. Now she studied him with the same assessing gaze he shot at her.

Quinn's even features were classically handsome. His unlined mouth and white teeth made Viola realize suddenly that he was younger than she'd first estimated. She doubted he'd seen thirty-five winters. His fair English skin had been bronzed by fierce Indian summers and lashed by its weeping monsoons. His stint in India had rewarded him with riches, but the subcontinent had demanded its price.

His storm-gray eyes were all the more striking because of his deeply tanned skin. They seemed to look right through Viola and see her for the fraud she was—a thief with pretensions of still being a lady.

And keep an eye out for Cynthia Eden's
NEVER CRY WOLF,
coming next month . . .

L ucas Simone paced the confines of the eight-by-twelve foot jail cell, a snarl on his lips. The wolf within howled with rage, and the man that the world generally saw, well, he felt more than a little pissed, too.

Collared for a murder he hadn't committed. Talk about shit-luck. Yeah, Lucas had played on the wild side, he'd even killed before, and the bastards had more than deserved the death he'd given them.

But this time, for this crime, he was innocent. Right. Like the cops would buy that story.

His hands tightened around the bars. If he wanted, he could rip those bars apart, and if they didn't let him out soon, he would. "I want my lawyer! Now!" His pack had to know where he was. A leader didn't just vanish, and if he didn't make contact with them soon, Lucas wasn't exactly sure what would happen.

Probably hell on earth . . . or wolves running wild in LA, which, yeah, that equaled hell on earth. Especially if he wasn't there to keep the wilder wolves on their leashes.

Everyone already knew that wolf shifters had a tendency to dance on the edge of sanity. Once those leashes were gone . . . *hello, hell.*

The bars beneath his fingers began to bend as the rage swelled inside him.

A human was dead. Tossed on his doorstep like garbage. *Not my kill.*

Because Lucas had a rule. Just one. *Don't attack the weak.*

As far as he was concerned, there wasn't any being weaker than a human.

"Guard!" His teeth burned as they lengthened in his mouth. No more fucking nice wolf. He was getting out, one way or another. The metal bars groaned within his grasp. "Simone!" Not the guard's voice. The dumbass detective who'd brought him in for "questioning." Only he hadn't been questioned. The cop had just thrown his ass into a cage.

Lucas's kind didn't do so well with cages.

He'd make sure the detective didn't make the same mistake again.

His eyes lifted, tracked to the left to meet that beady gray stare—

And instead got caught by a pair of green eyes.

His nostrils flared. The woman stood behind the detective, a slight frown between her brows. She was tall, curved just the way he wanted a woman to be, with sensual, full breasts and hips that would let a guy hold on tight for a wild ride.

Pretty face. Straight nose, tilted just a bit on the end—kinda cute. A light spray of freckles across her high cheekbones. Sexy red lips. Jaw that was a bit stubborn.

And gorgeous hair. A thick mane of dark, dark brown hair that curled around her face.

Her stare widened as he gazed at her. She licked her lips, a quick swipe of her tongue.

His cock began to swell, an immediate and instinctive response, even as suspicion rose within him. What was the sexy little human doing at his cell? Was she another cop? A lawyer?

Her eyes—the greenest he'd ever seen—stayed locked on his. That emerald stare didn't waver at all. Not even to glance toward the right, to catch sight on the jagged remains of his ear.

Most women looked. Like they couldn't help it. Looked, flinched. So did the men.

Lucas had never really given a damn. The top of his ear had been ripped off years ago in the worst fight of his life. He'd been ten at the time.

But she didn't look.

A guard came scurrying into the holding area, keys loose and jingling in his right hand.

"Get him out." The order came from Detective Dickhead.

Lucas let go of the bars, even as he tried to chain the beast that demanded he lunge for the ass's throat.

Playing it civilized sucked.

The door opened seconds later with a harsh moan.

The woman smiled—with her lips, not her eyes. "Lover . . ." A sexy purr of sound.

He felt that purr run the length of his body, even as the lie burned in his mind. He knew he'd never been *this* lady's lover.

Not yet, anyway.

"You're free to go, Romeo," Detective Dickhead drawled. "Your lady gave you an alibi for last night, one that we were able to back up with accounts from three other witnesses."

Bullshit.

Last night, he'd gone running solo. He'd let the wolf out so that he could howl and hunt as much as he wanted.

He'd come home with the taste of blood on his tongue, and then he'd found blood staining his front steps.

Lucas rolled his shoulders, trying to force the tension back, and stalked out of the cage. Then she was in his arms. Throwing herself against him. Wrapping slender arms around his neck and pressing her mouth to his.

Lucas wasn't a stupid man. If a sexy woman wanted to plaster her curves against him, he wasn't gonna argue.

But he was most certainly gonna take.

His hands lifted, caught her, locked right around the firm flare of her ass, and he pressed her closer. His mouth took hers, his tongue plunged deep.

Oh, but she tasted sweet.

Not the wild tang of his kind. Women like him, women who

could shift into the powerful form of a beast, usually tasted like aged wine.

She tasted like candy.

He'd always had a sweet tooth.

Her tongue moved against his, soft strokes, like a kitten, licking. A moan trembled in her throat.

His cock strained against the front of his jeans. Okay, so he didn't know who she was. Not gonna stop him. Because he'd sure like to screw h—

"Ahem." The Dickhead again.

The woman in his arms stiffened, just a bit.

For show. He knew she hadn't forgotten the detective's presence. And neither had he. Lucas just hadn't given a damn that they were being observed.

"Sorry I wasn't here sooner." Her voice was husky, sexual. Like a silken stroke right over his groin.

"No problem, babe." He curved his fingers under her chin. Two could play. He saw the small tremor that shook her, and he smiled. Deliberately, he let her see the sharp edge of his teeth. Way sharper than a human's.

But no fear flashed in her eyes.

Interesting.

The lady knew the score, he'd stake his pack's reputation on that fact. She knew he wasn't human. Probably knew exactly *what* he was.

And she was still coming to his aid.

Now, as a rule, Lucas didn't believe that people were good. No, he knew they were more apt to be influenced by the devil than any pure motivation . . . so he figured the lady had an angle.

"The Los Angeles police department apologizes for any inconvenience." The nasally voice of Dickhead told him.

Lucas released the woman. Gently, he pushed her to the side. His eyes narrowed as he cocked his head and waited for Dickhead to finish.

"Of course, you have a known history of affiliation with certain—"

He moved in one quick lunge. Lucas grabbed the detective, lifted the jerk by his too-thick throat, and slammed him against the bars.

The guard stepped forward.

Lucas's head snapped to the right. "Don't even think about it." Guttural. Because really, a guy's patience could only last so long.

The guard's Adam's apple bobbed.

"Good." He glanced back at the detective. "Bruce, I think you and I need to clear the air." So others were there watching—big deal. He wouldn't play subtle. "You've got a hard-on for me. You been dodging my feet for the last two months." He let the beast show in his eyes. Lucas knew the glow of the wolf would burn from his blue eyes. "You stay out of my way from now on . . . or you'll find out just what I do to bastards who piss me off."

The detective's skin bleached. "You-you can't threaten a cop—"

He let his claws dig into Bruce's flapping flesh. "I just did."

"What are you?" A whisper.

His smile faded. "Someone" something "You don't want to have as an enemy." His fingers loosened. The detective slid from his grip. Dropped to the floor. Probably pissed himself.

Lucas stared down at the man. He let Bruce see the intent in his eyes. Then he caught the woman's hand. "Let's get the hell out of here."